LITTLE HOUSE ON THE WASTELAND

LAURA INGALLS-WEI

ILLUSTRATIONS BY AMANDA PLATSIS

TRANSLATION BY CHRISTOPHER MCELWAIN

ISBN-10: 1-7338655-0-0
ISBN-13: 978-1-7338655-0-0

Translator's Note

This edition of *Little House on the Wasteland* is based on the
original manuscript by Laura Ingalls-Wei written in New
Merican Standard. For readability, the language has largely been
converted to conform with the conventions of Pre-Bust
English. However, the spellings of place names and a few other
select terms have been preserved in order to capture some of
the flavor of the time period.

"The world long divided unites. The world long united divides. Thus it has ever been."

CONTENTS

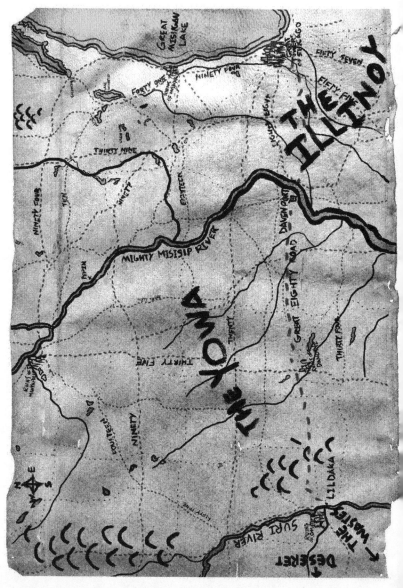

Map of Old Number Roads of the Illinoy and Yowa, parchment reproduction by Raskesh Halfsilver from pre-Bust papermap

ONE: THE BIG WOODS

There came a time when they had to leave their little house in the Big Woods of what was once Wisconsin.

It was a hard thing for Laura to imagine. She had been no older than Baby Grace when Ma and Pa had found it, that little cabin of log and stone, hidden safe among the tall trees in the hills north of the ruins of Greensbay. It was the only home she had ever known.

It was after Pa's last trip to market that the talk of leaving had begun. Twice yearly, Pa would travel down to the shores of Great Mishgan Lake to trade. He would leave with his handcar loaded up with bundles of furs and their surplus soy crop and perhaps a few blocks of Ma's handmade soaps, which smelled of lavender and pine and were famous throughout the Laketowns. He would return with powder for his gun and salt to cure their meat and a dozen other necessaries for life in the Big Woods.

But when Pa came back from market that fall, his face had been tense and troubled. Things had changed somehow in the Laketowns. It was no longer the safe place to trade that it had once been. Pa wasn't sure if he could go back, maybe not ever again.

Ma and Pa tried not to discuss it around Laura and Mary, but some nights, when Laura was supposed to be asleep, she would listen. She would crawl to the very edge of the loft where she and her sister slept and try to scoop up her parents' hushed voices into the tiny ladles of her ears.

Laura tried her best to make sense of what they said. The trouble in the Laketowns had something to do with the fighting in the East, she understood that much. Boats had always come and gone from the harbors along Great Mishgan Lake, but now instead of trade goods they brought people. Displacees, Pa called them. Laura heard him tell Ma that the Laketowns were full of them. Some came across Mishgan Lake, packed tight into their overcrowded boats. Others came staggering up the old number roads from the Illinoy. Whichever way they got there, all those displacees seemed to be part of what had gotten Pa so uneasy.

"Never known a time when the Laketowners weren't at each other's throats one way or other," Laura overheard Pa say one night. "But this is different. All these newcomers. It's like a pile of dishes, poorly stacked enough as it is, and someone comes along and wants to balance a whole heap more right on top. Won't be long 'fore the whole blasted mess comes toppling over, mark my words."

There was more, but Laura couldn't sort it out exactly. Ma and Pa spoke of town councils and taxes and shipping rights and other grown-up things that Laura didn't understand. All she knew was that things had changed somehow. They were one way, and now they were a different way.

Mary, who knew that spying was very bad, never joined Laura at the lip of the loft, but this did not stop her from badgering Laura to relate every word that had been said. Her pretty eyes, pale blue-gray like Ma's, had filled with tears when Laura told her that Pa had spoken of leaving the Big Woods.

Mary was older than Laura. She had memories. They were blurry but they were there, memories of a time before they'd found the little house, a time when they had moved from place to place, following the old number roads, scavving and foraging. The thought of returning to that life frightened her.

Laura didn't remember moving into their house in the Big Woods, but she knew the story of how Ma and Pa had found it. The house had sat all by itself, hidden deep among the trees, far from any settlement. Pa said that it had been built by the parkrangers, a people who had lived in the Big Woods long ago back in Lectric Times. Pa reckoned no one had touched it in many years, maybe not since before the Great Bust.

The house had been well hidden. Its walls had been covered

over in moss and creepers. What remained of its roof had been veiled amid a cacophony of branches. Yet, when the overgrowth was cleared aside, Ma and Pa found that the house's stone foundations were still strong. Its hardwood rafters still stood straight and tall.

Pa replaced the rotting beams with good new timber. He made shutters to fill in the empty windows. Ma sanded down the floorboards and furniture and waxed their surfaces smooth. She hung curtains and set down patchwork rugs. Before long, they had made the little house their own.

Its roof sheltered them from snow and rain. Its stone walls kept out bears and wolfdogs. And there was the big black stove that sat in its middle. That stove was a marvel, Pa always said. It burned wood, unlike the useless lectric stoves that he'd seen rusting away in other Merican ruins, and it burned with such efficiency that it could heat the whole house from loft to pantry on but a single cord. Once Pa had it working again, the heavy stove kept them warm night after night and cooked their suppers atop its flat iron surface.

The stove was not the only treasure the little house had kept for them, secret and safe for so many years. Many of Laura's favorite things had been found among the scav buried inside. Sealed in the underground room that would become their pantry, Pa had found Laura's favorite old paperbook, *A Children's Illustrated Book of Animals*. Among the rubble that had clogged the loft, they found the picture that now hung above Laura's bed, the one of an old Merican city at night, its gigantic towers wrapped in amber streaks of lectric light. Even Laura's ragdoll Oprah was made out of scav from the little house. The doll had shiny black hardmold buttons for eyes, buttons that had, like so much else, been left behind by the parkrangers long ago.

The woods no longer swallowed up the little house as they once had. Over time, the trees all around it had been pared away, further and further from its doorstep. In their place grew rows of crops.

Nor did the little house seem as lonesome as it once had.

Within its widening clearing, other structures, like the smokehouse and the forge, had risen up to keep it company. These things, which Laura's family had carved out of the wilderness themselves, were what made the Big Woods their home, every bit as much as the little house itself.

When Pa first suggested they leave, Laura could tell that Ma did not like the idea at all. Yet, as the weeks went by and the first snows arrived, they talked of it more and more

"Oh Charles, isn't there some other way?" Laura heard her whispering one night. "We can wait for spring at least, surely. Perhaps things will work themselves out."

Pa sighed. Laura listened to the pensive *scrape scrape* as he sharpened his hatchet with a broken piece of lectricmade glass.

"We can't afford to hesitate, Caroline. Come spring, I expect we'll find the old number roads near swarming with folks from the East. Things are changing fast, even way up here in the high country. We saw that today for ourselves."

Pa was referring to the strangers they had seen that afternoon.

For as long as Laura could remember, it had felt as if they were all alone in the Big Woods. There was Mr. Nguyen and his mother who lived a little ways up the creek and Fat Jorge down on the other side of the hollow who sometimes traded work with Pa. There were other more distant neighbors and the occasional passing trapper or scavman who might camp nearby for a season or two before moving on. Otherwise, the sight of other people in the Big Woods had always been unusual.

That had begun to change. More than once already that winter, Pa had encountered strangers when he went out hunting. He would come across their campsites sometimes, freshly abandoned and too near to the cabin for Pa's liking.

That afternoon, a group had come right up to the little house.

It was Laura who noticed them first. She was outside, making a tiny fort for Oprah out of the light layer of snow that had gathered overnight, when she saw dark shapes picking their way through the trees behind the smokehouse. She ran back to tell Pa.

4

"Stay in the house," Pa told her, but Laura lingered on the porch to watch. The strangers had emerged from the woods by then. Laura watched Pa approach them, the long barrel of his rifle resting casually on his shoulder.

Laura counted five adults and three children. They were skinny. Their clothes were dirty and ragged. Pa spoke with them, but Laura couldn't hear what was said.

Ma stepped out onto the porch a few moments later. Laura could tell that Ma was just about to scold her and tell her to go up to the loft, but just then Pa hollered back to them. He asked Ma to bring a few strips of smokemeat and some old soymeal biscuits up from the pantry. Ma hurried back inside. When she returned, she was carrying a bundle wrapped in hemp cloth. She brought it to Pa.

It wasn't much, Laura could tell. Yet the strangers appeared to thank Pa politely all the same. Then they turned and left. Whether it was the meat and biscuits that sent them on their way or whether it was Pa's rifle, Laura couldn't say.

"Were they fiends?" Laura asked later, tugging gently at the rough flannel of her father's sleeve.

The strangers' appearance had been so frightful that Laura thought they might be infected with the Ague, as folks in those days called that terrible sickness.

Pa gave Laura a stern look.

"Do you remember what I told you about that word, Laura?"

Laura remembered. People with the Ague were just people, Pa said. The disease might have stolen their wits and turned their skin a pallid yellow, but that didn't make them any less of a person than Laura was.

Laura understood that. Still, even Pa called them fiends sometimes, so the reprimand wasn't really fair.

"Were they . . . did they have the Ague?" Laura corrected herself.

Pa scratched beneath his great bushy beard. They both knew that Ma did not approve of Laura's preoccupation with fiends. During the outbreak in the Laketowns two summers back, the one that had closed the market for months, Laura asked so many questions that Ma had declared a ban on what she called "fiend talk."

But Laura knew that Pa seldom offered more than token resistance to her curiosity. After placing his rifle back on its pegs above the door, he sat and lifted Laura up into his lap.

"No, my little Soybean, they didn't have the Ague. Not that I could tell at any rate. Just displacees, heading west. Hungry. Tired. Sick in other ways, perhaps. But they spoke plainly enough. Their clothes were dirty and a might ragged, yes, but they wore them same as you or I, isn't that so?

"But you're right to be watchful of such things, I suppose. Fiends—folks with the Ague—are very dangerous. You're old enough to know that. If you see someone with yellow skin or eyes or someone with their clothes all in tatters or moaning or raving nonsense, you must not go near them. You must run away and tell me or your mother as soon as possible. Do you understand?"

Laura nodded, not feeling completely reassured.

It seemed as if the incident had troubled Pa as well, for that night he spoke more seriously of leaving the Big Woods, in tones more urgent than Laura had previously heard. Laura listened from the loft as, down below, his hushed discussion with Ma grew gradually louder, until even Mary was sitting up in bed, her eyes wide in the darkness.

"But the roads again, Charles?" Ma was saying. "With three girls? And Grace still nursing? It's not safe."

". . . no safer to stay," came Pa's reply. "Hungry desperate people mean danger, sooner or late. You know that. And what if there's another outbreak . . ."

"But where will we…?"

"West."

Laura heard Ma make an exasperated noise.

"I talked to Jim Cordry last I was at market," Pa continued. "He'd just returned from convoy not two weeks prior. 'Cording to Jim, Clan Ortega's lost their territory east of the Misisip, but they still hold the Old Eighty Road, all the way from Davenport to Lildaka. They keep the road open to travelers, those who can pay the tolls. There's forts that patrol for bandits and . . . and the like. If we can just make it as far as Davenport, we can apply with the Clan Council for safe passage all the way to the Wastes."

". . . the Wastes, Charles!" Ma's whisper rose sharply in pitch. "We've spoken of this . . ."

" . . . It's more than just showtales, Caroline! I've had it from folks seen it firsthand. Reliable folks. They say the rains have come again. Even as we sit here, those with the drive and determination to tame the wilderness are out there, raising up crops, building new lives . . ."

"I don't know," Ma repeated. "I just don't know."

"Jim says the Ortegas are keen to settle up the west. A hedge against losing their trade routes across the Illinoy, he says. Or maybe just to have a buffer between them and the nomads and Deseretis. Either way, the word is that Old Man Ortega will back the property claim of any man or woman willing to stake out a homestead out on the Wastes and farm it, up to three kims square. I don't doubt but what plenty of these displacees, those with strength enough to make the journey, will take Clan Ortega up on its offer.

"This could be our chance. If we go west now, ahead of the tide, we may yet arrive before the best land is taken. Think on it, that's all I ask. These woods have been good to us, I'll not deny it. This cabin was a mighty lucky find. But maybe we've gotten ourselves too comfortable here. A man who digs himself a rut is like to drown in it when the floods come. We've always been adaptable, you and me. Resourceful. That's why we're still around, when there's plenty who aren't.

"Just think on it is all. Wouldn't it be nice to start fresh, out in the wide open Wastes? To build a new home, one of our own, not one scavved up from another man's garbage? I hear talk of herds of bisox roaming the plains and flocks of birds tall as a man. The game around these parts feels used up, getting scarcer each year. Out west, we'll live off the land, free and self-reliant, just like our Merican ancestors."

As Ma began to respond, Laura shifted her weight, and the loft's floorboards gave an indiscreet creak. Ma and Pa paused, listening, then lowered their voices. Laura couldn't make out the rest of their discussion.

By the next morning, though, it had been decided. They would leave their little house in the Big Woods and strike west, out along the old number roads, bound for that vast unpeopled country that folks in those days called the Wastes.

TWO: THE HANDCAR

Laura placed a foot on the handcar's hub and hoisted herself up to look inside the cargo box. For the moment, it was empty. The bed of the handcar had been stained that morning with a fresh coat of pine pitch, and a sweet earthy smell wafted up from the flat oak boards. It would all have to fit in there, Laura thought to herself, everything they would take with them.

Seeing the handcar parked here, right in front of the house, ready and waiting to shoulder whatever belongings they chose to load upon its stout oak frame, it made everything feel suddenly less abstract. Suddenly, the realities of the coming journey were right here before her, resting atop those two wheels and the strong hickory axle running between them.

Laura ran her hands around the handcar's rims. They were made of bent splits of white oak framed all the way around by iron that Pa had pounded into long flat strips at his forge. Laura tried to imagine the sound they would make rolling across the creetrock of the old Merican number roads.

There had been little enough opportunity for Laura and Mary to take in the momentousness of what awaited them. Ma and Pa had allocated no time for such luxuries. No sooner had the decision been made than preparations began for the departure.

Laura had listened in bewilderment as Ma ran down her list of things needing to be done. Ma's manner was matter-of-fact, with no trace of the misgivings that Laura had heard during her eavesdroppings. They would settle out in the Wastes, and that was that. When Ma set her mind about something, there was no wavering. There was only planning and preparation and the making of lists.

Getting the handcar ready, that was one thing crossed off Ma's list, Laura thought as she hopped down from her foothold. Pa had inspected it that morning, staining the wood, mending spokes, greasing the axle. Apart from the streaks of rust around the rims, it looked brand-new built.

Meanwhile, Ma was busy with her needle. Mary sat beside her, watching her work and helping when she could. Laura joined them.

Ma was mending the stitching on Laura's winter coat. The coat was lined with fox skin, but its outer shell was a patchwork of lectricmade fabrics. Smooth to the touch, those old fabrics would let hardly a bit of rain or snow soak through. The scraps that made up Laura's coat had all been scavved by Ma and Pa, Laura knew, or else been bought from Rakesh Halfsilver or one of the other scav merchants down at the Laketown Market, for no one knew how to weave cloth like that anymore. Still, as marvelous as those lectric fabrics were, they would not keep Laura dry if they were not sewn good and tight. And so Ma looked over Laura's coat and Mary's too, inside and out, making sure every seam was double-stitched and would not come apart on the long road ahead.

When she was done, Ma turned to her buckskin apron and began to sew on extra pockets, where she could keep things that she would want within easy reach, without having to dig through the handcar.

Onto her back would go Baby Grace, Laura knew, wrapped up tightly like a butterfly in a cocoon. Ma would often bundle her up like that when out tilling the garden or picking berries. Laura, who found it difficult to sit still for more than a moment or two at a stretch, could not help but worry about her baby sister's well-being, cooped up like that for such a long trip.

Laura tried to concentrate on Ma's sewing, studying her technique like Mary was doing, but before long she was on her feet again. She found herself back on the porch, watching Pa load the handcar.

Into the car's cargo box went the bundles of furs that Pa had been saving for market. These he hoped to barter for safe passage along the Old Eighty Road or else trade for silver when they reached the market at Davenport. Into the cargo box went Pa's tools. Hatchet, chisel, and adze. Hewing ax and felling ax. Spade and hammer and goose-necked gouge. In went Ma's big iron stewpot and her skillet and her wooden stool. Bit by bit, the handcar was filling up.

Eventually, Laura made her way back inside and up to the loft, where her blue carrysack sat side-by-side with Mary's pink carrysack, both open and empty.

Pa had found those carrysacks many years ago. They were scavved from the ruins of an old Merican marketplace. They were both made of slick lectricmade fabric. The funny little hardmold teeth stitched around the mouths of the carrysacks no longer clicked together properly, so Ma had sewn in buttons to keep them closed. Painted onto the surface of Laura's carrysack was a faded picture of the Batman in his horned mask, just like in Pa's stories, while on Mary's carrysack there was a beautiful woman with yellow hair. Pa said he recognized the woman from other Merican artwork he'd seen but did not know her name. Mary and

Laura referred to her as Queen Lovely.

Laura stared down at her bag. They must choose carefully what things they wanted to take with them to the Wastes, Ma had told her. The handcar would be full enough with supplies. If Mary or Laura wanted to bring something with them, they must carry it on their backs. If it would not fit into their small carrysacks, Ma told them, it could not come.

Laura looked around the loft, overwhelmed at all that would be left behind. With a heavy heart, she sat down cross-legged beside her carrysack. Hooking a finger beneath one of its shoulder straps, she pulled it into her lap and studied the images decorating its stiff fabric shell. The Batman stared back up at her. The look on his face was one of determination, his jaw set as he raced ever forward, pumping his muscled arms. Laura felt her resolve strengthen. There was no sense putting it off any longer. She began to pack.

~~~

The next day, Ma and Pa set about digging up vegetables from the winter garden. In summer, the crops stuck up in proud rows in the fields surrounding the little house. There was soy and kale. There was hemp and squash. There were carrots and baicai and sweet blue peppers.

It was winter now, and the fields were nothing but little mounds and furrows, all dusted in snow. But the crops were still there, Laura knew. You just couldn't see them because they were buried. The best way to keep food from spoiling was to keep it in the ground, Ma always said. Each year when the cold crept into the Big Woods, Pa would cover the plants with mounds of loose earth and leaves so they wouldn't freeze. There they might have remained until spring, sleeping beneath their winter blankets, had Ma and Pa not decided to pluck them out and see what could be canned or dried or pickled and added to their provisions for the long journey to the Wastes.

Later that morning, Laura helped Ma make soymeal. First, Ma boiled up the soybeans. Then she heated the beans over the stove until they were a faded yellow-brown. Then she showed Laura how to grind the dry beans into flour using a long flat stone. It took them until well into the afternoon. Laura's arms got so tired she had to stop, and, after that, she just sat on the table with Oprah and watched Ma grind the soy.

There was a man who lived near the Laketowns named Mr. Abdullah who owned an iron machine that could grind soy. It was fitted with a crank and could make soymeal much more quickly than a stone grinder. After harvesttime, Pa would sometimes take his soy crop to Mr. Abdullah to grind, and he would give Mr. Abdullah some of the soymeal as payment. For years, Pa had been trying to put together his own grinding machine, but the metal pieces he molded in his forge never seemed to fit together quite right. Now, there was no time for Pa to make the trip down to the Laketowns, let alone to finish his stubborn machine. Ma had to grind that soy by hand with her stone.

Afterwards, they put the soymeal in a hemp sack and added it to the others that had been stored in the pantry. That made three big bags of soymeal, full to bursting. Those soymeal sacks would keep them fed on their long journey west. Beside them was another sack, smaller but more precious. That sack held their seedsoy. They would not touch that sack until they arrived at their new homestead, for they would need the seedsoy to raise their first soy crop out on the Wastes.

Other vegetables from the garden went into jars, as much as Ma could fit. Kale and carrots and peppers, all were sliced up and packed together inside Ma's glass jars just as tight as could be. Then Ma added boiled water and salt until the jars were almost full. Then she closed up the jars, put them inside her big iron pot and cooked them until steam shrieked from the tiny holes in the pot's lid.

Very carefully, Ma took the hot jars out of the pot and set them on the shelf to cool. They were all different shapes and sizes, those jars. Some had been passed down to Ma from her grandmother. Some of them, she or Pa had scavved themselves or gotten at market. Ma was protective of them all, and she would not let Mary or Laura touch them. Objects of good lectricmade glass were rare enough, but a jar with a lid that fit snug was as precious as silver, Ma said.

In all their preparations, they worked quickly, for Pa insisted that they mustn't delay their departure. Mid-winter was already past. Spring was just around the corner. Pa meant to cross the Mighty Misisip River while it was still frozen. If they didn't reach it before the thaw, they would need to travel south until they could find a ferry crossing, and Pa did not like the idea of venturing too deep into the Illinoy.

Pa also feared the spring thaw would bring more displacees streaming westward. They would have better luck hunting and foraging and scavving along the way if they did not have to compete with others, he said.

Pa told Mary and Laura that, when he was a boy, the Merican roads had been more crowded and more dangerous. Back then, many followed the old creetrock roads. Some were fleeing turmoil one place or another. Some sought fortune, hoping to strike it rich stumbling upon a hidden bunker or undiscovered ruins, for the scav left behind by the Merican Empire was more plentiful in those days.

Nowadays, the number roads were not so well travelled, Pa explained. Apart from convoy routes like the Great Eighty Road, folks no longer seemed to have much use for the creetrock byways that once linked the countless settlements of Old Merica to one another.

Many of the lesser roads had been forgotten entirely. That was why Pa put such value on the parchment map he had obtained from Rakesh Halfsilver, the scav merchant at the Laketown Market. The map showed all the old number roads between Mishgan Lake and the Wastes, no matter how obscure. Pa hoped that they might have some of those roads nearly to themselves. No doubt they would encounter others here and there, but Pa assured them that the days of vast displacee convoys—and those that preyed upon them—had ended long ago.

Even so, Laura could see that Pa was anxious not to delay

their journey west.

"Uncertain times always bring folks out onto the old roads," she heard him tell Ma.

~ ~ ~

Eventually, their provisions were ready. The garden was empty. The handcar was loaded. The day arrived.

They left the door to the little house unlatched. There was no sense wasting a good lock, Pa said, when someone would be along to bust it before long. Laura stood in the clearing that surrounded the empty cabin, trying to put on a brave face. She adjusted the shoulder straps on her carrysack as she watched Pa wheel the car down from the shed to the dirt trail that ran through the Big Woods.

The hide straps of Pa's beaver hat dangled undone against his chin as he steered the handcar back and forth to make sure it would not roll too fast. A wind blew through the trees. A chill went up Laura's back, and she cuddled Oprah close to her chest.

Finally, she felt Ma take her hand. Laura looked up. There was Baby Grace, hanging from Ma's back, cheeks rosy from the cold but otherwise looking cozy and content in her swaddling. Mary clutched Ma's other hand.

Together, they followed in Pa's footprints, tracing the meandering tracks the handcar had cut through the snow. The tall trees of the Big Woods rose around them, obscuring Laura's view of the little house sliver by sliver. By the time they reached the path that would lead them down to the Old Forty-Five Road and from into the unknown, the little house was swallowed up. Laura knew that she would not see it ever again.

THREE: THE GREAT TOWERS

Pa hacked aside the overgrowth. Beneath was a flat iron surface. Pa clanged it with the blunt side of his hatchet.

It was an old Merican signpost. Laura had seen many such signs in recent days, lying by the sides of the Old Thirty-Nine Road, the creetrock trail that had led them down through the wooded Wisconsin hills. Most of the signs were unreadable, the paint having long ago faded to a uniform grey or else been shed entirely from the rust-scabbed frames. This sign had been protected beneath a dense thicket of buckthorn that had grown up all around it, sheltering it from the sun and wind. The words on its face were faded, but they were still visible, white against a pale greenish backdrop.

"Can you read what it says, girls?" Pa asked Mary and Laura.

They could not. Pa had been taught his letters by his uncle, Frederick Ingalls, and he had been trying to teach Mary and Laura. Laura tried to sound out the faded markings on the sign, but the words were not familiar and she soon got stuck. To her relief, Mary fared no better.

"It says 'Shicago,'" Pa told them, "and this number tells you how far away it is."

Laura stepped closer, regarding the sign with a newfound awe. The Great Towers of Shicago were said to be one of the greatest wonders of Old Merica. Pa had seen them for himself as a little boy. He had told Mary and Laura amazing stories of what the ghost city must have been like before it had been abandoned during the Hard Years. Back in Lectric Times, people had lived inside the Great Towers. Those towers were so tall that on a cloudy day you could not see their tops, so tall that you might climb stair after stair all day long without rest and still not reach the highest levels.

Pa had told them stories, passed down from his Uncle Freddie, of long lectric wagons that roared through the skies and beneath the earth of Old Shicago, carrying people from place to place so that no one would have to walk. He told them of great libraries housing every book that had ever been written and vast menageries with cages full of every animal Laura had seen in the faded pages of *A Children's Illustrated Book of Animals*. Elephants and lions and polar bears and monkeys.

Laura could hardly contain herself, looking at the sign. She bounced from foot to foot. So excited she could barely form the words, she asked if they would see the Great Towers on their way to the Wastes.

Pa shook his head as he tossed his hatchet back into the handcar and hoisted its stiff handles back up to his hips. The sign pointed the other way, he told her, due south. They were going west, towards the Mighty Misisip and then across into the lands the Mericans had called the Yowa.

Laura's face fell. She had not really thought that she would get to visit the Great Towers, not deep down, but for a moment that old green-gray sign had made her imagination run away, out ahead of her good sense.

"But someday?" Laura said, as she continued down the road, walking in the tracks the handcar made through the snow. "Someday you'll take us to see the Great Towers. Right, Pa?"

Pa looked back at her and smiled. Someday perhaps, he allowed.

Ma was having none of it.

"You mustn't tease them with such promises, Charles," she called back to them from a few meters down the road. "The Ghost Cities are not places for little girls to go playing about. We'll stay well clear of them if I have any say in it."

Ma did not turn around or break her stride. Laura had not even realized she was listening.

"Everyone knows the old cities are haunted, Laura," said Mary, who was walking in the handcar track opposite her. "You wouldn't want to walk among the Great Towers. Not for truly."

"I would so!" answered Laura, "I'm not scared."

She looked to Pa, feeling that everyone was ganging up on her.

"Your mother's right, Laura," said Pa. "You know about the cannibal gang on the bridge, after all."

Laura cheered up then, for the story of Pa and the cannibal gang on the bridge was one of her favorite stories.

"Oh, tell it, Pa!" she cried, trotting ahead of the car to walk apace with her father.

"Oh, no, you don't want to hear that story again, about the time when I was a bad little boy," said Pa, though Laura knew he had already made up his mind to tell it.

"Please!" said Laura.

Mary had run ahead too, to walk on the other side of Pa. Even Ma dropped back a few paces to listen. Pa chuckled and shook his head.

"Well, it seems everyone could do with a story to help make the kims go faster. But you girls keep pace as I talk. Understand? This isn't an excuse for another rest break. Not so soon after the last."

Laura and Mary both nodded enthusiastically, pulling the straps of their carrysacks tighter around their shoulders.

THE STORY OF PA AND THE CANNIBAL GANG ON THE BRIDGE

"When I was a little boy, not much bigger than Mary, we had to leave the farm where I'd grown up.

"It was just my Uncle Freddie and me then, traveling the old number roads. We didn't know where we were heading precisely. We just knew we couldn't stay where we were. Reminds me of the journey we're setting off on now. Never ceases to astound me how the more the world changes, the more it seems to cycle through the same beats. 'Same song different key.' That's what Uncle Freddie used to say.

"Anyhow, that trip west with Uncle Freddie eventually took

us all the way up into the Wisconsin and beyond. But on our way we passed through the lands that the Mericans called the Illinoy. That was where we came upon the Great Towers.

"We'd been tracing the shores of Great Mishgan Lake. Lectric ruins were everywhere in those parts, so thick upon the ground I hardly noticed them anymore. But none of these ruins prepared me for when the Great Towers suddenly appeared on the horizon, rising up out of the flatness of the Illinoy like a single lonely mountain. Even from so far off, their sheer bigness was staggering.

"Uncle Freddie had visited Old Shicago as a boy, long ago back before the Great Bust. He had told me about how, back then, folks used to work and sleep and eat in the very tip tops of the Great Towers. Seeing them now for myself, I found I couldn't believe him. The thought of people living inside the peaks of those distant spires was just too fantastical.

"That day and into the next, we veered west of the ruins, but the Great Towers stayed constantly in view, sometimes drawing nearer, sometimes retreating. Then, one night, we camped on the banks of a wide, slow-moving river. According to Uncle Freddie, it was called the Shicago River, just like the city that once stood at its mouth. Just east of our campsite, the Great Towers loomed close and enormous.

"In the morning, instead of striking camp, Uncle Freddie packed his satchel and made for a trading post he'd been told about, which he reckoned lay nearby, on the outskirts of the Shicago ruins.

"It had been a good many weeks since we'd seen a settlement of any note, and we were starting to run fearful short on supplies. We knew of this Shicago trading post from other travelers we'd spoken to. As you can imagine, it was said to attract a rough sort. There's not a lot of honest folk would choose to settle beside one of the old ghost cities. Even if a man doesn't buy into the talk of haints and ghouls, you can't deny that living in the shadow of all that death and decay, there's something about it that just doesn't sit right. It would give me the shivers, I'll tell you that.

"In any case, this trading post's reputation being what it was, Uncle Freddie thought it best to go alone. He took with him a few choice trinkets we'd scavved along the road and just enough silver to buy us a week or two of whatever food these queer Shicago folk had for trade. I was to stay at camp and watch the rest of our supplies.

"He warned me many times not to stray from that spot on the river bank. He would try to be back by sundown. I watched him sling his satchel over his shoulders, tuck his rifle beneath his arm and set off.

"Now, at that age, I wasn't like you girls, who know well enough to mind. Oh, I tried my best to be good. But somehow or other I always seemed to find those misbehaving feet of mine trotting me down the wrong path before I even knew what was happening.

"I looked at the Great Towers in the distance. I thought about all that Uncle Freddie had told me about the old lectric cities and their wonders. Just like you, Laura, I wanted to see the Shicago ruins for myself. I wanted to walk along the tracks of those sky wagons, to hunt for rare lectric artifacts amongst the vaults and tunnels that were said to lie beneath the old city. I tried to mind Uncle Freddie, I truly did, but as I set about gathering firewood, I found myself wandering farther and farther from camp.

"The Great Towers on the horizon made me think of the stories Uncle Freddie had told me of Wane the Batman. The towers were just how I had always imagined the lost city of Gothim, where so many of the Batman's adventures take place. I began to play that I was a batman, fighting off fiends and cannibal gangs.

"All over among the trees and marshes along the riverbank, there were Merican ruins. Old creetrock walls and lectric cars and huge iron beams crusted over in rust. As I strayed further and further downriver, caught up in my make-believe, these ruins only grew denser and more striking. Up ahead, the Great Towers were now so close that I could make them out individually, which ones were made of stone and which of metal, which had lost their tops or sides and which were still mostly whole. I knew I'd gone too far from camp already. And I was just about to turn back, when I discovered the raft.

"Moss-covered and splintering, it had clearly been sitting there for some time. Yet, when I took off my boots and rolled up my pants, wading into the marsh where the tiny craft had washed ashore, I found that it was still quite seaworthy. I looked upriver, back towards camp, and downriver towards the Great Towers. The temptation was too great. I quickly found a long, flat branch that would serve as a paddle, and I pushed the raft out into the river and clambered aboard.

"My heart was pounding. I felt like Huckfin, the Merican explorer who had sailed a raft all the way down the Misisip, hunting for the whale that had eaten his leg. Using the paddle to steer, I drifted with the current.

"When we'd first come upon the Shicago River, Uncle Freddie had studied it with puzzlement. He remembered the river from his youth. He consulted his maps and compass for quite some time before satisfying himself that it was indeed the Shicago River. It was just peculiar, he said, for he was certain that it should be flowing in the opposite direction.

"Whether Uncle Freddie was mistaken or whether the course of the river had reversed itself somehow in the years since he had last been in the Illinoy, I can't say. Whatever the case, the Shicago River now streamed eastward, gently but steadily, towards Great Mishgan Lake and straight through the very heart of the Great Towers, taking me and my little raft deeper and deeper into the forest of brick and iron that was now rising from its banks.

"Old lectric buildings drifted by on either side of me. Steadily taller they grew as my raft made its way downriver. Most were mere skeletons, precarious stacks of metal beams with chunks of creetrock clinging to them here and there. The tallest all seemed to be missing their tops. Their peaks would suddenly dissolve into a nest of twisted iron threads, so that I could only guess at what their full height might once have been. Yet, even shattered and beheaded, these Merican buildings were grander than anything I had ever seen in my travels. I lay on my back upon the raft as they passed, awestruck.

"There were signs of habitation amidst the ruins. Campfires. Clothes strung out on lines beside the riverbank to dry. At one point, I passed a fisherman casting his net out from the side of a boat tethered near shore. I waved. He gave me a queer look as I drifted by on my ramshackle vessel but otherwise paid me no mind.

"I was drawing closer to the tallest towers, the ones that rose from the very center of the old city. I knew well that I'd let that little raft take me a good deal further than I should. I began to paddle towards shore. Just then, the river rounded a curve and abruptly picked up speed. I stopped paddling and turned.

"Immediately, I sat bolt upright upon the raft. Just ahead, the river seemed to flow straight into a wall. I wiped a hand across my face to clear my eyes of the spray that the river's current was now kicking up all around me, but, when I looked again, the wall was still there. It seemed that one of the lectric buildings had toppled straight across the river. Its crumpled skeleton lay there, all the way from one bank to the other. The iron frame sagged, tracing the slope of the riverbed and dipping down beneath the water. I was scared, sure I was about to crash right into it, impaling myself on one of the gnarled spikes that I now saw jutting out this way and that from its battlements. I began to paddle for my very life now, desperately trying to get to shore but knowing I would never reach it in time.

"Yet, as the current swept me perilously closer, I saw that the obstruction was not as solid as it first appeared. The river had eaten away much of the material that touched its gushing water. Boat-sized fissures had been torn throughout the fallen tower. With care, these gaps could be safely navigated, I now saw. I stopped struggling against the current and steered towards a wide, square hole that might once have been a window.

"As I entered the sunken monolith, darkness fell around me, as if my raft was floating through an underground cavern, full of splintered shapes dangling from above like stalactites or like vines from an overgrown jungle canopy. Other shapes rose from the water below, diverting the river's flow into pools and meandering channels. Much to my relief, these diversions slowed the current.

"Above me, a long unbroken stretch of hallway had survived. As I passed beneath, I could make out doors and alcoves. Here and there in the darkness, I saw markings plastered along the sideways walls, full of strange Merican designs and symbols whose meanings I could not begin to guess.

"Finally, I paddled my little raft all the way through the toppled tower, out another window and back into daylight. I whooped and hollered, I was so thankful to have passed through that treacherous tunnel alive. Turning my attention back to the path before me, I saw that the Shicago River made another sharp curve ahead. There, a second tributary, nearly as wide as the first and flowing southeastwardly, joined its force to the flow.

"Standing sentry upon the north shore of the river fork, gliding into view inch by inch from behind the rubble that loomed above my starboard bow, was a colossal structure. It appeared to be made of giant stone bricks. Not creetrock but solid brown stone that seemed to have shrugged off the passage of years.

"The ruins were taller on the south side of the river, among the heart of the Great Towers. In its own way, though, this stone fortress on the Shicago River's north bank was even more massive. Its walls just kept going, stretching on and on along the river's edge and sprawling away from sight beyond the corners of its parapets. I don't exaggerate a bit when I say this one building was big enough to swallow whole towns, whole cities. I had never felt so tiny, standing there on my little raft, a floating speck upon the river, staring mesmerized at the stone giant approaching around the bend.

"It was then that I first heard the voice. The sound ricocheted off the enormous wall of stone, echoing all around me as if channeled through a deep canyon.

"'*Eat!*' it cried.

"I looked about, startled. With no clue what direction the

voice had come from, I scanned the rubble-strewn banks of the river. But I saw no one.

"I floated onwards, directly beneath the castle's walls. Looking up, I saw a line of stone pillars guarding the fortress's front gate. Some were empty, but on some were mounted giant heads, forged in dark green copper. I watched them warily, still rattled by the strange voice.

"Then it came again. Closer now, it seemed. Hungry and insistent, even as it faded into a dull echo, dribbling down the face of the stone fortress.

"*'Eat! (eat eat) Eat! (eat eat)'*

"Uncle Freddie's warnings came flooding back to me. How cannibal gangs were known to make camp among the ghost cities. How the Great Towers were full of dark corridors and crevices, places where those driven mad by the Ague might shelter from the sun's rays.

"Up ahead, there was an iron bridge. Or what had once been a bridge. Much of the span had collapsed, but a thin spine of crisscrossing iron beams still spanned the river's width, patched here and there with rope and wooden planks. Tucked in among the shadows of its latticework, I thought I saw shapes, dark figures waiting in ambush.

"Terrified, I began to paddle once again for shore. The dark shapes above loomed ever closer, but I managed to steer my little boat into the muddy shallows of the river just before the water dragged me beneath the bridge's ominous trestles.

"I dragged the raft up onto land, and, for a moment, I squatted there in the tall marsh grass, unsure what to do. I watched the bridge, holding my breath, listening for the voice. Above the rush of the river, I could hear the Great Towers creak in the distance, their soft laments rising and falling. Otherwise, all was still and silent.

"I turned around and looked towards the river bend that had brought me here, towards the fork where the two tributaries smashed against one another. With only a mind towards escaping that current as quick as I could, I had found myself on the river's north bank, with no plan for how to get back to camp.

"Paddling upriver would be slow and tiring, if indeed I could manage it at all. And I was rightly worried that the shifting cross currents of the river fork might defy my limited seamanship. When I had set off on this adventure, my plan, such as I had one, heedless boy that I was, had always been to abandon my boat and walk my way back to where I started, but I had never counted on the river taking me so deep into the ruins.

"Suddenly, I heard a clatter from amid the ruins on the south bank. Whether it was movement or simply the sound of rubble settling, I couldn't say for sure, but it frightened me. I began to scramble up the mud embankment, trying to stay hidden behind the ridges of broken creetrock that studded its slope.

"When I reached the top, I found myself standing beneath the row of copper heads. Each had the face of a different man. Their expressions were severe, their features eerily lifelike. Atop their high pedestals, they stared blankly towards the gates of the giant stone citadel.

"From afar, the castle's gates had seemed small, a tiny cleft notched into the very bottom of its enormous cliff face. Now, those gates towered over me, taller than many a house. Huge metal beams, bent and rusted, lay diagonally across the opening. The threshold was choked with rubble, spilling out of its mouth like a fiend spewing yellow bile. Beyond was blackness.

"One of the copper heads lay on the ground near my feet, cheek down in the weeds and gravel. I kept my eye on it as I crept past. It had a pointed beard and serious, sunken eyes. Its dull green skull was cracked in two, and a gnarled, leafless shrub had sprouted in the gap. Twisted roots spilled over the copper man's brow and curled around his ear. I couldn't shake the disquieting sense that he was watching me.

"As I looked around, weighing the quickest and safest path back to camp, I was dismayed by how long the shadows of the Great Towers had grown. A foreboding dusk had settled into the winding alleys and corridors of the old ghost city. All over, the ruins were flecked in stark patterns as the fading daylight sneaked between the spires and reflected off a thousand shards of shattered lectric glass.

"How had it gotten so late? In the excitement of my adventure, I had lost track of the day. I started to panic.

"I was no longer Huckfin or Wane the Batman. I was a scared little boy. A little boy who had done a very foolish thing.

"And then, at that moment, I heard the voice again. So loud and clear, it spun me around in fright, thinking someone was standing right behind me.

"*Eat!* it said. *Eat! Eat! Eat!*

"I ran.

"Beneath the walls of the castle and around its corner, I fled headlong. I passed all manner of strange shapes as I raced through the ruins. Lectric cars of every description, sometimes piled in stacks of ten or more. Giant signs with words and pictures, all sculpted right into the metal and hardmold. I ran beneath a sky wagon, still sitting frozen on its elevated track. But I paid no mind to any of it. My dreams of treasure and adventure were forgotten. I wanted only to escape.

"It wasn't long, though, before I found my way blocked by the river. It was the north fork, the one that had joined its strength to my westerly branch just before I disembarked. Upstream, I saw another old lectric bridge. It was wide, wide enough for half a dozen wagons to cross all at once, side by side. And it seemed in fair shape, spanning the whole width of the river.

"I hesitated. Uncle Freddie had told me never to try and walk over any bridge left over from Lectric Times, no matter how solid it might look. Such bridges were like to collapse at any time.

"Besides, by now I imagined cannibals waiting in ambush around every corner. In my mind, I saw them lurking at the far end of the bridge, demanding their grisly toll.

"I decided to swim it. I stumbled down the riverbank and plunged into the cold water. Gasping, I flailed towards the far shore. The current began to pull me southward, taking me dangerously closer to the river's fork. For a moment, I was terrified I wouldn't make it, that the second tributary would crash down upon me, and I would be swept out into Great Mishgan Lake. But just before the two branches came together, curling eastward around the castle, my feet touched mud.

"Sopping wet, I climbed out of the river. Yet, as soon as I staggered up from the rushes and onto firm land, that sound once more froze me in my tracks.

"*Eat! Eat!*

"The voice seemed closer than ever. Had my pursuer followed me across the river somehow? Or was this another lookout from the same cannibal gang, calling out to his comrades in that same distinctive screech? I squinted at the bridge. Sure enough, I caught a glimpse of a figure making its way across, striding towards me at a threatening pace.

"Once more, I ran, my wet pants slop-slopping against my legs. After just a few steps, I tripped. My hands and knees were skinned bloody, but I barely noticed. I picked myself and stumbled onward. Behind me, I heard footsteps. Terrified, I ducked down an alley between two brick towers.

"I found the passageway blocked with rubble. By now, I was crying. I turned around. Through the narrow gap between the buildings, I saw a shadow fall across the creetrock gravel that coated the old streets. Its shape was deformed, neck and shoulders stretched into a slender, asymmetrical hunch by the waning sunlight, but I could tell that whoever was casting that shadow was hunting for me.

"I turned back, searching desperately for a way to clamber up the rubble blockade. Suddenly, a hand grabbed my shoulder. Strong fingers closed around my shirt, wadding up a bundle of fabric and squeezing the collar tight around my neck. The hand gave me a rough shake and spun me around. I opened my mouth to scream.

"But then I looked up. A confusing mix of emotions washed over me, for in that moment I found myself staring up into the face of Uncle Freddie. And he was furious.

"'So it's you after all, is it?' he said. 'When I heard that scavman at the trading post, telling folks about the boy he'd seen rafting down the Shicago River, splashing about in the middle of the Great Towers like a damned fool, I'd not believed it. Not Charlie, I told myself. He's a deal more sense than that. And yet something told me I should see for myself, just to be safe.'

"I began to blubber some explanation, but before I could get two words out, I stopped cold. Tongue suddenly stiff with dread, I held my breath, my jaw hanging limp and my eyes bulging. It was the voice again, filling the narrow alley with a shrill echo.

"*Eat!* it cried *Eaaaaat!*

"Uncle Freddie studied the terror on my face. He raised a curious eyebrow and glanced up over my shoulder before bursting into laughter. His unexpected reaction dampened my panic. Confused, I looked behind me, following his gaze upwards.

"Above my head, a twisted arch of metal scaffolding had come unfastened from one building and collapsed against the other. It hung there, suspended above the alley. Still holding my breath, I listened. I heard a faint scrape of claws against the rusted iron slats. And then I saw a flap of black wings, darting out momentarily from behind their perch.

"Uncle Freddie released me and gave me a clap to the back of my head.

"'I hope you've had a grand adventure, Charlie," he said. 'Chased through the streets of Old Shicago by mouthy little raven!'

"Well, now I felt double foolish, and I trudged silently after Uncle Freddie, feeling the mud squishing in my boots, all the way back to camp. And when we'd got back, Uncle Freddie thrashed me good with his belt for not minding.

"So I hope you girls remember," said Pa, and he stopped the handcar momentarily so he could look at Mary and Laura each in turn. "Never go playing around in ruins."

FOUR: RESTRANT

Night after night, they camped among the trees. Pa would pull the handcar off the road, into the cover of the woods. Once they found a nice flat place away from the road, Laura and Mary would sweep the ground clear of rocks and nettles. Then Ma would hang up the big tarp that she had stitched from hides and scraps of old lectricmade fabrics. Finally, snug and dry beneath their little lean-to, they would unfurl their bedrolls and settle in.

Most nights, unless it was snowing heavily, Pa would backtrack a ways to muddle their tracks.

Meanwhile, Ma would begin preparing supper. If Pa said it was safe, they could have a cookfire. Ma might boil a bit of saltmeat with carrots and pickled kale and perhaps a few herbs or moss that she had spied along the road. Sometimes, Ma would bake a big round wheel of soybread in her skillet, and Laura would have warm yellow bread to dip into her stew.

On some nights, after supper, Mary and Laura could stay up and watch the fire dwindle into embers. This was Laura's favorite time. If he wasn't too tired, Pa would tell them stories or bring out his two-string and sing them some of the old traditionals Uncle Freddie had taught him as a boy.

It was not easy, sleeping outdoors on the ground night after night. The woods were cold, even beneath Laura's layers of furs and blankets. The ground was hard and uneven, even lying atop her bedroll. But Laura knew she must not complain. She knew that she must be brave and strong on their long journey to the Wastes.

Late one day, they came to the ruins of a Merican town. They had seen the ruins from afar. The town lay at the bottom of a valley, along the shores of a tiny lake. From the mountain pass where the Old Thirty-Nine Road emerged from the wooded slopes above and began to twist its way downwards, Pa had pointed out the gray shapes of old creetrock buildings. They paused there for a time while Pa consulted his map. The place had no name, at least not one that anyone had bothered to record.

Pa studied the valley below. No traces of smoke rose from the ruins. Nothing stirred. No sounds of human activity were heard. Pa was certain that the town was long abandoned.

The Old Thirty-Nine Road wound down into the valley, taking Laura and her family right towards the abandoned town. Snow was falling gently but steadily by the time they reached the ruins and Pa said they might as well stop for the day and see if they couldn't find some shelter indoors for a change. He turned the handcar. They left the old number road and made their way cautiously down a side trail that seemed to lead deeper into the old Merican settlement.

According to Pa, that trail had probably been a road once, back when people lived in those parts, covered in creetrock just like the old number roads. The town's main street perhaps.

Laura looked up and down the trail, skeptical. If there had once been a creetrock road here, the Big Woods had done a fine job of covering it up. Along the Old Thirty-Nine Road, shrubs often sprouted from the cracks and nibbled away at its edges, but the road never disappeared entirely. That was because the old number roads have deep creetrock foundations that make it hard for plants to take root, Pa had explained. Besides, trade convoys still used those roads sometimes, trampling saplings beneath boots and carwheels and helping to keep the woods at bay.

This lonely, forgotten side road was something different. Here, the boundary between road and woods wasn't always clear. As they walked further, though, Laura began to see what Pa meant. Ahead of her, she could make out a long straight swath where the ground was flat and the trees were shorter and not gathered so closely together.

On either side, Laura began to notice square columns of brick and stone. They were evenly spaced, standing in neat rows. They began to pass one after another, and Laura soon realized that they were chimneys. The houses that once surrounded them had fallen away, their wooden boards and shingles absorbed into the nest of forest foliage from which the lonely pillars rose.

Pa weaved the handcar around the shrubs and brambles that choked the old main street. Every so often, he would hold up a hand, and Laura knew she must be still and quiet while Pa listened. But each time there was nothing but bird songs and the creak of pine boughs.

As they ventured further into the abandoned town, the chimneys gave way to bigger ruins. They began to come across old creetrock buildings, squat and grey. Their roofs were caved in, and Laura could see trees peeping up from inside some of them, like little walled gardens.

Eventually, the trail led them to a cluster of larger structures made of stone and brick. One of them rose three levels high. Its third level had partly collapsed, but still it towered over Laura, bigger than any building she had ever seen.

Pa squatted down next to her and pointed up. She followed his finger to a big circle set into the face of the building. The circle was made of smooth white stone, and a flat bar of copper had been hammered lengthwise across its center.

"That's a clock, Laura," said Pa. "Or it was. It was so everyone in the town could look up at that building and know exactly what time of day it was."

Laura didn't understand how someone could know what time it was just by looking at a big circle, but she thought the clock was very pretty, the way its white stone contrasted with the brown stone blocks that surrounded it. For a while, it seemed that they might stay the night inside the clock building, but when Pa inspected it he said it was too clogged up with rubble. The tall stone walls looked sturdy enough from the outside, but inside the upper levels had all spilled down into the lower levels. There would be nowhere to set up camp.

It was the same with the other big stone buildings. Finally, just as Ma was warning the girls that they would probably need to spend another night out of doors, Pa pointed to a plain square structure. It was separated from the clock building by a grove of young pines. They made their way towards it.

The building was made of creetrock, the lectricmade stone that seemed to characterize all Merican ruins, its surfaces dappled all over in the telltale grays and yellows. Cracks twisted and spread up and down its sides, and orange decay stained its ridges like frosting on a soycake. But every wall still stood. They would serve to keep out the wind. Its roof had survived as well, at least in part, enough to shelter them from the snow. After a brief inspection, Pa emerged, swung his rifle back over his shoulder and nodded. He wheeled the handcar around the back, out of sight, while Laura and Mary helped Ma push aside some of the rubble blocking the doorway.

Several large, empty windows invited the woods into the front room, but a short hallway connected this exposed area to a more sheltered space around the corner. Tentatively, Ma led Laura and Mary deeper into the abandoned building. When they came to the back room, Ma unwrapped Baby Grace and handed her to Mary.

Laura wandered about the room, examining the mysterious shapes that rose from the shadows. There had been ruins scattered around the Big Woods near their home. Buried nearby, Laura had sometimes found broken glass bottles and rusted pots and pans and Merican coins but never the great treasures of Lectric Times that Pa talked about in his stories. This abandoned creetrock chamber promised a better sort of scav, and Laura gazed about in awe.

Beams of sunlight broke through in patches from the dilapidated roof, and it gave the place an eerie quality. Laura stopped in front of a pile of rubble. It was more than twice her height. Bent metal bars and yellowed shards of hardmold weaved in and out of one another, all so twisted and weathered that it took Laura a moment to recognize the outlines of tables and chairs within the chaotic heap. A sunbeam fell directly down upon the rubble pile, illuminating its jagged surfaces and casting deep shadows into its hollows. Flakes of snow rode the sunbeam downward, gently settling and disappearing into the nest of broken furniture.

"Don't touch it, Laura. You'll get yourself cut again," hissed Mary in Laura's ear.

Mary stood behind her, bouncing Baby Grace against her shoulder.

"I wasn't!" Laura hissed back, though she had just been thinking of doing exactly that. A long rod that looked like it once had been the leg of a tall stool jutted off to the side of the pile, and Laura couldn't help eyeing it, wondering if she could pull it free without upsetting the rest of the pile.

The creetrock building had been a restrant, Ma told them. She too was taking stock of the room, noting where the snow sprinkled down through the ceiling's gaping holes and where it did not. When Laura asked what a restrant was, Ma explained it was a place where wealthy Mericans would go during Lectric Times and have their suppers cooked for them by servants. She pointed to a pile of broken clay plates lying in a corner.

"For a few coppers, you could come inside, and the restrant servants would cook you all manner of food and then bring it to you right at your table. Through that doorway's the kitchen, if I'm not mistaken," she said and pointed to a pair of rusted iron doors, one of which hung crooked by a single hinge.

Mary thought a restrant sounded like a marvelous place. Laura wasn't sure. What if she didn't like the food the servants brought her? She would have to eat all of it, for she knew it was very bad to waste food. She thought she would rather eat food cooked by Ma, who knew just what Laura liked and always gave her perfect Laura-sized portions.

But she knew that a special place like a restrant was probably full of special lectric scav, and she eyed the iron kitchen doors, wondering what treasures might be found in the chamber beyond.

Suddenly, just as Laura was considering this, she heard a noise. It came from behind the doors, from the room that Ma said had once been the restrant's kitchen. The noise was a clattering, as if a collection of objects had been knocked to the floor. Ma froze. Cautiously and quietly, she stepped in front of Mary and Laura. She put a finger to her lips to tell them they must not make a sound. Laura inched closer to Mary and clutched her sister's hand. They all stood still and watched the doors. They hardly dared to breathe.

That was how Pa found them when, a moment later, he came tramping down the hallway, dusting snow from his clothes. When he saw the looks of fear on their faces, he stopped in his tracks. His eyes met Ma's. Then he followed Ma's gaze towards the kitchen doorway. Now all four of them stood still, watching the iron doors. Laura felt her heart beating in her chest. Another clattering sound, fainter but unmistakable, came from the dark recesses of the restrant kitchen.

Pa nodded and unshouldered his rifle. He smiled at the girls to let them know it was ok. He was just being cautious. He crept closer to Ma.

"Place has sat undisturbed for quite a time by the looks," he whispered. "A fair bit of settling's to be expected after the knocking about we've been doing."

Still, he held the rifle's muzzle aloft as he approached the iron doors.

Pa peered as best he could through the gap left by the crooked right-hand door, which leaned drunkenly from its one good hinge. It did not seem as if Pa saw anything out of place. After pressing his eye to the gap from every angle he could think, he turned back to Ma and shrugged. Then, gingerly, he tested the door. The rusted old iron let out shrill creak, but begrudgingly the door gave way. Pa eased it open.

"Charles . . ." Ma whispered. The word hung there, floating. There was a breathless tone of fear to Ma's voice that Laura did not care for, not at all.

Pa's head disappeared behind the door for a moment or two. When he emerged, he shrugged again and motioned to Ma.

"Lamp," he said, mouthing the word silently.

Ma picked Pa's flint out of his satchel. Then she went to the lantern that sat beside their bedrolls and lit the wick. She crept towards the kitchen doors and handed the lantern to Pa. Pa kissed her on the cheek. Then he nudged open the door once again and squeezed his way through the narrow opening. Laura saw him set the lamp down on the floor just as the door creaked shut once again, leaving only a flickering glow dancing within the gaps in the doorway.

Ma backed away and crouched beside Laura and Mary. They listened to the sounds of Pa picking his way around the kitchen, sliding obstacles out of his way, rummaging in debris.

Then suddenly there was a more frightening noise. It was a growl, the growl of a wild animal. It was like a wolfdog's growl, only it was higher pitched, less resonant and guttural. Beside her, Mary gasped and clutched Laura's hand more tightly. Ma stood, placing herself between the girls and the terrible sound coming from the old lectric kitchen. Laura noticed for the first time that Ma had picked an iron table leg out of the pile of broken furniture. She gripped it in her fist like a club.

"Charles? . . ." Ma called, her voice forcefully level.

Suddenly, the door burst open as Pa stumbled backwards. It lurched back and forth on its single hinge until finally the hinge snapped.

The old iron door broke free at last. Briefly, it stood there teetering, as if unsure what to do next. Then, it came crashing to the floor. The door was lighter than it looked. Still, it made Laura jump when it landed with a hollow thud, kicking up clouds of dust and dried leaves that swirled towards them. Beside her, Mary shrieked.

As the dust settled, Laura peeked her head out from behind Ma. The kitchen doorway stood open. The lantern sat on the floor just past the threshold, throwing big enigmatic shadows across every surface. Black against the lamplight, Pa's silhouette stood in the doorway. He held his rifle high, aiming back towards the kitchen.

"Charles!" said Ma. "Charles! What's in there?"

All at once, the tension in Pa's body seemed to melt away. To everyone's surprise, he let out what sounded like a laugh. He set down his rifle. Turning to them, he wiped a hand across his forehead and then all the way down through his bushy beard. He shook his head and chuckled in relief.

"It's alright," he told them. "Just let myself get startled, that's all. It's alright."

"Is something in there, Charles?" Ma demanded. "What is it?"

"What is it?" said Pa. "I'll be hanged if I even know how to answer that. And you'll not believe me til you lay your own eyes on it in any case. Laura, fetch me a strip of saltmeat from my pouch. Let's see if we can tempt him out."

Confused but excited, Laura let go of Mary's hand and went to Pa's leather satchel. Never taking her eyes off the dark recesses of the kitchen, where shadows cast by the lamp continued to dance, she opened the satchel. She pulled out a bundle of dried meat wrapped in hide and removed a piece. Then she crept up behind Pa and handed him the hunk of salted deer.

Pa tore the meat into even smaller strips and placed one just outside the kitchen doorway, resting it on top of the fallen iron door. He then motioned for Laura to back away, and, together, they joined Mary and Ma and Baby Grace at the other end of the room. Pa told them to be very quiet.

Minutes passed. They stared into the flickering lamplight. Nothing happened. Then, softly at first, there was a skittering sound. It was the sound of claws scraping against the creetrock floor. Through the doorway, Laura saw a shadow rising within the kitchen. Slowly, the shadow grew. It rose tall and fearsome from its unseen source, its shape warped into grotesque proportions by the lantern lying on the floor.

As the skittering came closer, the shadow took the form an enormous four-legged beast, lumbering its way towards them. Mary squeaked in alarm and clutched Pa's coat.

"Shhh," he told her. "There's no danger. Watch."

The monstrous shadow loomed ever larger, growing more distended as the creature approached the lamp. Suddenly, it appeared in doorway. It crossed in front of the lantern. Instantly, the shadow shrunk back down, whipping around in the other direction. The creature paused there in the doorway, a black silhouette surrounded by the flickering lamplight.

Laura couldn't believe how tiny it was. The shadow had only appeared tall and ferocious because of the angle of the lantern. The little black shape crouching in the kitchen doorway was no bigger than a loaf of soybread.

The creature crawled tentatively forward. It snuffled, extending its head towards the bait that Pa had laid. As it approached, unable to resist the scent of the saltmeat, its features finally became visible.

Laura had never seen an animal like it, not even in the pages of *A Children's Illustrated Book of Animals*. It had a flat snout like a pig and cheeks that drooped down over its mouth in a comical grimace. Its coat looked black at first, but as it snuffled closer, Laura saw that it was brindled all over in light brown stripes like a tiger. Its head seemed too large for its body, and it waddled forward on a set of stubby, thoroughly impractical, legs. Queerest of all were its ears. They were enormous. They stuck straight up from its little round head like a bat's. Laura could not have imagined anything less terrifying.

"Pa . . ." she whispered, "What is that thing?"

Pa scratched his beard thoughtfully as the creature made its way to the strip of saltmeat. It was missing an eye, Laura now saw. Its remaining eye, unnaturally large and round, regarded them warily even as the little animal began gnawing at the meat.

"It's a dog," said Pa. "No doubt about it now that I've had a better look. But if it isn't the head-scratchingest dog I've ever laid eyes on, I'll eat my hat. I've run across packs of wild ratdogs not much bigger than this. But I can't say I've ever seen the like of those ears. Some jimmed-up breed from before the Bust I reckon. Where's a dog like that come from, that's the real question. Hard to imagine such a thing surviving long in the woods on those stubby little legs."

Pa approached the pigdog slowly. It backed away, abandoning

its treat, and began to growl its high-pitched growl. The sound now seemed adorable rather than frightening. Pa crouched low and extended a gentle hand. The little dog stopped growling. It tilted its head and examined Pa with its one bulging black eye. Finally, it crept forward to snuffle at Pa's hand. When Pa offered it another scrap of deer meat, the dog snatched it right from his hand. Pa laughed.

"Certainly tame enough," he said. "How'd you get here, little fella? Where's your people?"

The little dog allowed Pa to reach out and scratch it between its big bat ears. Giggling, Laura and Mary both rushed to Pa's side. The pigdog feigned a meager retreat but quickly bounded forward again to greet the girls.

"He's friendly!" Mary exclaimed.

They watched the dog bury its face once again in the deer meat.

"Hungry, but he's not malnourished," Pa observed. "Escaped from some bunker do you suppose? Uncle Freddie used to say, bunkerfolk have the queerest things squirreled away in their holes."

"Nonsense, Charles," said Ma. "I haven't heard talk of bunkerfolk since I was a little girl. They all died off years ago. Perhaps he ran off from a trade convoy that passed this way. Who knows what strange pets they breed out west?"

Pa and Ma continued their discussion in low, serious tones. Laura could not bring herself to pay any attention. She and Mary were absorbed by the slobbering antics of the little brindled pigdog. When he had finished all the deer meat, he licked Mary's hand. Then he licked Laura's. Then he yipped and spun around in a happy circle.

"What should we call him?" asked Mary.

Laura thought of the story Ma would sometimes tell them at bedtime, about a little boy who uses some magic soybeans to climb up to the moon.

"Let's call him Jack."

FIVE: TWO NIGHTS UNDER ONE ROOF

It was splendid to sleep indoors for a change. Their campfire heated that old creetrock building right up, and Laura slept warm and cozy.

When she woke up the next morning, it was snowing harder than it had the day before. Through the holes in the roof, the snow came in flurries, settling atop the pile of broken furniture like a snow-capped mountain. After some discussion, Ma and Pa decided that they would stay another night beneath the roof of the abandoned restrant.

Pa said that he had seen quail when he had gone out to disguise their tracks. He would use the day to go out hunting.

Laura and Mary were sent out to gather firewood. Trotting

along beside them was the little striped pigdog they had discovered in the restrant kitchen.

Jack was a bundle of energy. As Laura and Mary searched for kindling, he plowed right through the snow. Sometimes, he disappeared beneath the snowdrifts, and all Laura could see were his funny bat ears. Then he would pop his head up like a gopher from its burrow and give them a satisfied look, his tongue dangling limp from his open-mouthed smile.

More than once, Jack saw a squirrel. Then he would bark and give chase. Laura did not think he could ever catch one. Ma had said that there were mice nesting in the rubble inside the restrant and perhaps that's what Jack had been eating. Laura guessed Jack could catch a mouse, but a squirrel was something different. Jack's stubby little legs were not made for climbing trees.

They spent all day with Jack. When Laura and Mary had tired him out with playing, he sat beside Ma as she nursed Baby Grace. His big round eye watched and watched until finally Ma reached out to scratch between his ears and told him what a good boy he was.

When Pa returned, he didn't have any quail. Instead, he had a fat gray rabbit. He carried it by its hind legs, and its long ears slapped against his knees.

They cooked the rabbit over the fire. Laura and Mary each got a leg. The fresh meat tasted good. Once she had picked off all the flesh, Laura licked the juice off her fingers. Pa let them feed the scraps to Jack, who gnawed happily on the bones.

When they had finished supper, Pa brought out his map. It had stopped snowing outside, and there was daylight coming in through the holes in the restrant roof. Pa dragged one of the restrant's old tables out into the sunbeam. He straightened out the rusted legs as best he could with his hammer and steadied the broken table with chunks of creetrock. When it was as steady and level as it would get, Pa wiped down the yellowed hardmold surface with a rag, and there he unrolled his map.

Pa had bought the map at the Laketown Market from Rakesh Halfsilver, the scav merchant who sometimes traded metal scrap with Pa and had once paid a handsome price for an unopened bottle of Merican liquor that Ma had discovered in the cellar of their cabin in the Big Woods.

Rakesh Halfsilver's map was drawn with black ink on parchment, but Pa said it had been copied from an old paper map, the kind that the Mericans used to use when they would ride their lectric cars back and forth across the Old Empire from the Eastern Ocean to the Western.

Pa had seen the original with his own eyes. These old paper maps were so thin and so cleverly creased, Pa had told her, that they could be folded up and put in your front pocket. But, of course, Rakesh Halfsilver did not keep his paper map folded up in his pocket. It was too fragile and too valuable. The trader kept it pressed flat between two wooden boards in the back of his tent. He only brought it out when someone wanted to buy one of his parchment copies, and even then Pa said he was very stingy about letting anyone see it.

Laura knew that paper scav was very rare and precious. That was why she was always careful and gentle with *A Children's Illustrated Book of Animals,* keeping it wrapped up safe in its hide cover when it was tucked inside her batman carrysack. Pa said that when his Uncle Freddie had been a boy, folks mostly used their lectric screens for reading and writing and had no need for books of paper or parchment. What paper books they did have, most got burned up long ago in the May Madness, when the people living in the old Ghost Cities got so angry they lit those cities on fire.

Laura had often tried to imagine reading a book with a lectric screen. She had seen all sorts of screens. They were so commonplace in Merican ruins that scavmen hardly considered them worth collecting. There were little screens that could fit in the palm of your hand. There were big screens as big as a whole person. Big or small, Laura did not understand how someone could draw a map, let alone write a whole book, on one of those black hardmold planks.

Pa smoothed out Rakesh Halfsilver's parchment map and

weighted its corners down with creetrock stones. Laura stood on the tips of her toes, stretching herself as far as she could above the old hardmold table to have a look.

It was a very big map. Fully unfurled, it was nearly as wide as Laura was tall. On it were all the lakes and mountains and rivers that they would need to cross to get from the Big Woods to the Wastes. The map was covered all over in dotted lines. Those lines showed all the Old Number Roads and lots of other, smaller Merican roads besides. Whenever Pa brought the map out, Laura liked to crouch down next to him and trace their journey down along the many turns and forks of the map's inky web.

Down in the lower righthand corner, there was a little drawing of the Great Towers, standing at the edge of Mishgan Lake. Starting from the Great Towers, Laura ran her finger west along the bottom of the map until she found Davenport. There it was, right where the thick, meandering line of the Mighty Misisip River met the double dashes of the Great Eighty Road. Pa said that nearly ten thousand people lived in Davenport. Laura tried to imagine a town with so many people and found that she could not. The thought of seeing it made her feel excited and, at the same time, a little afraid.

From Davenport, Laura's eyes tried to trace the old number roads as they twisted and crossed, up up, through the map's empty middle and past the letters that Laura knew spelled out "YOWA." The dotted lines led her back over the Misisip and all the way up into the top corner of the map. That was where the Big Woods were and the Laketowns. On the map, it did not seem so very far between the Big Woods and Davenport. But Laura knew that tracing a road with your eyes was one thing. Tracing it with your feet was something quite different.

Pa's finger hovered over the map. It came down on a spot halfway between Great Mishgan Lake and the drawing of broken towers that represented the ruins of Twins City. Pa tapped that spot. Where his fingernail struck the parchment was a tiny sliver of a lake. Pa reckoned that was the lake they had seen. Of the village that once stood upon its shores and the little restrant where Laura's family had made their camp, however, the map had nothing to say. No nearby settlements were marked. If the town ever had a name, it was lost.

Finally, Pa rolled the hide map back up and tied it with hemp twine, tight and skinny. Now it was time to get their things ready. Tomorrow, they would leave early. In the morning, they must say goodbye to their little restrant in the ruins of the nameless village. Then they would return to the road.

Before bed, Mary and Laura both sat down by the fire to grease their boots. Ma had made Laura's boots for her the previous winter. They had thick buckskin soles and tall ankles that came up halfway to Laura's knees. They were too big, for Ma could not be restitching the leather every few months whenever Laura's feet grew. But when Laura stuffed the toes with cloth, her feet felt snug and comfortable. They were Laura's first pair of real, grown-up boots.

Because Laura's boots were newer than Mary's, they were a different color. Mary always took very good care of her boots. Over time, they had turned a pretty reddish brown. Laura's boots were still a drab sandy color. Laura felt a pang of jealousy when she saw the boots standing side by side, but she knew that if she kept treating the leather regularly, her boots would turn that deep dark color eventually too.

Mary set the jar of tallow down between them, carefully unfastening the lid. The jar seemed small compared to the big clay pots of tallow they had left sitting in the cellar of their house in the Big Woods.

Whenever Pa brought home a deer, before the meat was carved up to be smoked or salted, Ma would strip off the fat and *plop* it would go into her big iron stew pot. She would cook that fat all day, stirring and straining. The whole house filled with the smell, which always made Laura and Mary's stomachs feely queasy.

As soon as the fat was a pure clean liquid, Ma ladled it into containers. It became a hard white paste as it cooled. That was tallow. They could use that tallow for all kinds of things. Ma would use it to cook frycakes and to make her lavender soaps. She would coat pinecones with tallow to use as kindling when dry firewood was scarce. And, of course, it was good for treating buckskin.

Mary scooped up a spoonful of tallow and held it out over the fire to soften it. When it was good and drippy, she dolloped it onto the toe of her boot. With the corner of an old hemp rag, she started to rub the tallow into the leather. Laura did the same, trying her best to copy Mary's careful polishing motions. Jack trotted up beside them to watch, following their movements with his big black eye, a look of puzzlement on his funny smooshed face.

When the tallow was completely absorbed, Laura and Mary added more. They didn't stop rubbing until the leather glistened. Laura knew her boots must be kept well-greased if she wanted her feet to stay dry as she walked through the snow.

By the time they were finished, the fire was dying and it was time for bed. Laura crawled over to her bed roll, and Ma tucked the blankets snug around her. From her little cocoon, she watched Pa clean his rifle. After a while, he looked up and gave her a wink. He set his rifle down. Then he went to a corner and picked up his two-string. Laura had not even seen him bring the instrument into the restrant.

Pa pulled his stool closer to the flickering embers of their fire and rested the two-string's barrel in his lap. Then he picked up his bow and began to play. Softly, he sang. It was one of the old traditionals that Uncle Freddie had taught him. The words echoed off the creetrock walls and mingled with the smoke that snaked out through the hole in the roof. Even Ma set down what she was doing and sat and listened.

And all the roads we have to walk are winding
And all the lights that lead us there are blinding
There are many things that I
Would like to say to you but I don't know how
Because maybe, you're gonna be the one that saves me

"Play the one about the blackbird," Laura whispered when he was finished.

"Shhh," Pa told her. "Close your eyes now, Soybean." But even as he said it, he was already adjusting the frets on his two-string and feeling out the starting note with his bow.

As Pa began to sing about teaching the blackbird to fly on broken wings, Jack padded up to Laura's bed and tried to nuzzle his way beneath the blankets. Laura freed up a spot for him and put her arms around the little pigdog. Together, they drifted off into a warm, pleasant sleep.

SIX: A FINE WATCHDOG

Laura's eyes were full of tears. They couldn't leave him, she pleaded. They just couldn't.

"I'm growing fond of the animal too, Laura," Pa told her, squatting down to her height and placing his big hands on her shoulders. "But to take him with us would be no kindness. I can't have him riding atop the car, and he's not like to keep up. Not on those stubby legs."

"I could carry him!" protested Laura.

"I know you would try, my little pickled soybean. But we don't know what lies ahead of us on the long road. I need you taking care of yourself, not of a little pigdog. It would be best to leave him here. Perhaps he will find his way back to his people."

Laura did not think so. If Jack still had a home and a family that cared for him, why was he living in a crumbling old Merican restrant, eating mice? When she began to sob, Ma gave her a sharp "that's enough of that now," and Laura did her best to be brave.

Mary was clearly upset as well, but she knew better than to argue and cause a fuss. And so, in muted grief, the girls hoisted their carrysacks up onto their shoulders and said goodbye to their new friend.

When the car was loaded, Pa took its shafts in hand, and they started off the way they had come, past the stone clock building and down the long grove of chimneys, back to the old number road that would lead them towards the Misisip.

Laura trudged through the ruins of the nameless Merican village in the tracks that the handcar cut through the new-fallen snow. Suddenly, she heard a *yip* from the trees behind them, and she looked over her shoulder to see Jack scampering after them

46

through the snow drifts. Ma and Pa had seen the dog too, and Laura saw them exchange a look.

By the time they rolled the car back up onto the flat, treeless path that marked the Thirty-Nine Road, Jack had caught up with them. Pa wondered if they shouldn't try to scare him off. They could throw rocks or shout at Jack to drive him off. But Ma said she couldn't bear the thought of such cruelty.

"Leave the poor creature be, Charles. Please. He'll tire soon enough and turn back."

And so they continued down the road, with Jack following after them. Sometimes, he fell back to sniff the snow-covered hull of an old lectric car or to investigate some sound from the woods that flanked the old number road, but he was soon right back at their heels. He didn't tire. To everyone's surprise, he kept up with them all day.

"He's tougher than he looks," Pa admitted.

Indeed, as the sun began to dip lower in the gray-blue sky and Laura's shadow began to stretch across the snow like sap candy, it seemed that Jack was the only one who wasn't exhausted.

It had been a very long day of walking, but still they did not stop and make camp. Pa did not want to stop until they found the crossroads marked on Rakesh Halfsilver's map where the Thirty-Nine Road met another old number road.

According to the parchment map, they could follow this second Merican road west to the ruins of a town called Pepin. There, they would try and cross the Mighty Misisip into Yowa country. Pa was certain that the place where they would turn west was not far from the abandoned lakeside village where they had spent two nights.

The day grew late, and still the crossroads did not appear. Pa shook his head and muttered to himself every time he stopped to scan the horizon. Eventually, he announced that they must have passed the second number road without knowing. Laura looked around. Everything was covered in snow, and it was sometimes hard to tell where the road ended and the woods began.

Pa said that they had best make camp. In the morning, they

would retrace their steps. He pulled the handcar up off the road.

The place where they stopped was rocky and sparsely wooded. Nearby, they found a dry gully. Ma said that they would camp at the bottom, and that would provide some shelter from the wind. The sides of the gully were too steep for the handcar, so Pa found a thicket of short, gnarled shrubs on the ridge above. There, he tucked the car and its cargo in among the branches. Then he went back to cover their tracks while Ma and the girls carried the things that they would need that night down into the gully.

There was no singing or storytelling that evening. Instead of his two-string, Pa brought Rakesh Halfsilver's map with him when he joined Ma at their campsite. He squinted at it in consternation as Mary and Laura laid down their bedrolls. Even when the dusk light had faded and he could not possibly make out the ink trails on its face, he sat with the parchment on his lap, running his fingers through his beard.

For supper, there was hard saltmeat and leftover soybread. Then it was straight to bed. Laura curled up beneath her blankets thinking about the fat juicy rabbit they had enjoyed the night before. Even Jack seemed in low spirits. The little dog lay between Laura and Mary, his chin flat against the ground as his big bulgy eye followed Ma around the campfire while she doused the last of its flames.

~~~

Laura woke to the sound of Jack barking. It seemed to her as if only a moment had passed, but when she looked up she found that the moon had sunk low in the sky. She knew then that she had been asleep for many hours.

Jack was no longer lying beside her. He was somewhere above them, up at the top of the gully. He barked and growled and barked again. Suddenly, Pa was up, rifle in hand.

"Charles . . ." Laura heard Ma whisper.

"Stay here," Pa whispered back.

He circled around them, smooth and silent as a passing shadow.

Before Laura knew what was happening, Ma had grabbed her

beneath her arms and pulled her behind a dirt embankment where the gully gently curved. Mary huddled down next to her, Baby Grace still asleep in her arms. Ma crouched in front of them, flat against the gully wall. Both her fists were wrapped around the handle of Pa's hatchet. Moonlight glinted off the iron head, which waited, tense and ready, at Ma's shoulder.

Laura held her breath. There was more barking. The clatter of rocks. Then, voices. Pa's. But also another. Beside her, she heard Mary gasp.

Laura couldn't make out what Pa was saying, but as the minutes passed she felt she could hear some of the forcefulness fade from his tone. Jack stopped barking.

Finally, footsteps approached. Mary and Laura both sat up straight. Ma adjusted her grip on the hatchet.

Laura peeked around the embankment. Two figures climbed down out of the shadows that covered the walls of the ravine. When they reached the gully floor, moonlight fell upon them. One was Pa. The look on his face was calm and measured, but the barrel of his rifle was raised and pointed towards the other figure.

He walked a few steps ahead of Pa, holding his arms out to the sides, palms open, to show he had nothing in his hands.

As they approached, the stranger's features emerged from shadow. His face was smooth, except for two streaks of soft black hair smeared on either side of his upper lip. In truth, he was a boy, Laura realized as he and Pa drew closer, perhaps no more than a few years older than Mary. He wore a green jacket and matching green pants. Neither seemed to fit him. Even by the dim light of the moon, Laura could see how dirty he was. His feet were bare. He looked frightened.

Between Pa and the boy trotted Jack. He snuffled at the stranger's toes, then lifted his head and gave a quizzical yip before bounding over to Ma.

"It's alright," called Pa. "It's nearly dawn anyway, Caroline. Why don't we get a cookfire going?"

~~~

The young man's name was Marco. His manners were polite. He called Pa "sir" and Ma "ma'am" and was always thanking and apologizing. Laura found it hard to dislike him, even if he was a thief.

Marco never denied it. He had seen their smoke the night before and had waited until after dark to approach their camp. He'd been going through their provisions in the car when Jack raised the alarm. Tears welled up in his eyes as he admitted to the crime.

"Like I told your husband, ma'am," he said to Ma, "I was only lookin' for sum't eat, and I sure never meant to put a scare to you or your family. It's a shameful thing takin' food from the mouths of children, I know, and hateful in the eyes of the Prezdent Above. But hunger drives a man to things he mightn't otherwise."

Pa scratched thoughtfully below his neck whiskers.

"Dare say I've seen men do worse for hunger," he said.

The young man nodded towards the ground. He murmured something that sounded like "me too."

Dawn was turning the sky a pale gray violet. The fire was burning well, sending out tendrils of sweet earthy smoke. The smoke mingled with the morning mist which sat in the gully like soymilk settling into a cup of nettle tea. For the second time, Pa asked Marco if he was alone. Marco said he was. The way he said it, Laura believed him.

Pa and Ma exchanged a look that Laura couldn't interpret. Finally, Ma said, "Well, it sounds as if we'll all be better for some breakfast."

Ma placed her big flat iron skillet over the fire and set about making frycakes. As the soymeal gruel sizzled in its shallow bath of tallow, everyone seemed to relax. Eventually, Pa lowered his rifle.

The first frycake came out warm and steaming in the chilly dawn air. Ma spooned a dollop of wildberry jam on top and handed it to their guest. Marco looked overwhelmed, as if the fluffy yellow disc was the finest gift he had ever received.

More frycakes emerged from the pan and flopped down onto tin plates. They were best hot, so nobody waited for everyone to be served. They ate them up just as soon as they were ready. Laura liked to roll hers up like a parchment scroll let the jam squirt out the ends as she would take a bite.

At one point, Pa took over at the skillet so Ma could eat. As he flipped the soymeal cakes and spooned out the jam, he peppered Marco with questions. Where had he come from? Where was he bound?

Laura knew she was not supposed to speak while grown-ups were talking. But she could listen. She listened to everything the young man had to say, savoring her frycake in the meanwhile.

Marco had grown up to the south, Laura learned, in the lands called the Illinoy. He had been a soldier.

"General Rhee?" asked Pa, depositing another flat frycake on the stranger's plate.

Laura paused mid-bite. She looked from her father to the boy in the muddy green jacket, a wad of unchewed dough tucked into her cheek like a curious little squirrel. General Rhee was a famous caudillo. It was he that had founded the Army of Faith's Spear Triumphant, the men that had overrun the Illinoy and driven Clan Ortega west.

Laura had heard Pa talking about Faith's Spear with his friend Jim Cordry. Mr. Cordry often visited them when he was in the Wisconsin. He traveled far and wide on convoy and was always a great source of news. He and Pa would spend hours on the porch of the house in the Big Woods, smoking pipeleaf and conversing. Laura had liked to linger about to listen whenever she could get away with it. Sometimes it was boring, like when Mr. Cordry would argue with Pa about tariffs or silver inflation or the persecution of Lacorian missionaries. But sometimes they talked of far-off lands and great battles that were like something out of the adventures of Wane the Batman.

The names of powerful caudillos like General Rhee and Lucius Ortega and Roland the Hatchet, they had a fantastical quality, like something out of a storybook. Hearing Pa mention one of them now, in such a matter-of-fact manner, was startling.

Marco stared into the campfire. He nodded at Pa's question at first. Then, considering, he bobbled his head.

"The exalted general was called to Heaven last spring. His brother-in-law, General Albright—Glasseye the men all call him—now commands the Spear. Or some. Some chose to march east with Captain Sung . . . General Sung now, I mean."

"A great many generals," said Pa, as he took Ma's plate from her. Before she could protest, he'd scooped another steaming frycake and a spoonful of jam onto the dish and deposited the dish right back into her lap.

In fits and starts, Marco told them his story. He had been Laura's age when he was taken in by the Army of Faith's Spear Triumphant. Ever since, he had been a soldier. Laura could not bring herself to imagine it. She was nearly nine years old and could do a great many things, like grind soymeal and clean fish and even sew a cross-stitch. But she could not imagine herself as a soldier, carrying a gun and marching into battle.

Faith's Spear had been like a family to Marco, he told them. He would never have thought himself a deserter, and it seemed to Laura as if it pained him to even say the word. But a few months ago, everything had started to go wrong for Marco the boy soldier.

After General Rhee died, the commander of the fort where Marco was assigned had been purged. Laura wasn't sure what that meant exactly, but it sounded bad. The new commander was harsh with Marco, and it made him want to run away.

Then, a little while later, came an outbreak the Yellow Madness. Laura had never heard of Yellow Madness before, but from the way that Ma sucked in her breath and drew away from the stranger, she guessed it was another name for the Ague. A shiver went up Laura's spine.

Suddenly it seemed that everyone in Marco's fort was sick. Many soldiers were taken by the Ague, including one of Marco's childhood friends. Marco was very scared, and he decided to run away the first chance he had.

One night, some of the sick men somehow broke free of their restraints and escaped from the infirmary, into the dark underground hallways below the fort's armory. While the rest of the garrison was occupied attempting to subdue the crazed men, Marco stuffed what supplies he could into his marching bag and slipped over the wall.

He had been on the road nearly two months.

"Why north?" asked Pa. "Have you kin among the Laketowns?"

Marco shook his head and shrugged as Pa took his plate.

The soymeal and the jam had been put away. Pa splashed some water from a drinking sac into the iron pan and let the fire bring it to a boil. Though not a morsel of frycake was left on any of the tin plates, Pa plopped them one by one into the hot water anyway.

"Why not go west?" piped up Laura without thinking. "That's where we're going!"

Her parents both turned to her, a look of warning written on their faces. Mary too, though she was only two years older and had no right to be giving Laura such bossy looks. Laura's face reddened. She knew better than to be telling strangers about the family's comings and goings. She stared at the ground, fiddling with the drawstring on her cloak.

Marco glanced nervously back and forth between Laura and Pa, wiping the back of his hand across his wispy moustache, before breaking the tense moment of silence.

"That's a smart girl you've got there, sir. I asked myself much the same as the snow got deeper and food scarce. It's wilder country up here than I ever reckoned on, that's true enough. But you see, Miss, the way I saw it I didn't have much choice. South and east the Spear'd have caught me for certain and hung me for a deserter. And west, well, that's Ortega territory . . ."

The young man unbuttoned the collar of his jacket and pulled it aside. A line of dark blue ink ran up the side of his chest all the way to his neck. It ended in a sharp diamond-shaped point, ringed with a thin halo of flames. Laura wasn't sure what it meant, but she supposed it was something the people who lived in Yowa country wouldn't like.

Pa nodded as if he understood.

"Well, if you can make it as far as Greensbay, I'll give you some names. The situation in the Laketowns is complicated just at the moment. But these are good people, and they'll help you if they can. Tell them Charles Ingalls sends his regards."

Pa gave Marco the names of some of the Laketown merchants and farmers he knew. He told him about Mr. Abdullah and his soy mill and Mr. and Mrs. Johansen, who farmed the flat land east of Iron River and would need help with their planting come spring. He mentioned the Mwangi sisters who controlled the salt trade, and even Raskesh Halfsilver with his tent full of artifacts. Pa showed Marco the number roads to follow to make it through the Big Woods all the way to Great Mishgan Lake.

Eventually, Marco went back to fetch his belongings. He returned with a big carrysack. Then, he and Pa sat down to trade. Laura watched the piles of goods in front of them grow and shrink as the two bargained back and forth. Laura knew that Pa would give Marco a fair deal. He was always an honest trader. Still, she couldn't help but notice how the stranger looked like a frightened little boy sitting there next to her father.

In the end, they gave Marco a half-pound bag of soymeal, two jars stuffed with pickled kale, a fat bundle of saltmeat wrapped in hide, a spare set of gloves, and an old Merican coat made from lectric fabrics, which Ma had mended and lined with warm wolf fur. Marco traded them a half-filled pouch of gunpowder, a sack of special bullets for some kind of lectric gun, and three silver coins. The bullets wouldn't fit in Pa's rifle, but they were rare scav and might fetch a good price at market once they reached Davenport.

Once the trading was done, they packed up camp. The sun was bright in the sky, and it was time to return to the road. Marco walked with them for a little while, trudging beside the handcar with his big bag over his shoulder, telling Pa more about his life fighting for the Army of Faith's Spear Triumphant.

Before long, they came to a clearing bounded by short mounds of creetrock rubble. Nearby, the ruins of a big lectric wagon lay on its side, dusted in snow. Pa declared that this must be the crossroad. Laura looked east. Then she looked west. The faint outline of a road stretched over the hills and into the distance in both directions. Now that she had seen it, she didn't understand how they could have missed it the night before

"Well, lad, this is where we part ways," said Pa.

"Thank you for your kindness, sir," the young man said. "The Prezdent Above protect you and your family on your travels."

They watched him walk away, up the Thirty-Nine Road, bound for the country that they themselves had just abandoned.

"All that food, Charles," Ma said when he was out of hearing. "Can we spare it?"

"At that price, I dare say we can," Pa replied. "Three silvers for a week's provisions and an old coat? Plus the shells may fetch the same again at market. Don't fret, Caroline. We're well stocked yet."

When Laura thought about it, it was an awful lot of silver for the things they had given Marco. But she guessed that a fair price for something depended on how much a person needed it.

"Anyhow, we must count ourselves lucky. Last night could have turned out a deal worse. We'll need to be more careful in the future when we make camp."

Squatting at Pa's feet, Jack gave a little yip, as if he agreed. Pa looked down and smiled.

And so they started west, Jack riding happily on the back of the handcar.

SEVEN: SHOWTALES

One night, Laura and her family made camp by a lake. They had been following a road called the Ten Road. Or maybe it was called the Ninety-Four Road. Or else it had no name. Pa's map wasn't clear. They had turned down more crossroads and cutoffs than Laura could count as the old number roads led them zigging and zagging towards Pepin, the place that Rakesh Halfsilver had marked on his map and where Pa said that winter trade convoys sometimes crossed the frozen Misisip River.

They had been following their present road for three days. On the parchment map, it appeared as a squiggly trail of dots, cutting diagonally across the corner formed by two thicker ink routes. Whether the cutoff was called the Ten Road or the Ninety-Four Road, little remained of it. In stretches, the creetrock had crumbled away to nothing. Then the handcar's wheels would clang and rattle as they bounced over roots and rabbit warrens. The cutoff was plainly little used.

Because the old road was so overgrown with vegetation, they stopped often so that Pa could clear a path with his hatchet. Pa had hoped the cutoff would take them to Pepin faster, but after a day or two of fighting against the terrain, he admitted it would have been better to take the long way around.

At least it was pretty. The cutoff took them through a land of woods and lakes. Whenever they would spy another lake, Mary and Laura would ask if it had a name. If it didn't, they could give it a name themselves. There was Pretty Lake and Golden Lake and Star Lake and Jack's Lake and Lake of Pines and Skinny Lake and Jack's Lake Two. Soon, it seemed there were so many lakes, they would soon run out of names.

One night, they camped beside a lake that Laura and Mary had named Frycake Lake. Though the days had been growing warmer, Frycake Lake was still frozen over. From her place by the fire, Laura could see it, sprawled out between the wooded hills. Its dark glossy surface twinkled, reflecting the starlight above.

It was a clear, warm night, and Pa brought out his two-string. The strings sang as Pa's bow danced across them, their warbling notes sailing out over the frozen lake. Pa joined his voice to the instrument's.

And I was standin' on the side of the road
Rain fallin' on my shoes
Heading out for the east coast
Lord knows I've paid some dues
Gettin' through
Tangled up in blue

When he'd played a few songs, Pa set down his bow and told them a story.

THE STORY OF WANE THE BATMAN AND THE CANDLELIGHT OATH

"This story is about Wane of Gothim. You know him as Wane the Batman, one of the greatest batmen of Old Merica. But this story is from before he became a batman. Before he escaped from the labyrinth or fought the godzilla. Before he traveled to the Underworld or made his great journey to Mount Doom to destroy the Ring of Power.

"This story is from many years before all those adventures, from when Wane the Batman was just a boy, no older than you girls. Wane lived with his mother and father in their little house high in the sky above the City of Gothim.

"As you know, Gothim was the greatest city of Old Merica. Its lectric towers were taller even than the Great Towers of Shicago. More people lived in just one of Gothim's towers than today live in all of the big northern woods and the Laketowns and the whole darn Wisconsin combined. The richest merchants in the whole world came to Gothim, to live in the highest parts of its towers, enjoying the finest luxuries brought in from every corner of the Merican Empire.

"Yet, this was also a time of great turmoil. Old Merica was not the land of peace and plenty it had once been. Years of drought and floods had plagued the land. Harvests had failed. People were hungry.

"Wars across the sea had disrupted trade, and so Gothim's merchants began to fret as their convoys sat home idle. And it was these merchants, you see, who controlled the City of Gothim. Their wealth was legendary. They owned the towers and the sky wagons and the mills that made fuel for all the city's marvelous lectric machines.

"While the silver flowed freely, the powerful merchants of Gothim had worked with one another and ruled the city together in peace. But as the world became ever more treacherous, they grew fearful and greedy. With their stores of silver, they bought guns and hired soldiers. They became caudillos, you might say. They didn't hold towns or forts like General Rhee or Clan Ortega, but they began to wage war with one another for control of Gothim.

"Some of these warlord merchants were cruel and ruthless. But some of them did what they could to protect the people of Gothim and to keep the city from falling apart. Wane's family, they were of this second type.

"They were one of the richest merchant families in the city. Wane grew up in a house amid the clouds, in the tallest tower of all, surrounded by fabulous lectric toys and delicious foods and a library of paperbooks on every subject you can imagine.

"Wane was a smart boy. The best tutors in Gothim were brought in to teach him his letters and instruct him in science and art and all the wondrous secrets of Lectric Times. People said that young Wane was destined to be a great leader of the city, and he worked hard to prepare himself.

"Wane's father traded in screens and other lectric goods. He taught Wane the lectric arts, to forge the hardmold chips and the delicate iron threads that gave life to the screens and to fit them together just so. Just like his father, Wane loved to tinker, taking lectric contraptions apart and adjusting them and putting them back together.

"Wane's mother was a famous doctor. From her, Wane learned all about medicines and herbs and which shakras to treat for which ailments. Together, they all lived happily in their little house atop the tower.

"But, below Wane's tower, all was not well. Out in the streets, people were making a stir. They toppled over Gothim's statues and smashed its big beautiful windows. They set fires that threatened to climb to the very tops of its towers.

"Yet, for a time, life continued for young Wane much as it had. His family kept him safe in his tower, safe from rival caudillos and their soldiers, safe from the mobs in the streets.

"Then, one day, everything changed. The day the lights went out.

"Oh, it had happened before. From time to time, the lectric fuel that powered Gothim's towers would run out or else the underground canals that carried it from the mills would clog up or break. And then everything would suddenly go quiet and dark.

"Now, Wane, he was scared of the dark. Remember, he wasn't used to the long dark nights of the Big Woods like you girls. He knew only the bright lectric lights of Gothim, day and night alike. Whenever the lectric mills would fail, he would press his face against his tower window and look out. Where the glowing peaks and valleys of the great city had stretched out below him just a moment before, now there was only empty blackness. Just imagine how that must have felt for a boy like Wane.

"As things grew worse and worse in Old Merica, the darkness came to Gothim more and more often. The lectric light would disappear. Maybe for an hour, maybe for a day. And so, that night, Wane peered fearfully from his tower window, praying that the city's lectric fuel would flow again soon.

"But the darkness seemed thicker than usual that night. Wane stared down into the formless shadow that had swallowed Gothim, trying to make out the shapes of the buildings he knew must be there. Long hours passed and still the light did not return.

"Suddenly, he felt his father's hand on his shoulder. They must leave, Wane's father told him. Their home in the tower wasn't a safe place anymore. They must travel to a new home. I expect you girls know a bit of how Wane must have felt about that. But, just like you, he knew that his mother and father knew what was best and that he must be brave and helpful on the journey. So he quickly packed up his favorite things and readied himself to go with his parents to their bunker outside the city.

"They left that very morning. The lectric boxes that carried people up and down the towers had stopped, so Wane and his mother and father and all their guards and servants had to walk step after step down the endless stairs of their tall tower. They were all day on those stairs, and everyone was very tired by the time they came to the bottom, where they climbed aboard their lectric cars and set out for the bunker.

"Like a grand trade convoy, the cars made their way through Gothim, one following close behind another. It was slow. Thanks to the mobs, many parts of the city were impassable. Often, the streets were blocked with rubble, and Wane's father's guards would have to get out of their cars to clear a path. Soon, night was falling once again.

"Wane's convoy was crawling slowly through a part of the city that had been badly damaged by the fires, when they heard a cry for help. There was a young woman lying by the side of the road, holding her stomach in pain. Wane's mother told their driver to stop. Before anyone could argue, she had already opened the door and jumped from the car, clutching her doctor bag.

"The convoy halted. Wane's mother knelt beside the injured woman, attempting to treat her wounds. Wane's father ran to her, pleading with her to get back in the car, but it was her oath as a doctor to help the sick if she could. They both huddled there by the side of the road as Wane watched them from the car's open door.

"Wane climbed from the car and took a step towards them, about to call out, when, suddenly, the street was filled with commotion. All at once, his father's guards were out of their cars, rifles in their hands. Wane turned. Other men were emerging from the towers and crowding into the street on either side of the convoy.

"Some stories say these men worked for a rival caudillo. In other versions, they're simply bandits. For my part, I like to think Wane never found out. He would wonder his whole life who they were and what they wanted. To him, they would always just be men with guns, spreading chaos and pain because that's what men with guns do. They were a force of nature, as faceless as the droughts or the floods or the darkness.

"Swiftly, shouts turned to shots. Wane never saw it happen. He looked away for a moment. When he looked back, both his mother and his father were slumped over, motionless by the roadside. Wane tried to run to them, but someone grabbed him and dragged him back, kicking and howling.

"Who do you suppose it was?

"That's right. It was Alfred Butler, the captain of Wane's father's soldiers. Butler threw Wane into the back of the convoy's lead car. It was a fearsome car with heavy black armor. In the rear seat, Butler held Wane down and shouted at the car to drive away. The car heard the alarm in Butler's voice, and it knew how serious the situation was. And so the big black car took off, whirling around obstacles and slamming roadblocks aside with its strong iron armor.

"That faithful lectric car didn't stop until it brought them all the way to the secret entrance to the bunker that Wane's family had built on the outskirts of Gothim. The bunker was hidden away in the side of a mountain. When the car approached, rocks rolled aside like magic, making a doorway for the car.

"Only once they were safely inside did Butler release his grip on young Wane, allowing the boy to throw open the car's door and tumble sobbing out into the cavernous bunker. Now, you girls know that Alfred Butler and that marvelous black car will become like family to Wane the Batman and help him on his many adventures. But right then, Wane hated them both.

"'Take me back!' he shouted, his voice echoing off the bunker's high empty ceilings.

"But neither Butler nor the car would let Wane leave the bunker. Tears stinging his eyes, Wane ran from them, into the bunker's sprawling maze of underground rooms and alcoves.

"Deeper and deeper into the bunker he ran. Soon, he was passing through rooms that weren't yet finished, where the walls were nothing but the bare rock of the mountain, cold and wet. In a daze of grief, he plunged onward, down through winding tunnels leading him deeper beneath the mountain.

"The tunnels grew dark as Wane left the bunker's lectric lights behind, but he kept going, feeling his way along the damp cavern walls. Blackness and silence surrounded him. The only sound was the *drip drip drip* of the cave walls' weeping, echoing through the tunnels. For once, Wane was not afraid of the dark. There was no place inside him for fear. There was only grief and anger.

"Finally, he felt the tunnel widen. Only then did Wane pause and reach into his back pocket. There, he found a candle and a box of matches. He must have taken them from one of the supply rooms he had passed in his flight, he realized, though he had hardly been conscious of his actions.

"Wane lit his candle. The glow yawned and stretched, bringing shape to the cave around him. Jagged needles of rock hung from the ceiling and more stabbed upwards from below, reaching for him like a thousand withered claws. As the flame quivered and swayed, hostile shadows danced around him, leaping in and out of hidden corners and crevices. Taking a step forward, Wane saw that the floor of the cave dropped away. He held his candle over the precipice and peered down. He could see nothing but darkness, stretching down and down into a seemingly bottomless abyss.

"Even then, to his surprise, Wane did not feel fear.

"With his free hand, the boy wiped the tears from his cheeks. He walked along the side of the chasm, through the forest of stone needles that grew from the cave floor. The spikes rose all around him, straight and rigid, some no taller than the toe of his boot, some looming above his head, reminding Wane of the towers of Gothim.

"Eventually, he came to a stone tower, waist-high and flat on its top like a tree stump. Wane set his candle down on top of the stone and knelt before it. There, beside the mouth of that bottomless chasm, the reflection of the candle's flame flickering within his eyes, he swore his oath.

"'I swear by the spirits of my parents,' Wane whispered, 'to avenge their deaths. I will become a batman. I will spend the rest of my life warring on all lawlessness, and I will bring the light back to the City of Gothim.'"

EIGHT: ACROSS THE BIG RIVER

Laura and Mary had thought it another lake at first. They had been arguing about what to name it when Pa explained that the barren white expanse stretching before them was no lake at all but a giant river. The Misisip River. They had reached it at last.

In recent days, nearly every stream and river they encountered, Laura would ask if that was the Misisip. Now she saw how silly that was. Not even the biggest river they had seen so far on their journey could be compared to bigness of the Mighty Misisip River.

Standing there, gazing out at the icy expanse, Laura could not even see the river's other side. Yet, as they travelled along its rocky banks, Laura saw that Pa was right. This was no lake. The bank curved this way and that, but it never seemed to take them around to the other side. The Big River just kept rolling along.

By late afternoon, they came to a wide flat beach by a bend in the Misisip. There, Pa set down the handcar. Then he pulled out his map and compass and squatted down amongst the stones.

The beach's stones were smooth and round. The ground was covered with them. They emerged from beneath the frozen river and spread out all the way to the steep mud embankment that enclosed the beach. Some were as big as Laura's fist and poked up from the shore like buried eggs. Most were pebbles, thousands upon thousands of them, all packed together in a dense carpet that *critch crunched* beneath Laura's boots.

Further up the beach, the stones had been stuck together by ice and frozen mud, but here, sheltered by the embankment, they were loose. As Pa consulted his instruments, Laura dug her foot into the pebbles, feeling the satisfying crackle of the tiny stones giving way.

A flash of color caught Laura's eye. She peered closer down at the pebbles she had turned over with her boot. Amongst the ordinary stone-colored stones were sparkles of green and rose and blue, glossy and translucent. At that very moment, the sun seemed to come out from behind a cloud, making the little gems shine all the brighter. Laura looked around her. Suddenly, the entire beach seemed to glitter.

Laura quickly plucked up several of the gemstones and showed them to Ma. They were bits of old lectricmade glass, Ma told her, polished down into little round pebbles by the river. Laura held her handful of glass pebbles up and let them roll around in her palm, catching the light. They were so pretty.

Laura began to collect more. She found one that was turquoise and one was amber and several that were clear as diamonds. As she hunted, she also began to come across pebbles made of hardmold. They did not sparkle like the glass pebbles, but many were just as beautiful in their own way. Their vibrant, lectricmade colors jumped out amid the drab grays and browns of the natural stones. Oranges and purples and colors that Laura felt she had never seen before, colors for which she had no name.

Soon, Mary had joined the hunt, and together they scoured the beach, stuffing glass and hardmold pebbles into their pockets.

Meanwhile, Pa rolled his parchment map back into a skinny tube. He stood. He traced the river's bend with squinting eyes.

"Yes, I reckon this is it," he said.

This was the place the Mericans had called Pepin, Pa explained. This was where the winter convoys crossed on their way to Great Mishgan Lake. Somewhere on the other side was the Six Three Road, the old number road that would lead them to Davenport.

It was not what Laura expected. She had imagined in Pepin they would find the ruins of another Merican village like the one with the restrant where they had found Jack. But here there was nothing. Just trees and rocks and the endless frozen water.

"Charles, are you sure?" asked Ma. She looked from the

frozen water to the stony beach to the gnarled trees that crowned the top of the embankment, as if she too could not quite believe that a town had once stood here.

"We'll be able to orient ourselves a might better once the stars come out, but, yes, I reckon this is it. I just pray we're not too late in the season."

They made camp that night right on top of the stones by the river's edge. Laura was worried it would be too bumpy for sleeping, but Ma helped her dig out a place for her sleeping mat. When all the big pointy stones were gone and all the pebbles were flattened out just so, it made for a nice cozy cradle.

Pa said that he wished he had his pick and saw with him. He would cut a hole in the ice and catch them some fish. He didn't have those things, though, and so supper was once more a soup with saltmeat and pickled vegetables. The broth seemed thinner than it had been, but it felt warm and good flowing down into Laura's stomach.

As the cookfire dwindled, Laura asked about Pepin. Had there really been a town here once? Pa said he reckoned there had been. Laura wondered what had happened to it. Pa said he didn't know. Maybe the river had changed course and washed it away, he said. Maybe someone had come through and scavved everything away, bricks and all. Or maybe it had all just slowly fallen apart, year by year, until there was no trace of it left except a name on an old map.

~~~

The next morning, Pa went out onto the ice. Laura and Mary and Ma and Baby Grace and Jack all watched from shore.

Elsewhere, the river's surface was jagged, where waves seemed to have frozen mid-crest, reaching up out of the ice like grasping talons. But here beside the stony beach where they had made camp, the Misisip appeared flat and smooth. That was why trade convoys liked to cross here during the winter, Pa had explained. They knew the river was shallow and calm and the ice would be thick.

That made Laura feel better as she watched Pa walk out onto

66

the barren whiteness of the Big River. Still, there was a knot in her stomach, and she clutched Ma's hand tight as Pa's figure grew tinier and tinier in the distance.

To keep them occupied, Ma had Laura and Mary search the beach for the prettiest pebbles they could find and gather them up in a nice pile by the handcar. Laura threw herself into the game, trying not to think about Pa and the ice. She paced up and down the beach, plucking up the most promising looking gems. Eventually, she happened upon a hardmold pebble that was especially striking. It was nearly perfectly round, and a whole rainbow of colors swirled round and round its surface. Laura took it back to Ma.

Ma admired Laura's pebble and said that it was indeed very beautiful, but Laura could tell that her thoughts were elsewhere. Mary seemed to have already given up on the pebble-hunting game. She was sitting beside Ma and Baby Grace, her head resting on Ma's shoulder. Laura balled her pebble up in her fist and sat down at Ma's other shoulder. All four of them gazed out upon the frozen river.

When she was a little girl, Ma told Mary and Laura, she had lived for a time in a displacee camp near the Misisip. In those days the river seldom froze over. When it did, the ice was too thin to walk across safely.

"But the winters have been getting colder," she told Laura. "People say the Misisip freezes solid nearly every year now, all the way down into the Illinoy. Bad for ferrymen and farmers. But good for the winter convoys I suppose.

"My grandmother said it used to be so in olden days. Colder in winter. That's the way of things I suppose. The world goes one way and then after a while it goes back the other."

Laura thought on that a while. She spun the hardmold pebble around in her fingers, tracing its veins of color as they wound round and round and back round again.

Suddenly, Jack began to bark. A shape had appeared on the horizon. It was Pa. He was walking back to them.

"Well, thank goodness," Laura heard Ma mutter under her

breath.

Pa nodded when he returned. The nod didn't seem to satisfy Ma, and she handed Baby Grace to Mary before pulling Pa aside. They walked away from the car, towards the edge of the beach. They talked in hushed tones, but the wind carried their words right back to Laura's little ladle ears.

"You'll hear some crackling," Pa was saying, "but the surface still seems mighty solid to me. We can cross, I'm confident of it."

"Confident?" said Ma, her voice rising so high and sharp that it caused Laura and Mary to turn to one another. "That car's as heavy as a bisox. If the ice should break . . ."

"What would you suggest, Caroline?" Laura heard Pa answer. "That we doubleback the way we came? Try to follow the river's edge north until we find a better spot? Cut our way blindly through the bush down into the Illinoy? The ice is solid, I say. We can make it."

The winds shifted, and Laura could not hear the rest of her parents' discussion. But a moment later they were back, Pa's arm around Ma's shoulder and both smiling, as if nothing could be amiss. Ma hummed as she knelt down to pull Laura's hood tighter around her cheeks and tuck her scarf snug down under her coat.

When they were ready, Ma took Mary in one hand and Laura in the other. Baby Grace was wrapped cozy across her back. They all stepped carefully out onto the ice, while Pa wheeled the handcar up the beach to find a separate spot to cross.

"Slow and steady, girls," Pa called after them. "It can be slippery in places. Don't worry. I'll see you soon on the other side."

Pa was right. Laura immediately felt her left boot slip out to the side. She waved her arm around to keep her balance. But she didn't fall. With Ma helping to steady her, Laura soon regained her footing, and together they made their way further out onto the river.

"Oh, and girls?" Pa called again when they were almost out of earshot. Laura turned back to look at Pa, who waited on the stony riverbank with the big heavy handcar.

"Keep your eyes out for the boat," he said.

Laura and Mary looked at one another, wondering if they had heard him right.

Step by careful step, they journeyed deeper out onto the desolate whiteness of the frozen Misisip. Laura looked behind her towards the receding shore. In the distance, she could see Pa, dragging the car behind him, a small dark shadow against the featureless ice. She tried to wave.

Whoops! Laura slipped again. She hadn't been minding her steps, and her feet slid out in opposite directions beneath her. Ma lurched forward, twirling to a halt as Laura's weight pulled against her arm. After that, she made Mary and Laura walk ahead on their own. It wouldn't do for Ma herself to topple over, not with Baby Grace on her back.

Laura tried to be careful, taking tiny steps and sliding her feet back and forth without even lifting them. But before long that slippery ice stole her feet out from under her again, and she crashed all the way down onto her bottom. It didn't hurt much. Her long thick coat cushioned her fall. Still, it took a few moments sitting on the ice, telling herself to be a big brave girl, before she was able to push herself back up to her feet. No sooner was she upright than she saw Mary, who had continued walking on ahead of her, slip and fall just as hard onto her own bottom. Instantly, Laura felt better.

On they went. Sometimes, a thin, brittle layer of snow crunched under Laura's boots. Then walking on the river was easy. But sometimes the wind swept the river clean and smooth. Then there was nothing beneath Laura but the deep dark ice, streaked in tangled cracks. That was when it was most treacherous. Laura walked especially slowly across these naked patches of ice, arms held high out to her sides.

Suddenly, a noise made Laura stop in her tracks. It started as a low rumble and ended with a creak and a pop. Mary gasped and turned back to look at Ma, but Ma just waved her hand.

"It's nothing," she said quickly. "That's the ice settling. Like the floorboards back home on a winter evening. Just keep moving, girls."

At the mention of home, the flat gray landscape suddenly seemed all the more alien and formidable to Laura. She found herself wishing she were safe and warm back inside their little house, sheltered by the tall trees and the steep hills of the Big Woods.

There was another loud boom and a ferocious crackling. It seemed to come from somewhere nearby, down beneath Laura's feet. Laura bit her lip. For a moment, she was too scared to continue. Then, she felt Mary next to her. Mary squeezed her arm. Together, they walked forward.

The river kept on making its alarming sounds, *tick-tick-tick*-ing beneath them before erupting in a terrible crash. Laura tried not to think about it. But then she remembered Pa and the heavy handcar, and she was more frightened than ever. Would the ice be thick enough to support all that weight? Despite herself, she imagined a chasm opening underneath the handcar and swallowing her father up, sucking him down into the freezing depths of the Misisip. She dared not even glance back behind her. Instead, she kept her mind on her feet, telling herself that if a whole trade convoy could cross the river, then so could their little family.

"Laura, look," Mary suddenly whispered, yanking at Laura's arm.

Laura looked up. With relief, she realized she could see the other side of the river approaching. But there was something else, something giant looming before them. At first, she thought it was the ruins of old lectric building. It rose up at an angle, its bottom half-sunk down into the distant riverbank.

"I think that's the boat," said Mary.

Laura supposed that Mary must be right, but it was hard believe a boat could be so big. Laura thought of the boats she'd seen anchored in Mishgan Lake. Those boats had been wood. The monstrous shape before them seemed to be made of iron, dappled in the same oranges and browns as the lectric cars that slept along the old number roads. Its gigantic prow hovered high in the air, scraping at the sky like an enormous spoon. Laura could not imagine how such a thing could float, let alone how many sailors it would take to row it.

Laura was so wonderstruck by the enormous metal boat that she hardly noticed when the ground around her began to change. First, rocks appeared, poking their heads up out of the ice. Then, the brown skeletons of bushes and brambles and small trees popped up here and there. Soon, her feet were not walking on ice at all but hardened, snow-frosted mud. They had reached the other side of the Misisip at last.

Ma led them up the side of the riverbank. There, they found a dry spot to sit amid a group of young birch trees, sheltered from the wind by a long box-shaped hill. Ma wiped a hand across her face, and her muscles seemed to relax ever so slightly as she loosened her cloak and unbundled Baby Grace. She fussed over each of the girls in turn. Then, she stood and hurried back out to the edge of the embankment.

Grace had started to cry, so Laura picked her up. Bouncing her sister in her arms, she walked up beside Ma. Mary followed. They all looked east, back out over the frozen expanse they had crossed. The stranded iron boat lay some ways upriver, and Laura could see its shadow creeping across the ice.

Finally, Laura located the dark shape of the handcar. She watched it weave in fits and starts over the treacherous terrain. Her fear returned for a moment, but soon it was clear that Pa had made it into the river's shallows. He was almost to the other side. They had all crossed the Big River safe and sound. Laura held Baby Grace high in the air, twirling and shouting in excitement.

"He's going to make it! He's going to make it!" she told her little sister, who was so startled she stopped crying and looked at Laura with big eyes.

"Well," was all Ma said. "There's that done."

NINE: IRON BOXES

Pa left the handcar down by the riverbank. Then he climbed up to join them beside the long earthen mound where Ma had chosen to wait. He gave them each a big long hug.

"Seems to me we've all earned a quick rest," Pa said. "What say we stop here for a spell and get our bearings. Plenty of time to find the Six Three Road before nightfall."

It was pleasant, that spot above the riverbank. Shielded by the mound on one side and a grove of birch trees on another, the wind no longer lashed their cheeks as it had while they crossed the Big River. Even the snows seemed unable to conquer the little sheltered promontory. Tufts of grass and here and there a wildflower peppered the brown earth. The branches of the birch trees were bare, but moss crept up the sides of their trunks, adding more splashes of color.

Pa brought the stool up from the handcar for Ma, and she sat down to feed Baby Grace. Then Pa pulled out a bag from his pocket. It was full of dry-roasted soybeans.

Dry-roasted soybeans were one of Laura's favorite snacks. When they lived in their little house in the Big Woods, Ma would make a batch most every week. First, she would soak the beans in cool water. Then, Laura would help her scoop them up with a big slotted spoon onto an iron pan rubbed slick and shiny with tallow. Ma liked to sprinkle the beans with salt and herbs. Then onto the stove would go the pan, and Ma would roast those beans for an hour or more, shaking the pan from time to time, until they were crispy yellow-brown.

Pa told Mary and Laura to hold out their hands like tiny bowls. Then he poured them each a big handful of soybeans. Laura stuffed as many into her mouth as she could fit. They were salty and crunchy and good, and they made Laura skip happily round and round the skinny white birch trees, grinning through her bulging chipmunk cheeks. Jack bounded right along with her, just as happy as anyone to be safely on the western side of the Misisip.

As Laura skipped past the mound, which sat lonesome at the far end of the grove, she stopped. She had not looked closely at the funny little hill until just then. She had been too caught up in the excitement of crossing the river and reuniting with Pa and enjoying her tasty snack. Now, for the first time, she saw that it was no kind of regular hill. The sides were too steep. Laura walked along its flat face, the soybeans turning to mush in her mouth. Beneath the dirt that clung to its surface, she saw that the mound was not made of rock or soil, but rather iron. It was a box. An immense iron box.

The box had tried to hide by blending in with its surroundings. Slopes of moss-covered earth were piled around its bottom, and creepers climbed their way up its ridges and hung down over its top. But, beneath, it was mottled in dark yellows and oranges just like the stranded boat that lay upriver. All down the long sides of the box, the iron rippled in and out like tree bark.

Laura felt Pa walk up behind her. She could tell that he had noticed the half-buried box too. He knelt down to scratch Jack behind his silly bat ears as he regarded the indentations that ran along the box's surface in neat vertical lines beneath the moss and creepers.

"Well," he said. "This is quite a box."

Pa stood. Stepping closer, he banged a fist against the rust-dappled metal. It answered with a hollow *bong bong* that reverberated through the birch trees and rattled down the bank and out over the frozen river.

Laura held her breath, listening to the echoes die away. Then she let out a squeal of delight. She scurried up the mound to bang her own tiny fist against the metal wall. It gave a curt *clang* but not much more. She tried again, pounding both fists against its side. For good measure, she also gave it a few sharp kicks.

She was just beginning to coax a few satisfying noises from the box when Pa pulled her gently away.

"Ok. I think that's enough of that now, Laura," he said. "Stay close to me, and we'll investigate just what we've got here."

He took her by the hand, and, together, they walked in a slow circle around the big rectangular structure. When they reached its short side, Pa pushed away the creepers and ran his hand across the metal ripples.

"Hm," he said.

There was a seam running down the middle, but nothing moved when Pa pushed against it. If the box had once had doors, there were no knobs or handles left that Laura could see. Anyway, if they wanted to open it up, they would need to dig away the built-up piles of earth, for the ground seemed to have risen up to swallow the box.

By this time, Mary had joined them, standing a wary distance away from all the banging and scraping.

"What's inside?" she asked.

"Hard to say," confessed Pa. "And I don't know it's worth finding out, half-buried as it is. Most likely scavved clean long ago in any case I reckon. The convoy trail from Davenport is supposed to pass through here somewhere nearabouts. Still, I wonder . . . Let's us take stock, girls. Follow me."

He took Laura by one hand and Mary by the other. Jack trotted by their feet. Together, they marched through the grove of birches. Mary and Laura took two steps for every one of Pa's. And Jack took two steps for every one of Mary and Laura's.

"Don't stray too far, Charles," Ma called out to them as they passed.

The ground sloped gradually upwards before falling away. Soon, the trees thinned out, and they found themselves looking upriver. The west bank of the Misisip stretched out before them. They stopped. Pa scanned the landscape.

There was the giant iron ship, standing at a crooked angle a short distance away. From this vantage, Laura could see just how far from the river the poor old boat had gotten itself. Its tail was sunk down well into the rocks and shrubs that rose away from the Misisip's banks and only its nose hovered above the icy beach, as if straining to find its way home.

She could now see the boat's deck. It was a lighter gray than the hull but streaked in the same burnt yellows and oranges. It was so flat and so smooth that Laura found herself imagining what it would be like to take her sled up to the tip top and ride all the way to the bottom. As her eyes sledded downward across the deck, to where it crashed beneath a rolling ocean of foliage, Laura saw that the base was clogged with a great pile of rubble.

They were boxes. From far away, they looked just like the little wooden building blocks that Pa had carved for Laura and her sisters. The messy heap they made reminded Laura of a carefully constructed building-block castle that had just been knocked down.

Other piles of boxes ringed the shipwreck. The longer she looked, the more boxes Laura saw. They were strewn along the riverbank, lying in ones and twos, hiding behind trees or jutting out from under the ice and mud near the water's edge. You could trace the trail of boxes straight from the boat all the way to back the overlook where she and Pa and Mary stood. It made Laura think of the trail of soybread crumbs that Hukfin used to find his way back to his raft after escaping the evil witch's bunker.

Laura looked up at Pa. She could tell that he was tracing his way along the trail of boxes too. His eyes paced in thoughtful zigzags, silently taking it all in.

"Well now," he said finally. "That's a good many boxes."

They went back to tell Ma about what they'd seen. She and Pa agreed that they would stop a little longer by the riverbank and see if anything of value could be scavved from the shipwreck.

Pa rummaged through the handcar, pulling out tools. Into his satchel went his heavy claw hammer. Into the pocket of his overcoat went his framing chisel. He scooped up a long-handled adze with his left hand and, with his right, his trusty hatchet.

When Pa handed Mary and Laura an empty soymeal sack, they looked at each other with big eyes. They would be allowed to come along and help Pa with the scavving!

Mary on one side and Laura on the other, they followed Pa along the frozen shore of the Misisip, towards the shadow of the stranded lectric boat. Ma moved her stool up to the overlook and watched over them, Baby Grace tucked into the crook of one arm and Pa's rifle in the other.

Mary got to hold the bag because she was older, but Laura didn't care. She just wanted to see what was in all those giant old boxes from Lectric Times. Her imagination filled with treasures. Stacks of paperbooks. Big bolts of untearable lectric fabrics. Rows of glass jars with nice snug lids so Ma could pickle all the vegetables she wanted.

As if seeing the wonderful bounty flickering behind Laura's eyes, Pa warned the girls again that anything of real value would likely have been scavved away long ago. He was looking mainly for metal scrap, he told them.

Pa was always after scrap. Iron was his favorite. Beside his forge in the Big Woods, there had been a pile of iron scrap. Ma would tease him sometimes when he would return home, sweating and wheezing from the exertion, dragging a sled loaded down with yet another iron door torn off some old lectric car.

"For goodness sake, Charles," she would scold him. "Don't you have enough metal for your projects? That scrap heap out back is taller than you are."

But, to Pa, no two pieces of iron scrap were alike. He seemed to see subtleties in metal scav that weren't obvious to Laura: which iron would be easiest to shape, which iron would make for the hardest ax head and which the sturdiest nail.

Pa had taught Laura how to scav for copper. In the Big Woods, she would often come across old Merican coins and bring them back to Pa. Laura knew that the silver-colored Merican coins had the most copper. The copper-colored coins had the least. That always seemed funny to Laura, but Pa just said that it was a good lesson not to judge things by how they look on the outside.

Once, Pa had heated up one of those copper-colored coins to show her. Its thin copper skin had cracked and a dark silver-colored liquid had dripped out into Pa's mold. The metal inside was called zink, Pa told her. Zink had its uses, but it wasn't as valuable as copper, which could be traded at most markets almost as readily as silver.

Now, though, as Pa hacked a path through a thicket of shrubs with his hatchet, he explained to Laura and Mary that it wasn't iron or even copper he was looking for in the big lectric boxes. He couldn't melt such metals over a campfire. Until he set up a new forge out in the Wastes, iron scrap was just useless weight. It was scrap for casting bullets he needed most, Pa told the girls. In the Big Woods, Pa might make bullets from zink or nikel. He liked to experiment with different mixes and, sometimes, he would even cover his bullets in a hard outer layer of copper. But nikel and zink would be no easier to work than iron while out on the open road, Pa told them. He needed softer metals like lead or tin.

Good soft lead was hard to come by. The Mericans had seldom used it. But you could find it if you knew where to look. The best place to look for lead was the wheels of lectric cars, Laura knew. If you pried off the iron wheel caps, there were sometimes tiny little lead nuggets tucked around their edges. Whenever they would pass a lectric car, Pa would squat down to look at the wheels. If there were any bits of lead hidden inside, he would pry them off and pocket them for making bullets. Unfortunately, they hadn't seen many lectric cars of late, and Pa had begun to worry about his supply of ammunition. Laura supposed that was one reason he was so keen to scav through the iron boxes.

The first box they came to was missing a chunk from one of its corners, as if someone had taken a big bite out of it. Pa only had to widen the hole, knocking away a few ragged metal flaps that hung loose, and they could all step right through.

Inside, the box was filled with tall black blobs. They were piled in distended columns that bulged and slouched and leaned against one another. Laura nudged the nearest one with her foot. It was the same black softmold that sometimes clung to the wheels of lectric cars. Looking around, she realized that the big ugly pillars were actually stacks of individual rings, though they were so warped that you could hardly tell they used to be round. The old softmold artifacts oozed into one another, forming shapes like hideous swamp creatures emerging from a bog.

There was a strange, sharp smell inside the box. Pa coughed, pressing his handkerchief to his face, and immediately shooed Laura and Mary back outside.

"Rotting softmold!" he exclaimed, "Pyoo! What a stench."

The next box Pa had to pry open. That was a good sign, he told them as he banged his hammer against the rusted-out iron rods that held the doors in place. The box hadn't been opened in some time, perhaps not since the Hard Years. Whatever scav lay inside might not be so picked over. Once the latches had been broken off, the doors gave easily, creaking apart at the insistence of Pa's chisel.

But inside there was nothing but dirt and dust, piled as high as Laura's knees in some places. Some of it rose into the air when the box's door swung open, escaping in a puff of gray out over the riverbank. A piece of fabric tumbled past Laura. It was stamped with faded green letters and a picture of some sort of bean in a deep reddish brown. Laura tried to pick it up, but as soon as she touched it, it crumbled into nothing.

Pa peered inside the dirt-filled box and tapped his chisel against the door in disappointment before moving on.

They found another box nearby lying at an awkward tilt, half-sunk into the mud and covered over in moss. Its latches were already rusted clean off, but, when Pa tried to pry open its doors, he found they were jammed. Pa worked long and hard to pound his chisel deep enough into the gap to open up a space for his adze. Finally, working with adze and hammer both, he pulled one of the metal doors free.

An avalanche of square black objects poured out of the box and into the mud. One landed near Laura's foot. She picked it up. It was a lectric screen, a small one, flat as a frycake and narrow enough that Laura could wrap her fingers almost clear around it. Laura wiped the dust away with the corner of her cloak. She had never seen a screen that looked so perfect and new. Sheltered inside the iron box, the little screen had managed to defy the ravages of time. Its rounded hardmold corners were smooth and even. And its black surface, made of polished lectric glass, sparkled in the sunlight, as brilliant as any jewel.

Laura held the screen up. Suddenly a face appeared within the black rectangle. Laura nearly dropped the screen she was so startled by the clarity of the features peering back at her. It was a little girl. Though the colors were dulled beneath the screen's dark tint, she could make out the nut brown color of the girl's eyes and hair and distinguish each one of the tiny blemishes that ran across her nose and down her cheeks, some of which were freckles and some, no doubt, merely dirt.

Laura angled the lectric artifact back and forth. Was that really her in the screen's deep black face? She shook her head in disbelief. The girl in the screen did likewise.

Meanwhile, there was a great commotion as Pa shoveled the screens aside. Eventually, he climbed up over the pile and into the box. There was more clatter from within. Screens came flying out the door, skittering down the heap to join their companions in the mud and reeds. Finally, Pa emerged, drumming his hammer softly against his thigh in disappointment.

For good measure, Pa set one of the screens on a stone and gave it a good smash or two with the hammer. Then he peeled apart the black glass and the hardmold shell. He scraped out the screen's innards, spreading its little lectric bits out across the stone. He pulled out the thin green slice of hardmold hidden in its core. He flipped it over once or twice, inspecting the metal ridges and tiny lectric threads that studded its surface, before flicking it dismissively into the bushes.

"Junk," he said with a shrug. "A bit of copper, maybe a trace of silver if you could get at it. But not worth the trouble, not by half."

Laura took another look at her reflection in the glossy black rectangle. Quietly, she slipped the screen into the pocket of her overcoat, right beside Oprah. It might be junk, but it was just too pretty to leave lying there to get washed away by the Misisip.

Laura saw that Mary had picked up a shiny screen of her own. Following Laura's lead, she pocketed it. They both smiled at one another, sharing in their little secret.

Further up the riverbank they went. Laura could now see the stranded boat looming up ahead. Soon they came to a clearing where three boxes had come to rest, all facing each other in a tight circle as if they were holding an important box meeting. They seemed relatively undisturbed.

Surely one of these boxes would have some useful scav, Laura thought.

Pa pried open the first box without much difficulty. The big iron door swung open with a groan and a screech, and Pa climbed in. Mary and Laura peeked in after him.

It was dark inside the box. Pa was squatting down, inspecting something big and round that looked to Laura like a giant bird's nest.

"Well, here's a find, girls," he said.

Pa tried to drag it closer to the doorway and into the light.

Laura could tell it was very heavy, for Pa could barely lift it, and it scraped along the box's metal floor as he tugged it haltingly inch by inch. He didn't get even halfway to the door before Pa let it drop with a heavy clank.

Mary and Laura stepped up into the box beside Pa. Lying at his feet was a mass of metal rope, coils upon coils of it. The rope was as thick as a man's thumb and stacked nearly as high as Laura's knees. She tried to imagine how far it must stretch end to end fully uncoiled.

"Not copper," Pa said. "Iron I'd say. Hard lectric iron. There's plenty a man could do with a good length of iron rope like that. If only we had the means to haul it. Or to slice a few meters off somehow. Ah, well, no helping it. This fine treasure will just have to wait here for the next scavmen to come along I reckon. A shame. But let's have a look around and see if there aren't some shorter iron ropes hiding in this box as well."

Pa pushed open the other door to let in more light. A hinge broke loose as he did, and the big door nearly swung free entirely before the remaining hinge caught it mid-collapse and held it askew above the shrubs. Mary and Laura wandered deeper into the box to help Pa look for more iron rope. Unlike the other boxes they'd opened, this one didn't seem to hold one single type of scav. In one corner, there was a stack of iron cabinets with broken drawers gaping open like slack jaws. In another, there was a pile of warped hardmold forms that might have once been chairs or tables. Elsewhere were mounds of other debris in varying shapes and sizes.

Pa began prying open cabinet drawers and rummaging around inside. Laura stepped carefully over a twisted ribbon of hardmold and around the iron cabinets, deeper into the box. It grew darker as she approached the far end, and Laura had to squint long and hard at each object.

"Be careful now, Laura," Pa called to her. "Don't touch anything."

As she came to the back wall, Laura realized that its surface was covered in markings. Words had been scratched into the metal. And pictures, crude human figures arrayed across a rust-covered canvas, etched in ragged lines across the ridges and crevices that textured the iron wall. Peering out from the shadowy recesses of the box, the images had an eerie and menacing feel.

Laura tried to pick her way through the debris to get a better look. That was when her foot struck something. It was light and brittle and rolled away from her with a hollow rattle. Startled, she stepped to the side and felt something crunch and snap beneath her boot.

Laura froze. She suddenly had a bad feeling in her stomach, though she couldn't say why. Holding her breath, she let her eyes drop from the carvings on the wall down to box's iron floor.

Lying scattered around Laura's feet were bones. Dirt and shadow clung to them, obscuring their shapes, but there was no mistaking what they were. They lay in jumbles of yellow and gray, gathering in denser piles towards the back of the box.

In the furthest corner, some of the bones came together into an unmistakably human shape. The skeleton was huddled against the iron walls, its arms tucked against its ribs in a posture of weary resignation, its knees propped upright, as if it might turn and rise to its feet at any time. Nearby, Laura could make out a second skeleton lying on its side across the floor. She glanced over at the object she had kicked. A broken skull stared back up at her with hollow misshapen eyes.

"Pa?" she called softly.

He was already there, his hand on her shoulder. Pa let out a heavy sigh. He touched Laura's cheek and gently guided her face away from the piles of bones, back towards the open end of the box, where, beyond the confines of the iron tomb, a square slice of the riverbank seemed to glow.

"I believe I've had my fill of scavving," said Pa, once he'd led Mary and Laura back into the sunlight. "Suppose we head back up the hill to Ma. Past time we quit fooling about in old junk heaps and focus on the road ahead."

TEN: THE ROLLING HILLS OF THE YOWA

The days that followed were warm. Laura didn't need to wear her mittens or her wool cap any more. A few days later, when they stopped for a midday rest on a bluff overlooking a river valley, Ma let Laura unlace her traveling cloak. Ma folded the cloak up and stuffed it deep into the handcar so that it disappeared, swallowed up among the other supplies.

Laura was glad to be rid of it. She was more than warm enough in her patchwork coat of buckskin and lectric fabrics. Oprah's floppy cloth head peeked happily out from the biggest of the coat's many mismatched pockets, glad to be able to enjoy the passing scenery without some cloak blocking her view.

Whenever one of them shed another layer of clothing, Pa remarked again how lucky they were to have crossed the Misisip when they did. One morning, they forded a swift stream. Its cold waters hissed in delight, finally free to race across the land after being cooped up so long off in some snow-capped mountain. By now, Pa reckoned, winter's failing grip would no longer hold the Mighty Misisip still. The Big River would be rolling once more, its many waters dividing east from west.

The lands west of the Misisip were called the Yowa. It was empty country. At times it seemed like they were surrounded by a vast wilderness. Laura would play explorer, imagining herself the first person to ever lay on eyes on these strange uncharted lands.

Pa said this wasn't so. Trade convoys came this way most every season, bringing goods north from the market at Davenport. He would point out stacks of rocks that the traders had placed to help mark the route. Every time a thicket of shrubs came across their path, threatening to bar their way, they always seemed to find some place where the overgrowth had been thinned, hacked aside by the axes of the traders who preceded them.

Still, the land did seem very much untouched. They followed a trail marked out on Rakesh Halfsilver's map that wound down through the Yowa. It was called the Six Three Road. Yet, there was rarely any sign of the creetrock that had marked the old number roads on the other side of the Misisip. At first, Laura assumed the old Merican road must be there somewhere beneath the snow, but, as they continued to make their way south and warm days were followed by more warm days, the last traces of snow faded away, revealing nothing but bare earth beneath. From time to time, they still passed the remnants of an old lectric car or wagon, but if the Six Three Road had once been made of creetrock, it had all crumbled away.

They saw no other people. Pa remarked that the Yowa might make a good place to settle if they could count on it remaining so peaceful.

"There's a good many folks would like to lay claim to these lands, though," he reflected. "You've got Clan Ortega to the south and the Spear pushing in from the Illinoy. And there's more than one caudillo in the Northlands who likely sees the Upper Yowa as part of his sphere of influence I'd wager. It'd make a man mighty fretful to try and build his home smack dab in the middle. And with the fighting in the East like to get worse before it gets better, all those displacees might just be to spark to light the whole darned tinderbox up. No, the way I see it, we need to keep on heading west, away from it all. The Wastes, that's where our new life awaits."

Laura was glad when Pa said that. She wanted to see the wild bisox herds and the wastebird flocks and the wide open skies.

At first, the lands on the western side of the Misisip had looked much like the lands on the eastern side. But, as they traveled south, deeper into Yowa country, the woods disappeared, and the landscape became more alien to Laura. In place of trees, there was only grass. It wasn't soft grass like in the glades and meadows that hid among the Big Woods. It was tall grass, strong and stiff. When the wind picked up, it danced, fluttering around Laura's waist and billowing in great waves that rolled down one hill and up another.

There were a great many hills in Yowa country. Every day their journey took them up and then down. Then usually up and down again. The hills were never steep, not like the mountain passes that led from the Big Woods down to the Laketowns, but they kept coming, one upon the other. The land bobbed and rolled. Each hill looked the same as the last, rising towards a gentle summit before slumping right back down to where it had started. Laura wished the Yowa would make up its mind.

With no trees around, it was hard to gather firewood, and so their nights grew darker and colder, even as their days were warming up. Pa tried to make fires by gathering handfuls of the tall grass and tying the straws together in tight bundles. Then he'd dig a trench and stack the bundles up inside. It worked, but the fire needed to be tended constantly and produced such thick black smoke that Mary and Laura would soon be coughing and covering their eyes. Ma refused to bring Baby Grace anywhere near Pa's smoky grass fires.

Eventually, Pa gave up. One night, shielding his face with his kerchief, he kicked the dirt back into his hole, smothering a fire that had developed a particularly unpleasant odor. As he stood over it, watching the embers fall dark, he gave a deep sigh.

"Well, no point in a campfire anyway, I don't suppose," Laura heard him mutter. "It's not as if we've anything to cook."

Pa had found the hunting to be poor on the Yowa's rolling hills of grass. He had managed to shoot a few birds, but just as often they had flapped away, chased over the horizon by the hollow echoes of Pa's gun. Pa had grown more careful with his shots, mindful of wasting precious bullets.

Without game, their supplies dwindled. There were more empty pickle jars in the back of the handcar than full ones, and they'd eaten up the last of their saltmeat. They rationed their soymeal carefully.

When they couldn't get a fire hot enough to make bread or frycakes, Ma would soak the soymeal, and they would have to make do with a cold gruel for supper. Ma sweetened the yellowish mush with a bit of date syrup she had saved away in a secret little jar, but the gruel still tasted chalky and unpleasant in Laura's mouth.

Some nights in Yowa country, as she curled up under her blankets with Jack and Oprah, beside the empty space where the campfire should have been, Laura felt the slender fingers of hunger wrap around her belly and begin to gently squeeze. She never complained or asked for more. Neither did Mary. They both saw how small the bowls of soymeal gruel that Ma and Pa poured for themselves had gotten. They both knew that Ma needed good nourishing food to nurse Baby Grace and that Pa needed his strength to keep pulling the car over the rolling hills.

At first, Laura worried about Jack. Jack couldn't eat soymeal. When their saltmeat ran out, she pictured the poor little pigdog shriveling up into nothing but skinny bones beneath his handsome brindled coat. As the days passed, though, Jack proved better adapted to life on the Yowa than the rest of them. He was always rooting around in the dirt around their campsites, searching for fat little grubs and gnawing on the roots of plants. Sometimes, he would pounce into the tall grass and emerge a moment later with a grasshopper sticking out from under his floppy jowls. It was a meager diet for a dog, Laura thought, but Jack appeared to thrive on it. In fact, as the weeks wore on, he was the only one whose energy and enthusiasm seemed undiminished by the journey.

Pa noticed Jack's skill at foraging as well, and he was clearly much impressed with the pigdog's show of self-reliance.

"That's the way, Jack," Pa would say whenever he saw Jack scoop up a worm or snatch another grasshopper off its swaying perch. "I hope you don't expect to depend on anybody else. A body can't do that. Learn to live off the land, yes sir, you'll never have to go begging for scraps off another man's table."

Once, right after praising Jack on another successful kill,

Laura saw Pa turn his back and slip his hand into his coat pocket. He pulled out the silvers that Marco the boy soldier had given them in trade for supplies. Laura saw him run his thumb along their edges, shaking his head. For a moment, Laura didn't like the look on Pa's face, but when Pa saw that she was watching him, he smiled and quickly stuffed the coins back into his coat, the stiffness in his jaw instantly banished.

~~~

One day, they came upon a pair of giant stone legs.

The Yowa held few ruins. From time to time, especially when the land had flattened out for a stretch, Laura had spied the remains of abandoned lectric plows in the distance, rising like lonely islands of rust amid the grass. There were bigger shapes too, the iron skeletons of yet stranger machines that the Mericans had used to tend their fields. But there were no signs of any towns or cities, no brick chimneys or creetrock walls.

Then, late one morning, Pa pointed to something on the horizon.

At first, it appeared to be just another of the stone piles built up by the convoy crews to mark their path, but as they got closer Laura saw this wasn't so. The vague gray form in the distance grew taller. Gradually, it divided itself into two distinct columns, each too thin and straight to be piles of rocks.

Strangely, the two columns appeared to be all on their own. No other ruins surrounded them. They seemed to be the only landmark amid the featureless hills of grass that stretched out in all directions. As they passed alongside the queer monument, Pa set down the handcar to take a closer look.

They were made of creetrock or something like it. One column was taller than Pa, the other a little more than half that size. The tops of both were broken, a suggestion of greater heights that either destruction or decay had cut short. Tangled webs of iron sprouted from the tops of the pillars like ragged crowns and drooped down their sides.

It was only as Laura circled round them, following close in Pa's footsteps, that she realized what they were. Both columns were anchored to the same creetrock base. There, the bottoms of the columns splayed out into shapes of feet. Above those feet, Laura thought she could make out the outline of boots carved into columns' surfaces. Further up the taller pillar, she saw the faint dimple of a knee and the curve of a thigh.

Mary grabbed Laura's arm.

"Laura," she whispered in Laura's ear. "These are the legs of a giant creetrock man!"

The creetrock man must have been giant indeed. In Laura's estimation, if the rest of him had been built to the same proportions as his legs, he would have stood as tall as a house. Rubble of iron and creetrock was scattered all around the broken legs. Lying a few meters away, Laura found something that looked like a giant ear. She was crouched down, examining the ear, when Pa called out to her and Mary.

"Come have a look at this, girls," he called.

Further along, Pa had found an old iron sign, half-buried. It was crusted in a uniform swirl of dull oranges and grays, but Laura saw that the surface was raised in places. The iron sheet was dimpled with the shapes of letters.

Pa squatted down and found a handhold. Grunting, he pulled that heavy sign up out of the dirt and dragged it to where they could get a better look. Laura tried to make out the words that had been stamped into the metal, but Mary was faster.

"Happy Vvv. . . V-vay. . ." she said, slowly sounding the words out. "Valley. Happy Valley Or. . . Orchards. Restup and Re-reptilsoo? Five mie. Five mee? G-gaz. Food. Fun."

Pa was very impressed with Mary's reading, but Laura felt only the faintest tinge of jealousy. She was too eager to know what the sign meant to worry too much about Mary being perfect at everything.

Unfortunately, Pa seemed just as puzzled as Laura and Mary by the sign. He pulled out Rakesh Halfsilver's map. There was no town called Happy Valley Orchards nor any sign of ruins called Reptilsoo. He muttered something to himself as he ran a finger along the parchment. Finally, he shrugged. He rolled up the map and gave Mary and Laura each a playful shake by their shoulders.

"Well, we'll just have to see what we see."

That afternoon, shortly after leaving the giant legs and the iron sign behind, Laura began to notice, for the first time in many days, the remains of an old creetrock road peeking out for short stretches amid the grass. The faint old road led them gradually up up up a hill and then down again. There, where the road levelled off before preparing to climb again, they came to a creek.

The creek sighed and sputtered, as it made its way through the roots and fallen branches of shrubs that sprouted along its banks. Pa took off his boots, rolled up his pants and waded in. The creek was wide but shallow, and Pa determined that the tall wheels of the handcar would keep their belongings dry. He found a good firm grip on the car's handles and squared his shoulders. Then he led the car down the bank and into the creek. Its wheels clattered and bounced over rocks as brown water rushed through the spokes, sending up a fantastic spray.

Before they could stop him, Jack dove into the creek and swam after Pa. Laura worried he would get swept away by the current, but Jack paddled fast, and soon he had passed right by Pa and was climbing out, sopping and happy, on the far bank. He shook himself dry and yipped for the rest of them to hurry up.

Laura and Mary and Ma and Baby Grace all waded in together. The water was cold. Laura and Mary both gasped when their bare feet first touched it, but Laura soon got used to it. As she waded across, Laura savored the sensations of the muddy creekbed squishing between her toes and the smooth moss-covered rocks gliding across the pads of her feet.

Laura and Mary had rolled their pants all the way up past their knees, but it did no good. The stream came up nearly to their waists, and they were soaking by the time they reached the other side.

Pa set down the handcar. Up ahead, the faint path of the old Merican road wound between two hills and disappeared from sight. Pa decided that he would scout ahead a ways while Ma and the girls dried off beside the creek. Rifle over his shoulder, Pa marched off and soon vanished behind the hills.

While they waited for him to return, Ma pulled out her stool and found a nice shady spot to nurse Baby Grace. As she was about to sit, she paused and squinted down at something lying on the ground. She picked it up and spun it in her hand. It was some kind of fruit. The round object was squished and blackened, but pink hues were still visible on its leathery skin.

"Mary, Laura, come look at this," she said. "Do you know what this is?"

They didn't know. It was smaller than a melon but much bigger than a berry. It reminded Laura of a picture she'd seen in the tattered book of Bible stories that they'd left behind back in the Big Woods. But she didn't know the fruit's name.

"It's an apple," said Ma. "This one's old and rotted. But they're delicious when they're fresh. Near one of the camps where I lived for a time when I was a little girl, there was a grove of apple trees. It was one of the few nice things about that place. I remember the children would gather them and . . . "

Ma trailed off. Baby Grace sensed that her meal had been interrupted and began to fuss, but Ma just bounced her absent-mindedly against her shoulder as she looked back down at the apple. She spun it around again in her hand, lost in thought. Then, as if abruptly snapped back to the present, Ma suddenly pursed her lips and gave a quiet "hmmm." It was a sound that Laura knew well. Ma liked things to be just so. This was the noise she made when they weren't.

"Odd," she said. "I should think it's far too early in the year for apples to be ripening. These lands are a deal warmer than where I grew up, I suppose. Or perhaps these are just a different sort of apple. Some jimmed-up breed the Mericans cooked up before the Bust."

Ma scanned the bushes and trees growing alongside the stream, looking for where the apple had come from. Apparently, none of them looked right, because she turned her attention to the hillside.

"There's some trees up on that ridge yonder," Ma said,

pointing up towards the rise behind which Pa had disappeared. "Why don't you girls scamper up a little ways and see if there's any apples to gather. But don't you go eating anything until you show me first. And mind you don't stray to where I can't see you."

Mary and Laura raced up the hill, leaving their carrysacks at Ma's feet beside the handcar. Mary looked back at Laura as they ran. They both laughed, and Laura knew that they were thinking the same thing, how good it was to run free for a change instead of trudging slowly down the road with their belongings on their shoulders.

When they came to the trees that Ma had pointed out, they stopped. Laura saw something lying in the grass. It was big and round, half pink and half yellow. But before she could reach down, Mary snatched it up. Laura scrunched up her face but said nothing. She would just have to be quicker next time.

Mary started hunting around nearby, but Laura saw that there were bigger trees further up the hill. She darted towards them. Up and up she ran. Looking behind her, Laura could no longer see the bottom of the hill where Ma was, and she knew she shouldn't go any further. But she was almost there now, and those trees at top of the hill looked like they would have lots of apples.

Laura pictured herself marching triumphantly down the hill, her arms piled high with ripe apples. The image put lift into her steps. She bounded onwards even faster.

As the hill crested, Laura was suddenly surrounded by bushes and brambles. She almost turned back, unsure about picking her way through the unexpected thicket, but then she saw three round shapes hiding in the dappled shadows of the underbrush. She dropped down to her hands and knees and crawled towards them.

The apples weren't as big as Mary's, and two were a little squishy. Laura stuffed them into her pockets anyway. Then she crawled further, ducking under branches until she found a spot to stand up straight. There, she found herself at the foot of a big tree. It was not tall like the trees in the Big Woods, but its trunk was thick and its branches spread in all directions above her head like the roof of one of the tent stalls at the Laketown Market. Among that sprawling canopy of branches, Laura saw apples.

They looked small and green and hard, but surely they would be nicer than Mary's moldy old ground apple. From the second she saw them, Laura knew she simply had to climb that tree. There really wasn't any other choice.

Laura was a good tree climber, and the apple tree's limbs fanned out perfectly. She had no trouble hoisting herself up from one to the other. For a moment, she forgot all about the apples, caught up in the thrill of just climbing higher and higher. Before she knew it, she had reached the uppermost branches. Wrapping her arms around an upright bough for support, she looked out.

From up in the top of that tree, Laura could see all around for many kims in every direction. Far below, she could make out the old road that Pa had followed, and she traced it with her eyes as it wound around the hill, hoping to see him.

Taking care not to lose her footing, Laura shifted in her perch so that she could gaze out in the opposite direction.

Suddenly, she stopped, frozen dumbfounded in place, as rigid as if she were one of the apple tree's branches. What she saw made her close her eyes and give her head a shake, hoping to rattle the scene before her into a more comprehensible shape. Yet, when she opened her eyes, it was still there.

The far side of the hill was steeper than the one she had ascended, and Laura found herself looking down on a wide valley below. Through this valley ran a creetrock road. It ran east-west, crossing the smaller road that Laura's family had followed south. Directly below her, sitting astride that old road, were the strangest ruins Laura had ever seen.

Tallest was the iron spire. It rose higher than the biggest trees in the Big Woods, yet it was skinny like a soystalk. Lofted high in the air near the spire's tip were three lectric cars, stacked one on top of the other. The great spike appeared to have punctured the cars right through their middles, skewering them like rabbits over a cookfire.

But that wasn't all. Standing alongside the great car spike, guarding it perhaps, there were monsters. They were huge, towering above the brick and creetrock buildings. One creature had a long neck like a snake. The other stood on two legs, its mouth open in a wide grimace, showing off a set of impossibly sharp teeth. Both were a bluish green that glistened in bright contrast to the brick and creetrock buildings that surrounded them.

For a terrifying heartbeat, Laura thought they might be alive. She stared. As the monsters remained motionless, only then was she convinced that they must be statues, just like the broken creetrock legs she'd seen beside the road. She supposed that the monsters had been erected by the same mysterious hand that had set those lectric cars atop their spire. Still, the sight of them made her skin tingle. What sort of people would build such monuments? And for what purpose?

Laura wanted to race back down the hill, to tell Mary and Ma and Baby Grace what she had seen. Yet, at the same time she felt transfixed, afraid that if she looked away from the ruins for a single moment they might vanish like a mirage.

Finally, she managed to tear her eyes away and began lowering herself down the tree. She was feeling for the next limb when, suddenly, something rustled in the bushes below. Laura paused, her foot suspended in mid-air.

"Mary?" she called. "Mary! You have to come look at this. You'll never believe it. Not in a million years!"

But the answer that came was not Mary's. It was not human. From the bushes came a burbling, guttural shriek.

Laura clutched tighter to the tree. She craned her neck around, searching for the thing in the bushes beneath her, but she found her gaze drawn to the valley floor, where the giant monsters stood. As Laura stared down at them, her terror mounting, she had the sensation that they were looking back up at her, watching her with their tiny monster eyes.

The rustling from the bushes grew louder and closer. Laura

began to panic, imagining all manner of sharp-toothed, snake-necked creatures emerging from the foliage below. Then the cry came again, that same burbling shriek. Laura scrambled through the branches, trying to keep the tree between her and the direction of that horrible monstrous sound.

Part of her wanted to drop to the ground and run, but she was scared to leave the tree. Grasping the limb above her for support, she peeked around the trunk.

There was a dark shape lurking among the brambles. Laura's eyes went as round as saucers. Her palms felt cold and clammy against the tree bark. The limb began to tremble in her grip.

And then a face burst forth from the thicket, a face with flared nostrils and slitted eyes. And then that terrible burbling shriek once more.

Laura screamed and tried to back away. Her hands slipped, and her footing faltered. A branch snapped.

She fell. Everything went dark.

ELEVEN: TOBIAS GOATHERD

It was dark when Laura woke.

Everything was a jumble. She couldn't sort out at first where her memories ended and where the dreams began.

She remembered something stalking her. She could still feel it, icy on her skin, the terror of being treed by some unseen predator. That had been real, surely. But the demon face in the bushes? Yellow eyes with square black pupils. Long snout. Had she seen that truly or was that a part of the nightmares that followed?

She remembered falling, down down, and that was about where things began to blur. The face stayed with her, hovering over her, its features twisting and changing, dissolving in and out of focus. She felt as if she were still falling, while at the same time she saw herself from above, lying there asleep beneath the apple tree.

At some point, the face in the bushes began to take on new aspects. Its snout and misshapen pupils faded away. Its yellow eyes became those of a person driven mad by the Ague. The look in them was savage and threatening, but now they flickered with an unmistakable humanity that only made the face more horrible.

She dreamt they came for her then. Laura watched helplessly from above as the fiends came shambling out from the bushes in ones and twos, converging on her paralyzed body. And at the same time she was back inside that body. She felt the touch as one of the yellow-skinned horrors scooped her up. She saw herself hanging limp in its skeletal arms. She could do nothing but wait in mute terror for the fiend to begin tearing into her flesh in its delirium.

But then she was back home. Safe in the little house in the Big

Woods. It was morning. The smell of soybread drifted up to the loft where she lay, and she could hear Pa playing his two-string on the porch and singing one of his old traditionals.

I gazed a gazeless stare
We walked a million hills
I must have died alone
A long, long time ago

Who knows? Not me
I never lost control
You're face to face
With the man who sold the world

The scene meandered, with little regard for coherence of time or place. Jack was there. And Marco, the boy soldier who had deserted the Army of Faith's Spear Triumphant.

Finally, Laura woke again. This time, it was dark. She was inside, abed, but it wasn't her loft back home. Someone was squeezing her hand, and Laura turned her head to find Ma gazing down at her.

Laura tried to sit up. She opened her mouth to speak, but Ma shushed her gently and pressed a damp cloth to her forehead.

"Easy now, Laura," said Ma. "You took quite a fall. We need to make sure nothing's broken."

Disoriented, Laura tried to look around. She was lying on a bed, built low to the ground, on a mattress stuffed with hay or straw. Twilight trickled in from a small window above her head, but otherwise the room was illuminated only by a lantern hanging from the far wall. From within its metal cage, the candle cast a flickering glow across half of Ma's concerned face.

Only as her eyes adjusted could Laura make out the figures standing behind Ma, crowding the small room. There was Pa, holding Baby Grace in his arms, and there was Mary right beside him, hanging onto his coat. When Laura looked in her direction, Mary let out a little sob of relief and clutched Pa tighter.

But there were two other figures that Laura did not recognize. They stood a few steps apart from Mary and Pa, nearer the curtain-covered door. Laura stared at them for a moment, half convinced that they were lingering phantoms from her dream. The fickle lantern light obscured them in dancing shadows. Yet, as Laura stared, the strangers did not disappear.

The first was a man. He was shorter than Pa, and his back was stooped. His head was bare but for a ring of long gray wisps circling the back of his skull from ear to ear and a single lonely tuft sprouting from the very top of his forehead. His beard, long and white, hung from his chin in wild curls.

The second figure appeared to be a girl, perhaps a bit older than Mary. She fidgeted beside the doorway, as if afraid to fully enter the room. Her hair was short but tangled. She had been staring intently at Laura, but when Laura made eye contact, the girl looked away and ducked deeper into the shadows.

Seeing that she was awake, the old man approached Laura. He looked her over, scratching at the underside of his beard and bobbing his head up and down as if in appreciation of a song that only he could hear.

Laura's body was wrapped in a wool blanket, but her right leg stuck out from underneath. Laura looked down, and there she saw half a dozen little metal pins sticking up out of her knee. Laura knew that they were medicine needles, and she made an effort to keep her leg still so as not to disrupt their healing effects.

The old man tapped each of the needles in turn. Then he held up a crooked finger in front of her face and asked her to follow it with her eyes as he waved it slowly back and forth. He raised two more fingers and asked Laura how many there were. She said that there were three.

"Leg may have a minor sprain," the old man said at last. His voice was thin, and it whistled faintly as his words made their way past a mouth missing half its teeth. "But it don't seem the bump to her head is like to do any lasting harm. The Prezdent Above was watching over her, I don't doubt. I'd keep those needles in another hour or so to be safe, but with a bit of rest, I warrant your girl will end up no worse for her tumble."

He turned to Ma, straightening up as much as his crooked back would allow.

"She can spend the night here, in Mabel's cottage," he told her. "Best not to move her unnecessarily. You'll want to stay with her here, I suppose. I'll have Mabel prepare a room in the main house for your man and the other girls. It'll be a deal less cramped."

"We really don't want to trouble you more than we already have," said Ma.

"Trouble? Pshaw, not a bit, Ma'am," the old man said. "The Prophet teaches that every guest is a blessing. And I'm sad to say we don't get as many guests out this way as we used to, not with the situation down in Davenport being what it is."

"Well, sir, we're mighty obliged to you for your hospitality," Pa said.

As Pa stepped forward into the candlelight, Laura saw the lines that worry had creased into his face. She felt a pang of guilt at all the trouble she'd caused.

"Try and get some more sleep, little one," the old man said, turning to Laura, the whiskers around his mouth curling upwards in a kindly smile. "In the morning, if you're feeling better, Mabel will take you around on a tour of the grounds. Would you like that?"

Laura wasn't sure how to respond, but the old man's smile was disarming. She nodded.

"Yes, I'm sure you would. Have you heard of Happy Valley Orchards? Pilgrims once traveled from all corners to pay tribute to the relics housed here. As I was telling your daddy just before you woke, it has been my honor to be its custodian for more years now than I care to say. My name is Tobias. Tobias Goatherd folks call me down Davenport way. You just let me know if you need anything. For now, I'll fetch you back a nice cup of nettle tea to help you sleep."

"Thank you, Mr. . . . Mr. Goatherd," Laura managed to say.

Tobias Goatherd smiled again.

"A resilient girl you've got here, Ingalls," he told Pa.

As the old man turned to leave, there was a sudden flurry of movement from beside the door. The girl with the short, tangled hair ducked past Tobias Goatherd and emerged next to Laura's bedside. She stood there a moment, looking down at Laura with an odd expression on her face. Then, without a word, she thrust a hand toward Laura. In it was Oprah the ragdoll.

Caught off guard, Laura stared at the doll a moment. Finally, she reached out and took Oprah from the young woman's stiff, outstretched hand.

"Thank you," Laura murmured, looking up with curiosity at older girl. The girl didn't say anything. She just cocked her head and stared back.

Finally, clutching Oprah to her chest, Laura cleared her throat. "I'm Laura," she said.

The girl's mouth twitched. Then, she spun around and dashed abruptly from the room. Laura watched her go in bewilderment, wondering if she had done something wrong, but Tobias Goatherd was quick to reassure her.

"Don't mind Mabel, sweetheart. That's just her way. It was her what found you after your fall. Carried you all the way back here and fussed over your wounds while I tracked down your Mommy and Daddy. She's taken a shine to you if I'm not mistaken. I hope you'll forgive her acting a bit queer. I don't know but what she's never met a little girl before."

Laura just nodded, unsure what to make of any of this.

"I'll let you folks get settled in," the old man continued. "Ingalls, perhaps you'll join me on the porch of the main house before you retire? It's been a spell since we've seen any travelers out this way, and I'd be obliged for any news you have to share from the north country."

Pa said that he would. Then Tobias Goatherd gave them a little bow and left. Pa handed Baby Grace to Mary and approached Laura's bed. Brushing aside a damp strand of hair, he planted a small kiss on her forehead before following the old man out the curtain-covered doorway.

Mary came over to lie at the foot of Laura's bed. Ma dampened the cloth and pressed it again to Laura's brow. Feeling overwhelmed by the day's events, Laura was about to shut her eyes when, from somewhere outside, somewhere just beyond the open window above her bed, Laura once again heard the monstrous cry that she remembered coming from the bushes on the hilltop just before her fall. At the sound of that horrible, burbling scream, her forgotten terror suddenly returned. She tried to sit up, but Ma gently guided her back down.

"Shhhhh," Ma told her. "It's only the goats."

~ ~ ~

Laura tossed and turned in bed. As tired as she felt, the questions rolling about in her head would not let her sleep.

Who was this Tobias Goatherd? And what were those frightsome statues she had seen from the hilltop? Who had set those lectric cars atop their iron spike?

Why couldn't that odd Mabel girl speak? Were goats friendly animals and may Laura pet one?

Eventually, Ma removed the needles that were mending the energies in Laura's leg. Then, she left to help get Mary settled in wherever she and Pa would be sleeping.

The bleating of the goats continued from time to time as Laura lay awake, but the sound no longer frightened her. At some point, in between the sound of the goats, Laura heard talking.

She scooted up in bed and listened more closely. It was Pa and Tobias Goatherd. Their voices were coming from somewhere outside, drifting in through the bare window above Laura's head. Soon, Laura began to smell the sour, earthy smell of Pa's pipe. As the men smoked, their conversation became louder and more jovial. Tobias Goatherd said something that made Pa laugh, and that laughter gave Laura a warm feeling. She leaned towards the window and tried to make out their words.

"And you, sir?" she heard Pa say. "How does a man come to make his home in a place like this, tending to these queer monuments?"

Tobias Goatherd's chuckle drifted in through the window on

the heels of another whiff of pipesmoke.

"Oh, that's a long story," he said. "But I'll try to sum it up as best I can, if you'll indulge me. I was born east of here, across the Illinoy, on the outskirts of Old Shicago, a place that folks in those days called Southside."

"I saw the Great Towers in my youth," came Pa's voice. "My uncle Frederick often spoke of a trip he took to Old Shicago, long ago, before it was abandoned. Do you have memories of it then? From before the Great Bust?"

There was a pause, long enough that Laura thought that the men might have gone inside or lowered their voices. But then she heard something that sounded like a sigh or maybe a laugh, and Tobias Goatherd began speaking.

"From before? Hard to say, Ingalls. Hard to say. You know, old timer like me, back in my day, no one talked about no such 'Great Bust.' This beard of mine was already turning white when I heard that name used first time. Good deal after the fact. And never been quite sure what this 'Great Bust' refers to, to be honest with you. Seems to me some folks mean the one thing, some folks 'tother.

"Are we talking about the storms and drought and such? The money crisis? Some say the Year of the Five Prezdents, that was the beginning of the end, but others say no, it was the May Madness what drove the nail in the coffin. I was born after the First Hyperflu, mind you, but that was still a good many years before the arrival of the Ague. So where's that put me? This so-called Great Bust mighta happened a hundred years ago or two hundred or just fifty-odd, depending on who you talk to.

"Well, I'll leave those questions to the scholars. All I know is the world had gone to hell long before I came into it. But I'll tell you this, Ingalls. I'm old enough to remember the lights. Yes, sir. That's true enough. I remember the lights."

THE LIFE OF TOBIAS GOATHERD

"When I was a boy, I lived in a little house beside the big city.

"We could see the Great Towers from out our kitchen window. Or that's the way I remember it anyhow. I can still picture the way the lights glowed from the lectric towers at night. Not always, mind you, but from time to time. Whenever the lectric fuel was flowing.

"I remember we had all manner of lectric contraptions inside that little house. One for washing clothing and another for washing dishes. And a lectric screen with the most marvelous pictures inside, all moving and talking and acting out all the old showtales.

"It's all a bit fuzzy, what I recollect of old Shicago Southside. I left when I was a deal younger than your girl, the young tree climber in that hut yonder. Haven't laid eyes on the Great Towers since.

"My mother was a teacher. My father . . . I confess, I no longer remember what my father did. They both perished in the fires during the May Madness. I fled Southside soon after with my older sister, and we never returned.

"We ended up in a displacement camp. It was run by soldiers what called themselves the Nashnell Guardsmen. They claimed to be under the command of the Merican Prezdent himself, though in those days there were more than one person who claimed that title. Later, the Guardsmen were driven out, and operation of the camp was turned over to a local militia loyal to the Illinoy Governor.

"Those were difficult years most everywhere. I had it easier than most, I reckon. My sister took up with one of the Guardsmen. He gave us food and kept us safe from some of the camp's rougher elements. When the Guardsmen went east, he defected to the Illinoy militia and thus continued to look out for us.

"He was a good man, or better at any rate than many of the men who oversaw that camp. He treated my sister with kindness and respect as best I can remember. They both died in an outbreak of the Yellow Madness a few years later. May the Prophet be at their sides.

"I was fourteen when my sister died. Or fifteen or thirteen. Or older maybe. Who can say? At any rate, it was around then I left the camp.

"Life in the camp had been harsh. I'd witnessed my share of death and suffering. But it didn't prepare me for the things I saw in the years that followed, not by a stretch.

"I moved from place to place for a time. I travelled with a group, other boys and girls who had survived the displacement camps and had nowhere to go when the militias melted and the chaos of the Hard Years set in. I was their leader, I suppose, in retrospect. We roamed back and forth across the Illinoy, scavving and foraging and doing what we could to survive. During that time, I saw things . . . And we did things . . .

"Well, but that's the past. 'The past is a rhyme etched in sand,' as the Prophet says. My little bandit gang was eventually absorbed into the army of a caudillo named General Blair. Weren't given much choice in the matter, though I don't recall anyone protesting the conscription. The General's men promised us three meals a day, something most of us hadn't known for some time.

"I knew a bit of soldiering thanks to my sister's benefactor back at the camp. He'd taught me how to care for a rifle and some basic military theory and tactics and so forth. As a result, I rose quick through the ranks of General Blair's forces. Constitutional Patriot Front, we called ourselves. Before long, I was commanding my own brigade.

"I can see now that the CPF was up to much the same sort of banditry as me and my roving gang of hoodlums had been. But we had uniforms, and we always had some excuse or other for our pillage. Now, if that uncle of yours taught you any history, you might know that Blair's army was routed by Lucius Ortega at the Battle of Beardstown. That's Lucius Ortega the First, mind you, not his son. Anyhow, General Blair was killed in the fighting and that was the end of the CPF.

"I was there at Beardstown. And I tell you without the slightest shame that my unit surrendered before the explosions even began. Ortega had offered amnesty to any soldiers who laid down their arms, and I'd seen men shift their allegiance from one flag to another plenty enough times in my life. Loyalty was something leased not sold, that's how I looked at it. To me, treason was just one more survival tactic.

"After Beardstown, I found my way across the Misisip to Davenport. And it was there that I first heard the words of the Prophet, Deshawn LaCore. The conduit of the Davenport fellowship was a woman we called Mother Chloe. She was one of the First Called, one who had known the Prophet himself in life. Listening to her relate the Prophet's teachings, I looked back upon my life, on the violence I had witnessed and the suffering I had caused, and I was ashamed. But when Mother Chloe laid hands upon me to cleanse my aura, I could feel the toxins leaving my body. The shame was gone. I was reawakened.

"I spent many years in Davenport, working first as a ferryman and then a wheelwright and finally as apprentice to a doctor. The doctor was a fellow member of the Faith to whom I'd been introduced at prayer meeting. It was he that taught me what I know of needlework and such.

"Then, one day, the Prezdent Above appeared to me in a dream. I know how foolish it sounds, but that's the plain fact of it. I don't know how to say it any other way. He came to me and told me to strike out into the wilderness, and so I did. I settled my affairs, packed my meager belongings, and left Davenport, following the old number roads. Finally, the Prezdent Above led me here, to this valley, a valley filled with fruit, like the garden of Paradise that once covered the world before it was corrupted by man.

"When I saw the dinosaurs, I knew it to be a sign, for there is a passage in *The Collected Sayings* that speaks of such creatures. They are ancient beings. Before God created man, they roamed the earth for millions and millions of years. But 'what grows must die, what waxes must wane and what comes together must fall apart,' as the Prophet teaches. The Prezdent Above brought the cycle of the dinosaurs to an end, leaving mankind their bones to remind us of the impermanence of all things.

"It's my belief that in Lectric Times, this must have been a place of worship, a holy site. As I explored the ruins, I came across its other monuments. The axman and his bull. The tree of cars. And then in that brick building yonder—it once housed a menagerie of sorts, if I understand the Merican inscriptions—there I found the relic that I had been brought here to seek. Hidden in this forgotten outpost, far from any settlement or convoy route of any note, were the earthly remains the Herald, the very angel God sent to call the Prophet to his mission.

"I knew then my life's work. The Prezdent Above sent me here to care for these relics. And I've strived from that day on to create a fit home for them, a place where folks of the Faith can come to ask the Herald's blessing. As you can see, I've tried restore the site's monuments to some of their former magnificence. The better glorify the Prophet's teachings.

"For some good many years after, pilgrims flocked to this holy place once more. Word spread. Time was when I'd have more travelers showing up at my door than I could properly house. But that was before the persecutions began in Davenport. The whole Lacorian Fellowship fell under suspicion thanks to General Rhee and his zealots, to where Old Man Ortega—that's the son, mind you, not the Butcher of Beardstown—he went and practically outlawed the Faith all together.

"Oh, the Prophet's light burns brighter than ever in people's hearts, don't you doubt it. But outward shows of piety like going out on pilgrimage? Well, it's just too much risk for most folks.

"The Ortegas don't much bother with the likes of me, not way out here, and I keep good relations with the local supervisory. But I don't talk so freely about the Herald's Shrine as I used to, that's true enough. I suppose the time may come soon when it will be forgotten once more.

"But that's the way of things, Ingalls. I've no complaints. No bitterness, no, not a bit. Why, as I near the twilight of this long life, I find myself more blessed than ever. Just look around you. The hills are abundant with fruit. And my flocks are thriving.

Brought a single pair up from Davenport some time back, and the Prezdent Above has seen fit to multiply their numbers year upon year.

"And then, as if these blessings weren't enough, one day He sent me Mabel. I'd never had the opportunity for children of my own, and perhaps He sensed my loneliness.

"Early one winter, I realized that someone was raiding my supplies. If it had just been food that was disappearing, I'd have suspected some wild animal. But when tools began to go missing, I knew that there must be someone camped in the hills beyond the old number road. So I lay in wait one night. Hearing a rustling, I crept up to my shed. Flinging open the door, my lantern light fell upon a child, disheveled and naked.

"I thought for certain she must have the Ague, and I might have shot her if I had been able to aim my rifle with lantern in hand. Instead, she escaped, and God gave me the chance to reflect. I'd seen Yellow Madness up close, mind you. I knew the signs, and this child had neither the look nor the behavior of a fiend.

"Over the course of months, I slowly won her trust. Began the long process of taming her, one might say, for she was like a wild animal when the Prezdent Above first sent her to me. She'd been on her own a good while, her whole life maybe or near about. I'd seen children like that in the years after the camps broke up. Ferals. I never have managed to teach her language, though whether there's some physical malady that causes her muteness or it was simply too late by the time I got to her, I do not know.

"Wild she remains in many ways, but she has a good heart. Her aura glows with greater kindness and gentleness than many who are a good deal more acquainted with the society of men.

"It's an odd thing to happen to one so late in life as me. My little bandit gang roaming the Illinoy shared a certain bond of necessity, I suppose. So too with my regiment in the CPF. And of course I knew the solace of being united in Faith during the years I spent worshipping with Mother Chloe and the Davenport

Fellowship. But it's only now, in this final chapter of my life, for the first time perhaps since my sister left all those years ago, that I finally feel as if I have a family. Look out for yours, Ingalls. It's the greatest blessing the Prezdent Above can bestow upon a man.

"Pshaw. What a sentimental old bore I must sound like! I blame this pipeleaf of yours, Ingalls. It's got my mind running off all wistful and contemplative-like. Is this what you folks grow up in those big north woods? I dare say it's a good deal stronger than what they smoke down in Davenport, I'll tell you that.

"Well, yes, I suppose one more small bowl before bed won't tip the scales one way or 'tother. You're a good man, Ingalls. You take care of that family of yours. A blessing. A blessing."

~~~

The smell of pipeleaf wafting past Laura's window grew stronger and then subsided. Pa was speaking. His voice was softer than the boisterous old man's, and Laura found she could not make out his words. The goats were bleating again. At some point, the sounds from outside worked their way into Laura's dreams, as the wily hand of sleep gently brushed her eyelids shut.

TWELVE: HAPPY VALLEY ORCHARDS RESTUP AND REPTILSOO

By the time Laura opened her eyes, morning had crept into the room. She sat up and worked her fingers through her hair. There, towards the back of her skull, she could feel a bump. It felt sore but only when Laura touched it.

She got out of bed. Then she lifted her scraped knee and let her leg swing up and back. It didn't hurt at all. Tobias Goatherd's medicine needles had done their work.

Laura walked in a circle all the way around the little hut. As she padded barefoot around the soft dirt floor, she reached out and let her fingers crawl along the wall like a spider, *tap tap tap*. The walls were made of stacked logs. The wood felt rough and raw, not like the ancient pine beams that had supported Laura's house back in the Big Woods. Through the gaps between the logs, pinpricks of sunlight pierced the hut.

Laura hopped back up onto the bed to reach the hut's little square window. She pulled aside a ragged cloth curtain and peered out into the dawn. There, the first teasing rays of morning cast zig-zag shadows through a weed-covered yard. The yard was divided into neat squares by the remains of several criss-crossing creetrock walls. Beyond these ruins, just a short distance from Laura's window, there was an old brick building. Jutting out from the building was a covered wooden porch that did not look like it had been part of the original construction. Its deck and posts and awning were all painted a milk white that clashed with the weathered brick. A pair of wicker chairs sat beside the railing. Laura supposed that was where Pa and Tobias Goatherd had been sitting when Laura had overheard their conversation the night before.

Laura leaned a little further out the window to better scan her surroundings. She took in a long breath, filling her nose with the fresh morning air. Before she could exhale, her eyes landed on something that made that breath stop where it was, lodged right at the top of her chest. Rising up from behind the brick building's roof was one of the monsters Laura had seen from the hilltop. Only now she wasn't gazing down on it from afar but looking right up into its lizard eyes, which peered down at her from a tiny head perched at the end of its long snake neck. Instinctively, she jerked her head back inside the window.

As soon as the cloth curtain flopped back into place, Laura released the breath she had been holding in. It poured out in a giggle of relief. She knew the monster was just a creetrock statute. She had just been startled to find it looming over her, so big and close. She peeked out of the window once more to prove to herself she wasn't afraid. Then she hopped down from the bed.

Laura found her coat, shrugged it on, and stuffed Oprah snug into the pocket. Then she walked over to the curtain which was draped over the doorway of the little log hut. She pulled it aside, letting the sunlight wash over her.

Before Laura could even take in her surroundings, she heard

Mary call out.

"Laura!"

A dirt path led from the hut towards the brick house with its white porch. A little ways up the path, sitting beside the ruins of an old wall, were Mary and Ma. Alongside them sat the silent, tangle-haired girl Laura had met the night before. Ma sat on her stool, and Mary sat cross-legged on the ground, Baby Grace in her lap. The girl—Mabel she had been called—crouched across from them, hugging her knees tight against her chest.

"Laura's awake!" Mary cried, rising to her feet.

Mary handed Baby Grace to Ma and ran to Laura. Close at her heels was Jack. Mary wrapped Laura up in a joyous hug, while the little striped pigdog raced in circles round and round them.

Mary at her arm and Jack at her heels, Laura was swept up the path. There was a fire going. As Laura approached, the smell of frycakes greeted her. Soon, she could hear them sizzling. Her stomach squealed in anticipation.

The old stone wall that sheltered Ma's cookfire ran parallel to the footpath. The wall rose and fell in an erratic succession of peaks and valleys before sinking with finality beneath the weeds just short of the main house. Near the spot where Ma was preparing breakfast, an apple tree had knocked down an entire section of the wall and was busily wrapping its roots about the rubble. The tree's branches spread upwards, stretching out over Ma and the wildgirl and the skillet of frycakes. Sitting there beside the fire, Laura saw a whole basket of apples.

Ma pulled Laura close and pressed the back of her hand to her forehead. Then she felt around for the bump on the back of Laura's head.

"All in all, I'd say you look well enough," Ma said, finally. "Do you feel dizzy? Tired?"

Laura shook her head. Ma kissed her forehead and then handed her a tin plate piled with three steaming frycakes. Laura looked down at the plate and couldn't believe her eyes, for there were fat chunks of apple baked right into the soymeal. The tallow-coated skillet had turned their flesh a sticky caramel. Laura looked over to Mary to share her delight and found that her sister's face was already stuffed with frycake.

Laura was about to follow Mary's lead, when Ma told her to lower her plate. Right on top of the warm apple frycake, Ma plopped down a spoonful of cream. Laura had never had cream before. It was so thick that it just sat there in a thick glop on top of the frycakes for a moment before slowly spreading across the spongy surface, soaking into the little holes that the bubbles had made. Finally, Laura took a bite. Between the tart apples and the rich cream, Laura's mouth was full of flavors she had never tasted, and she chewed slowly, savoring the delicious newness.

On the other side of the cookfire, the wildgirl seemed to be enjoying the breakfast as well. Judging from the way she eyed the sizzling soymeal in fascination and sniffed each morsel before it passed her lips, the frycakes were just as much an exotic treat for Mabel as the cream and apples were for Laura. As the girl ate, her eyes bounced back and forth between Ma and Mary and Laura and the food on her plate. It reminded Laura of Jack when they'd first found him, the wary way he'd watched them as he gnawed the saltmeat Pa had set out as bait.

Ma explained that Pa had gone off with Tobias Goatherd to help the old man mend some fences down by the creek.

"He said that Ms. Mabel would show you and Mary around the grounds if you're feeling up to it. Would you like that?"

Laura looked back to Mabel. The girl's expression was impossible to read. Gazing back at Laura, she wrinkled her nose like a rabbit and pursed her lips. Perhaps that was her version of a smile, Laura thought. Over Mabel's shoulder, Laura could see the lectric cars suspended in the air atop the great iron spike. She nodded to Ma.

When their tin plates and the big iron pan had been scraped clean and the soymeal sack tied up tight with hemp string to keep the air out and everything stacked up neat and put away in the handcar, Mary and Laura looked to Ma expectantly.

"Alright," Ma said. "I suppose there's no harm in you girls exploring for a few minutes while we wait for Pa to get back. Just

111

see you don't go far. And be careful around any old ruins. Don't touch anything. And stay together. And see that you mind what Ms. Mabel . . . well, you just mind her, understand?"

Mabel raised her eyebrows when Laura and Mary turned to her and pursed her lips in that same cryptic maybe-smile. Then she squeezed through a gap in the old stone wall and looked back at them, cocking her head, before skipping off down another dirt path that led winding off through the ruins in the direction of the giant car spike.

That look meant "follow me," Laura thought, and so, after a moment of hesitation, Laura rushed over to the wall, clambered through, and raced down the trail after Mabel, Mary and Jack right behind her.

The wildgirl led them down a rocky path. It wound its way in between weed-covered creetrock foundations, which Laura knew were the footprints of vanished buildings. Suddenly, the iron spire rose up ahead of them. High above, the column of lectric cars hung suspended in the air, speared through their middles like chunks of meat on a skewer. Mabel led them right up to shadow of the car spike. Skinny beams of sunlight rained down on Laura from the many holes that pierced the cars' age-encrusted armor. Instinctively, she and Mary hung back, as if the heavy lectric machines might topple down on them at any moment.

The spike had looked so spindly and delicate from far off that Laura was surprised to see how thick it was about the base. Mary and Laura and Mabel might all have joined hands and still not been able to wrap their arms around it. She could also see now that, while the spike had seemed solid from far off, like a single nail crafted in some gigantic forge, its surface was covered in sections of iron plating, joined edge to edge. One of the plates, a few feet above Laura's head, was missing, and she could see shadows of iron scaffolding within.

Mabel danced round and round the spike, seemingly oblivious to the rusted hulks dangling precariously above. Finally, Laura made up her mind that she was going to touch it.

"Laura!" Mary said when she stepped forward.

Another step and then another, into the shadow, and soon Laura was face-to-face with the monolith. She reached out and pressed her palm against it. The iron surface was coarse with rust, streaked in deep reds and grays. Slowly, Laura lifted her chin upwards until she was staring straight up at the strange metal canopy. The shapes of the cars were dark against the sun, but when Laura shielded her eyes with her other hand she could make out the undersides of the old machines. Twisted pipes hung loose from their bellies like the innards of a deer strung up for cleaning.

Mabel stopped beside Laura. She too placed a palm against the base of the spike. They looked at one another. Suddenly, the winds shifted, and the great tree of iron above them groaned and creaked. Laura gasped and dashed backwards, and Mabel followed her lead.

The car spike quieted. When her initial alarm subsided, Laura looked up at Mabel. The wildgirl wrinkled her nose, making a soft snuffling sound that sounded bit like a laugh. Laura found herself giggling too.

Mabel gave them another follow-me look before running back up the path. Laura and Mary and Jack all ran after her. Almost immediately, Mabel stopped beside a hill of rubble and clambered up its slope. Mary and Laura climbed after her, hoisting themselves up and over the remains of an old creetrock wall. Poor Jack couldn't find a way around. He dashed back and forth, growling piteously, until Laura turned back and lifted him across.

At the top of the rubble slope, they found a flat plateau covered with tallgrass and brambles. Nearby, a stray goat munched on the vegetation. Jack bounded over to it with a yip. The goat was startled at first, but then it turned to Jack and planted its hooves. The goat snorted and lowered its head, showing Jack its horns.

For a moment, Laura was worried the goat might hurt Jack. But Mabel walked up to the goat and grabbed it by the horn. She waggled a finger in front of its face and clacked her tongue. Then she gave it a smack to its hindquarters, sending it loping off through the grass with an indignant bleat. Jack yipped and ran around in a tight circle as if it had been he that had faced down the goat.

Next to where the goat had been standing was a long mound. It was covered in weeds and brambles, and Laura had taken it for simply another pile of creetrock debris from some toppled building. When Mabel beckoned them closer, though, Laura saw that the mound was more than mere rubble. Beneath the overgrowth, the creetrock was carved with the details of another huge statue. And there were even streaks of color, faded blues and pinks.

Mabel lifted up her roughspun tunic. Hidden beneath, tucked into a sash wound tight around her hips, was a leather sheath. From the sheath, Mabel pulled out a knife, so long and sharp that Laura couldn't believe it had been there the whole time. Mabel twirled it, its bone handle sliding through her fingers while the long blade spun end over end, as casually as one might stir a bowl of soymeal porridge. Mary and Laura turned to one another in surprise. A look of uneasiness creased Mary's brow as she watched the wildgirl, but Laura mostly just found herself wishing that she had such a knife and could learn to twirl it just so.

Mabel knelt down and began to hack away at the brambles and pull up weeds by the root. As she worked, Laura and Mary walked along the length of the fallen statue. It was a man. A huge man. When he had stood, he must have been as tall as a house. A huge ax lay across his chest, clutched against his sleeping body. Along the undersides of his bulging arms and shoulders, Laura could see faded pink squares that had once checkered his shirt.

When she came to the axman's head, she paused. Half his face was missing, and his nose was broken off completely. But the features that remained were sharp and lifelike. Curls of creetrock hair peeked out from beneath a cap still flecked with traces of pink paint. His jaw was covered with a bushy creetrock beard. It rose in a majestic arc from the axman's ear, half buried in soil, to an apex where it abruptly stopped, hewn clean away along with the rest of his face. His one remaining eye was open. It stared unblinking skyward.

When Mabel finished clearing weeds, she put her knife away. She stepped back. Pressing her hands together, she closed her eyes and made a respectful bow towards the fallen axman. Mary and Laura exchanged a puzzled look. Finally, Laura stepped forward and put her own hands together and copied Mabel's bow. She wasn't sure why, but the gesture felt right. Mabel seemed pleased, and, after a moment of hesitation, Mary bowed towards the statue as well.

And, with that, they were off again. Mabel led them from place to place all around the abandoned Merican outpost, pointing out other strange ruins. There were more statues. Most were little more than wayward limbs or creetrock mounds weathered down to shapeless gray blobs, but some were nearly as well-preserved as the giant axman. Laura's favorite was the horned rabbit, whose head and front limbs they found propped against a brick wall.

Then there was the chain of small lectric cars. They were all strung together like the long skytrains of Old Shicago, but Laura could not imagine this train ferrying people around the Great Towers. Each car had only one seat, each seat barely big enough to fit a child. Mabel climbed in one anyway, her knees squished up between her chest and the car's rusted iron prow. She slapped her palm against the side as if imagining herself drawn along by the train's vanished lectric power. A smiling face was sculpted into the front car. There was something unpleasant about its warped grimace, the way the streaks of rust dripped down its pock-marked cheeks. Laura was glad when they moved on.

Elsewhere, they came across big letters etched into a metal sign. According to Mary, they spelled out "World's Largest Apple." Laura was much impressed until she inspected the ruins that lay just beyond the sign. Not much of the building remained, but the base had clearly been round. One of its walls lay at an angle, propped up by a fortuitous tree. The creetrock was curved, cresting up and over like a wave before crumbling away into a web of iron rods. If this was what the sign had called the world's largest apple—nothing more than a modest-sized apple-shaped building—Laura couldn't help feeling a bit cheated.

Finally, Mabel led them to a structure that stood at the edge of Happy Valley Orchards. It seemed better maintained than the other ruins, its walls free of creepers and the ground around it cleared of weeds and rubble. Its brick doorway was tall and wide and flanked by ornate creetrock columns, each carved with the image of a snake winding up and down its length. Whatever doors had originally stood between those snake columns were gone. Instead, the doorway had been filled in with a crude wooden fence, into which, in turn, a smaller doorway had been cut. A curtain was draped across the entryway, much like the hut where Laura had spent the night. Above the doorway, a stone slab was set into the brick. Letters were etched into the stone.

"Reptilsoo," Laura heard Mary whisper, sounding out the building's name.

Mabel pulled aside the curtain. Everything beyond was darkness. Laura and Mary stood there at the threshold of the old building, hesitant to follow. For some reason, Laura felt a tingling at the back of her neck, causing her to glance around. Emerging from behind a corner of the mysterious reptilsoo, she was confronted by the second of Happy Valley's twin monsters, the one that stood on two legs. Its face loomed above her. It smiled a smile, full of crooked knifelike teeth, gaping wide in eerie silhouettes black against the morning sun. Turning again to the dark doorway framed by serpents, Laura felt an unaccountable chill.

Suddenly, Mabel disappeared behind the curtain. A moment later, she peeked back out and regarded them with that same enigmatic tilt of her head before ducking back inside. Laura squared her shoulders, reminding herself that the sharp-toothed monster guarding the building was nothing but creetrock. With a deep breath, she plunged in after Mabel.

Laura stood there a moment, just inside the curtain. Gradually, her eyes adjusted to the darkness. Though the roof had clearly been repaired at some point in the recent past, gaps remained, letting stray fissures of light slip through its high ceiling. Eventually, Laura was able to pick out Mabel's shape from among the other shadows. The wildgirl was crouched just a few steps away, fiddling with something on the creetrock floor. There was a clacking and a scratching. Then a spark. Then a blossoming orange glow.

Mabel stood and lofted a lantern. Around her, the shadows shifted and danced. She walked past Laura. As she moved along the wall, she thrust her lantern out, splashing light across a patchwork of brick and plaster.

The sweep of the lantern gradually revealed a breathtaking scene. The walls of the reptilsoo were covered with murals. The images stretched from the floor all the way to the rafters, interrupted only by cracks and the irregular blotches where decaying plaster had given way to bare brick.

Even beneath the pale orange tint of the lantern light, the paintings were vivid. A green shape crept along the bottom of the mural. As Laura approached, she saw it was a creature. Its long snout was filled with many sharp tiny teeth, and its short legs seemed unable to keep its belly from dragging along the floor.

Above the long-snouted animal was a giant snake devouring a deer whole. Nearby, beside a mountain that spat fire and smoke into the air, was something that looked very much like the monster statue standing outside. It had the same little two-clawed hands, the same big toothy mouth.

"Oh my," said a hushed voice at Laura's back.

Laura had been so absorbed by the paintings, she hadn't noticed Mary slip in behind her. Together, they stared, mouths agape at the strange animals and exotic landscapes flickering in the lantern light.

The paintings seemed to go on and on. Jungles faded into deserts which gave way to swamps, each crawling with a different collection of clawed and scaly beasts.

As Mabel led them deeper into the abandoned structure, she turned her lantern away from the mural-covered walls. The big room seemed to go on and on, cavernous and empty, but Laura began to discern peaks and valleys cut into the featureless creetrock floor. Vague shapes rose up here and there. Elsewhere, the ground was sunken, with steps leading down into shallow pools. In one corner, there were stacks of boxes made of pure lectricmade glass. Their crystal walls were cracked and dusty but still hauntingly beautiful.

Mabel walked on, illuminating their path so Laura and Mary wouldn't stumble. Even so, it made Laura nervous. She knew Ma and Pa wouldn't want them crawling blindly through old ruins, and she did not think it would make them feel better to know they were under the care of a wordless knife-wielding young woman whom they'd only just met.

She could hear Mary getting more and more upset.

"Laura . . ." Mary kept saying, her voice hushed, as if afraid of the echo that would bounce back at her from the far corners of the vast dark chamber.

Finally, Mary grabbed Laura's arm and tried to tug her back the way they'd come. Laura thought Mary was probably right. They shouldn't go any further. She was about to give in and follow her sister back out into the light when suddenly Mabel stopped. Her lantern clanked as she set it down. Mary stopped tugging Laura's arm, and they both looked.

Mabel stood before a rock shelf. At first, the shelf appeared to have been chiseled from a heap of boulders, piled incongruously in the middle of this abandoned building and somehow arranged to form a series of flat outcroppings. On closer look, though, Laura saw that the shelf was made of creetrock that had merely been shaped to imitate natural stone. On top and on each of the lower outcroppings, there were candles. Mabel lit them one by one until an eerie, flickering radiance surrounded the shelf of false boulders.

Between the candles, there were other objects, big and small. As the candlelight bloomed, brighter and brighter with each sweep of Mabel's hand, Laura's attention was drawn from one strange item to another. Small statuettes, ornate jars and bottles, painted wooden crosses, and still other objects that Laura couldn't even begin to comprehend lurked everywhere among the creetrock boulders' ramparts and alcoves. In a place of prominence, there was a framed picture, a faded portrait of a man with dark skin and long, braided hair.

Finally, Mabel lit the topmost row of candles, illuminating a shelf above the portrait of the man. Sitting there, at the very pinnacle of this strange display, was the biggest object of all. Laura took it for a large stone at first or perhaps a remnant from another creetrock statue. But as its contours took shape, the spreading candlelight gradually revealing the depth of its black eye sockets, she realized that the thing was bone, gray and smooth like the skeletons they'd found in the great iron boxes beside the river.

Only these bones did not belong to a person. These were the bones of some creature, some ancient horror from a forgotten world.

The skull stared back at her. Tooth upon jagged tooth crissed and crossed from beneath a long snout. This was the same snout, the same teeth, she'd seen on the snarling green creature from the mural. In the flickering light, the skull seemed to move, the hollow shadows of its eyes looking Laura up and down as its jaws twisted upwards in a savage grin.

"Laura . . ." Mary said again, the word quivering off into nothing.

From somewhere in the shadows, she heard Jack growl.

Laura clutched tight to her sister's hand, and together they dashed headlong toward the exit.

THIRTEEN: THE HERALD'S SHRINE

Pa and Tobias Goatherd returned from the creek around midday. By then, Mary and Laura had recovered from their experience inside that eerie old building that the Mericans had called the Reptilsoo. In the light of day, Laura felt a little foolish for getting so frightened of a silly old skull.

Nevertheless, Tobias Goatherd apologized to Ma and Pa for letting Mabel take them inside.

"Your girls weren't in any danger, I promise," he assured Pa. "Those brick walls are sturdy, old as they are. The Mericans who built that place knew what they were about. It's not like to collapse on anybody any time soon. And I cleared the worst of the hazards out myself years ago, in days when this back of mine was a good deal stronger."

As he and Pa unloaded a wheelbarrow full of rotted fence posts, Tobias Goatherd tried to explain the mysterious chamber that Mary and Laura had followed Mabel into, with its dramatic murals and strange bones. Back in Lectric Times, he told them, the Reptilsoo of Happy Valley had housed all manner of exotic animals, brought in from the far-flung corners of the Merican Empire and caged there under that very roof. Those animals had all died long ago, of course, but Tobias Goatherd seemed to think that there was still something special about the place. He told them how he had worked for years to restore the site and invited travelers from far and wide to come marvel at the old murals and the strange artifacts he had recovered from the reptilsoo's hidden chambers.

The candlelit shelf with the monstrous skull, he called the Herald's Shrine.

"You wouldn't know it nowadays, but folks used to come

from all over to pray at the Herald's Shrine," Tobias Goatherd said. "From up in the Northlands. From way down in Flannerista Territory and the so-called Holy Gulf Confederation. Even had a pair of Tang envoys visit once. Not just Lacorians, neither. Had plenty of Deshi folk from out Lildaka way, even a Desereti or two. Word got out about the relics of Happy Valley, and people just wanted to take a gander."

When the fence posts had all been tossed atop a pile of scrap wood, Tobias Goatherd began wheeling his empty barrow back up towards the main house. He continued talking as he went. He was speaking mostly to Pa, but Laura and Mary trotted alongside, listening in.

"That all changed quite some time back, mind you," the old man said, his breathing growing heavy with the effort of pushing the wheelbarrow up the path. "Been years since we've seen that kind of traffic out this way. Not since Old Man Ortega started suppressing the Faith. Then of course the Spear cut off trade from the Southeast, which was pretty well the nail in the coffin. And beyond that, well, I suppose it's been a combination of causes, like anything else. Things were one way, and now they're a different way."

Tobias Goatherd grunted as he struggled to force his barrow past a rocky patch. Pa tried to take the handles from him, but the old man waved him away.

"Even so," he continued, once the barrow's wheel found traction and began to roll again, "we keep up the shrine to this day, Mabel and me. Try our best to care for the valley's monuments. You never know when a stray pilgrim may show up at our doorstep, seeking the Herald's blessing."

They reached the main house, with its wide white porch, where Ma sat with Baby Grace. As Tobias Goatherd set down his wheelbarrow, Laura tugged on Pa's shirt sleeve. When he bent down towards her, she tried to whisper in his ear.

"What's a herald, Pa?"

Her whisper was too loud, and the old man heard. He turned and laughed.

"That's a right fair question, my dear," he said. "Nowadays, my mind does get jumbled up so. Can't hardly keep straight who I'm talking to nor what I told them not five minutes back. No, you'll not know the first thing about the Prophet's Herald, I suppose. Why, probably your pa has no idea what I'm talking about neither. That fair to say, Ingalls?"

Pa grinned sheepishly and shrugged.

"You're a kind man, Ingalls, humoring the ramblings of an old graybeard like me. No, of course you'll not have heard the story of the Herald. Why would you? These days, there's many good Lacorians don't know it. You won't find it in *The Letters of Deshawn LaCore* nor in *The Collected Sayings*, and I hear tell that in some fellowships, there's conduits—otherwise godly men and women mind you—they dismiss the tale as nothing but a bit of folklore made up long after the Prophet's death. The story's true, though, every word of it."

Tobias Goatherd climbed the porch's wooden steps, clutching tight to the railing. Slowly, wincing every time another one of his joints was conscripted into the effort, he sat down on the top step. He took off his straw hat and wiped the sweat from his bald head with a handkerchief. As he fanned himself with the brim of the hat, he looked down at Mary and Laura and raised his bushy white eyebrows.

"I don't suppose you girls would like to hear the story?"

Laura very much wanted to hear the story, especially if it involved the monstrous beast whose skull she'd seen in the reptilsoo. She dashed over to the foot of the porch steps and knelt down in the grass expectantly. A moment later, Mary sat down beside her.

Mabel, who seemed to have grown more bashful since Mary and Laura had run from her and the candlelit shrine, had been watching from up in the branches of a nearby tree. Now, she climbed down and disappeared behind the house, emerging a moment later with a ladle of water. She handed it to Tobias Goatherd and then hopped down the porch steps to sit in the grass, close but not too close to Laura and Mary.

Tobias Goatherd took a long grateful drink from the ladle. Wiping the moisture from his whiskers, he opened his mouth to speak. Suddenly, he paused. Glancing over at Pa, he cleared his throat.

"Begging your pardon, Ingalls," he said. "It's not my intent to missionary to you or your family. I don't know how much they know of Deshawn LaCore or his teachings up in the north country where you're from, but every man has his own path to trod. You folks are decent, good-hearted people, I could tell that from the start, and how you worship, well, that's your look-out. I'd just be pleased to share just this small anecdote from the Prophet's early life, if you'll indulge me, and leave it at that."

Pa tugged at his beard and looked over to Ma, who sat beneath the porch's awning on the other side of the old man. Ma scooted her stool forward. To Laura's relief, she said that they'd be delighted to hear Tobias Goatherd's story.

"Well then," the old man said happily and began.

THE STORY OF DESHAWN LACORE AND THE FORTY DAYS IN THE SWAMP

"A long time ago, back in the days of the Merican Empire, there was an island called Norlins. It lay in the southernmost reaches of Old Merica, right where the Mighty Misisip River meets the sea. And it was there, in the tumultuous final years of the Lectric Era, that a young boy named Deshawn LaCore was born.

"This boy would one day become the last and greatest in the long chain of prophets sent by the Prezdent Above to guide mankind. Yet, his early life could not have been more humble and inauspicious. He was an orphan. Poor. And, like so many who would be touched by his ministry during the coming Hard Years, he was born into a world that had already descended into chaos and darkness, one that promised a child like Deshawn LaCore little but struggle and sorrow.

"You see, by the time of the Prophet's birth, the island of

Norlins had endured tremendous suffering. Elsewhere in the Merican Empire, the lectric light still glowed. This was before the worst of the wars and the riots, before the Hyperflu and the Ague. But, for Norlins, the Great Bust had come early. Terrible storms had ravaged the island, one upon another. And with every storm, the waters around Norlins rose bit by bit.

"The people of Norlins, those that could, fled to other parts of the Empire or to displacement camps away from the encroaching floods. As the island emptied, bandits and pirates descended on Norlins to scav the abandoned towers and terrorize those who remained. Soon, what had once been a great Merican city like Shicago or Gothim had become a soggy wasteland, all but forsaken by the outside world. A lawless place, devastated by hunger, disease, and the relentless storms.

"Deshawn LaCore's parents likely perished in one such storm, though nothing is known of them. It is said that he was found floating in a reed basket, tethered to the steeple of an old church that had become submerged beneath the rising waters. The captain of a pirate gang came upon him there. He brought the babe into his boat and took him home—back to the little tin shack on stilts where he and his outlaw brothers slept—to be nursed by a woman in the pirate lord's hire.

"And so it was that the future prophet of the Prezdent Above came to be raised by a gang of petty thieves and bandits, growing up among them in their little house perched above the floodwaters. To survive, his adoptive family scavved and stole and traded in intoxicating tonics and pills. All in all, the boy seemed destined for a short and wicked life.

"Then, one day, when Deshawn LaCore was nearing his eleventh birthday, he saw a member of his gang being beaten by a Merican Guardsman. It was during the reign of Prezdent Augustus West, who had sent the Guardsmen down to pacify Norlins and restore the Empire's control over the island. But the Prezdent's soldiers had quickly grown corrupt and cruel, and soon they were hated by the people of Norlins almost as much as the bandit gangs.

"Young Deshawn LaCore, he was loyal to a fault. Seeing his brother being treated with such brutality, he ran home to his gang's little tin shack on stilts. He returned with a pistol and shot the Guardsman dead.

"Now, you must understand that, in those days, the killing of a Guardsman was the greatest crime that you could commit in the land of Norlins. The Mericans who occupied the island might turn a blind eye to banditry or the selling of forbidden pills, but a man who killed a Guardsman, they would never rest until he had been hunted down. Deshawn knew this. He knew that he would be a danger to his friends and family. He knew that he must run far away. And so he hurriedly packed supplies into an old canoe. And then he fled into the Swamp.

"Have you girls ever seen a swamp? I've no doubt you have marshes up north, come across a bog or two in your travels I reckon. But the Norlins Swamp was something different altogether. It surrounded the island city, beginning at its edges and stretching for kims and kims in every direction.

"The Swamp, it was like a labyrinth. Shadowy corridors. Twisting canals filled with murky brackish water and flanked by gnarled trees. Everything obscured beneath a shroud of moss and hanging creepers. The Swamp was deep and dark and unknowable, and many a man entered the Swamp never to return.

"For forty days and forty nights, Deshawn LaCore wandered the Swamp alone. He ate snakes and lizards and swampmoss, and at nights he slept beneath his overturned canoe. But gradually the Swamp consumed him. Insects tormented his skin. The damp, fetid air settled into his lungs. He grew sick.

"Finally, one day, as a fierce storm began to batter the Swamp, the Prophet's canoe ran aground amid a tangle of tree roots. There the boy lay, on the floor of the little boat, shaking with fever, too weak to extricate himself from the twisted claws that entwined his vessel. He closed his eyes against the rain which pelted his face and tried to accept the numbing embrace of the end.

125

"But the Prezdent Above had other plans for Deshawn LaCore. Suddenly, the water beside the canoe began to bubble and churn. Waves rocked the boat, knocking it violently against the tree roots. Deshawn opened his eyes and struggled to drag himself to the side of the canoe. White-knuckled, he grasped the lip of the boat and pulled himself up to peer over the side. To his astonishment, from the swirling water beside him there arose a gigantic alligator.

"Do you girls know what an alligator is? They are ancient creatures, as old as the dinosaurs depicted in those creetrock idols yonder. I've never seen one in the flesh myself, but I've spoken to travelers from the Gulf Confederation who say they still lurk among the rivers down south. Been on the earth long before us and aim to be here long after I reckon. They are reminders from the Prezdent Above that the works of man are but one cycle in His design.

"But this was no ordinary alligator, mind you. This was an angel of the Lord. Long ago, the Prezdent Above had chosen Deshawn LaCore to be His prophet and to guide His people through the changes that would soon come. And so He sent the Herald to protect His chosen one and direct him towards his destiny.

"The Herald was larger than any alligator Deshawn had ever seen. What's more, its skin was a ghostly white, and its eyes were red. Seeing the great scaly body emerge from the swamp, fear overwhelmed the boy, and he fell backwards into his boat. Too weak to cry out, his mouth hung open in mute horror, broken only by soft, ragged gasps. Somehow, the white gator managed to lift itself fully from the water, its head and shoulders looming above the canoe. The creature looked down upon the Prophet and spoke.

"'Sit up, Child of Dust,' it said. 'And fear no more. For I come not to deliver you unto your death but unto your call. I am the Herald of the Prezdent Above. You have been chosen to bear His light among the peoples of the world that they may know His design and not despair.'

"Closer the great white alligator approached. It tilted its head to stare down sidelong at the boy with a single reptilian eye, and Deshawn could see his own terrified reflection glistening within the terrible pink sphere.

"'God knows you, Deshawn LaCore,' the Herald continued, and the deep hiss of its voice seemed to echo from everywhere at once. 'You have walked a path of darkness. But that is over. You have been called. You shall emerge from Swamp changed. You shall return to your town and your tribe, and there you shall share the sacred light that the Prezdent Above has already hidden within you. And when you have knit their hearts to yours in fellowship, you and your sisters and your brothers, together you shall spread God's light to other towns and other nations until the world is united once more by faith in the design of the Prezdent Above.'

"Deshawn could only stammer. Fervently did he wish to appease this frightful Herald, but how could he explain to the creature the futility of what it asked? Deshawn had long since lost his way in the boundless Swamp. He was not certain he could even find his home again, much less muster the strength for the journey. What was more, even if managed to return to Norlins as the Herald seemed to demand, the Guardsmen would surely kill him for his crime. Whatever sacred light might lie hidden deep within him, there it would surely stay once his body was left to bleed out upon the streets of island city.

"Though Deshawn could not form the words, the Herald knew his thoughts. It made a low guttural noise that might have been a laugh.

"'Do you doubt the sovereignty of He that made and renews the world, Child of Dust?' it said. 'The Prezdent Above made men free that they might craft their own hope and be their own salvation. But He has filled the world with tools for your use if you but have the wisdom to reach out and grasp them.'

"The Herald lowered his head until his giant white snout filled the boat. It opened its jaws, revealing an endless procession of knife-sharp teeth, each bigger than Deshawn's thumb.

"'Reach into my mouth, Child of Dust. There you shall find a loose tooth. Pry it out. Take it with you when you return to your home. This shall be your talisman. While you carry it, men will sense its power and hesitate to do you harm. The path ahead will not be straight or easy. You will be met with scorn and hatred. You will be slandered and obstructed. But draw strength from this talisman you bear, and let it remind you that you do not face these trials alone.'

"What could Deshawn do but as the Herald instructed? He leaned forward into the beast's waiting jaws, half expecting them to snap shut at any moment and cleave his body in two. He spied a tooth, smoother and larger than the rest, near the back of the creature's mouth. Warily, he reached out and grasped it.

"No sooner had he touched the tooth than Deshawn felt his fever subside and his hands steady. Gingerly, he nudged and twisted. He felt the tooth give way. A moment later, he had pulled it free of the Herald's bone-white gums. He clutched the enormous fang in his fist and backed away to gaze once more into the big red slitted eye.

"'Well chosen, Child of Dust,' the Herald said. 'Now climb upon my back. I will bear you to the swamp's edge. You shall return to your people before day next breaks.'

"And so the Prophet rode the great white alligator through the swamp and all the way to the outskirts of Norlins. What he did when he arrived, well, that is a separate tale. Enough to say that, indeed, God saved him from execution at the hands of the Merican Guardsmen, though whether it was his talisman or the Prophet's own wits and words that stayed their guns, as to that the stories differ. In time, many Guardsmen would set aside their uniforms to follow the Prophet and would be counted among the most fervent of the First Called.

"As to the Herald, little else is said. Most assume the ancient creature vanished, its role fulfilled.

"But you girls know better, do you not? That's right. A hundred years later, long after the Prophet was martyred and laid to rest, God sent a dream to a man who was a former bandit himself. A man who, like the young Deshawn LaCore, had done many shameful things in the name of survival. The dream led that man here to this very place, this valley full of strange idols from Lectric Times.

"When I first laid eyes on these ruins all those years ago, I sensed that a sacred energy must flow through this place. Why else had its Merican builders chosen this remote site to erect their monuments? I knew right away that I had reached my destination, that this was what the Prezdent Above had sent me out upon the old number roads to find.

"And then, as I cleared out the rubble from the abandoned buildings, I discovered old lectric pictures buried within. And what do you suppose they showed? A huge alligator. White with red eyes.

"Astonished at the revelation, I continued to excavate. From the ruins, I began to pull bones, the skeletons of all manner of exotic creatures. Until, one day, I came upon the relics that I was seeking. The true earthly remains of the Herald.

"How this divine being made its way from the Lost City of Norlins all the way to Yowa Country, I cannot rightly say. Perhaps it was sent here by the Prezdent Above to perform some further service or to bless this place with its presence. Or perhaps, once the Herald's duty was complete, its earthly vessel remained to live out its days as a simple creature of the swamp. Perhaps it was later snared and brought here in captivity.

"However it came to pass, I knew it was my calling to build a shrine here, a proper place to house these holiest of relics. And so I have. And here the Herald lives. And many a Lacorian pilgrim has felt its power.

"And if you doubt, as some have, that the Holy Restup and Reptilsoo of Happy Valley Orchards holds the true remains of God's own messenger, I invite you to stand once more before the Herald's Shrine. Feel its presence. Look upon that skull. Observe how unnaturally well preserved it is. Then examine its jaws. You will notice—through what can only be judged a miracle—that every one of its teeth is still present.

"All but one. Look closer. You will notice, on its bottom jaw, near the back, in a gap larger than the rest, the space for a single missing tooth."

FOURTEEN: JIMAPPLES

Laura stood on the tips of her toes, straining to reach her paintbrush just as high as it would go. Everywhere her brush swished and dabbed, the monster's creetrock skin glowed like new, protecting the ancient beast from wind and rain and sun.

Of all her chores at Happy Valley Orchards Restup and Reptilsoo, caring for the old Merican statues was one of Laura's favorites.

She wasn't allowed on the wobbly wooden ladder that Mabel scrambled up and down to paint the high places, but Tobias Goatherd had given Laura a brush lashed to a long pole. With that pole brush, Laura could reach all the way up almost to the monsters' knees to coat them with fresh paint.

The paint had a funny smell because it was made from curdled goat milk. Laura had helped Mabel make it. First, buckets full of milk and apple vinegar were left out to age inside the shed behind the main house. Laura had watched Mabel separate out the curds floating on top and scrape them into another pail. Then they stirred and stirred until all the lumpy curds just disappeared, melting away into a cloudy pool of liquid, smooth as you please.

Then it was time to mix in the colors. Laura liked that step especially. There seemed to be no recipe. It was just a drop of this, a sprinkle of that from the clay jars arrayed on a small shelf in the shed, adding and stirring and adding again until the shade was just right.

The milkpaint in Laura's pail that morning was a greenish-blue to match the long-necked monster's skin. When she had coated every last bit of the statue's legs that she could reach, Laura lowered her brush down, hand over hand. The pole was taller than she was, and she very nearly toppled over as she tried to spin it bristle-side-down. When she had managed to balance the long polebrush across her shoulder, then she carefully squatted down to pick up the pail with her free hand. The milkpaint inside had all but disappeared. Just a faint green film clung to the sides. With pail and pole in hand, she started back up the path towards the shed.

Nearby, Pa was squaring timber to replace some of the old rafters that held up the roof of the main house.

The logs were white ash, which Pa and Tobias Goatherd had harvested from the wooded hills that overlooked the valley. First, Pa would prop a log up in place using piles of rocks. Then, he would climb on top with his adze. Walking methodically down its length, he made deep notches across the top of the log, each an ax head's width apart. Then he would hop down and turn the log a half-turn onto its side. Trading his adze in for his broad ax, he would walk along the side. Right in between each pair of notches, he brought the ax down with a great *thwack*, hewing off chunks of wood in big square chips that flew spinning from the force of Pa's blows.

As Laura passed by, Pa had just climbed back on top of the ash beams to begin notching another side. Laura saluted him with her polebrush. Pa lifted his adze to return her salute.

So many things needed to be tended to around Happy Valley Orchards. It was a wonder that Tobias Goatherd and Mabel had managed to keep it up all by themselves all these years.

Pa had agreed to stay on just long enough to help Tobias Goatherd repair the roof of the main house and finish digging a new well. The old man had insisted on paying Pa in trade for the work, and soon two small barrels had been set aside next to the handcar. One was filled with salted goat meat. The other was filled with thick loaves of cheese coated in a hard gray wax.

Tobias Goatherd also said they could take as many apples with them as they could gather. Taking him at his word, Ma had immediately set about mashing and boiling apples until all her empty jars were full of sweet smooth apple butter. When she ran out of jars for apple butter, she sliced the apples up and spread them out on a blanket in the sun to dry into leather strips. Laura's jaw ached just thinking about how tough and chewy those apple leathers would be after days and weeks bundled up in the cart, but she knew they would not be so bad after being soaked and stewed.

Pa protested at first that it was all too generous for a few days' labor.

"I'd have lent him a hand just out of gratitude for the hospitality he's shown us so far," he told Ma one evening. "It feels like too much. I like the pious old graybeard well enough, but you know I don't like to feel indebted to any man."

"It's not charity, Charles. He needs help, and we need provisions. What's wrong with that? Honestly, I don't know what we'd have done if we hadn't found this place when we did."

Pa relented. He knew they would need fresh supplies to make it the rest of the way to the Wastes, especially if they chose to bypass the market at Davenport as Tobias Goatherd suggested.

Apparently, their path through Yowa Country had led them further west than Rakesh Halfsilver's map made it look. The road to Davenport would take them many days in the wrong direction. Meanwhile, somewhere due south of them stretched the Great Eighty Road, the road which would lead them all the way to the Wastes.

Tobias Goatherd told Pa of a settlement that lay along the Great Eighty Road, no more than a week or two journey from Happy Valley if a person knew how to find their way along the lesser-travelled Merican roads. There, the old man said, they would find the local supervisory for Clan Ortega. Some of the guardsmen in the supervisory's garrison would make the trip up to Happy Valley to trade from time to time, and Tobias Goatherd was certain that Pa could arrange with the supervisor for permission to travel the Eighty Road without having to backtrack to Davenport.

When she reached the shed, Laura put away the pail of milkpaint and her polebrush. No sooner had she finished than Ma appeared, walking up the path from the main house, an empty basket in her arms.

"Laura!" she called. "If you're finished tending to the . . . those things, why don't you and Mary pick us another basket of apples. Mr. Goatherd says there's trees on the west slope of that hill just yonder that may have some ripe ones. Gather as many as you can. Those I can't use for supper tonight, we can set aside for Mr. Goatherd's next batch of cider."

Laura accepted the basket from Ma and set off.

She found Mary on the porch of the main house. Mary was at her thread and needle, stitching the hem of a hemp curtain. Laura herself had no patience for needlework. Mary, on the other hand, could focus for hours at a stretch, her movements always fine and precise so that her cross-stich would always come out straight and even and pretty.

Laura waited while her sister finished up the edge she was sewing. Finally, Mary tied the thread off, in and out and under and through, in a neat little knot you could hardly see. She gave a satisfied nod. Then, together, she and Laura started up the path that wound through the ruins, past the car spire and the round creetrock shell that might have once been the World's Largest Apple, up towards the hill where Ma had said they might find ripe apples.

Happy Valley's apple trees didn't congregate in one single place. They grew in ones and twos, spread out all across the valley and the hills around it. It was still early in spring, so many of the trees were bare or had only tiny green buds clinging to their branches.

But some of the trees produced fruit all year round. Laura had heard Tobias Goatherd call these jimapples. According to the old man, all of Happy Valley's apple trees were descended from orchards planted by Merican farmers long ago. During Lectric Times, he reckoned the land around the Restup and Reptilsoo had been filled with jimapples, all grown from special seeds bred with forgotten lectric knowhow. These jimapples would have been huge and sweet, he said, and the trees that produced them so hearty they would have needed hardly any water at all.

Many of the trees that grew on the hills around Happy Valley still had some of these qualities, inherited from their jimapple ancestors. But Tobias Goatherd lamented that most were slowly losing their marvelous lectric traits over time. In the decades since he had settled among the ruins, he told them, he had seen the valley's apple trees grow ever more fragile, more vulnerable to drought and disease and insect infestations. And with every passing year they produced fewer and smaller apples.

"Going feral I fear," he had said. "Just like my darling Mabel. That is the way of things, I suppose. 'What is gathered, God shall disperse,' to quote the Prophet. 'And what is dispersed shall in time be gathered anew.'"

Laura thought about the old man's words as she and Mary went from apple tree to apple tree, basket in hand. The first trees that they came to had all been picked clean. Only as they climbed further up the hill, with the ruins of Happy Valley growing small below, did they have better luck. By a rocky outcropping near the hill's summit, Laura found a promising tree. Hidden among its leaves, she spied a cluster of ripe-looking fruit, all bunched up atop a branch just out of reach. Laura slipped off her coat and threw it over a lower branch. She rolled up her sleeves and tucked the cuffs of her pants into her boots and started to climb.

"Be careful, Laura," said Mary as Laura's boot found its first toehold. "That's just how you hurt yourself the last time. What will Ma say if you fall again?"

"You know I won't!" Laura shot back. Being bossed only made her climb faster and more recklessly. "Besides, Ma said I could," she added, swinging her leg up over the branch and hauling herself up.

This was true. Ma had been fretful about Laura's tree climbing after the accident, but Pa had convinced her to allow it.

"Let her go, Caroline," he had said. "The man who burns himself twice on the same hot stove is a fool, that's true enough. But if we let a single misstep scare us off the whole journey, we'd never get anywhere. I warrant Laura's a better tree climber now than she was before her fall."

And so Laura climbed. When she reached the branch she'd set her sights on, she locked her legs beneath her and reached out for the apples. They were so big and bright, Laura thought they surely must be close cousins to the jimapples of old. She plucked them with a twist of her wrist and dropped them down into the basket. One. Two. Three.

Just as she was starting to shimmy back towards the trunk of the tree, she heard Mary's voice from down below.

"Laura!" Mary said.

Laura expected a warning about climbing so far out onto the branch and was prepared to ignore her sister. But then she heard Jack barking somewhere in the distance.

"Laura!" Mary said again. "Look! Come here."

Laura scrambled down the tree and dropped to the ground beside Mary. Mary was pointing, and Laura followed her sister's gaze down the hill, out across the valley below.

The outlook where they stood offered a perfect view of the ruins. From there, Laura could see the brick walls of the Reptilsoo and the circular foundations of the World's Largest Apple and the field where she knew the axman lay hidden among the weeds. She could see Mabel perched atop her ladder, leaning against the statue of the sharp-toothed monster. A short distance away, she picked out Pa, still hewing beams for the roof. And, beside the main house, there was Tobias Goatherd, milking a goat.

But Mary was pointing beyond the monuments and the buildings, beyond Mabel's ladder and the clearing where Pa stood swinging his ax. She was pointing towards the far side of the ruins, towards the big number road that ran along their northern edge. There, Laura saw two shadows, stark against the sprawling ribbon of creetrock. Laura squinted at them. Attached to the shadows were two men, following the old creetrock road westward towards the ruins of Happy Valley Orchards.

Jack must have seen them too. Laura couldn't find the little pigdog, but she could hear his yips, faint but insistent.

Laura turned to Mary.

"We have to go tell Pa!"

She was just about to dash down the hill, but Mary grabbed her arm.

"Laura, wait! Look!"

Pa was going somewhere. His stride was swift and steady. Was he going to see what had got Jack to barking so? Laura watched him disappear behind the main house. When he emerged on the other side a few moments later, he had swapped his broad ax for his rifle. Now he was walking towards the old number road. Jack had stopped barking. Maybe he had found Pa, Laura thought.

The two strangers were closer now. When Pa reached the road, he stood there, looking east. Laura could tell he had seen the men.

They saw him too. The two figures paused. From across the long stretch of road that still separated them, Pa and the strangers regarded one another.

Eventually, the two men began walking again. Laura and Mary watched in silence as Pa turned around and made his way back towards the main house. A few moments later, they saw him speaking with Tobias Goatherd. Meanwhile, the strangers kept approaching, closer and closer.

Laura wanted to run down the hill to Ma and Pa, but at the same time she was scared to look away, scared of missing something important. Instead, she and Mary merely crept forward to find a better vantage, crouching behind a rock that sat at the very edge of the overlook.

She could see the men more clearly now. One was taller, with a mane of curly yellow hair and a bushy yellow beard. The other was squat and bare-faced. They appeared lightly provisioned. Both wore identical cloaks dyed a silvery gray. Laura cupped her hands against her brows to shade her eyes, studying the figures as they marched down the old creetrock road.

To the left of each man's head, there was a spike, sprouting rigid from his shoulder like a pine sapling. An icy tingle ran over Laura's cheeks as she realized that the pointed shapes were blades, each attached to the end of a long gun barrel. As the men marched, the bayonets swayed in rhythm with their footsteps.

Laura watched them with such intensity that she did not see Ma coming up the path until she was practically right beneath the outcropping where Laura and Mary were perched.

"Ma!" Mary called out in a hushed voice. "Down on the road…"

"It's alright. I know," said Ma, as she stepped up around the rocks and sat down beside them, Baby Grace in her arms. "Mr. Goatherd says they're probably Ortega men from the supervisory east of here, come to trade for cheese and cider. But just to be safe, we'll stay right here until they leave or Pa says it's alright to come down. Keep your voices low and try to stay out of sight."

Ma looked inside their basket, remarking what fine-looking apples Mary and Laura had picked. She handed Grace over to Laura and fumbled through the pocket of her hemp apron for her paring knife, suggesting they all enjoy a slice while they wait.

Laura knew Ma was trying to distract them. As Ma pulled the leather sheath from her knife and began to cut up an apple, Laura scooted stealthily back towards the edge of the overlook, her gaze drifting back down to the valley floor.

Pa and Tobias Goatherd were on the porch of the main house now. Laura saw that Pa still had his rifle, and that made her feel relieved. For a moment, she lost sight of the strangers. But then they reappeared from behind the ruins of an old building. They had left the old number road and were making their way down one of the dirt paths that led through the ruins, past the Reptilsoo and its monstrous guardians.

They were within sight of the porch now, and the tall blonde man raised his arm in greeting. Tobias Goatherd returned the gesture.

Baby Grace fussed then, and Laura lifted her from her lap to shoulder. There, Grace clung to Laura's tunic and twisted her head to look down the hill with her big baby eyes, as if she too were watching to see what would unfold.

The men were climbing the steps of the porch now. Laura tensed. But when they reached Tobias Goatherd and Pa, they stopped. They just stood there, all four of them in a circle beneath the shadow of the porch awning.

The minutes ambled on, and still nothing happened. At one point, Tobias Goatherd disappeared into the house and returned with a jug of cider, which the men passed around. Otherwise, they continued to just stand around on the porch. Laura assumed they must be talking, but she was too far away to hear.

Eventually, Laura allowed Ma to tempt her focus away with a fat slice of apple. The apple was crisp and sticky as Laura bit into it. It was the sweetest she had tasted yet, a true jimapple for certain. Ma began cutting up another, and she and Laura and Mary all sat there cross-legged for a time, passing Baby Grace back and forth between them and savoring the delicious fruit. Laura turned occasionally to glance back down the hill towards Pa on the porch, but gradually her apprehension ebbed.

The warm sun and her full belly was beginning to make Laura feel a bit sleepy, when suddenly the sound of raised voices in the distance shook her alert. Laura whirled around and scrambled back to her perch overlooking the valley floor. Ma whispered sharply to her to come back and keep still, but Laura couldn't help herself. She had to see what was happening.

The figures on the porch were all where Laura had left them, but the mood communicated by their bodies had changed. The shorter stranger stood just inches from Tobias Goatherd's face and waved his arm emphatically. The one with the shaggy blonde hair had his rifle out. So did Pa. There was more shouting.

What came next happened so rapidly that Laura struggled to make sense of it. There was shoving, back and forth, and suddenly Tobias Goatherd was on the ground. Pa was backing away, the barrel of his gun raised. At the same time, movement drew Laura's attention up to the awning above the porch. There, perched on top, was Mabel. Had the mute wildgirl been there the whole time? Laura had not noticed her until that very moment.

Laura had barely begun to formulate these thoughts when Mabel leapt from the porch roof. She seemed to change direction in mid-air, as she swung from one of the posts that held up the porch's awning, twirling around it to drop down directly behind the blonde, shaggy-haired man. No sooner had her feet touched the floor than her arm swung upwards, and for a second Laura saw the glint of the Mabel's knife.

There was a horrible scream. All at once, the stranger was flailing, clutching his neck. At the same time, Mabel was spinning away, pouncing in a single fluid motion at the other man. One moment he was reaching for his bayonet, the next he was flat on his back, the wildgirl on top of him. Pa was shouting. There were more choked cries from the blonde stranger as he stumbled backwards, hands still at his throat. He tripped over the porch railing and tumbled head over heels in a sloppy cartwheel to the gravel below.

And then, as abruptly as the commotion had started, Happy Valley Orchards fell quiet. Laura watched as Pa helped Tobias Goatherd to his feet. Mabel rose to her feet as well. The man lying beneath her did not.

FIFTEEN: CARRYING ON

"It's time for us to go," said Pa when he found them there.

Laura lay cradled in Ma's lap, beneath the shade of the apple tree. Mary and Baby Grace huddled close beside. Somewhere up above them, birds chirped. Pa knelt down with them and took Laura and Mary in his arms both at once and pressed his face against their cheeks each in turn. His voice was steady, but Laura felt his hand shake as it squeezed her shoulder.

"It's alright," he told them. "Everything's alright. It's just time for us to go."

Laura said nothing. Her mind felt all muddied up, as if her thoughts were struggling to catch up with her senses. The world around her still seemed muted and distant, as if reaching her through some fog. She could not even begin to guess how long she had been there beneath the tree, huddling together with Ma and her sisters.

She remembered feeling a tug on her arm and hearing Ma's

voice repeating her name, but the tug and the voice had both seemed to come from far away, as if they were happening to someone else. She remembered being pulled backwards, away from the edge of the overlook. but even as her view of the house and the valley below had disappeared beneath the curve of the hillside, the images stayed with her. Part of her was still there, down on the porch of main house, with Pa and Mabel, and Tobias Goatherd and the two bodies.

If she closed her eyes, she could see those bodies even now. One lay on the deck of the porch, the other in the brambles beneath the railing. With their gray cloaks bunched up around them, they might have been mistaken for bundles of rags.

Yet, by the time Laura and her family reached the house, the bodies of the two strangers were gone. Laura wondered what had happened to them, but she didn't ask. She had tried to voice some of her questions as she followed Pa back down the hill, but Pa had hushed her before she could even find the words.

"Later, Soybean," he told her. "Right now you must get yourself ready to leave. It's past midday, and we should try to get some road behind us before dark."

And so without questions and without further discussion, Laura gathered her things. Then she helped load up the handcar.

Pa lifted their barrels of saltmeat and goat cheese into the car. Then he set about greasing the axles with a fresh coat of tallow, while Ma rummaged through the cargo box, finding crevices into which to tuck the new jars of apple butter and bundled strips of apple leathers, shifting their belongings around until everything was packed up just as tight as could be.

Tobias Goatherd emerged onto the porch at one point. He watched them work, a somber expression on his face, but he said nothing.

Finally, when Pa had satisfied himself that the handcar was ready to travel, he joined Tobias Goatherd on the porch. The two men spoke in low tones, before disappearing together into the house.

They were gone a long while. Ma finished loading and

securing their supplies. When that was done, she took Baby Grace and set her stool down beside the car to nurse. Nearby was Mary, sitting on the ground beneath the shade of the handcar, her knees pulled up against her chest.

Laura went over to join her sister. Her blue batman bag hung from her hand by its straps, swinging and slapping against her ankle as she walked. Laura tossed the bag down next to Mary before flopping to the ground beside her. Together, they sat quietly shoulder-to-shoulder in the handcar's shadow, picking at the weeds that poked up through the gravel.

At one point, Laura looked up. Directly across from them, on the far side of the yard, was Mabel. The wildgirl was perched atop the remains of a creetrock wall, her bare feet dangling just above the weeds. She had been sitting in that same spot for quite some time. From there, she had watched as Laura and her family gathered their things, her expression as cryptic as ever. Now, Laura found herself returning the girl's gaze. In silence, the two of them stared at one another from across the yard.

Laura twisted a dandelion stem thoughtfully round and round her pinky. That very morning, she and Mabel had sat side-by-side in the shed, mixing milkpaint. Now, the wildgirl seemed almost a stranger. The distance between them felt enormous.

"Should we be scared of her, do you think?" Laura whispered, without breaking Mabel's gaze.

Mary looked over at the creetrock wall. After a pause, she shook her head.

"I don't know," she said. "But I don't think she would hurt us. I don't believe she's bad."

"I don't think so either," said Laura.

It was hard to reconcile the scrawny barefoot girl seated on the wall with the violence Laura had witnessed from the hilltop. Could she have been mistaken about what she thought she'd seen? But no. The image was too fresh and crisp in her mind. The flash of the knife, the way the man in the gray cloak had flailed and cried out.

"She saved Pa," Mary whispered. "Those men might have . . .

we don't know what mightn't have happened."

Mary reached behind her for her Queen carrysack. She unbuttoned one of the pockets that Ma had stitched into the side and pulled out a band of braided hemp. She held it up.

"I was making this for her," she said. "It was almost finished."

Laura looked at the necklace. She had seen Mary working on it but had never examined it up close. It was lovely. The hemp fibers were expertly woven, spiraling round and round and criss-crossing one another in mesmerizing patterns. And between each hemp knot, the necklace held some tiny treasure. Smooth glass pebbles, copper coins, colorful chips of hardmold, and other tiny lectric charms sparkled as the braided cord swayed beneath Mary's fist.

Laura thought for a moment. She dug something out of her own carrysack and stuffed it in her pocket. Then she stood.

"Come on," she said to Mary.

Together, they walked towards Mabel. Ma called out to them as they passed. She looked like she was about to stop them, but then she just sighed.

"Go on," she told them, with a weary shake of her head. "Just don't stray. We must be ready to go as soon as Pa is done speaking with Mr. Goatherd."

Mabel hopped down from the wall as they approached. The three of them stood there facing each other. A gust of wind made the weeds dance around their ankles. Laura's eyes momentarily drifted down towards Mabel's hips, where the smallest tip of the girl's leather-sheathed knife was peeking out from beneath her tunic. She looked away and tried to pretend not to have noticed.

Mary showed Mabel the necklace.

"It's for you," she said. "It's not finished, but if you just tie off the end like this, you can hardly tell. Here."

Mary twisted the loose threads together in a pretty little knot and then lifted the necklace up to the girl's throat. Mabel flinched and backed away. But then she stepped hesitantly forward again and bowed her head. Mary reached up and tied the braid loosely around her neck.

The necklace came to rest just above her collarbone. Mabel touched one of the glass shards that hung suspended within the web of hemp, feeling it between thumb and forefinger. Her face withdrew into her neck like a turtle as she tried to get a better look at the necklace. Laura stepped forward.

"Here," she said. "I wanted to give you something too."

She held out the small black screen she'd found in the boxes by the Misisip.

"You can see yourself in it. Look."

Mabel took the screen and held it up to her face. She tilted it this way and that, transfixed by her reflection. She toyed with the hemp necklace, adjusting the way it draped around her throat. Finally, she looked up at them. Her lips were pinched in an ambiguous grimace, but the smile in her eyes was unmistakable.

Tentatively, Mary stepped forward and put her arms around the wildgirl. Then Laura did the same. Mabel seemed to go limp. She let her weight fall against them until finally they all tumbled over into the weeds. Laura and Mary both sat up giggling. It was one of the strangest hugs they had ever had.

Just then, Pa and Tobias Goatherd came back out onto the porch. Laura and Mary stood up and brushed themselves off. They made their way back to the car, followed by Mabel.

Pa had the parchment map, rolled up and tucked under his arm. He stuffed it into the back of the cart before circling around, making sure everything was secure. Tobias Goatherd watched from the porch, running his fingers down his long white beard. Mabel scampered up the steps to stand behind the old man. She clutched his arm and rested her head against his shoulder.

While Pa finished checking the car, Tobias Goatherd called down to Ma.

"I'm awful sorry things fell out how they did, Ma'am," he said. "There'll be candles burning for you and your family at the Herald's Shrine, asking that the Prezdent Above guide you safe and true to your new home out on the Wastes. You're always welcome at Happy Valley Orchards. I hope you and your girls will make your way back here someday. When times are different."

~~~

They left along the road that ran down the middle of Happy Valley Orchards. The road had no name, not on Rakesh Halfsilver's map and not as far as Tobias Goatherd knew about, but it must have been one of the old number roads. It was the biggest Merican road they'd seen since they'd crossed the Misisip. It was wide enough in some places to fit three or four cars across, and its creetrock foundations were so deep that hardly anything grew on top.

It was the same road that had brought the two strangers in the gray cloaks. They had come from the east. Laura and her family took the road in the opposite direction, westward, chasing the sun. As the great car spike of Happy Valley disappeared behind them over the horizon, Laura thought again about those men.

"Who were they, Pa?"

Pa didn't answer at first. He kept his eyes fixed on the road ahead. Laura fell in beside him, trying to match him step for step.

"Were they bandits?" she pressed. "Cannibals?"

Pa gave a short, hollow laugh. He shook his head. Glancing back at Ma and Mary, who had fallen a few paces behind, he took a deep breath.

"I don't mean to be keeping secrets from you, my little soybean," he told her. "The world's complicated sometimes is all, and some things, well, I just don't know how to go about explaining them to you and your sister so you'll understand. I'm still trying to get the whole business straight in my own head. But you're right to ask, and I reckon I'll just have to do my best. You see where the road ahead curves around that hill yon? We'll make camp for the night on the other side. And then we'll all have some words about what happened back there, best as I understand it. Now is that a fair bargain?"

~~~

They camped that night in an open field beside the road. There was no wood for a fire, and they ate a cold supper of cheese and apples as dusk settled over the Yowa countryside. Pa sat

146

beside the handcar, his back resting against its wooden spokes. He looked tired, but he called Laura and Mary to him.

They curled up on either side of him, and he wrapped an arm around each of them. Ma pulled her stool up next to them, Baby Grace swaddled up in her lap.

"Ma tells me you girls saw some of what fell out," Pa began, "and I'm sorry for that. I imagine you were scared, seeing those strange men with guns and then things boiling over the way they did. I was scared myself, I don't mind saying. And when the wildgirl swooped in from nowhere . . . Well, it's a serious thing to see a man meet an end like that. I've been witness to the like more than once over my years, and I can tell you. Doesn't matter who they are or what the circumstances. A thing like that stays with you. I wish I could tell you different, but that's the way of it. I'm sorry."

The men had wanted silver. That seemed to be the short of it.

The explanation didn't feel especially satisfying to Laura. As the stars came out overhead and a cool night wind began to blow through the tall grass, she kept asking questions. Pa did his best to answer.

Laura knew that she was just a little girl and couldn't expect her parents to tell her everything. Yet, as Pa tried to explain to her what had happened back on Tobias Goatherd's porch, Laura began to realize that Pa himself didn't really understand. And that thought upset her far more than Pa keeping things from her.

"I had a pit in my stomach, right from the moment I saw their shapes coming up the road," Pa said at one point. "But when I ran back to tell the old man, he didn't seem over concerned. Some Ortega boys up from the local supervisory, he reckoned. Some in the garrison'd grown fond of his cheeses over the years, I was to understand, and they sent someone up from time to time to trade. Even so, when your Ma told me you girls were away picking apples, that set my mind a good deal at ease. You did the right thing staying put where you were."

As the men approached the porch of the main house, however, Tobias Goatherd confessed they didn't look familiar.

New recruits perhaps, he told Pa, scratching beneath his beard. At that, Pa's uneasiness had returned.

The tall stranger, the one with the long curly hair, greeted them warmly. But there was something studied about his smile that Pa distrusted. His stouter companion, on the other hand, hardly met their eyes. According to Pa, he kept looking about, as if taking stock.

The strangers claimed to work for one of Clan Ortega's supervisors, but the name wasn't one that Tobias Goatherd recognized. The shorter man kept trying to ask questions. How many people lived on this settlement? How many livestock did they have? How many acres under cultivation? How many guns? How many bullets?

The taller man laughed the questions off, apologizing for his companion. Pa had felt a certain tension in the air, but, despite the short man's pointed manner, the conversation struck a cordial enough tone at first. Tobias Goatherd had fetched a cool jug of cider from the cellar, which the travelers seemed to appreciate. They'd discussed weather and the latest news out of Davenport. Pa asked them whereabouts they were from, and their answers seemed forthright.

It was when the men began talking about taxes that things began to go bad. Tobias Goatherd explained that he had an arrangement with an official named Malcolm Syed out of a place called Hawkeye Crossing. But the shorter man snapped how Hawkeye Crossing had nothing to do with it.

"Now for my part, I can't say I exactly knew who had the right of it," Pa admitted. "The old man, he was perfectly matter-of-fact. He's got papers that show his claim to the land, he tells them just as cool as you please, all legal and proper and stamped by this man Syed. But even I know it's a tricky business, when folks start talking of territory and sovereignty and land claims and the like."

Pa reckoned that it might all have something to do with the situation down in Davenport. Regional supervisors were appointed by the Clan Council, Pa explained. And, for as long as Pa could remember, the Clan Council had been controlled by Old

Lucius Ortega. Only, now, talk was that Old Man Ortega was very sick. And people seemed to disagree about who should be Clan Chairman next. It was a confusing time to live in Ortega territory, it seemed. Pa figured that, with all the uncertainty and everyone picking sides and all, it might be tough to always know who was in charge of what.

The two strangers had looked the part of Ortega men, Pa allowed. But he supposed that anyone could find themselves a gray cloak. After it was all done, Tobias Goatherd had insisted that the men hadn't been official tax collectors at all, just some bandits roaming the frontiers and intimidating honest folk. He said that the seals were wrong on the papers they'd shown. Sloppy forgeries, he told Pa. And when he'd asked after men he knew in the local supervisory garrisons, the strangers had been vague and evasive.

Still, whether the men were real tax collectors or just bandits, Pa was of a mind they should have offered them something just to send them on their way. They'd wanted silver. How much seemed open to discussion. Tobias Goatherd claimed he had none, though even Pa found that difficult to believe, what with his trade in fruit and cheese, not to mention donations by pilgrims visiting the Herald's Shrine. In any case, Pa reckoned the strangers might've accepted their tax in kind. Tobias Goatherd could have offered them fresh supplies at least.

Instead, the old man had been amiable but firm. He knew their sort, he told Pa later. Such men take and take. Appease them, let them think for a moment that you recognize their power over you, and they will never stop. He recited some passage from *The Letters of Deshawn LaCore,* though Pa couldn't recall its relevance.

Laura thought a lot about that after Pa explained it to her.

"I think Tobias Goatherd was right," she said finally. "If you showed those men what you had, they'd just take it. And they'd know they could just come back and take more. Whenever they want."

The evening was growing chill, and Pa pulled a blanket from the handcar and draped it over Laura's shoulders.

"You may be right, Laura," said Pa. "But if there's one thing I've learned about people, it's that no two are alike. I'm cautious about judging a man by his 'sort' or pretending I know what he's like to do. We'll never know now, I suppose. I just can't help thinking things didn't have to go as they did. But done is done."

The killing had shaken him, Pa confessed. He told Laura how the barrel of his rifle had rattled about uncontrollably as he tried to steady his hands. Tobias Goatherd, on the other hand, had maintained a composure throughout that seemed to trouble Pa. When he had risen to his feet, the look in the old man's pale eyes was one of sad resignation. There was no trace of the shock or the horror that Pa felt. With the shorter man still bleeding on the ground beside them, Tobias Goatherd had gone to Mabel and gently cupped the sides of her face with his hands. Pa had watched speechless as the wildgirl bowed forward and Tobias Goatherd planted a kiss on her forehead.

Pa began telling Laura and Mary about how he had helped Tobias Goatherd carry the shorter man's body down the porch steps and hoist him into a wheelbarrow. Suddenly, he stopped himself with a wince. Laura realized then that Pa hadn't meant to say as much as he had, that somewhere along the way he had forgotten he was talking to Mary and Laura and started talking more to himself.

Pa gazed up at the stars. Laura could see his eyes tracing one constellation then another, as if making sure that each was in its proper place.

"Have I told you the story of the time I saw the horses?" he said at last.

Laura knew the story, but, as Pa began to tell it, she quickly realized that it was different this time. There were parts she had never heard. She cuddled closer into Pa's side and listened.

THE STORY OF PA AND THE HORESEMEN

"When I was little, I lived on a farm in a land called Upstate, with my Uncle Frederick and his husband Louis. Uncle Louis died in the Second Hyperflu not long after, but at the time it was the three of us living on that farm, raising oats and jimtaters and chickens.

"There was a lake beside Uncle Freddie's farm. It was the best source of fresh water for some ways around, and so it wasn't unusual for travelers to stop there. On the far side of the lake, there was a cluster of abandoned houses where they would stop and make camp. Mostly, they were heading north. These were the days when the old Ghost Cities were still emptying out. We saw plenty of displacees from Baltimore and Filidelf and the like pass through our way, folks fleeing the endless wars, looking for a new home not so ravaged by chaos and disease.

"But one summer a group of men arrived going the other way, towards the very places everyone else seemed to be trying to get away from. That wasn't the only thing that made these particular visitors so memorable, though. What really got folks around Upstate to talking was that these men had horses.

"Now, I had never seen a horse before. Uncle Freddie had owned one, but all the horses in those parts had died some years before I was even born. Killed off by the same fever that took most of the cattle. So these were the first horses anyone in Upstate had seen for some time, and they created quite a stir.

"The men made camp in the ruins across the lake. A neighbor had seen the riders arrive, and I listened in fascination as she and Uncle Freddie discussed the visiting horsemen. When Uncle Freddie announced his intention to pay a call on the group to see what they might have for trade, I begged to go too. I wanted to get a closer look at the animals I had heard about in so many stories. But Uncle Freddie and Uncle Louis wouldn't allow it.

"When Uncle Freddie returned, he told us more about the mounted travelers.

"'Hard-looking men,' he said. 'Not talkative types, but courteous enough. They didn't volunteer what their business is down south, and I didn't pry. They're well-provisioned but naught in the way of surplus. They're not here on trade convoy, you can be certain of that.'

"He couldn't resist asking them about their horses, though.

"'Mentioned as how seeing mounted men is a mighty unusual sight in these parts,' Uncle Freddie said. 'Told them how, even before the cattle fever, no one hereabouts had managed to breed a healthy foal for as long as I could remember. Where had they come by their animals, I asked them. Well, these fellows, they were cagey on that point too. "Up north" was all I could get out of them. And that's about when I took my leave. They say they aim to stay for a day or two and fish the lake. I told them they were welcome to it.'

"Word about those horses spread quick. The next day, I was working in the fields when I saw a group of children coming up the path towards me. Leading the way was a girl whose family tended the next farm over from Uncle Freddie's. She was joined by two boys, brothers who lived with their granddad in a bunker in the woods not far from the lake. The older one was nearly a grown man, tall and broad-shouldered, with the shadow of a beard around his chin, but there was something wrong with his wits. He would often come down by the lake and splash around for hours in the muddy shallows. Folks around there called him Turnip, though I've no idea why.

"The girl—I wish I could remember her name but it's fled me—she calls out to me. 'Hey Charlie Ingalls,' she says. 'We're going to go see the horses! Want to come?'

"Well, I knew my uncles wouldn't want me going near the men's camp. And I tried to shake my head no, but somehow it nodded yes. And the next thing I knew I was skipping and laughing with the other children, making my way towards the other side of the lake, my hoe lying abandoned in the jimtater field.

"We quieted as we approached the old houses, creeping cautiously through the trees. Turnip kept making excited little grunts and had to be shushed. Finally, we came to an old stone wall, overgrown with moss and creepers. I slipped my boot into a toehold and lifted myself up to peep over.

"There they were. Four of them, each a different pattern of

dappled white and black and brown. They were tied up beside an abandoned stone cottage. Wonderstruck, I watched them stamp their legs as they jostled with one another and tossed their manes into the air. They were beautiful.

"The others had climbed up beside me. They were watching the horses too, peeping their faces up over the wall. There was no sign of the men anywhere. Then, Turnip decided to climb over. He hoisted himself clumsily up, then sprawled belly-down over the top of the wall, before tumbling head-first down the other side.

"Turnip's brother called out to him to come back, but the simple-minded young man just clapped his hands as he bobbed closer and closer to the horses, bouncing from foot to foot in that funny tip-toed walk of his.

"Suddenly, there was a shout. *Hey you*, it said, *get away from them horses*. Immediately, I ducked down behind the wall. *Ooooooooh*, I heard Turnip moan in confusion. The horses made agitated noises. There were more shouts, closer, angrier. Don't move, the voice warned, get your hand out of your pocket. Get your hand out—

"And then the gunshot that made me run. I leapt down from the wall, and I ran, and I didn't stop until I was back home.

"I was scared to say what had happened at first, but Uncle Freddie eventually got it out of me. He and Uncle Louis argued about what to do. Finally, as evening fell, they locked the farmhouse doors and barred the shutters. All night long, they took turns at watch. When morning came, they found that the men on the other side of the lake had pulled up stakes and moved on.

"Uncle Freddie never scolded or faulted me over what had happened with that boy and the horsemen. But I felt awful with guilt just the same. The next day, I stayed on the farm and tended to my chores while Uncle Freddie and Uncle Louis went to inspect the deserted campsite. After that, it was seldom spoken of. I saw Turnip's brother once or twice more down by the lake, but he disappeared soon after, and Uncle Freddie said he'd heard their granddad had abandoned his bunker and gone west.

"Uncle Louis died the following winter. And it wasn't long after that we left Upstate behind ourselves, Uncle Freddie and me. We just carried on. After a while, the memory got to feel distant, like something I'd just heard about in a story. The sound of that gunshot stayed with me for some time though. I'd hear it sometimes in quiet moments, and I'd feel the fear and guilt again, the same as I'd felt scrambling down from that wall."

SIXTEEN: THE GREAT EIGHTY ROAD

It wasn't long after their abrupt departure from Happy Valley Orchards that Laura and her family turned south. Mid-afternoon the very next day, they reached a fork in the road. The wide old number road that led from the ruins kept going west, up and over the horizon, and a smaller road branched away. They stopped there while Pa consulted the map. Then he nodded to Ma and began to turn the car.

Their new road was little more than a trail of creetrock gravel. For long stretches, it would disappear entirely beneath soil and grass. That first day, they followed the patchwork path as it meandered through groves of buttonbush and hazelnut. Eventually, they came to a creek, and there they made camp for the night. The banks of the creek provided wood enough for a nice roaring fire, and they all felt their spirits much improved.

Ma boiled up a pot of apple leathers and saltmeat until both were soft and juicy. Then she took a handful of hazelnuts that Laura and Mary had helped her gather, wrapped them in cloth and struck them over and over with a rock. She sprinkled the crushed hazelnut into the boiling pot along with a few pinches of other herbs from her jars.

The stew was sweet and spicy and thick, and it warmed Laura all over. When they had all had their fill, there was hardly a drop left inside the pot. After supper, Laura went to the handcar and returned with Pa's two-string. Slyly, she laid it on the ground beside him. Pa laughed and allowed as how he could take a hint.

He rested his back against a log and stretched his legs out, crossing one over the other. Then he rested the drum of the instrument on his thigh and picked up his bow. The taut snakeskin across the barrel's mouth thrummed. He began to sing.

A lonely mother gazes out of her window
Staring at a son that she just can't touch
Walking down the road with no one by his side
But he doesn't realize he hurts her so much
All her praying only quickens his footsteps
'Cause he can't help lying wake nights to wonder
So he leaves to make his fortune the best way he knows how
Trading hither for the perilous yonder.

Don't go chasing waterfalls
Please stick to the rivers and the lakes that you're used to
I know that you're gonna have it your way or nothing at all
But I think you're moving too fast

The next day and the next and for a good many days after, they followed that winding little road south. It was tiring at first. Laura's legs had forgotten what life on the road was like. But soon they remembered. Before long, walking was once again as natural to her as breathing, and it was the moments of rest, lingering in one place for too long, that felt strange.

She told Ma as much. That's your father's wanderlust, Ma told her. She made it sound like it was some dreadful disease that Laura had caught.

The familiar rhythm returned. One foot in front of the other, propelling her steadily forward, towards new places and new experiences. There was something soothing about it, entrancing. How far away Happy Valley Orchards seemed and how quickly. More and more, Laura's questions about days past were crowded out by her curiosity about what lay ahead.

Soon, they would see the Great Eighty Road, Pa promised, the enormous old number road that once stretched the whole length of Old Merica, from Eastern Sea to the Western. Laura imagined walking it end to end, seeing all the wondrous sights and meeting all the strange peoples who must surely live in between those far-flung oceans.

One day, the road wound down through a wooded basin where the land was soft and marshy. Pa had to go slow and careful to make sure the wheels of the handcar wouldn't sink down into the moist earth.

Laura saw animals she had never seen before. They stopped that afternoon beside a little pond bristled all over in reeds, and Laura watched tall white herons stalking through the water on their spindly legs, trying to spear fish with their long beaks.

Later, she came across a big snake with the dark brown stripes and a diamond-shaped head coiled up behind a log. Pa said it was a viper and warned her to stay well away. Laura took one last look back at the snake. It was motionless as a stone, but its black eyes seemed alert, cold and watchful.

It was good land for game, and in the days that followed they often camped early so that Pa would have a chance to go out hunting. One evening, he came back with the biggest bird that Laura had ever laid eyes on slung over his shoulder. Pa said that it was called a turkey. They roasted it over the campfire that night. The meat was mild and savory, and there was so much of it that they could hardly eat it all before it spoiled. Even Jack had all the turkey he could eat.

"If you think that turkey was something, just wait until we get to the Wastes," Pa told Mary and Laura, as he carved up the meat, plopping the choicest cuts into Ma's stewpot and tossing the scraps to Jack. "The wastebirds that roam the plains out west can grow to be taller than a man, to hear some tell it. I reckon that's an exaggeration. You know how folks are. But they're mighty big as birds go, you can believe that much. That big tom I bagged yesterday, why he'd look like a woodpecker next to a wastebird if you credit even half the tales."

As they passed through that moist green country, the Merican road vanished as often as not, swallowed up by clubmoss and creepers. Every so often they passed the burnt orange shells of lectric cars and wagons and plows. Crusty tufts of lichen clung to their shoulders, and branches curled out through their ribs. Laura sometimes mistook them for part of the vegetation.

At first, it seemed to Laura that few people passed this way. A few days later, however, they began to encounter signs of recent habitation amid the wilderness. That was because they were nearing the Great Eighty Road, Pa told her. As their destination approached, they began to come across the traces of campsites, clearings where trees had been felled and every so often a ring of stones arranged around a cold fire pit.

Late one day, they stopped by a cluster of creetrock ruins. Timber beams had been erected against several of the old walls, forming a series of simple lean-to shelters. Pa called out, asking if anyone was around. After scouting the site further, he decided that it had been abandoned for some time, and that night they camped cozy beneath a lean-to.

That was a good thing, because the next day they awoke to a light drizzle.

The rain continued all morning. Mary kept her hood up, but Laura couldn't bear to shroud her face for long, with nothing to watch except her boots trudging along the soggy road. Inevitably, she would toss her hood back and just let the rain speckle her cheeks and forehead, droplet by droplet, until enough droplets gathered together to drip from her nose or chin. Ma would make her cover her head then, and for a while Laura's world would narrow once again behind a tunnel of stitched lectric fabrics and buckskin.

Early that afternoon, their road ran straight into a river. When he saw the trail drop off ahead, Pa set down the handcar. Laura followed at his heels as he walked carefully out onto a creetrock precipice that overlooked the riverbank.

Pillars rose out of the water where a bridge had once been. They seemed to get shorter and shorter as they approached the middle of the river, as if slowly wading down beneath its surface. Down in the mud beneath the creetrock overlook, an iron beam, bowed and rusted, slithered out of the water and up onto the banks like a great brown river snake.

It was the widest river Laura had seen since the Mighty Misisip. From where she stood, the trees on the other side were

158

nothing but a distant green curtain. And, unlike the Misisip, which had been eerily still when Laura's family had crossed it that winter, this river rushed rumbling past her, hissing white foam as its waters collided with the creetrock pillars. Laura watched the ripples of raindrops sweep across the river's span and knew they could not cross.

Pa did not seem concerned.

"End of the line," he announced. "The old man warned we'd lose the road at the Yowa River. The going may get a might rougher from here out. But not to worry. Shouldn't be far now to the Eighty Road."

They made their way down a muddy trail that ran alongside the river. Pa kept his hatchet handy, tucked through the loop of his belt, for he often needed to stop and chop aside encroaching bushes to make way for the handcar. Their progress was slow.

Downriver from the collapsed bridge, they saw their first people. The side trail had led them back down to the riverbank, near a bend where the waters slowed. There, on the other side of the river, they saw a group of women. They were fishing. Their poles hung out over the water and bobbed up and down as the current tugged them. Pa tried to hail them.

"Bound for Hawkeye Crossing!" he shouted. "How far?"

Some of the women waved. Laura heard one of them shout something, but she couldn't make out the words over the rumble of the river. Pa tried again.

"The Old Eighty Road! This way?" he shouted, pointing downriver.

More indistinct voices came from the other bank. Pa shook his head and shrugged. They continued down the trail.

When the way became impassable, they were forced to leave sight of the river. Pa dragged the handcar up a path that turned and backtracked so many times that Laura soon lost any sense of which direction they were heading. The sound of the river faded into the distance and disappeared.

"Charles, are you sure this is the right way?" said Ma when they had walked what seemed to be a good many hours. "I fear we're going in circles."

"We're close, Caroline," Pa assured her. "Did you see those ruins we passed some ways back? The Eighty Road can't be far off. If we can just make it through this last rough stretch, we may yet lay eyes on it by day's end."

Unfortunately, the day was ending quickly. The rain had stopped by then. Light streamed sideways through the trees, painting their trunks in checkered patterns of amber and gray.

Finally, Ma and Pa resigned themselves to making camp for the night. They had just begun to look for likely spots to set down their bedrolls when the little trail they had been following burst from underneath the trees and out into open sky.

One moment Laura's boots were sloshing up a muddy hill, and the next they came slapping down onto a plateau of creetrock, as firm and flat as could be. She stopped. Her gaze slowly panned up. The gray, lectricmade stone beneath her boots just kept spreading out and out and out. Laura turned in a circle. Behind her and ahead of her both, as far as Laura could see, there it was. The Great Eighty Road.

It was wider than all the other Merican roads they had travelled laid side by side together, as wide as the wide river that had separated them from the fisherwomen.

Cracks arced across the creetrock like lightning forks or else coiled in upon one another like spiderwebs. Little islands of soil and vegetation sprouted here and there from its fissures. Yet, as the Eighty Road unfurled out into the distance, its imperfections were swallowed by the road's sheer scale. Out into the farthest west and out towards the farthest east, the old number road stretched, straight and smooth, a thick unbroken band of gray, stark against the corridor of trees that framed it.

While Laura gaped, Pa was still struggling to drag the handcar up the final slope. Ma had turned back to help. Finally, the car's wheels found traction at the road's crumbling edges, and Ma and Pa joined Laura upon the gray vastness of the Eighty Road. Ma murmured a prayer under her breath. Pa wiped the sweat from his forehead and stared out across the endless ribbon of creetrock with a look of wonder. He let out a whistle of appreciation.

"Well, here it is," he said. "How do you like it, girls? The road that will take us to our new home on the Wastes."

SEVENTEEN: HAWKEYE CROSSING

The next morning began with a bath, for Ma wanted them to look presentable when they reached Hawkeye Crossing.

Hawkeye Crossing was the name of the settlement where Laura's family would obtain papers permitting them to travel the Great Eighty Road. Tobias Goatherd had marked its location down on Pa's parchment map, right where the thick dashed line of the Eighty Road met one of the rivers that forked diagonally up through the Yowa. That river was the same one that they had seen yesterday, said Pa, so Laura knew that Hawkeye Crossing must be very close, somewhere just west of where they had camped that night beside the Eighty Road.

Hawkeye Crossing was just a small village and trading post, according to Pa, but it was also the location of an Ortega fort. Inside the fort was the Clan's regional supervisory office. Tobias Goatherd had given Pa a letter of introduction to the supervisor in charge of the Hawkeye Crossing garrison, a man named Malcolm Syed. If all went well, they would be allowed to continue on, following the Great Eighty Road all the way to Lildaka and to their new home in the Wastes beyond.

Ma did not want them to look like desperate displacees when they petitioned the Hawkeye Crossing supervisor. And so, when Laura woke that morning, Ma was already busy with her thread and needle, stitching tears in Mary's coat.

Pa was nowhere to be seen, for he was hiking back towards the river to fetch water. When he returned, he carried a jug in one hand and a sloshing bucket in the other. Slung across his broad shoulders were two bulging waterskins.

The night before, Ma had worried about smoke so close to the big road. They had kept their cookfire small and doused it quickly. Now, though, the firepit crackled and glowed. Ma instructed Mary to boil a big pot of water so that they could all have a good thorough wash.

When the pot began to bubble, Mary removed it from the fire and carefully poured the steaming water into the basin that Pa had forged from scrap aluminum. Mary then mixed in cold water from the waterskins until the temperature was just right.

Laura bathed first, lathering up a washcloth with one of Ma's lavender pine soaps and scrubbing her skin all over until it glowed a happy pink. She even washed her hair. Undoing her braids, she worked soapy water through the matted clumps and tangles until her fingers massaged her scalp. It was bracing, standing there with damp hair and skin in the cold morning air. Laura hopped from one foot to the other to fight off the shivers. Still, goosebumps and all, it was marvelous to feel so clean.

Meanwhile, Mary set out the jar of tooth powder. As Laura bathed, Mary mixed a spoonful of the fragrant powder with water and some ashes from the campfire to make a sticky paste. She spread the paste across her teeth with her finger. Then she took the bone-handled toothbrush that Ma had made for them and dutifully scrubbed the inside of her mouth with its soft hemp bristles. When it was Laura's turn, Mary handed her the toothbrush and the bowl of paste. Laura hated the burnt taste of the gray ointment, but Ma always said that they must clean their teeth with paste at least once a week if they wanted to keep them. She forced herself to brush up and down, front and back, until the foul mixture frothed over her lips. Then she spit into the bushes with a theatrical "blech!" before rinsing the taste from her mouth.

When they were both brushed and bathed and dressed, Mary and Laura sat together to comb out one another's hair. They used Ma's comb. It was an antique from Lectric Times, with dozens upon dozens of stiff iron prongs that never seemed to rust or stain. Laura bit her lip, wincing as Mary coaxed wet brown knots of hair through the comb's narrow teeth.

Not for the first time, Laura wished her hair would flow like Mary's and not coil into such tight kinks. Mary had teased her about it when they were younger. Of course, Ma's hair was the same way, and no one could deny that Ma was beautiful. Still, Laura couldn't help feeling a pang of jealousy when she looked at her older sister's sandy curls. Neither of them would ever have golden hair cascading down their shoulders like the Queen on Mary's carrysack, but Mary's hair was a good deal closer than Laura's.

Meanwhile, Ma continued her mending. When Mary's coat was patched, she turned to Laura's and then to Pa's. She even asked to see Oprah and declared that the ragdoll could fresh thread and stuffing.

The handcar got a cleaning too. Pa wiped down the sides of its oak frame and scraped dried mud from its hubs and spokes. One of its wheels had begun to squeak, and so he applied a fresh coat of tallow to the axles.

Later, while Pa combed out his beard and Ma pinned her hair, holding Mary's handscreen up to inspect herself in its smooth black surface, Mary tried to give Jack a wash with the leftover bathwater. The brindled pigdog wanted nothing to do with the damp washcloth, and Laura laughed and laughed watching her sister wrestle with the squirming, kicking loaf of fur. When Ma admonished Mary that she was getting the dog no cleaner and herself a good deal dirtier, Mary finally gave up and let Jack be.

All this activity kept them at camp until mid-morning. Eventually, Ma looked them all over and announced that they were as respectable as they likely to get under the circumstances.

"Might even pass for decent folk in a bad light," joked Pa.

With that, they started on their way down the Great Eighty Road.

It made Laura feel tiny, walking down the center of that wide creetrock road. The cars that used to travel this way back in Lectric Times must have been gigantic, she imagined.

Yet, when they began to come across the remains of lectric cars, they seemed much the same as those she'd seen elsewhere. They passed toppled lectric wagons, those great rectangular cars that Pa said were used by Merican traders in Lectric Times to carry their goods from town to town. As huge as they were, those old wagons would have taken up only a small sliver of the Eighty Road's span. Laura estimated that the road could easily fit five or six of the biggest lectric wagons side-by-side, with plenty of room left for travelers on foot to pass safely in between.

Most of the abandoned cars and wagons had been dragged off the road. They lay in heaps, one atop the other in the ditches alongside the long flat plateau of the Great Eighty Road. As often as not, the lectric cars had come to rest on their sides or flipped completely on their backs, their wheels straining uselessly skyward, stray threads of distended softmold clinging to their stunted metal rims.

Laura saw more and more lectric wreckage as the morning wore on. The clusters of cars grew thicker and more frequent. Sometimes, there were too many for the roadside ditches to hold. Then they spilled out over its edges like a swarm of insects, crawling over one another as they invaded the creetrock road.

They had been walking for several hours when Laura saw shapes ahead that seemed to block the road completely. Several lectric wagons appeared on the horizon. Their enormous rectangular shells reminded Laura of the iron boxes that had spilled from the stranded boat beside the Misisip. The wagons lay end-to-end, all the way across the road and down over its side. From Laura's vantage, they seemed to form a wall of rust-coated iron, barring their way. She looked up at Pa. He smiled back at her, but Laura saw that he had begun to drum his fingers restlessly against the grips of the handcar.

As they drew closer, Laura noticed something on top of the iron wall. It looked to be a little hut. It was a simple thing, no more than a canopy suspended by four posts over open air, with low lumpy walls made of what seemed to be piles of heavy sacks. Beside the hut, a silvery gray flag hung limply from the top of a pole, stirring itself occasionally when a breeze kicked up. Another flag hung below the hut, draped down across the front of the iron box. A red shape was sewn onto its silver field. It was the face of some sort of red bisox, Laura eventually realized, with pointed horns and flared nostrils and dark, scowling eyebrows.

At the same time, Laura realized that the lectric wagons were not arranged into a single wall as she had first thought. Instead, the iron barricade ended halfway across the Eighty Road. Behind it, a second row of wagons obstructed the other half of the road. Anyone who wished to pass through would have to snake around one wall and then the other. Pa would not have any trouble navigating the maze with the handcar, but a bigger bisox-drawn car might find the turn awfully tight.

They were almost to the first wall when suddenly a head popped up inside the hut from behind the pile of sacks. The face looked startled to see them, as if jolted from a slumber by the rattle of the handcar or the crunch of its wheels over the creetrock gravel.

Pa stopped, and Ma took Laura's hand, guiding her and Mary back behind the handcar. Perched atop their belongings, Jack yipped, but Ma gave him a harsh shush, and he immediately ducked back down, head between his paws in embarrassment.

There was a frantic commotion inside the hut and a sharp exchange of hushed voices. Something bumped and clattered, and someone shouted a very impolite word. Ma and Pa looked at one another. Pa raised his eyebrows and shrugged.

Finally, a figure scrambled from the hut, fumbling with a bayoneted rifle, and called down to them.

"Ho there!"

It was a young woman. A gray cloak hung askew from her neck, as if hastily fastened. Beneath, her rumpled tunic was half-tucked into the waist of baggy trousers. The roof of the hollow iron wagon clanged under her boots as she stomped to the edge to peer down at them. She held her rifle high, at the ready, but she did not point it at them.

"Ho!" Pa shouted back. "My name is Charles Ingalls and this is my wife Caroline! We come from the north country, up Lake Mishgan way! We mean to take the Eighty Road to Lildaka to settle a homestead out in the Wastes! I was told we could petition for passage with Supervisor Syed!"

The woman straightened out her cloak. Some of her composure seemed to return. Looking them over, she allowed her rifle to fall back across her shoulder.

"You're in the right place, Mr. Ingalls!" she called down to them. "You'll be wanting to pay a visit to the eastbank office and see Big Jasmin or whoever's on duty there this time o'day! Supervisor's office is 'tother side of the river, but folks at the east office they'll help get your papers sorted and ferry you 'cross to the fort proper! It's just a short jaunt downroad yonder! Tyreek'll take you there! Tyreek!"

At the sound of his name, a second figure stood up inside the

167

hut from behind the lumpy sack wall, struggling with buttons on a gray vest. Hastily grabbing his rifle, he stumbled out onto the roof of the old lectric wagon to stand beside the woman. He waved down at Laura and her family before turning around and climbing down an unseen ladder on the other side of the iron box. A moment later, he appeared again, rounding the corner of the roadblock's winding alley.

"Good afternoon to you, sir," he said as he approached. "Ladies. Welcome to Hawkeye Crossing."

The guardsman looked to be of an age with the young woman standing atop the barricade. He was clean-shaven and had a wide, bashful grin. He was bare-chested underneath his gray vest, and series of crude tattoos, barely visible against his dark skin, paraded from his shoulders down his skinny arms.

"If you follow me, I'll get you over to see Big Jaz," he said, shaking Pa's hand and then Ma's.

"Big… ?" Ma began.

"Jasmin Perez," said Tyreek. "Assistant Supervisor. She'll start getting you processed. Maybe get you a hot meal in the bargain. How's that sound?"

Pa said that it sounded fine indeed and stooped to hoist up the poles of the handcar. Together, they followed the young man through the checkpoint, weaving between the immobilized lectric wagons, all under the watchful eye of his companion up above, who waved them off before returning to the shade of her little watchpost.

As they walked down the Eighty Road toward Hawkeye Crossing, Tyreek asked them about their travels and what life was like in the big northern woods.

Tyreek had grown up near Davenport, he told them. He'd entered service with Clan Ortega years ago but only just been assigned to Hawkeye Crossing the previous summer. He liked it here, he said. Life was more peaceful out in the hinterlands, and Supervisor Syed always made sure the garrison was well fed and the barracks heated in winter.

Pa asked if the outpost had seen many travelers of late. Tyreek told them traffic along the Eighty Road had picked up a good deal since the spring thaw. Most came through by way of Davenport, attaching themselves to trading convoys. A single family showing up at their doorstep out of the blue was a might unusual, he confessed.

Laura smelled cookfires. Up ahead, wisps of smoke were rising from a spot just south of the road. As they passed, she saw that the smoke was coming from a thicket of creetrock ruins that lay at the end of a dirt trail, a little ways off the main road. Eventually, a flat clearing appeared from behind the trees and ruins, and Laura could see tents and people.

"Convoy," Tyreek said, indicating the camp. "Arrived day before last. Heading west. If the supervisor gets your papers approved quick enough, you folks may be able to attach yourselves. Road's a good deal safer traveling with a decent sized party."

Just past the campsite, the Eighty Road dipped gradually downward through a meadow speckled with pretty blue wildflowers. At the bottom was the river that Laura's family had encountered upstream the day before. It seemed even bigger now, as it surged down across the Yowa plains to cut short the Great Eighty Road, just as it had the previous day with the smaller road that had brought them south. Down the road ahead, Laura could see the spot where the river swallowed up the wide creetrock trail that had seemed so indomitable just a moment before.

Rather than follow the Eighty Road down to where it disappeared beneath the water, however, Tyreek turned down a dirt path. The path meandered up and down across the gently sloping meadow. These gentle slopes overlooking the riverbank were studded with old lectric buildings of brick and creetrock, Laura now saw. The more she looked, the more there were. Most sat roofless and abandoned, but several showed signs of recent repair. In places, in between the ruins, land had been cleared and the soil furrowed into neat rows for crops. Here and there, chimneys breathed their faint gray breath.

By then, the other side of the river had come into view. There, the signs of habitation were even more apparent. On the river's west bank was some kind of fort, surrounded by a long fence of spiked wooden posts. Within that fence, a tall stone tower could be seen and the tips of a dozen or more thatched rooves. From these buildings rose more trails of smoke, all mingling together into one great cloud that spilled lazily across the water. Beside the gates of the fort, Laura could just make out the faint gray ribbon of the Eighty Road, reemerging from the river's western shore.

As they continued to follow Tyreek down the meandering dirt trail, Laura noticed people walking amongst the fields and ruins ahead, some carrying buckets of water sloshing from yokes across their shoulders, some pulling small handcars. At one point, they passed a man splitting firewood outside an old shed, who called out to them

"Ho, Tyreek!"

"Ho, Darryl!" Tyreek called back. "New arrivals heading west! Big Jaz in the east office?"

"Last I saw!" the man replied. He gave Laura and her family a wave.

Eventually, they stopped in front of a stout square house that stood all alone, surrounded by a field of leafy green vegetables. The building was a queer patchwork. Its foundation and most of its outer walls were creetrock, but from within this gray shell grew timber beams. They rose to fill the gaps that time had torn into the upper reaches of the creetrock frame. There, they blossomed into rafters propping up a slapdash roof cobbled together with wooden boards and sheets of old lectric iron. It was almost as if the house had another smaller house sprouting inside of it.

The wide windows of the original structure had been plugged, and its big creetrock entryway had been narrowed and fitted with a wooden gate. The gate hung open. Tyreek climbed up the uneven stone steps that led to the house and peeked his head inside.

"Ho, Big Jaz!" they heard him say. "Got a new intake for you. Just arrived through the east checkpoint."

Tyreek turned back and beckoned them inside. Pa set the handcar down by the side of the path, and he and Ma and Mary and Laura and Baby Grace all followed Tyreek up the crooked steps and through the open door.

As Laura entered, she passed a woman slouched on a stool just inside the doorway, her back leaning against the wall. She had a small knife in one hand and a wooden block in the other, which she seemed to be whittling into some kind of misshapen animal. She had something wadded up inside her mouth, and she chewed it slowly while watching Ma and Baby Grace, then Mary and Laura and finally Pa, step inside the building. Her eyes followed them, but she made no attempt to rise. Tyreek led them right past the woman on the stool, making his way straight towards the far end of the room, where an older woman sat behind a large desk.

The inside of the assistant supervisor's office was as much a jumble as the outside. The floor was bare creetrock, clean but discolored. A big crack that ran diagonally all the way across the center of the room had been filled with some sort of clay and smoothed down. Two of the walls had been painted white, but the paint stopped halfway through a third wall, as if someone had run out of material or simply gotten tired.

The office was spacious, but it somehow still managed to feel cluttered. A big thick post had been erected right in its middle to hold up the roof. More wooden beams, some painted and some not, crisscrossed between floor and walls and rafters at eccentric angles. Crates were stacked in one corner, barrels lined up against another. Here and there were shelves displaying a haphazard collection of old artifacts and lectric scav.

Colorful artwork hung from the walls. As they followed Tyreek through the office towards the woman at the other side of the room, Laura passed beneath a painting of a beautiful, smiling woman holding up a bottle filled with some dark brown liquid. The portrait, partially hidden behind a row of barrels, stretched nearly from floor to ceiling.

Daylight came in through the open door and through shutters that had been installed within some of the boarded-up windows.

171

But the deeper recesses of the room were streaked in shadow, adding to the sense of clutter.

Tyreek stopped in front of the big desk, Pa beside him.

"This here's Big Jasmin," said Tyreek. "She'll sort you out."

Like the building in which it sat, Big Jasmin's desk was cobbled together from mismatched parts. Its base was made of two iron tables. They were clearly old Merican antiques, lectricmade, but they looked remarkably well cared for, with only the faintest stains of age creeping down their sturdy legs. Across their top was laid a long stone slab, its surface perfectly flat and smooth. The stone was glistening white, but faint veins of pink ran through it, giving it a pretty rosy hue. On the wall behind hung another gray flag, decorated with the same red bisox head Laura had seen at the checkpoint.

Big Jasmin was hunched down over the marbled stone desk, making marks in chalk on a writing slate. When she tilted her head to the side, something glinted from her face, and Laura realized that there were a pair of glass circles covering the woman's eyes, thick and round and held in place by copper wires that twisted round her ears. Her dark hair was salted with strands of white, and it blossomed from her head in short, stiff tendrils.

Beside her writing slate lay a stack of thin sheets and a quill poking out from inside an inkpot. The sheets were not parchment, Laura saw, but rather hemp papers, crinkly and brown. Their edges were ragged, not like the neat squares that filled old lectricmade books. Still, the sight of so many papers stacked together caught Laura's attention. At the Laketown Market, each one would have fetched a hefty price, for few craftsmen in those days knew the secrets of papermaking.

The woman at the desk did not look up as they approached. Instead, she continued to study the symbols on her writing slate. Finally, she turned to a sheet of paper. Taking up the quill with a *tap tap* to the mouth of the ink jar, she made a tiny, precise mark. Then she replaced the quill and returned to the writing slate. Pa watched her for a moment then cleared his throat.

"Good afternoon, ma'am. My name is Charles Ingalls. This is

172

my wife Caroline and our three daughters. We're making our way west, Lildaka bound. I was told we could see you about arranging safe passage on the Eighty Road. I've a letter of introduction addressed to Supervisor Syed."

Pa pulled out Tobias Goatherd's letter from the pocket of his coat.

"And what is your business in Lildaka, Mr. Ingalls?" the woman asked without looking up.

"We mean to settle out in the Wastes, ma'am," Pa answered. "Claim a homestead."

The woman grunted. It sounded derisive, but it might have just been her own curt way of acknowledging what Pa had said.

"The Wastes . . ." said the woman absently, almost to herself.

"Yes, ma'am," said Pa. "I'm told rains have come again. The soil's not so used up out west, and they say folks are making a go of working the land. I'm to understand the Clan supervisory in Lildaka will register a man's claim up to a hundred acres."

The woman's chalk scratch-scratched on her slate. Pa frowned, giving Ma a sidelong look

"Cargo?" the woman asked, finally.

"Just our own supplies," said Pa. "And a few bundles of furs and hides to trade. Our car is outside. We've a few coppers set aside for tolls if your Supervisor will not take barter, but our means are modest. I'm just a poor trapper from the northern woods I'm afraid."

After a few more terse scratches, the chalk in the woman's hand paused, hovering above the writing slate. She lifted her eyes, tilting her face upwards no further than absolutely necessary to examine them. Her eyes were magnified and distorted by the glass circles strapped to her face, giving her a bug-like appearance. Her humorless expression only made the effect more comical, and Laura felt a sudden urge to giggle.

The big bug eyes snapped from Pa to Ma to Mary and Laura. Finally, the woman set down her chalk. She placed a stone on top of her sheet of hemp paper to keep it in place. Then she stood, removing the glass eyecovers from the bridge of her nose so that they rested atop her forehead.

"My name's Jasmin Perez, Mr. Ingalls," she said curtly. "Senior assistant supervisor. I'll get you started on your forms. Once your cargo's inventoried, you'll have to take the ferry over to see Supervisor Syed. I can't promise he'll stamp your papers. Every other week, the Clan Council seems to have a new policy on displacees. Not much reason to any of it. But that's none of my concern."

Big Jasmin made her way around the stone desk. To Laura's disappointment, the woman seemed to be of perfectly average height and build. But Laura supposed that, whoever Little Jasmin was, she must be a good deal smaller.

"Send Darryl up on your way back to your post," Big Jasmin told Tyreek. "Grita, let's get the inspection started on the Ingalls family's cargo."

The young woman on the stool set down her whittling and picked up a rifle that had been leaning on the wall beside her. She shifted whatever she was chewing to the other side of her mouth and gave them a lopsided smile through her stuffed cheek. She gestured towards the open door, inviting them to lead the way outside.

Out by the handcar, they discovered Jack engaged in a tense confrontation with a fat orange cat. The cat was bigger than the poor little one-eyed pigdog, and he had a mean look to him. Jack, normally so indomitable, cowered beneath the car. The two animals stared at one another through the spokes of the big wooden wheel.

The guardsman that Big Jasmin had called Grita shooed the cat away with the butt of her rifle.

"Oi! Marlo! You leave that doggy alone! Scat you! Go on!"

The cat flinched away from Grita's waggling weapon, but then he turned and sauntered away slowly, as if leaving at his own discretion, giving Jack one last growl before disappearing into the vegetable patch beside Big Jasmin's office.

Tyreek shook Pa's hand and wished them safe travels before turning to walk back the way they'd come. Meanwhile, Grita began to circle the handcar, peering inside. Big Jasmin emerged from the building a few moments later, another writing slate tucked under her arm, and soon they were joined by Darryl, the man they'd passed earlier by the side of the path. A light gray cloak was now about his shoulders and a rifle in his hands.

Laura and her family stood there and watched as Grita and Darryl went through every inch of their belongings. Bit by bit, the Ortega guardsmen unloaded everything from the handcar.

"Don't worry, folks. We'll put everything back right where we found it," Darryl assured them, but Laura could see it upset Ma to have her careful organization so disturbed.

Meanwhile, Big Jasmin asked Pa questions, making notes on her slate. Where were they from? What roads had they taken? What had they brought with them? Had any of them been sick of late?

Occasionally, Grita or Darryl would announce some item they'd found in their search, and Big Jasmin would write that down as well. She emptied out Pa's coinpurse and counted what was inside. She even made Ma and Pa turn out their pockets and had them hand their coats over to Darryl, who patted the garments down and inspected them inside and out.

At one point, Grita slung her rifle across her back and came over to crouch down beside Laura.

"Hi there," she said. "What's your name?"

"Laura."

"It's very nice to meet you, Laura. I'm Margarita. That's a fine blue carrysack you have there. May I have a look inside?"

Laura looked over to Ma, who nodded. Laura shrugged her batman bag off her shoulders and unfastened it. Grita peered inside.

"My what a pretty doll!" she said, picking up Oprah and handing her to Laura. "And what's her name?"

"Oprah."

"Why, that was my mother's name! Died during the Second Hyperflu when I was about your age, God rest her. Well, you take good care of your Oprah, sweetheart."

175

She buttoned Laura's bag back up and took a quick look through Mary's bag.

"Nothing to speak of over here, Big Jaz" she announced.

When all their possessions had been pawed over and tallied and all of Big Jasmin's questions had been answered, the assistant supervisor slid a cover across the face of her writing slate and buckled it tight. She handed it to Darryl with instructions to ferry Pa across the river to the fort and escort him to Supervisor Syed.

Laura watched them all the way. Pa followed the gray-cloaked guardsman down through the meadow until they were both tiny figures by the riverbank. Laura watched these figures walk out onto a square shape that jutted into the river. Laura had mistaken it for a dock, but then it began to move away from shore, her father aboard.

Gradually, the ferry crept further out across the water. Laura thought she saw Pa standing at the boat's stern, waving, and she frantically waved back, jumping up and down to make herself seen.

There was nothing to do then but wait. As time passed, Laura began to feel apprehensive. Pa knew how to take care of himself in the woods and out on the old number roads, but this place was something new. There were so many people, so many papers, so many rules. Laura found it all overwhelming. She gazed at the big fort across the river, with its looming walls and trails of chimney smoke. Somewhere inside was Pa.

As Laura and Mary waited with Ma beside the handcar, Grita brought them all a supper of soymeal biscuits smothered in a chunky fish gravy. The gravy was spiced with peppers that made Laura's tongue tingle and burn. It was too much for Mary, who scraped her biscuits dry before eating them and then discreetly set her plate down for Jack to lick the gravy clean. Once Laura had gotten used to it, though, she decided that the fiery sensation was not completely unpleasant, and she ate every bite.

Big Jasmin had returned to her desk and her papers by then, but Grita kept them company, chatting away with Ma about the latest fashions in Davenport and the best way to gut a fish. The fat orange cat returned, and Mary and Laura lured him close enough to scratch beneath his jowls, much to Jack's indignation.

Pa was gone a long time. After a while, Laura began to pace, hopping up every few minutes to scan the river for signs of his return. Finally, she saw the dark shape of the ferry stirring itself and moving back in their direction.

Three figures disembarked on the other side. As they made their way up the path towards her, Laura saw that Pa and Darryl had been joined by a woman. She was nearly as tall as Pa, with black hair pulled back into a long tight braid that coiled down around her neck and back over her shoulder like a pet snake. She did not wear a gray uniform like Darryl's or Grita's. Instead, she had on a long coat of a lightweight, tan-colored material that flapped about her knees. It was broad-shouldered and covered all over in pockets.

As the woman approached, Laura found herself looking at that coat with longing, thinking of all the things she could carry in all those pockets. Something else was odd about the long coat, but it took Laura a moment to realize what it was. One of the sleeves was empty. It was folded up and pinned against the woman's chest where her left arm should have been.

"Ho, Priya!" Grita called out to the woman when they were within hailing distance. "Mr. Ingalls! How'd you fare? Good news I trust!"

Laura couldn't restrain herself any longer. She ran to Pa, who scooped her up and carried her with him the rest of the way back to Ma and the car.

"The supervisor's stamped our travel papers," Pa said when he reached the hancar. He brandished a carefully folded sheet of hemp paper. "The toll's a bit steeper than I might have liked, but fair all things considered. Caroline, this is Priya Syed. She's captaining the convoy we passed camped by the Big Road yonder. She's agreed to let us join her company if we're prepared to leave by first light tomorrow."

"Oh!" said Ma. She seemed a little flustered by the tall one-armed woman. "Well, that's wonderful news, Charles. I'm very

177

pleased to meet you, Ms. Syed. Are you and the supervisor . . . ?"

"Malcolm's my brother," answered the woman with a laugh. "Half-brother, truthfully. But family counts for quite a bit in Ortega country. We're of old Deshi stock ourselves, me and Malcolm. You'll find plenty Syeds out Lildaka way. Got roots there stretching back generations, from back before the Hard Years. But Malcolm, he married into the Clan, Old Lucius Ortega's very own niece if you want to know, and now he's got himself a big-shot title and a fort full of graycoats to order about. Me, I don't have any interest in politics. I'm a trader, like my daddy. But I won't lie to you, ma'am, if you want to run cargo back and forth along the Eighty Road, it don't hurt to have a brother high up in the Ortega bureaucracy."

The woman spoke with a confident, unbroken patter, as if Ma and Pa were old acquaintances and not strangers just arrived from far-off lands. When she began to lead the way, back up the path towards the Eighty Road, it seemed the most natural thing in the world to follow.

They thanked Big Jasmin and said their farewells to Grita and Darryl. Then they hurried to catch up with the tall, one-armed convoy captain. Captain Syed led them all the way back to the convoy's campsite, amongst the ruins beside the Great Eighty Road. Laura could hear voices as they approached. The smell of campfire was in the air and a hint of something unfamiliar cooking. Laura thought of all the new people she'd encountered already that day and about the prospect of soon meeting many more. A feeling of exhaustion came over her.

Ma took her hand.

"Come, Laura," she said. "I know it's been a long day. We're almost at an end."

They found the convoy in a clearing ringed with trees and ruins. Skinny gray aspens sprouted here and there between the remains of creetrock walls and pillars.

At one end of the camp sat a large wagon. Its four big wooden wheels made the ones on Pa's handcar look tiny, and it was roofed over with a great billowing patchwork tarp. A clothesline had been strung between the wagon and a creetrock pillar. Tents were spread out across the rest of the clearing, along with a few smaller, two-wheeled handcars.

Suddenly, a loud snort from just over Laura's shoulder made her jump. Standing right beside her were two enormous horned shapes.

Bisox. Laura had seen a pair once on her trip to the Laketown Market, but not from so very close. These animals seemed bigger than the ones she remembered. Shaggy hair cascaded down from their mountainous humps. One was a chestnut brown, the other a darker shade, nearly black, with a patch of white across its forehead and mane. The brown one looked at Laura and grunted, sending shivers through threads of mucus that dangled from its gaping nostrils. Laura watched the creatures with wonder, her neck twisting like softmold as she passed.

Faces turned towards Laura and her family as Captain Syed led them through the camp.

"Make yourselves at home, Mr. Ingalls," the convoy captain said. "There's some nice flat ground on 'tother side of that wall there, might offer you a touch of privacy. But you're welcome to set down stakes wherever you can. When you're settled, come share our fire, and I'll introduce you to the rest. Or not, suit yourselves. Just be ready to strike camp at first light. I keep my convoy moving at a steady, sensible pace, but I don't wait or turn back for stragglers. If you fall behind, you're on your own."

Pa thanked her, and he guided the handcar through a gap in the ruins to a clear patch of ground covered with dried leaves and twigs. They began to sweep the area and lay out their bed rolls.

"How much did they take?" Laura heard Ma ask in a quiet voice.

Pa glanced over his shoulder before answering.

"Syed and I agreed on half our coin. Two silver pieces and a handful of coppers. Plus the bullets we picked up from that deserter from the Spear. And I've promised a half-bundle of pelts to the sister when we make it safely to Lildaka and a generous commission on the remainder if she can find us a buyer at a good price."

Ma sighed.

"Well, not as bad as it might've been," she said.

Laura knew that such talk was not for her. Yet, something bothered her about what Pa had said. Something didn't add up, and she couldn't seem to let the thought go. She was just about to speak up when Mary did it for her.

"Pa?" Mary asked, as she rolled aside a chunk of creetrock rubble to make room for her sleeping pad. "You said two silver was half our coin. But we have more silver than that. Don't we?"

Ma and Pa looked at one another. Pa crept back to the ruins that separated them from the rest of the camp, peeking his head around the other side.

"Mary, may I see your coat for a moment?" he said quietly, after making sure no one was nearby.

Confused, Mary handed Pa her patchwork coat. He turned it inside-out, pinching and prodding at the lining.

"Ah, here we are," he said, offering the coat back to Mary. "You never fail to amaze me, Caroline. Truly, if I hadn't known where to look, I'd never have noticed."

When Mary felt the spot on her coat where Pa indicated, she looked up in surprise. Laura hurried over to feel it too. At first it seemed like just a wrinkle or fold where two different fabrics had been stitched together, but as Laura worked her fingers deeper, she realized there was something round and hard buried deep in the lining.

"Silver?" she whispered.

Pa winked at her.

Meanwhile, Ma had scooped Oprah up from among Laura's things. She handed Laura the ragdoll, an uncharacteristic look of mischief in her eyes.

"And as for you, Laura," she said, "that young lady told you to keep good care of Oprah. I know that you will."

Laura held the doll in her hands, noticing for the first time how much heavier she felt than normal. Prodding the back of Oprah's head, she felt another lump. She gaped up at Ma and Pa.

"We lied to them?" she whispered. "Big Jasmin and the rest?"

"Pshaw! Lied nothing," said Pa. "We agreed on a fair price, Malcolm Syed and me, and both of us walked away satisfied with the bargain. A man's not obligated to disclose everything he owns just because some folks with guns ask him to. Besides, officials like Syed, they expect a bit of honest cheating when it comes to tolls and such. It's all baked into the system."

Laura suddenly felt more tired than ever. It had been a very long day.

She lay down on her mat with Oprah in her arms, telling herself she just needed to rest for a moment before they joined the others for supper by the campfire. But, before she knew it, her eyes were closed, and she was lost in dreams.

EIGHTEEN: THE FERRY

Captain Syed had said the convoy would leave at first light, and so it did. By the time Laura and her family joined the others, the two bisox were already hitched to their wagon. Laura stood there in the clearing beside the cold firepit, her carrysack tight around her shoulders, and watched the big hairy silhouettes shuffle and snort in the pre-dawn darkness.

Hector Chavez, the man who drove the bisox wagon, was perched silently at the reins, a shadow beneath the arch of fabric that sheltered the trade goods stacked up inside. At a whistle from Captain Syed, Mr. Chavez gave the reins a snap. The bisox strained forward, and the wagon wheels began to turn. Everyone fell in behind, and together they began their twilight procession up the trail to the Great Eighty Road and then on towards Hawkeye Crossing and the unknown lands beyond.

Laura's sense of adventure soared, only to be yanked back to earth a short while later to strain feebly against its tether, for, as it happened, their journey was delayed almost as soon as it was begun. When the convoy arrived at the Yowa River, not a quarter hour after departing its camp, there was no ferry waiting. Instead, they came to the end of the Eighty Road, right to the precipice of its ruined bridge, to find Big Jasmin making her way down towards them from her office on the hill, writing slate tucked beneath her arm. Grita, the guardsman from the day before, trudged sleepily behind her, practically dragging her bayonet along the ground.

Big Jasmin and Captain Syed's words became heated when the two women came within arguing distance.

"Malcolm said we were cleared to cross," Laura heard the convoy captain say. "I have the papers right here."

"That you are," Big Jasmin replied. "As soon as we complete the medical inspection. Supervisor Syed mentioned it, I'm sure. Davenport's issued new travel restrictions. New cases of Yellow Madness down Cedar Valley way, as you know. We'll be lucky if the Clan Council don't shut the roads down for good come summer. Don't you fret yourself, Priya. The doctor's already been roused. We'll have you on your way soon enough."

Captain Syed stormed and cursed, but there was nothing to be done. And so they all waited there on the riverbank, beside the creetrock precipice where the Great Eighty Road rose and fell away, the travelers once more setting down the baggage they had so recently taken up.

Mr. Chavez climbed down from his wagon and set about preparing a big iron pot of chia pudding. As dawn's light began to creep slowly across the timber walls of the fort looming on the other side of the river, the members of the convoy gathered around to share a breakfast.

Laura had never had chia pudding before. She dabbed the speckled substance experimentally with her spoon before lifting a dollop to her lips. The pudding was mixed with soy milk and sweetened with honey, and Laura eagerly dove back in.

As she ate, she studied the other travelers. There were over a dozen of them in the convoy when Laura and her family were included. It was too many for Laura to keep straight that first morning, but, in the days and weeks that followed, she would come to know them well.

There was Captain Syed of course. The tall, one-armed woman spoke rapidly and often and had a laugh louder than Pa's. Beneath her pocket-crowded coat, she wore a thick leather belt that held a pistol, holstered to her right hip. Her pants were tucked into tall boots that rose nearly to her knees. And she was always chewing on some sort of leaf, which stained her teeth black and caused her to spit frequently, a habit she used to punctuate her many proclamations.

After her confrontation with Big Jasmin, Captain Syed paced the ferry dock for a time, chewing and spitting and muttering to herself. When Mr. Chavez handed her a bowl of pudding, though, she seemed to resign herself to the delay and began to mingle among others, joking and telling stories.

Captain Syed's manner was a curious mix of warm and cold. She was amiable, over-familiar even, but there was something aloof about her as well. She was quick to engage in conversation or, indeed, to share her observations with no one in particular. Yet, over time, Laura began to notice that she seldom made eye contact when she spoke, frequently glancing over her shoulder or squinting into the distance, as if taking constant stock of her surroundings.

Laura knew better than to ask outright what had happened to the woman's arm, but it did not take long to learn the story. That very first morning, in between bites of pudding and with no apparent prompting, Captain Syed began telling them about how, when she was just a little girl, there had been an outbreak of the Ague in Lildaka, where she'd grown up. One night, she was attacked by an uncle who had fallen ill. She escaped, but not before the man had sunk his teeth into her arm. Afterward, her family had tried to stop the spread of the infection by severing the limb above the bite.

"Got sick anyway, sorry to say," she remarked as an afterthought, rising briefly to her feet to scan the river for the ferry before sitting back down to her pudding.

Laura's eyes went wide when she heard that. She looked the woman up and down, searching for signs of froth trailing from her lips or madness lurking behind her eyes. Could her dark skin be obscuring the Ague's telltale jaundice?

Captain Syed noticed Laura's reaction and laughed.

"Didn't wager you'd be sharing the road with a bona fide fiend, did you, girl? Well, don't you go burning my corpse just yet. I got better. The Yellow Madness ain't ever a dinner party, but you'd rather you get it when you're little if you're gonna get it. Rare for a grown-up to make a recovery, but in children it ain't unheard of at all, specially if you get to it early enough to stop the spread. Fact of the matter, they say childhood survivors like me, we're immune to the sickness, though I've got no mind to put that theory to the test."

Laura listened in fascination as Captain Syed described her struggle with the Ague. The horrifying details were rattled off casually, in the same tone the convoy captain might have used to inventory her cargo. She had spent weeks kept in darkness, she told them, tied down tight to her bed so she couldn't harm her caregivers. Ever since, she couldn't stand to be indoors for long. Just the thought of feeling restrained made her sweat with panic. Maybe that was why the life of a trader suited her, she said, out on the open road. Then she spat for emphasis.

No one quite knew what to say to that. There was a lull in conversation, as the others all contemplated their breakfast bowls or else stared pointedly across the river, wondering what was taking the ferry so long. Captain Syed seemed not to notice. She just scraped up the last lingering trails of chia pudding with a *scritch scratch* of her spoon across her wooden bowl, smacked her lips, stood, and returned to pace the dock once more.

Laura turned back to her own breakfast, continuing her examination of the other members of the group. None were as forward or as talkative as the one-armed convoy captain, and so it would be some days before she learned their stories.

There was Hector Chavez, the bisox driver. He and Captain Syed had worked together for many years, Laura later learned, and they seemed to have developed a wordless, intuitive form of communication, full of nods and subtle hand gestures.

Mr. Chavez was not a handsome man. Beneath a short, patchy beard streaked with gray, his cheeks were pock-marked. Yet, despite the scars, his face was kindly. That first morning, he smiled at Laura when he handed her a bowl of the gummy concoction he'd been stirring.

So reserved was Mr. Chavez, it was only much later that they managed to piece together the particulars of his rather interesting life. He had grown up far away, across the mountains, in the lands that people in those days called the Occupied Territories, though Mr. Chavez told them that he had left there long before the arrival of the invaders from across the sea.

As a young man, he had made his way to Deseret. There, he had been recruited by a convoy company which was organizing an expedition east, through the treacherous mountain passes and all the way across the Wastes.

It was a risky but profitable trade route, and Mr. Chavez made the journey several times. Then, on one expedition, his convoy met with disaster. He alone had survived. Somehow, he made it out of the Wastes by himself, staggering into Lildaka near death. After that, he settled in the Yowa, finding less hazardous work running cargo back and forth along the Great Eighty Road.

Also in Captain Syed's employ was a man named Abu Malla, though everyone called him Bucky. His head was shaved, covered in short black stubble except around a scar that snaked behind his ear from his temple to the back of his skull. He was a big, thick-necked man with smooth, pudgy cheeks that gave him the look of an overgrown baby. His job was to protect the convoy. He carried a rifle and bayonet, and, along with Captain Syed, he patrolled beside the bisox wagon, keeping watch for bandits and other threats.

The rest were not traders like Captain Syed and Mr. Chavez and Bucky Malla. They were simply travelers, going west like Laura and her family and joining the convoy for safety along the Great Eighty Road.

There was Caleb, a skinny young man with pale blue eyes and an eager disposition. He was a guardsman for Clan Ortega, gray cloak and all. He was garrisoned at a supervisory west of Hawkeye Crossing called Badger Creek, but he had returned to Davenport over the winter to care for his sick mother and was now going back to resume his post.

Then there were Oprah and Janice Khan. They were cousins, though they looked enough alike to be sisters, both stocky and plain-faced, with the same bushy eyebrows. They were returning to their family's compound on the outskirts of Lildaka and brought with them a small handcar stacked with boxes that hummed and buzzed. When Laura saw tiny black shapes swirling around the boxes, she realized they were full of bees. The cousins had travelled all the way to Davenport to obtain the hives, and they watched over them as if they were chests full of silver.

Also joining the convoy were Mr. and Ms. Aguilar and their son Devonte. The Aguilars had left a settlement south of Davenport to strike out west, and, just like Laura and her family, they too meant to claim a homestead out in the Wastes. They had a handcar as well, slightly smaller than Pa's, and all three of them took turns pulling it. Devonte Aguilar was only a little older than Mary, but he was already nearly as tall as his father. He had a lean, athletic build. Thick curls of brown hair spilled halfway down his neck and swept across his forehead, threatening to cover his eyes.

Finally, there was the scruffy-looking bachelor named Bill Keo. It was difficult to know where Bill Keo was from or what he was doing on convoy, since so many of his stories turned out to be elaborate jokes or fantastic showtales. At times, he hinted that he was a displacee, forced to flee the Holy Gulf Confederation after having composed a dirty song about the head of the local Virtue Committee. Other times, he insisted that he was an ambassador from one of the Lantic States, on a mission to see the Tang Emperor.

In the story that seemed most likely to Laura, though, he too was bound for Lildaka and meant to file a claim on a homestead out in the Wastes, though he seemed to regard the matter with less sobriety than Pa or the Aguilars.

"Mean to bag me a couple of these wastebirds I hear tell about," Laura heard Bill Keo tell Pa, "then like as not I'll be moseying on my way. Spent so much of my life drifting, I don't think about destination no more. Figure I'll pick up my land claim from Wolfdog Ortega, shoot me enough wastebirds to make a fine feather headdress, then sell my claim to the next bigger fool. That's Bill Keo's plan."

Bill Keo's companion was a large dog that he simply called "Dog." The two of them looked alike. Dog's hair was the same deep black as Bill Keo's beard, which hung long and wispy about the man's throat in the same manner as Dog's shaggy coat. They had the same dark rings sagging beneath bloodshot eyes, eyes that seemed to regard the world with the same look, placid but watchful.

Bill Keo had no handcar. Instead, he traveled with a great big carrysack strapped over his shoulders and buckled across his chest. Dog had a bag too, two bulging bundles draped over his sides, which the big black animal patiently bore as he trotted beside his companion.

That morning, Bill Keo sat alongside Dog at the furthest edge of the Eighty Road. His legs dangled over the cliff where the creetrock spilled over the riverbank, splintering into crooked slabs before disappearing beneath the mud. With sleepy eyes, he looked out upon the river.

As the sun rose further, gradually sprinkling the gray twilight with streaks of color, Laura followed his gaze. Below them, creetrock pillars peeped out of the water, the only remnants of the old Merican bridge. Beside these pillars sat the ferry dock. It was little more than a simple wooden platform hanging over the water. A post stood at its far end, anchoring a thick rope that stretched towards the far bank before vanishing into the dawn shadows.

Eventually, Laura saw movement on the surface of the river. It was the ferry. She watched it drift slowly towards them.

The ferry looked like a floating version of the dock, another simple wooden platform, flat and square. As it grew closer, Laura could see two men aboard, both shirtless. One was Darryl, she realized, the Ortega guardsman who had helped inventory their supplies the day before. The two men were hauling the ferry forward, hand over hand, along the rope that ran from the dock and through a pair of timber posts rising from the ferry's otherwise bare deck.

Only when the ferry was practically below her did Laura see that there was a third person aboard. An older woman was seated on a stool by the ferry's stern, a black bag in her lap.

"That'll be the doctor," Laura heard Bill Keo tell Dog. "Don't you go telling her about that thing I picked up from that girl in

New Hewston, and I won't mention your worms. Bargain?"

A moment later, the ferry collided with the dock. The two platforms united with a hollow thump. The doctor stood and hopped ashore. When she reached the convoy, she set her stool and her bag down beside Big Jasmin and began to look over her instruments.

One by one, everyone in the convoy had to go see her. After the doctor had examined their tongues and their auras, Big Jasmin would check their names off a list.

Laura had never been examined by a doctor before. When it was her turn, Ma took her hand and led her over to the old woman. The doctor asked Laura many questions. She asked about what kind of foods Laura ate, about whether she often felt hot or cold, about her dreams, about her sweat. Then the doctor asked her to stick her tongue out as far as she could. The doctor looked at Laura's tongue for a long time, prodding it with a small metal rod, all the while humming softly to herself.

"Hmmm. Fiery disposition, this one," she said to Ma, finally.

Then she turned to Big Jasmin and said, "Clean. Next."

While Big Jasmin and the doctor completed the medical inspection, Mr. Chavez drove the bisox wagon down to the ferry. The bisox seemed reluctant to step out onto the water at first. They stamped their hooves on the dock and groaned and shook their manes. But Mr. Chavez had a way with the animals. With the Ortega guardsmen steadying the ferry and Bucky Malla helping to guide the car, they got both the bisox and their cargo aboard.

The ferry was just barely long enough. Its deck sank down under all the added weight but managed to stay just above the surface of the river. When the wagon's wheels were locked and the bisox quieted, Mr. Chavez and Bucky Malla and the Ortega guardsmen began to haul the ferry back across the river.

Later, just as the doctor was examining the last of the travelers, the ferry returned, empty but for Bucky Malla and the guardsmen.

"Ingalls, you take next crossing," Captain Syed told Pa.

"Come on, girls," said Ma. "Our turn."

Mary called Jack out from under the handcar. The pigdog scampered over to them, and Mary scooped him up in her arms. Pa spat on his hands before lifting the car's shafts and rolling their belongings down towards the dock.

While Bucky Malla trekked back up to the ruined bridge to speak with Captain Syed, Darryl and the other guardsman helped Pa drive the car onto the ferry. Mary and Laura and Ma followed cautiously behind. For a moment, they stood at the lip of the dock, hesitant to step from the stable platform onto the one that bounced and swayed in the river's current.

Pa took Ma's hand and helped her onto the deck. Then he picked up Mary, Jack still wrapped tight in her arms, and set them both down beside the handcar. He turned back for Laura, but she had already hopped over.

"Careful now, Soybean," Pa told her. "We don't want you tumbling overboard. Caroline, why don't you hold on to that post there. Mind the rope. Girls, you hang tight to your mother once we get moving."

Bucky Malla returned. He was accompanied by Caleb, the guardsman from Badger Creek, and by Bill Keo and his shaggy black dog. All of them boarded the ferry. It was crowded, but Laura was grateful that at least the Khan cousins and their bees weren't coming with them.

They tied Jack up to the handcar. He scampered back and forth across the deck at first, barking at the water on one side and then running back to bark at the water on the other side. But then Dog arrived. At Bill Keo's instruction, the big black animal slumped down beside his master's baggage, as if he had been aboard a ferry his entire life. Dog's serenity seemed to shame Jack, and the little pigdog stopped his antics, content to stand at the edge of the deck and stare down into the river with his one bulging eye.

Pa and Bill Keo and Bucky Malla and Caleb and the other two guardsmen positioned themselves along the rope. With a "hup hup hup," they all began to pull, hand over hand, and suddenly the ferry was drifting away from the dock.

Laura held tight to Ma. The deck rocked and jounced as the river rolled beneath them. Laura felt her stomach clench as she imagined the ferry tipping over or sinking. But then she thought back to crossing the great frozen Misisip all those weeks ago. Compared to that, this little boat ride was nothing, she decided. If she plunged beneath the water here, at least she wouldn't end up trapped beneath ice.

The men at the rope shouted encouragement to one another as the river hissed louder and louder. Swaddled to Ma's back, Baby Grace began to cry. Laura stretched up on tip toes to brush a reassuring hand across her sister's cheek.

Finally, the ferry thumped against the dock on the far side of the river. Bill Keo and Caleb hoisted their bags back up onto their shoulders. Pa unlocked the handcar's wheels, and they all made their way up onto the riverbank.

On the western side of the river, the splintered creetrock rose from the mud and coalesced once more into the flat gray expanse of the Eighty Road. Mr. Chavez and the bisox wagon were waiting. They gathered there, where the road began again, beneath the looming walls of the fort, and waited for the ferry to bring the rest of the convoy.

At last, they were all assembled. Captain Syed exchanged a word or two with Mr. Chavez. Then she lifted thumb and forefinger to her lips and whistled the most piercing whistle Laura had ever heard, before raising her one hand high above her head and twirling her wrist with a commanding flourish.

The reins cracked against the backs of the two bisox. The big wagon wheels began to roll. They were on their way.

NINETEEN: ON CONVOY

The Great Eighty Road stretched on and on, gray and unwavering, day after day. Laura sometimes found herself despairing at its oppressive straightness, longing for the days when her way had meandered and detoured in all manner of surprising directions. Every day, from when the convoy embarked at dawn to when they made camp for the night, Laura's whole world was bound by that narrow corridor of creetrock.

It began to feel hypnotic. Relentlessly, the Great Eighty Road pulled them along, through a landscape so unchanging that Laura would have thought they were going in circles but for the fact that they never, ever seemed to turn.

The country through which the Eighty Road gouged its rigid path offered little to mark their progress. Each day since their departure from Hawkeye Crossing had brought much the same passing scenery. The Yowa's hills rolled by, steady, small, and featureless. Though spring was now well upon them, the land was far from lush. There were trees, but nothing like the vast woods where Laura had grown up. Instead, they stood in patchwork islands amid seas of pale grass.

Meanwhile, the only ruins to be seen seemed to be the Great Eighty Road itself. Rarely was there any other sign of the people who had laid down the endless trail of creetrock. The road stood as an isolated monument, all the more grandiose in its loneliness.

One day, Laura overheard Pa ask Captain Syed why there were no settlements in this part of the Yowa. The convoy had just finished fording a small creek and was passing through a rare woodland. The hills to the east had looked comparatively green. To Pa, the land seemed to have all the ingredients from which to make a living.

"There's some," Captain Syed answered. "Head up beyond them hills yonder and you'll run into folks here and there, farmers and shepherds and the like. Paying taxes to the Ortegas or supposed to. Most who try and make a go in the Yowa midlands, though, after a season or two they move along or... Well, or they just don't stay long-term, I'll leave it at that. I heard a man tell me once the soil's no good in these parts. Used up. I wouldn't know anything about that. Never been one much for settling down and raising crops. But soil or no, this ain't the easiest country to set down roots. You've got Cooley's Army and all them other gangs of rascals running about, not to mention raiding parties from the north whenever one of the caudillos up that way starts feeling their oats. The supervisory garrisons don't offer no protection you can count on. Clan Ortega don't have it in 'em to pacify the

Yowa this far west, and they don't try."

Pa nodded, as if satisfied with the explanation, but Captain Syed kept talking.

"Only reason the Clan Council mans outposts so far west is to keep the Eighty Road open to Lildaka. And they ain't doing such a fine job of that lately neither, not if you ask me. Too busy squabbling 'mongst themselves over this so-called succession crisis to mount proper patrols. I'll tell you one thing, they're going to find themselves in a right fix if they let the Great Eighty get cut off. Where do they think their graycoats' wages come from? Davenport might be where the decisions get made, but it's the trade coming through the City of Mounds what keeps the wheels of their little empire greased. Stop that silver flowing and you'll see the whole blasted supervisory system collapse by next winter, mark my words."

Laura might not have understood every word of Captain Syed's discourse on Ortega trade networks, but she knew that the City of Mounds was another name for Lildaka. It wasn't the first time Laura had heard Captain Syed talk about the frontier town that lay at the end of the Eighty Road. Lildaka was home for Captain Syed, as it was for Bucky Malla and for the Khan cousins, Janice and Oprah. Laura supposed that made them partial. Still, she listened with interest whenever the town was mentioned.

According to Captain Syed, nearly everyone there lived underground. Even the town's meeting hall and its supervisory were dug straight into the earth. Captain Syed described hundreds of underground houses pimpling the landscape. And, on a clear day, you could see the ruins of the Ghost City of Oma looming in the distance.

Lildaka was remote, kims and kims from any other settlement. According to Captain Syed, it was located at the very center of Old Merica, the exact middle point between the western and eastern oceans.

"The town was founded by Deshi displacees," Laura had heard her explain more than once. "Round about the time of the Great Bust. I can trace my family right back to them. Barsha

194

Syed—that was my pa's gran—she was Lildaka's first mayor. Story goes they came from a land that was sinking beneath the sea. After watching those floodwaters swallow up their old homes, it's said our great grandmothers and grandfathers wandered about til they found a place just as far away from any ocean as it was possible to get!"

Captain Syed admitted she didn't know how much truth there was to that old story. But however it was that those Deshi pioneers came to choose that remote spot to settle down, it had proved to be a good one. Over the years, Lildaka had grown to become an important crossroads where several important convoy routes came together. The Great Eighty Road connected it to Davenport and the Illinoy. The Suri River brought down timber from Wolf Point and further up in the Northlands, while grain and soy flowed in the other direction from the Southern Yowa. Precious metal from Deseret and textiles from the Occupied Territories came by way of the Suri's smaller tributaries or else by the straighter but more perilous convoy routes overland across the Wastes.

To hear Captain Syed tell it, goods from all over the world found their way to Lildaka. Laura listened with fascination to her description of the Lildaka Market, which stood just outside the town proper. She told of colorful stalls, packed shoulder to shoulder. There, you'd find all manner of traders, Desereti and Lakota and even Tang, all haggling and shouting.

It all sounded quite exotic and fantastical to Laura. She could hardly believe that she would soon get to see such a place for herself.

And so, as Captain Syed continued to lecture in Pa's general direction, Laura hurried her steps to stay apace. Captain Syed barreled forward from topic to topic in her distinctively assertive patter, pausing only long enough to stuff another wad of chewing leaf into her cheek.

"Marius Ortega—Wolfdog we call him out west—he's been the local supervisor for ten years now or close enough," she was now saying, "I barely remember myself, but there was hard feelings for quite some time after the annexation. Wolfdog Ortega, though, he's always had a light touch. Long as the silver keeps flowing back to Davenport, the Wolfdog's mostly been happy to leave things to the old Deshi families who run the Merchants Guild.

"These days, though… Well, I ain't never seen relations with the supervisor so tense as they been lately."

Captain Syed looked back along the convoy's procession. Her gaze seemed to linger on Caleb the Ortega guardsman, who was walking a few paces back, chatting with Bill Keo. For some reason, Laura expected the woman to lower her voice, but Captain Syed just spit beside the road and continued talking at the same volume.

"Losing the Illinoy's been mighty bad for trade. You ain't heard it from me, but I'd be surprised if there ain't folks in the Merchants Guild asking themselves just what exactly they need Clan Ortega for anyway. And that was before Old Man Ortega took sick. If this succession crisis don't get sorted out, who can tell which way the old Deshi families are likely to bolt?

"What do you suppose is behind these land claims they're so keen to dole out? You think Davenport cares two beans about cultivating the god-forsaken Wastes? No sir. Wolfdog Ortega, he feels his grip on the City of Mounds slipping away. He means to surround Lildaka with homesteaders, all carrying Ortega papers, all loyal clients of the supervisory. Something to balance out the power of those stubborn Deshi tradesmen."

Pa said nothing to all this, but Laura could tell that Captain Syed's words had troubled him.

~~~

Later that evening, when the convoy stopped to make camp, Laura saw Pa pull out the parchment map from the handcar. Map in hand, he approached the clearing beside the bisox wagon where Hector Chavez was chopping onions for supper.

It wasn't the first time the two men had sat down together. Pa often tried to engage the bisox driver in conversation whenever the opportunity presented itself. Captain Syed might be a fine source of information about Lildaka and the Great Eighty Road, but she seemed to know little about the lands west of the Suri River.

It was Mr. Chavez who had actually seen the Wastes firsthand, and Pa was keen to learn all he could from the old man's recollections. What was the weather like in the Wastes? How hot was it in summer, how cold in winter? What kind of game could they expect? Was the better unclaimed land to be found to the west or to the south? Unrolling his map, Pa would point to locations along the parchment's leftmost edge.

Unfortunately, Mr. Chavez's approach to conversation could not have been more different from Captain Syed's. Where the convoy's captain volunteered a dizzying abundance of observations and opinions without prompting, the bisox driver was inclined to answer even direct questions with little more than a smile and a shrug.

Sometimes, though, Pa's pipeleaf could loosen up the man's words enough for Pa could shake a few of them out. That evening, Laura watched Pa produce his wooden pipe from a coat pocket and offer Mr. Chavez a smoke. They began talking. Under pretense of gathering firewood, Laura gradually made her way close enough to listen.

Mr. Chavez was telling Pa about a dust storm that his convoy had once weathered while crossing the Wastes. He described a wall of dark clouds had appeared suddenly on the horizon, rolling towards them. When it finally crashed down upon them, the world around had vanished. Mr. Chavez hadn't been able to see his hands held out in front of his face. The dust storms sometimes lasted days, he said, showering brown grit that would choke a man's lungs and threaten to bury him neck deep.

Mr. Chavez shook his head at the memory and took another deep pull from Pa's pipe. He was silent a moment, gazing thoughtfully at his half-chopped onion as the smoke trailed from his nostrils. Seeing Laura lingering nearby, Pa gave her a look but said nothing. Already, this was an unusually detailed account by Mr. Chavez's standards, and Pa seemed afraid to disrupt the old man's momentum.

He hadn't seen the Wastes in a good many years, Mr. Chavez finally continued, letting more smoke leak from his mouth alongside his words. He reckoned the land was a good deal changed if the stories were to be believed.

There were no settlements in the Wastes in his day, he said. No farms. No homesteads. The only people were the small gangs of nomads that the Deshi traders called the Yaya and the Deseretis called Zoramites. No one seemed to know who they were or where they had come from. The Yaya had no permanent homes. Instead, they roamed from place to place across the vast Wastes, following the wastebird flocks. A savage folk, Mr. Chavez told Pa. They were known to attack convoys, and it was said that they ate human flesh.

When Mr. Chavez said this last part, Pa spit his pipe out, right in the middle of inhaling. Coughing violently, he looked over to where Laura was milling about, barely concealing her eavesdropping.

"But this was all some time ago," Pa said between coughs. "Before the rains returned."

Mr. Chavez smiled and shrugged.

~~~

After Pa shooed her away from his conversation with Mr. Chavez, Laura wandered about the camp. In every corner, the convoy was unburdening from the long day's journey. They took stock, tended to their equipment, and prepared for the arrival of darkness.

On some nights, the convoy stopped right alongside the Great Eighty Road. Other times, they would turn down a side trail and might walk for near an hour to reach their endpoint. Either way, Captain Syed always seemed to know just what she was aiming for. Inevitably, just as dusk was threatening to creep upon them, the convoy would find itself standing on the perfect campsite. Some flat place sheltered from the wind. A place with high enough ground to give them vantage over the surrounding area. And there always seemed to be a stream or a source of groundwater nearby. As often as not, these places bore the signs of past convoys. Carvings on the trees or rings of stones enclosing old firepits.

That night, the convoy had camped uphill from the Great Eughty Road, in a clearing in the shadow of a little sandstone bluff.

Sitting atop the bluff overlooking the camp, Laura spied Bucky Malla. The big man squatted, resting his thighs against his calves, with his rifle balanced across his knees. When he saw Laura looking up at him, he smiled and waved.

Laura knew that he was on lookout, watching for any sign of bandits. The convoy had to be careful as they ventured further and further away from any settlement, out where the guardsmen of Clan Ortega seldom patrolled. Laura had heard Captain Syed warn the others about Cooley's Army, which was not an army at all but just the name for some bandit gangs that roamed in those parts. They were mostly small gangs and didn't have much to do with one another, except they all claimed to follow some man named Cooley who everyone seemed to all agree had died a long time ago if he ever existed at all.

Captain Syed didn't seem very worried about Cooley's Army. They were poorly armed and even more poorly fed, Laura had heard her say, and more like to attack one another than a properly defended convoy. That was no excuse not to be careful, though, and so Bucky Malla kept a watchful eye on the surrounding hills as the other travelers bustled about below him.

Laura was accustomed to the routines of life on convoy by now. Making camp each night was a much livelier business than when it had been just Laura and her family on the road, for there was always much to do. Whenever Captain Syed called a halt to the day's journey, it seemed to release a sudden burst of activity, like a long-simmering pot suddenly boiling over, as everyone hurried to make use of whatever precious daylight remained.

They all had their own cargo to tend to, but the fellow travelers also helped one another. Everyone pitched in, seeing to the things that needed to be done for the convoy's common safety and comfort, making sure that the whole group would be ready to move again the next morning.

At one edge of the camp, Janice and Oprah Khan were fretting about their hives, counting up their bees to see how many had gotten lost along the way. Laura stopped and watched them for a moment. It must be very confusing for the little bees, she thought, to have their home moving all the time.

Nearby, Caleb the guardsman was helping Mr. Aguilar patch some of the boards on his handcar that were rotting away. Pa, who had apparently gotten all the information he could out of Mr. Chavez, came over to join them, offering his opinion on how best to fix the joints of the car's cargo box.

After watching them for a time, Laura turned and began to make her way back to her family's corner of the camp. Along the way, she stopped to pay a visit to the bisox. She was becoming good friends with the two beasts. The one with the white patch was named Pretty, she'd learned, and the chestnut brown was Penny. It could still be frightening to stand close to the big, horned animals, but their deep black eyes were never threatening. They were gentle creatures, though Pretty could be stubborn when she wanted to be, snorting and stamping her hooves when Mr. Chavez tried to turn the wagon. The bisox even tolerated Jack, who now trotted over to greet Laura, before turning to Penny to snuffle at her shaggy legs.

Laura chatted for a moment with the animals. Then she called Jack to her, and together they made their way back to Ma. They found her scrambling over the handcar, retying bundles and shoving barrels that had jostled loose back into place.

When Ma looked down at Laura, she frowned at the meager bundle of branches tucked under her arm. Laura had forgotten that she was supposed to be looking for kindling. Ma sent her right back out to join Mary and Devonte Aguilar, who were gathering firewood in the thicket downhill from the campsite.

As she made her way down the trail, Laura heard Devonte explaining something to Mary in a very self-important voice. Suddenly, Mary let out a loud girlish laugh. It sounded unnatural to Laura, and she doubted that anything Devonte Aguilar had said could possibly be that funny.

Laura's sister had started acting funny around the older boy, always changing her voice as if to make herself sound more grown up. A few days previous, Mary had asked Laura if she thought Devonte was handsome. Laura had made a face and said she guessed he probably was, but he was also stuck up and a know-it-all.

When Laura reached them, Devonte turned to her. Placing a hand to his chest, he bowed low. That made Mary fake laugh again. Laura just rolled her eyes and set about scooping up kindling.

When they had all they could carry, Laura, Mary, and Devonte returned to camp. They set down their firewood next to Mr. Chavez, who was preparing the cookfire. Mr. Chavez made a show of surprise when Laura dropped her armful of branches, raising his bushy eyebrows and remarking on her strength. Laura knew he was only teasing her, but it made her feel good anyhow.

Before long, the aromas of supper were wafting across the camp. Mr. Chavez was always in charge of the cooking. Soon after leaving Hawkeye Crossing, though, Ma had started assisting him, and each night she seemed to assert herself more around the convoy's makeshift kitchen. Meals were richer for their collaboration. By agreement and tradition, most of what supplies people had brought with them on convoy were pooled together, and Ma and Mr. Chavez made the most of the varied ingredients. For Laura, each supper was a revelation, flavors new and familiar overlapping one upon the other.

After the sun had gone down, Captain Syed and the other Deshis unrolled their mats and went off to say their evening prayer. By the time they returned, the rest of the convoy was gathered around a roaring fire, and Mr. Chavez was ladling out bowls of a rich, sweet stew with barley from the stores in the back of the bisox wagon, apple leathers that Ma had pulled out of one of their barrels, and even a touch of honey from the Khans' hives.

Now was the time when the convoy would truly come alive.

On some nights, there was singing. The others had been delighted when they learned that Pa played the two-string, and, if there was fuel enough to keep the fires glowing after supper, they would often convince him to bring it out, shouting requests as he adjusted the two tuning pegs that stuck out from the instrument's skinny neck.

Other nights, they told stories. Some told stories about their lives. Others just told story stories.

Bill Keo told second type. The wispy-bearded bachelor was cagey about his life and his travels. But he was an enthusiastic teller of showtales.

"I don't reckon a couple sensible young ladies like you is interested at all in stories about the Batman," he said that night, as Laura and Mary passed by on their way to sit down beside the fire, bowls of apple barley stew in their hands.

He had seen Laura's carrysack and knew very well she was interested.

"I know all the Batman stories," she told him. "Pa's told them to me."

"Oh I see. Well then," said Bill Keo, shrugging in disappointment as he tucked his legs beneath him and blew theatrically across his bowl. "Don't mean to bore you. Suppose you know all about how the Batman saved the whales with help of his space friends."

Behind her, Laura heard Captain Syed snort.

"Saved the whats?" she said. "Bill, what nonsense are you telling those girls?"

As Bill Keo cackled to himself and slurped his stew, others gathered closer to listen. The Khans pulled their stools around to Bill Keo's side of the firepit. Bucky Malla and Caleb, who had been standing nearby eating their stew, both turned. Even Devonte Aguilar, whose parents seemed to disapprove of showtales, sat down beside Mary and Laura.

"Saved the *whales*, Priya," Bill Keo was saying. "Why, everybody knows it was the Batman that brought whales back to the sea after they'd all died out. How else do you think he calmed the Storm God's furies? Though, if you ask me, he couldn't have done it without the help of his space friends: Mighty Prime, the Lectric Man, and a clever moon goblin by the name of Spok. Those two don't get near their share of the credit, that's always been my view."

Space friends? Storm gods? Moon goblins? This didn't sound like any of the Batman's adventures that Laura knew about.

"There's no such thing as whales," Laura heard Devonte whisper to Mary in his know-it-all voice.

Bill Keo must have heard it too.

"Well there weren't until the Batman brought some back in his moonship," he said, waggling his spoon in Devonte's direction. "I can't believe not one of you has heard the story of the Batman and the whales. Don't you folks out west have any culture? Well, sit back a spell, and let Ol' Bill tell you how it goes."

HOW THE BATMAN AND HIS SPACE FRIENDS SAVED THE WHALES

"It was a time of great storms," he began.

"Deep in his bunker, Wane, the Batman of Gothim, was safe. But he knowed that up above people were suffering. Well, Wane the Batman, he brooded on that. He'd defeated countless enemies. Bandits and fiends and corrupt caudillos. But even a batman can't fight wind and rain, can he?

"He's just about fixing to despair. Those tall old towers of Gothim are sure to blow right over any moment, he figures. And then one day there's a knock at his bunker.

"Who could that be with these storms a-raging as they are? he thinks. Well, danged if it ain't the Batman's old friend, Spok. Now, Spok, if you ain't heard of him, he's from a people that live in a city up on the moon. Goblin I said? Well, fine, goblin if you like. He don't look like a regular fella, that's for sure. Like all moonmen, he's pale and short of stature, with pointy tips to his ears, sharp as daggers, and naught but three fingers on each hand.

"Well, the Batman knows it must be something important if

old Spok's come all the way down from the moon. And sure enough it is. Turns out Spok knows just what's been causing these terrible storms. Seems that something's got Thor in a right foul mood, he says.

"'Of course!' thinks the Batman. Why hadn't he thought to go see Thor sooner? He's the god of storms and such after all! If anyone's responsible for this calamitous weather, it'd have to be Thor.

"There's no time to lose, says Spok. He tells the Batman they ought to hop aboard his flying moonship right away, sail up to Thor's castle in the sky, and make him knock it off with the storms before he floods the whole blasted world.

"Right you are as always, my friend, says the Batman. Only this Thor, he's a tough character. Stronger than twenty men. And he's got a magic hammer what shoots lightning. We need help, says the Batman, and I've a notion just where we can find it.

"Now who do you suppose the Batman went to see next? Why, who else but his old friend, Prime the Lectric Man!

"You girls have heard of Prime, sure. No? Why, he's one of the greatest heroes of Old Merica! No sense of culture out west, and that's a fact.

"Mighty Prime! The Lectric Man! As tall as a house and made of solid iron. He looks like just a lectric wagon but with great brawny arms and legs and a pistol what shoots beams of white-hot flame, straight as arrows. Now does that sound like the kind of warrior Spok and the Batman want at their back when they fly up to Thor's castle? You bet your bottoms it is.

"Prime's from space too, legend goes. Some star or other. But in those days he lived here on Earth, in a cave on top of a mountain. And that's where Spok and the Batman find him. Meditating. Just a-waiting to be called to adventure.

"Prime! says the Batman when they get to the cave. We've got to get that rascal Thor to quit making these storms! Will you help us? I will, says Prime. And he grabs his flame pistol and off they go.

"So the three friends, they fly Spok's moonship up into space, straight towards the storm god's castle. It's a sight, that castle. Made of gleaming silver and hardmold as white as pearl. And it floats through the sky, circling the whole Earth round and round. On clear nights like this, if you know what to look for, sometimes you can still see it pass overhead, a-blink-blinking as it passes.

"When they get there, sure enough, there's Thor, standing right there on top one of the space castle's silver towers, whipping up those awful storms with his magic hammer. He's got a furious look on his face and just the craziest of crazy eyes. Right away, the heroes set down their moonship, and Prime rushes at Thor, thinking to tear that hammer away from him.

"But Thor's too strong! He swats the mighty lectric man away like he was a child and not a giant iron wagon with arms and legs and a flame pistol and all. Oh no, thinks Spok and the Batman, and they get ready for Thor to come for them too. Only, when the storm god turns towards them, he doesn't look angry. More sad-like. He doesn't attack them. He just kind of hangs his head and walks away.

"The three heroes, they watch him, wary. Thor climbs to the tip of a spire what juts up from the castle tower, just a-hanging out among the stars. There he sits. He sets his hammer down and pulls a flute from his cloak, and he begins to play.

"Now, the song that comes out, it ain't like a normal flute. Beautiful and sad, it was. It seemed to come from everywhere at once. Well, something about that sound tickles at the back of the Batman's mind. So he pulls his lectric handscreen from his belt. That screen knows everything or nearabouts. The Batman asks the screen, 'Screen, what is that song that Thor is playing?'

"'Why, that's the whale song,' the screen answers. 'When whales swam the oceans, the sea was filled with their song. It soothed the world and kept all nature in harmony.'

"Suddenly, the Batman thinks he knows what's got Thor in such a blasted rage. Screen, he asks, didn't these storms start just after the whales disappeared, right about the same time the oceans went silent? Sure enough they did, says the screen.

"The Batman calls out to Thor. 'God of thunder! If my friends and I can return the whales to the seas, will that quell your fury? Will you then forsake these terrible storms and let mankind once more live in peace?'

"'You have my word,' says Thor.

"So the heroes climb back aboard their moonship. That was some quick thinking, says Prime, but where are we going to find some whales from? I thought they all died a long time ago.

"I've got an idea, says Spok. We'll fly the moonship backwards! All the way around the Earth, so fast that we'll fly back through time. Then we'll scoop up a couple of those whales, fly forwards to right now, and plunk them back into the ocean.

"What are you grumbling about back there, Priya? You heard me. Backwards through time. You ever flown in a moonship? Then how do you know that's not how they work?

"Anyway, that's just what they do. They fly backwards around the Earth. Faster and faster, until finally Spok reckons they've gone back far enough. Then they sail back home, back to Gothim. Only when they get there, it's all changed. The towers are all aglow with lectric light. The streets are full of lectric cars and wagons, just driving around all by themselves. Why, it seems the Batman and his space friends have gone and flown themselves all the way back to Lectric Times.

"Prime decides he ought to try to blend in, so he tucks his arms and legs into his body so he looks like just a regular lectric wagon. Spok and the Batman climb inside, and together they drive around Old Lectric Gothim looking for someone who can tell them where to get ahold of some whales.

"Well, it ain't long before the Batman sees something what makes him tell Prime to hit the reins quick. There's a set of gates up ahead. The Batman, he recognizes this place. They're standing in front of the entrance to Zoo, a great big old palace what the Mericans built, full of gardens and a famous menagerie with two of every kind of animal thre is.

"Now, the Zoo of Gothim was abandoned during the Hard Years, and the Batman, he knows it only from the ruins. But back in Lectric Times, rich Merican folks would all pour into Zoo to spend their leisure days, strolling the gardens and gawking at beasts brought in from the farthest corners of the Empire. The Batman and his friends watch the crowds swarming all about. There's all sorts of activity. And what's this Zoo got out front but a great big painting of a whale!

"So in they go, through the gates of Zoo. They pass tigers and monkeys and unicorns and all sorts of strange animals what you'd never even have heard of. Finally they find the place where they keep all the fish and other water critters. They've got this pool, see, big as a lake. The Batman and his friends step up to the edge of the pool to take a closer look. And wouldn't you know it but there's a pair of whales swimming around down there!

"Now there's only two problems. For one, Zoo is crawling with guards. How are they going to sneak those whales out without anyone's notice? For two, whales are big. Real big. No way they're going to fit inside Spok's little moonship.

"So the heroes get to planning. They leave and wait for dark. Then, late that night, Prime races back to Zoo, still pretending to be just an ordinary lectric wagon. The gates are closed and locked now, but Prime just drives himself straight into them and busts them right down. The Zoo guards on nightwatch all start shouting and chasing Prime around, but they can't catch him. The Lectric Man's too fast.

"Meanwhile, out hops the Batman, and he goes about opening cages. Pretty soon there's bears and monkeys and all the rest running loose all over, and you've never heard such a ruckus. The guardsmen, they're having a time of it, trying to round up those animals, so Prime and the Batman manage to sneak off to the whale pool. There, the Batman opens a door in the back of Prime's wagon, and he pulls out the giant net that the three friends have spent all day weaving.

"The Batman dives into the pool, trailing the net behind him. Beneath the water, he can hear the whales' song, rising and falling. He swims up to them. 'Mankind needs your help,' he says to them. The song changes pitch, and the Batman knows the whales have understood. He swims in circles around them, wrapping them in the net. Then he grabs a corner and swims back to the surface.

"The Batman pops his head out of the water. There in the sky, it's Spok in his flying ship. Spok sails down to the Batman. The Batman attaches the net to a hook on the bottom of the moonship. Then he and Prime get aboard, and the ship sails away. Now, if you can picture a sparrow who's caught himself a trout, then you can begin to imagine what Spok's little moonship looked like, climbing into the air with that net dangling beneath it, holding as it did two giant whales!

"Back up into space they fly. Then around the Earth. Forward this time. Faster and faster. Until they arrive back into their own time, whales and all.

"The Batman and his friends drop the whales into the sea. They watch the two mighty beasts swim away, singing their whale song all the while. And then, from somewhere up above, another song rises in answer. The Batman looked up to see the blinking light of Thor's castle passing overhead, like a shooting star in slow motion. The notes from the sea and the notes from the sky came together in harmony.

"From that day forward, the storms grew quieter. And whales once again roamed the oceans, protecting mankind from the heavens' wrath. All thanks to the Batman and his amazing space friends."

TWENTY: THE GHOST CITY OF DAMOYNE

Laura's teeth rattled as the bisox wagon clattered over a rough patch of creetrock. The rest of the convoy, following in her wake, became a jittering blur.

After so many months of travel, Laura was a very good walker. But on the straight, flat Eighty Road, the convoy was able to cover more miles each day than her short legs were used to. Pa had protested at first when Captain Syed suggested that Laura and Mary ride on the back of the bisox wagon, but Mr. Chavez insisted that the two girls combined weighed less than a single sack of barley and that Pretty and Penny would never know the difference.

It was fun at first, to sit on the back of the big car, her legs dangling over the road as the great hairy bisox tugged her along. After a day or two, though, the thrill had worn off. Laura was growing fidgety, and her bottom hurt from all the jouncing. On their next stop, she decided, she ask if she could walk again for a while.

She did not have to wait long, for it was not yet midday when the convoy abruptly halted. They had come to a creek that ran right across the Eighty Road. It was shallow enough to ford, but the waters were rapid.

After some discussion, it was decided that any excess weight should be removed and carried across individually, and Mary and Laura were the first cargo expelled from the bisox car. Laura hopped down, grateful for the chance to stretch her legs.

As the rest of the convoy set about unloading or bolting down their belongings and applying fresh coats of wax or tallow to the wheels and bottoms of their cars, Laura decided she would go inspect this creek and maybe dip her fingers into the cool water.

As soon as she stepped out from behind the bisox wagon, however, she suddenly stopped. In the distance before her, where the Eighty Road seemed to narrow and vanish, rose enormous jagged shapes.

They were old Merican towers, bigger and more numerous than Laura had ever laid eyes on. They must have appeared on the horizon some time ago, but they had been invisible to Laura, seated backwards as she was on the bisox wagon.

The ruins were still a good ways off, but already the towers dominated the landscape. The tallest was a skinny tower that seemed to list slightly to the side. Its top was cleaved by a wide gash, and what remained hung bent and splayed around its peak like a ragged crown. Beside it was a second tower, slightly shorter than its neighbor but much wider about the base. On either side of the twin monoliths, a dozen or more lesser peaks of varying shapes rose and fell, stark against the smooth Yowa countryside.

"Mary!" Laura called out. "There it is! Da— Dommin— Dom—"

"Damoyne."

Laura looked up to find Devonte Aguilar standing beside her, shading his eyes as he too stared out towards the ruins. Laura felt a swell of irritation at his know-it-all tone. A moment later, Mary squeezed in between them.

"Father says it was a great city once, like Gothim or Shicago," Devonte said, studying the towers. "The Supervisor of Damoyne ruled over the whole Yowa, all the lands between the Suri and the Misisip. He lived in a great palace with five golden domes. The palace still stands. Father knows a man that's seen it."

Laura had seen Daymoyne marked out on Pa's map and knew that the Great Eighty Road passed nearby, skirting just north of the old ghost city. There had been talk around the cookfire that morning about the ruins and what precautions the convoy must take to pass around them in safety. But this was the first Laura was hearing of golden domes.

"Oh," she said, trying to sound uninterested.

"Father says the Supervisor of Damoyne rebelled against the

Merican Prezdent. A great battle was fought here. As we near the city, we may see signs of it. Have you ever seen a Merican warcar?"

"Bunches," said Laura, though she hadn't.

"Some had guns as big as chimneys," Devonte went on. "Mounted right on their tops. Just a few shots from a warcar's gun could knock down whole towers. *Pow. Pow. Pow.*"

"Then how come those towers are still there if you're so smart?" Laura retorted.

Devonte made an annoying show of growing somber.

"By the plan of the Prezdent Above. Father says He left them here for us, that we might look upon them and reflect on man's pride and the futility of his works."

Mary made a thoughtful humming sound as if this was the wisest thing she had ever heard. Laura bit her tongue to stop herself from saying something mean. The Aguilars were devout Lacorians, she had learned. Pa said that Mr. Aguilar had been a conduit back in the settlement where they had come from. That was why they had left, Pa seemed to think, though Laura didn't really understand what one thing had to do with the other.

The Aguilars had been close-lipped at first about their faith, and no one talked about it. The further west they traveled, however, the less guarded the Aguilars became. Recently, Mr. Aguilar had taken to reading every evening by lantern light from a thick book full of ragged parchment pages, bound in a plain leather cover. It was called *The Letters of Deshawn Lacore*. Anyone who wanted to listen was welcome, and Ma had started attending the reading nearly every night.

Laura had listened once, mostly because Mary had wanted to. Laura thought she probably just wanted to sit next to Devonte.

Laura had been bored to the point of anger by *The Letters of Deshawn Lacore*. She had expected something like Tobias Goatherd's story about the fantastic white alligator that haunted the swamps of the Lost City of Norlins. Instead, Mr. Aguilar's story was hardly a story at all, just a bunch of words. Laura wasn't sure if this man Deshawn Lacore was really a prophet like people said, but he sure repeated himself a lot.

One day, Mary had told Devonte about visiting the Herald's Shrine. She probably thought that he'd be impressed, but Devonte had seemed dismissive, even offended. He proceeded to lecture them on what his father had to say about the Prophet's childhood and about shrines and so on. He said that people like Tobias Goatherd weren't true Lacorians at all. When Laura asked what the difference was, though, he couldn't explain.

That was Devonte Aguilar all over, Laura thought. Lots of high and mighty talk, but when you pressed him, he didn't know half as much as he pretended. Still, as the three of them stood there beside the bisox wagon, waiting for the convoy to proceed, Laura couldn't help taking one more look out towards the ruins of Damoyne, hoping to see some hint of a golden-domed palace.

~~~

Eventually, when all the cargo had been removed or bolted down, the convoy began to ford the creek. First, items were carried across individually on foot. Laura watched Pa wade into the creek with two barrels hoisted one on each shoulder. At its deepest point, the water rose nearly to Pa's waist, and Laura worried he would be swept away. A moment later, though, he was emerging on the other side and setting his load down on the dry creetrock bank.

The water was too deep for Laura and Mary, and so Pa carried them across as well. As she clung to Pa's back, her feet dangling down into the rushing water, Laura looked back and was surprised to see Bill Keo splashing through the creek behind them with one of the Khans' beehives balanced atop his shaggy head. Little black dots buzzed and swarmed around him. Laura could even see a few clinging to the man's cheeks. Bill Keo growled some rough words to himself but kept a firm grip on the hive.

When the girls were safely ashore, Pa crossed back to retrieve the handcar. Laura watched him pull the car down into the creek, with Ma helping the steady and guide the wheels. Nearby, Devonte Aguilar and his father were dragging their own handcar through the rushing water. They had taken off their tunics, and Laura could see the identical crosses that were inked in dark blue on the center of both of their chests.

Laura looked over and saw that Mary was watching Devonte too. The boy seemed to take such pride in being tall and strong enough to help his father get their handcar across the creek that Laura couldn't help but grin when at one point he lost his footing and was dunked, handsome hair and all, beneath the cold water. He came up a moment later, gasping and sputtering and flailing for the side of the handcar. Laura turned to her sister, but the look on Mary's face was one of genuine concern, which spoiled Laura's fun.

When everyone and everything was across, Ma and Pa made Laura and Mary climb back onto the bisox car.

"You can walk for a spell once we're clear of the ruins," Pa told Laura when she protested. "You can't be too careful around such places."

The towers looming in the distance seemed to set everyone on edge. As they continued their journey, marching ever further down the Eighty Road towards the old ghost city, Laura noticed that the procession was eerily silent. With each passing kim, the convoy seemed to grow more tense and watchful.

Ma followed close in the tracks of the bisox wagon. In her hands was Pa's gun, which was unusual. She wasn't the only one armed, Laura noticed. A few paces behind her, the guardsman Caleb kept his weapon aloft and ready, its bayonet flashing whenever it caught the midday sun.

Bucky Malla and Captain Syed walked ahead of the bisox for the most part, invisible to Laura, but occasionally they hung back, patrolling the convoy's flanks even more vigilantly than normal. Bucky Malla's rifle was unshouldered as well. His bayonet was shorter and less polished than Caleb's, but it had a toothy edge that gave it a meaner, more savage look. For Captain Syed's part, whenever she paced into Laura's field of view, the woman's long coat always seemed to be pulled to the side, her one hand resting on the handle of her pistol, which peeked up from her thick leather belt, holstered but unbuckled.

Even Bill Keo seemed on alert. He and Dog walked silently down the road, drawing up the rear behind the Khan cousins and their hives. Beneath his wispy black beard, his mouth was curled into its typical smirk, but Laura noted that his long felling ax was gripped in his fists instead of strapped down through his carrysack as it usually was.

As the bisox car continued to rattle along, facing backwards became more intolerable than ever to Laura. She kept trying to crane her neck around to catch a glimpse of the Damoyne towers that she knew must be rising bigger and bigger up ahead.

Yet, before long, even Laura's rearward vantage offered her plenty to look at. The scenery slowly rolling into her periphery began to change. More and more Merican ruins began to appear beside the Eighty Road. They were isolated and unremarkable at first—here a toppled iron column, there a roofless creetrock cabin—the sort of things that one expected to find sprouting along all the old number roads.

By the time midday turned to afternoon, however, the abandoned works of Old Merica were all around them. The empty creetrock buildings grew taller, and they clustered more tightly together. There was no doubt now that the convoy was passing through what had once been the site of a settlement of fantastic size.

Eventually, the Damoyne towers themselves made their way into Laura's view. She had to lean out of the wagon at first, but soon she could see them just by turning her head. They loomed larger now than they had at the creek, and Laura could make out their individual windows, staring out towards the convoy like rows of empty eye sockets.

The Eighty Road continued to give the heart of the old ghost city a respectful berth. The towers now stood due south by Laura's reckoning, close but not too close. Before long, the convoy would pass right by them, and the towers would begin to recede.

Yet, though the Eighty Road seemed determined to lead them

well north of the tallest ruins, that did not mean that the convoy had steered clear of Old Damoyne entirely. The further west they went, the more the roadside filled with evidence of the ghost city's former grandeur. Ruins covered the landscape, heaped upon one another so close that hardly a bit of the Yowa countryside could be seen beneath. Instead of grass and trees, the Great Eighty Road now led the convoy through fields of brick and creetrock, through groves of hardmold and iron. Old Merican structures were everywhere, one level or two or even more. Most had collapsed, leaving behind the craggy remains of walls, with valleys of rubble lying between. Lectric cars of every shape and size lay in piles. Everywhere that Laura looked, she saw toppled columns, tangled nests of iron rope, and all manner of lectric wreckage that Laura couldn't even begin to identify.

More than once, she found herself leaning out of the bisox car to catch a glimpse of a towering Merican signpost, still standing defiantly atop its tall iron pole, even after so many years of neglect. Mostly the faces of the enormous skyward signs were a rust-covered blank, their messages lost to time, but sometimes Laura thought she could make out the faded outlines of lettering. At one point, a huge slab of pinkish hardmold appeared above her. Outlined upon its surface were the head and shoulders of white-faced man, who grinned benevolently out across the ruins from behind a trim white beard that framed his gray-blue lips.

The convoy's progress slowed as lectric rubble increasingly clogged the road. Sometimes, they had to leave the Great Eighty Road entirely, following rough side paths in order to bypass the obstructions.

It was mid-afternoon when they came to another of these detours. Laura felt the bisox car slow and eventually come to a stop. Somewhere up ahead, Captain Syed was shouting instructions. Then, Laura felt the heavy wagon begin to turn. As they gradually wheeled around, Laura caught a glimpse of the road ahead. The Eighty Road seemed to rise slightly before disappearing over a sheer cliff. It looked to be the remains of an old bridge, and Laura assumed at first that they had come to

215

another creek or river. Yet, when she strained her ears, listening for the rush of water, she couldn't hear any.

The bisox pulled the wagon down a side trail, off the Great Eighty. The trail was bumpy. Laura and her sisters had to hang on tight to one another and to the sides of the wagon to avoid getting bounced right out. Slowly, they clattered their way down into a shallow ravine. There, Captain Syed called a halt to wait for the rest of the convoy. Ma and Pa and some of the others were having difficulty with the side trail, the smaller wheels of their handcars struggling over the uneven terrain.

At the bottom of the ravine was another old number road that had once crossed the Great Eighty Road. It ran north, climbing up out of the canyon before curving away from view. Once, it seemed, this second road had tunneled right underneath the Eighty Road. Now, the route was impassible. Just a few meters away from where the convoy now gathered was an impenetrable wall of rubble. The crossroads' passageway was now filled up with the remnants of the creetrock bridge that had collapsed from above.

Laura heard Mr. Chavez climb down from the front of the car to soothe and water the bisox. Pretty and Penny grunted and shuffled their feet. Their noises echoed against the walls of the rubble-choked corridor. Up above she could hear Mr. Aguilar's voice shouting "steady" as the handcars continued to make their way down the trail into the ravine.

Laura stood up in the back of the bisox wagon and leaned out, looking around. All around her, the afternoon sun bathed the old road in whites as pale as milkpaint. But, just ahead, shadows fell upon what remained of the corridor where one old number road had once leapfrogged over the other. There, sheltered from daylight by the walls of the narrow canyon that split the road above in two, a thicket of creetrock slabs and iron beams lay shrouded in darkness.

Laura found herself staring into the dark recesses of the rubble. The broken, intersecting shapes seemed to harbor a hundred little caves and tunnels.

216

Then, suddenly, she saw something move. Something crawled over the rubble, out from one crevice and into another. Something big.

Laura's nails dug into the wooden post that held up the bisox wagon's canvas roof. She spun around to see if Mary had seen it, but Mary was occupied with Baby Grace, cooing into the infant's face to stop her fussing.

When Laura turned back towards the passageway, the thing was gone. She wiped the back of her hand across her eyes and looked again, wondering for a moment if she might have imagined it. But no. The pale shape had been too vivid, its movements too precise. She looked around. Bucky Malla was standing nearby, observing the convoy's progress down the hill. Laura's mouth felt dry and stiff, but she somehow managed to force her lips to form the words.

"Mr. Malla!" she cried.

The big, smooth-headed man turned. When he saw Laura pointing towards the rubble, he stiffened. The barrel of his rifle jerked upwards in the direction of the collapsed bridge.

"Priya!" he said in a soft but pointed voice.

Immediately, Captain Syed's whistle rose sharp and shrill from nearby. At her gesture, the handcars coming down the trail stopped where they were. No one spoke. No one moved. Even Baby Grace stopped fussing. The ravine fell quiet. The whole convoy waited and listened.

Then came the *crunch crunch* of Bucky Malla's boots across the creetrock gravel. He crossed the threshold of shadow and approached the obstructed passageway, gun raised. Methodically, he patrolled around the rubble, peeking into crevices, nudging fragments aside with his bayonet. Eventually, he turned around and shrugged.

"Clear!" he called to Captain Syed.

Finally, Captain Syed whistled again, and the convoy's stragglers resumed their trek down the hillside.

Meanwhile, people gathered around Laura. Captain Syed and Bucky Malla at first, then gradually joined by Ma and Pa and the rest as they made it down to the bottom of the ravine. Laura told them what she'd seen. Then she had to tell it again and then again as others arrived, so many times she began to get confused between the memory and the telling of it, until the whole thing felt very muddled and uncertain.

"Wolfdog most like," Bucky Malla reckoned. "There's dens all over the ghost cities. Probably coming round to get a sniff of the bisox. The packs prowling Old Oma will venture out to nab livestock from the ranches 'round Lildaka from time to time. Bolder every year, if the talk around the market's to be believed."

Still, he kept a close watch on the rubble as the convoy assembled on the canyon floor and an even closer watch once they began to move again, with Mr. Chavez and the bisox leading the slow procession up the dirt trail on the other side.

Laura kept watching too, scanning the shadows for any further sign of movement. Once the wagon began to rattle back up the hill, though, it became difficult to fix her gaze on any one place. She gripped tight to Mary's arm and closed her eyes.

It took even longer to get all the cars back up to the top of the ravine than it had to get them down, but finally the convoy all gathered again atop the Great Eighty Road, ready to move on. The sun was getting low in the sky by then, but Captain Syed said that the worst of the old city was behind them. The road ought to open up from there out, she told them. They'd make better time now and be clear of the ruins by nightfall.

The bisox car rattled along, jostling Laura away from the old ghost city. But, even as the towers began to grow smaller and smaller in the eastern horizon, Laura couldn't shake the feeling she had felt back at the crossroads. Every time the car drove over a rough patch, causing her view of the road behind to shake and blur, she saw that rubble-choked passageway. She remembered the shape in the shadows, remembered the way it moved, clambering over one pile of creetrock to duck behind another.

It did not look like a dog to Laura.

TWENTY-ONE: THE FLOODED VILLAGE

The afternoon was quickly waning, but the convoy was now making better time. As the Great Eighty Road continued to lead them westward, past the sprawling ruins of Damoyne, there were fewer lectric cars, fewer iron signposts, less nameless lectric clutter lying in piles and creeping across their path. The hollow houses and crumbling creetrock walls that lay alongside the Eighty Road began to shrink, and the great leaning towers of Old Damoyne began to recede ever further.

Captain Syed had assured them that they would be clear of the ghost city by nightfall. When she called an end to the day's march, however, it did not feel as if the convoy was free of the abandoned lectric city completely. With the sun hanging low and red in the sky before them and dusk threatening to envelop the Eighty Road, the echoes of Old Damoyne were still all around them. To the southeast, its towers were still visible. Indeed, as the sun retreated, their shadows only grew more stark upon the horizon, cutting fangs into the purple sky.

The ruins that radiated from the city's center had never disappeared entirely either. Remnants of Merican structures still pockmarked the landscape in small clusters.

Eventually, the convoy came to a gravel trail that intersected the Eighty Road. A short distance to the south, according to Captain Syed, lay a stream where they could take on fresh water. There, they would make camp for the night. And so, wheels creaking, the bisox car turned down the path that Captain Syed had indicated, and the rest of the convoy fell in behind.

The trail led them past rows of roofless creetrock houses. Empty doorways and windows gaped in upon courtyards overgrown with gnarled vegetation, their foliage gray and inscrutable in the twilight. Finally, in a flat clearing encircled by these sorts of ruins, they stopped. Mr. Chavez unharnessed the bisox, and everyone began to set down their loads.

The stream that Captain Syed had promised could be heard murmuring nearby, and Mary and Laura were sent down with Devonte to gather wood from the trees that grew along its banks. When Laura reached the stream, she was surprised to find more ruins standing right in the middle of the water. Upstream and down, the water meandered undaunted through a maze of old walls and columns.

Laura wanted to get a better look, so she set down her armload of kindling and hoisted herself onto a tree branch that hung over the current's edge. She scooted forward on the branch and leaned out to inspect the ruins that lay upstream. There, the water flowed through a large brick building with three intact walls. Daylight was quickly disappearing, but, as she stared and let her eyes adjust, Laura could see how the stream pooled up behind the building and spilled out in a burbling torrent through its half-sunken doors.

Devonte Aguilar had hopped up onto a low creetrock wall which jutted out into the water and now stood there atop his narrow perch, also admiring the flooded ruins.

"The river must've moved since Lectric Times," he announced to Mary and Laura, making a great show of maintaining his balance as he tip-toed further out onto the creetrock wall.

Laura was always reluctant to acknowledge that Devonte might be right about something, but she supposed his theory made more sense than someone building their house right in the middle of a stream.

Laura swung back down to the ground. She was crouching down to pick up her bundle of kindling when she heard Devonte splashing in the water. For a moment, Laura hoped that he had lost his balance showing off for Mary and fallen in, but when she looked up she saw that his pants legs were rolled up. He appeared to be deliberately wading into the cold stream. Mary watched from the bank as Devonte leaned down, digging something up from the mud.

"Hello! What's this?"

Devonte raised his hand up high. There was something in it. Laura came closer to see what it was, stepping down to the water's edge beside Mary. The sun had just set, but the moon was already rising big and full above them, making the stream's ripples glitter. Moonlight glinted through the glass object that Devonte held aloft. It was a drinking cup with a long stem, wrought in pure lectricmade glass. Devonte wiped the cup down with the hem of his tunic, rinsed it in the stream and held it up again. It shined even brighter, smooth crystal curves shimmering as Devonte twirled it in his fingers.

"It's beautiful," said Mary, and even Laura had to admit it was a very fine cup.

Playfully, Devonte bowed to them. Placing a hand behind his back, he dipped the glass cup into the stream and then raised it towards them.

"A toast to the Ingalls sisters," he said, adopting a tone of teasing formality. "The most elegant ladies in the Golden City of Damoyne."

Even in the dim moonlight, Laura could see that the contents of the cup were murkier than she would have drunk, but Devonte either didn't care or had come too far with his joke not to follow through. With another dignified nod, he raised the gleaming cup to his lips and drank down every drop of that river water.

~~~

Ma helped Mr. Chavez prepare supper that night, a gravy full of dried peppers and herbs and served over soymeal biscuits. The convoy seemed in good spirits, relieved to have made it safely past the haunted old city. By tomorrow, they would likely reach the supervisory at Badger Creek. With luck, they might be in Lildaka in little more than a week. In the City of Mounds, the merchants would offload their cargo and the settlers would begin looking for their homesteads.

With the fat round moon lighting up their camp and plenty of

221

wood to burn, the convoy lingered longer than usual around the firepit. The smell of pipeleaf, earthy and sour, began to mingle with the smoke of the campfire. Bill Keo reached deep into his giant carrysack and pulled out an old hardmold bottle plugged up with a wooden stopper. Declaring he'd squirreled away a few drops of doju for just such a night, he passed the bottle around, though most of the others declined the pungent liquor.

Finally, though the hour was late, someone convinced Pa to bring out his two-string. Ma made sure that Laura and Mary were tucked in atop their bed rolls but said that they could stay up and listen, at least for a little while.

It was Bill Keo that took the lead on the first song. Laura was surprised to find that, despite the raspy timbre with which the man spoke, his singing voice was not unpleasant.

I remember when we used to sit
Round the displacement camp in Hewstown
And my friend Georgie would make the fire light
As if it was log wood burning through the night

Then we would cook soymeal porridge
Of which I'll share with you
My feet is my only carriage
So I've got to push on through

But while I'm gone
Everything is gonna be alright
Everything is gonna be alright
Everything is gonna be alright

It was not a song that Laura had ever heard, but Pa didn't miss a note. He knew all the old standards.

Next, Janice Khan led them in a few rounds of *Annie, Are You Ok?*. As soon as that was done, Pa launched into *So Sorry Ms. Jackson*. Finally, Pa rested his bow for a spell, and, as sleep's first caresses began to blur her senses and jumble her thoughts, Laura listened to the hushed conversation of the adults gathered around the dwindling fire and, more faintly, to the gurgle of the nearby stream making its way through the flooded village.

~~~

Something was wrong. Laura knew it before she opened her eyes. Before her dreams had faded completely, before she even remembered where she was, she felt the tension in the air.

Laura rolled over, blinking away the sleep. It was still night. The moon had climbed higher in the sky. It was just as round and bright, but it felt further off. The glow it cast across the campsite had grown colder and more fickle.

Pa was sitting up. His gun was in his hands. Nearby, Jack growled. Laura watched the pigdog's silhouette pace, sniff the air, then growl again.

When Pa saw that she was awake, he reached down and touched her shoulder. Then he put a finger to his lips. Trying not to move too much or too fast, Laura raised her head. A short distance away stood a big broad-shouldered figure that could only be Bucky Malla. Moonlight glinted off his bald head. From the shadows, someone whispered something to him. The big man shushed at the voice, waving his arm in irritation.

Bucky Malla faced a ring of disjointed brick walls that lay along the edge of the camp. Shadebush and spindly birch trees had grown up around them, consuming sections of the walls within their branches and toppling other sections with their roots. In the dark, the ruins and the vegetation seemed to form a single misshapen structure. Bucky Malla crept slowly towards this thicket of darkness, bayonet raised high.

Then, everything seemed to happen all at once, with such chaos and fury that Laura couldn't separate cause and effect.

"Bandits!" Bucky Malla bellowed.

His rifle exploded, deafening. Was it before he shouted or just after? Or had he fired twice? Laura couldn't say. But when the burst of flame erupted from the gun's barrel, that was when she glimpsed for the briefest instant several pale figures creeping among the bushes.

Suddenly, the whole convoy was awake. Voices were raised from every corner of the camp. In the darkness, there was a tremendous clanging as someone tripped over a stack of pots and pans. Somewhere, a lantern was lit. Its beams careened wildly around the clearing, this way and that, adding to the confusion.

Laura tried to rise, but Pa pushed her back down. Mary and Ma and Baby Grace were beside her by then. All of them crouched, huddled together. Pa's rifle jerked back and forth in uncertain semi-circles, unsure which direction danger might come from.

Ma and Pa closed in around Laura and her sisters. Shoulder to shoulder, her parents' bodies formed a barricade separating Laura from whatever madness had consumed the camp. But as they shuffled back and forth, trying to better position themselves, the smallest of gaps opened up between them.

And, through that gap, Laura saw. She saw people rushing towards Bucky Malla. Three of them. No, four. Five.

They lurched wildly towards him, limbs flailing. The moon and lantern light flashed across their pale skin. Two were naked. Scraps of clothing hung indifferently about the others, trailing from their bodies in tatters. These were not bandits, Laura thought. No, these were not bandits.

Bucky Malla fired again. One of his attackers staggered, knocked off course. The rest kept coming. He thrust his bayonet towards the nearest figure, plunging the blade deep into its stomach. As they struggled, the others leapt at him, tackling him to the ground.

"Fiends," Ma whispered, the end of the word strangled by a terrible sob. "Devils. Prezdent Above preserve us. I beg you."

Laura turned away, squeezing Mary's arm. Mary squeezed right back.

Bucky Malla was screaming. There was more gunfire. The sharp *pop* of Captain Syed's pistol. She was shouting. Everyone was shouting. And something else. Wails. Inarticulate and inhuman. Savage wails. Full of pain and blind rage.

"Ingalls!" someone cried.

In an instant, Pa was on his feet.

And then Laura saw it. It was rushing towards them. A man. Or something that had once been a man. He was close enough that Laura could see the silver-gray of the cloak that still clung around his throat, could see the sores on his face, could see the crazed expression in his yellow eyes.

Pa's gun fired, and for a moment the chaotic sounds of the campsite vanished beneath the ringing in Laura's ears. She saw but didn't hear the fiend twist and drop to the ground, only to pull itself back to its knees and stumble onward. She saw but didn't hear Pa strike the fiend with the butt of his rifle, kick it in the ribs to stop its furious scratching, and pin its arm beneath his boot as he shoved the barrel of his gun against its skull.

She covered her eyes just in time to hear but not see the blast of Pa's rifle as it went off a second time.

~~~

Never had dawn been so slow to come.

Huddled there between Mary and Ma, it seemed to Laura as if the familiar rhythms of night and day had been broken forever, as if the warm sunlit world she thought she remembered was nothing but a distant dream, far too faint to ever overthrow the infinite dark in which she now lived. No one spoke. Pa would stand sometimes, pace, speak softly with someone before crouching back down beside them. Otherwise, they simply waited. Waited and listened with a lingering, tedious dread. It was this dread that made Laura feel that this night, unlike all the nights that had come before, might never end.

Yet, finally, morning did come. The black sky gradually turned an ashy gray. Shapes began to differentiate themselves from the shadows. Outlines of the vine-covered ruins that ringed the camp emerged sharper and sharper against the dawn horizon. Further off, the row of trees that marked the course of the stream showed themselves once more.

At some point, the scales tipped, and now it was night that seemed a fantasy, its terrors unthinkable in this new world where birds chirped and soft clouds drifted peacefully against an ever-bluer sky.

As the camp brightened, the convoy took stock of its causualties. Oprah Khan had twisted an ankle, and Mr. Chavez had been cut by Caleb's bayonet as the young guardsman swung wildly at an approaching fiend.

But these injuries were nothing compared to what had happened to Bucky Malla.

Once the immediate danger had passed, the others had dragged the big Deshi trader towards the center of camp, laying him out near the firepit. He had screamed in pain as they moved him, but, afterward, he had quieted, making only the occasional moan or feverish murmur. Mr. Chavez sat beside him, trying and failing to produce a fire from spent coals and what scraps remained of their woodpile.

Bucky Malla still lay there as dawn rose over the camp. Laura was not allowed near him, but even from afar it was plain that he was badly hurt. His face was bruised and beaten, one eye swollen shut, and he seemed unable to sit up straight. At one point, Laura heard him gasp in pain. She looked over and saw that Mr. Chavez was trying to roll up Bucky Malla's tunic sleeve. The sleeve was sticky with blood. As his meaty arm came into view, Laura could see the dark crescents where the fiends had bitten him.

The convoy's cargo was untouched, for the intruders had come for flesh, not silver. Frightened by the chaos, Penny the bisox had torn free of her hitching but was soon found a half-kim downstream.

As for the men and women who had attacked them—it was easier now, beneath the light of day, to think of them as men and women—they were eventually all gathered into a pile behind an old creetrock wall for burning.

Mr. and Ms. Aguilar protested that the bodies should be buried, but Captain Syed wouldn't allow it. Their sickness might make its way into the groundwater, she said, maybe even sneak into the stream and glide downriver like a poisonous water snake towards the Badger Creek settlement.

So instead Mr. Aguilar said a prayer over the dead men and

women, while Pa and Bill Keo hauled wood up from the riverbank to place beneath the bodies. Ma went to the handcar and pulled out a few pinecones dipped in tallow to use as tinder.

There had been seven of them all told. The five that had swarmed over Bucky Malla, the one that Pa had killed and another that had tried to creep into camp from the opposite direction only to be cut down by Bill Keo's ax. As Laura watched the bodies being dragged off one by one, she found herself thinking back on the showtales where great swarms of fiends, hundreds or more, might descend upon a village all at once, only to be fought off by a team of courageous batmen who arrive just in time.

Whether there were a hundred of them or just seven, though, you always heard about fiends attacking in groups. Only after seeing it firsthand did it occur to Laura how peculiar that was. Why should people with the Ague stick together? Was it their disease that made them seek one another out? Or was it rather that, even after so much of their humanity had fled, there remained deep within them some need for community?

Laura knew that this was not the time to be thinking such thoughts, but she couldn't shake them away. She was still wrestling with them when Captain Syed announced that the convoy must move on.

Bucky Malla was in no shape to travel. His eye, the one that was not swollen shut, was alert, but he seemed unable to rise. Wrapped in a blanket, he lay propped upright against a rock. Even though the sun was well risen by now and a healthy blaze had finally been coaxed from the firepit beside him, the man continued to shiver.

Captain Syed said that she too would stay behind until Mr. Malla was able to walk, and she instructed Mr. Chavez to lead the convoy onwards towards Lildaka as quickly as possible. They left the two of them there in the clearing as the first wisps of a foul-smelling smoke began to rise from behind the ruins.

They would catch up with the rest of the convoy later, once Bucky Malla was feeling better. That was what Laura kept telling herself that morning as the bisox wagon rattled down the Eighty Road. And so it was with surprise that, just a few hours later, she spotted Captain Syed's silhouette on the horizon, striding rapidly after the convoy, her long coat flapping in the wind. She was alone.

Mr. Chavez called a halt to wait for her. When she approached, she gave the bisox driver a curt, grim-faced nod. Mr. Chavez seemed to understand. He nodded back and removed his hat. Pa did likewise, and Mr. Aguilar tapped his chest in the spot where the ink cross marked his skin.

Nothing more was said of it.

TWENTY-TWO: BADGER CREEK

The whole convoy was quiet, but no one was quieter than Caleb the Ortega guardsman. As they approached the crossroads to Badger Creek, the young man's silence stood out, even amid all the other silences.

Yesterday, Caleb could not stop talking about the Badger Creek supervisory and the first things he would do when he returned. Laura had heard him telling Bill Keo all about the fort where he was posted. It lay west of the ruins of Damoyne, a few kims south of the Eighty Road, keeping peace among the settlements scattered along the rivers and streams that branched across that part of the Yowa. He described all the things he'd brought back from Davenport for his friends in the Badger Creek garrison. A pouch of good pipeleaf for Hal and the boys. An old paperbook for Shauna the Doctor, who knew her letters and would read to the guardsmen some nights in the fort's common hall. A little wooden wolfdog, painted in vibrant colors, for the supervisor's young son.

That was yesterday. Whatever Caleb's thoughts were now, he kept them to himself. He trudged wordlessly down the road, staring straight ahead, into the empty distance.

It was around midday, soon after Captain Syed had caught up with the convoy and Bucky Malla had not, that they reached the crossroads. The road that led south was rough and narrow, made of dirt and creetrock gravel, but it seemed well traveled. On a nearby hill, there was a watchtower. A silver-gray flag with the red bisox of Clan Ortega still hung limply from its ramparts, but the little square perch on top, shaded beneath a crinkled iron sheet, stood deserted.

Captain Syed called a halt.

Looking up at the abandoned watchtower, the creases in Caleb's brow deepened. Laura felt as if she could practically see the lump rise in his throat. Finally, he squinted down the road south, adjusting the shoulder straps of his carrysack.

"Well, I suppose this is where I leave you folks," he said.

The words had a forced gaiety and trailed off into a nervous chuckle.

Captain Syed announced that she meant to accompany the young man back to his garrison to see if she couldn't exchange a word or two with the Badger Creek supervisor.

"Fort's not a far walk as I recollect," she said. "Why don't you all just rest yourselves here a spell beneath them trees, get some food in your bellies. I won't be long."

Captain Syed turned to Pa then.

"I hate to ask this, Ingalls," she said. "You mind tagging along with us to the fort? If you feel you ought to stay with your family, I won't press you. But you're our ablest shot now that Buck… that he's no longer with us, *Allah yarhemuhu*. And, well, I'd just feel a might better knowing we've got your rifle at our backs."

Pa looked at Ma. She didn't say anything. She didn't move her head in one direction or the other. But her eyes said "no."

The tiniest shadow of a grimace passed over Pa's lips.

"Of course," he said. He wheeled the handcar to the side of the road and shouldered his rifle.

"Hector, convoy's yours," said Captain Syed. "Two hours, you understand? Let's say two and a half at most. Then you call it no matter. That clear? We'll catch up down the road if we have to."

Laura stiffened at that, thinking how they had left Bucky Malla behind. He too was supposed to catch up down the road.

Mr. Chavez only nodded. He squinted up at the sky as if taking a mental reading of the sun's position. Meanwhile, Captain Syed, Caleb, and Pa all started south, down the road towards Badger Creek.

~~~

There was an unopened barrel of dried turnips in the back of the bisox car. Mr. Chavez scooped up piles of the shriveled, salty turnip chips onto plates and handed them around, along with a helping of saltmeat and soymeal crackers.

When Ma handed her a plate, Laura thought at first that she would surely break her teeth. She had grown to hate the hard, dry soymeal crackers that the convoy ate so often, and the turnip chips seemed like they would be little better. Laura gnawed on one experimentally, twisting and pulling it between her jaws, unable to bite off a manageable chunk.

But then Mr. Chavez passed around tin bowls of apple core vinegar. The amber liquid was mixed with spices, and a dark puddle of fermented soy paste floated on top. When Laura dipped the turnip slices into the vinegar, they softened and plumped.

She flinched in surprise when she bit into one of the vinegar-soaked chips. The bold sour taste made her face pucker. Yet Laura soon decided she liked the sensation, and she began soaking up as much sauce as she could with each slice of turnip. She tried the same thing with the saltmeat and crackers and discovered that was good too.

Devonte Aguilar seemed less satisfied with the food. Laura overheard him refusing the plate that was offered to him, insisting that he wasn't hungry. When his mother kept urging him to eat, he grew angry with her.

"I said I don't want any blasted turnips, Mother!" he snapped loudly.

Many people turned to look. They had not heard Devonte speak to his mother this way before or use such strong language. Complaining of the midday heat, Devonte retreated to the shade beneath the Aguilars' handcar to sulk as the rest of them finished their meal.

Eventually, the plates and bowls were all wiped down and put away. The turnip barrel was sealed and hoisted back into the wagon. Still there was no sign of Pa or Captain Syed.

They waited. It seemed to Laura as if two hours passed and then passed again, many times over, but each time that Mr. Chavez clambered down from the bisox wagon to consult the position of the sun, he climbed right back up again without any sense of urgency and made no effort to ready the convoy for departure.

Just as the fear bubbling up in Laura's belly felt like it was about to boil over, three shapes appeared on the horizon. There were the two tall figures of Pa and Captain Syed and the somewhat shorter figure of Caleb the guardsman. Everyone stood to watch as the figures marched their way back to the crossroads.

"Thank you, Lord. Thank you," Laura heard Ma whisper to herself.

Laura was happy that Pa was back, but she was surprised that Caleb was returning as well. She knew that must mean something was wrong at the Badger Creek supervisory.

The faces of Pa and Captain Syed were solemn as they approached the convoy. Caleb looked worse, face white and eyes downcast. Captain Syed stopped, slipping her thumb into her heavy belt, hand resting in the space between her pistol and the pouch where she kept her chewing leaf. The others gathered around.

Pa told Mary and Laura to take his rifle back to the handcar and to give the axles a fresh greasing. Laura nodded, but she walked with tiny, slow steps, dawdling back as long as she could to listen.

"Fort's abandoned," Laura heard Captain Syed say, spitting emphatically onto the creetrock road. Her tone seemed to say that she'd half-expected as much.

"Didn't venture further," she continued, "so I can't speak for the rest of the settlement. But I expect anyone's fled west towards Lildaka who's well enough. Small wonder we ain't passed any eastward convoys. Wolfdog Ortega's probably got the City of Mounds locked down good and tight. We've got some time in quarantine to look forward to if nothing else."

Janice Khan asked a question, but her voice was too hushed to hear. Mary was tugging Laura's arm, and Laura finally allowed herself to be led across the road to the handcar, away from the adult discussion.

~~~

And so the convoy carried on westward.

During the day, it was hard to be scared. As long as they were following the Great Eighty Road through the open Yowa countryside, danger felt far away. What's more, the days that followed were stubbornly beautiful. There suddenly seemed to be not a single cloud above them. With the sun shining so bright, it was easy to forget about all the bad things that lurked in the shadows. Surely, no harm could befall them under such a blue blue sky.

Nights were different. They kept watch in twos now. Everyone took their turn, staying awake in shifts throughout the whole long night. Where they could, they strung twine from the trees or bushes surrounding their campsites. These hemp webs they decorated with tin plates and other objects that would clank and jangle when disturbed. Sometimes, they would gather sticks into delicate piles that would crunch underfoot, concealing the noisy traps in a wide ring around the convoy's camp.

In some ways, the rhythms of life on the road continued. Ma and Mr. Chavez continued to fix suppers. Captain Syed and the Khan cousins continued to lay out their mats for evening prayer. Mr. Aguilar continued to read out passages each evening from his books. Everyone continued to help one another maintain their cars and cargo. Yet, all of this was colored now by what had happened. Every activity had taken on a darker, more serious hue.

Evening was no longer a jolly time for singing and showtales. They kept their fires smaller now and extinguished them earlier. When the convoy now stopped to make camp after a long day of travel, it was not a welcome rest as it had once been but something to be endured until morning came.

One evening, a few days after leaving the deserted Badger Creek supervisory behind, Laura sat with Ma and Mary, listening to Mr. Aguilar read from *The Letters of Dashawn Lacore*. The passages were as boring as ever, but nights of late it felt good just having a human voice to fill up the gathering darkness.

That night, in addition to Ma and Mary and the Aguilars, Caleb had come to listen as well. He sat across from Laura, staring at his boots. Whether he was getting more out of the prophet's latest proverbs than she was, Laura couldn't say.

When the reading was finished, they all continued to sit there around Mr. Aguilar's lantern. It seemed that no one was ready quite yet to leave that tiny circle of light.

After a while, Ma began telling a story. Mary and Laura both looked to her in surprise. Ma was not ordinarily a storyteller. Unlike Pa, she disliked attention and tended to keep her thoughts to herself, especially in front of a group of people like this.

Storytelling did not come naturally to her. She began haltingly, telling things out of order and having to go back and start again. But everyone waited patiently as she groped to find the flow of her narrative. Even Caleb looked up, following attentively to Ma's words as gradually her story fell into place.

THE STORY OF MA AND THE CAUDILLO IN THE KITCHEN

"When I was a little girl, I lived with my grandmother in a house in the north country near the ruins of Duluth.

"It felt enormous to me at the time. The house was two levels. It was made from sturdy brick. There were three or four sleeping rooms upstairs and a big open common room downstairs with a long dining table and a working fireplace.

"It sat all by itself, that house, but there was a minor convoy route that passed right by on its way to a trading port on Great Mishgan Lake. And so my grandmother ran a boarding house of sorts, providing the occasional traveler with a place to rest and a hot meal.

"In those days, a new caudillo had recently seized control of that part of the Wisconsin. El Osito the people called him. He was much feared. Folks spoke in whispers of the man's ruthlessness and the brutality with which he treated all who opposed him. It was thanks to him, though, that the roads stayed open and some measure of law in those parts was observed. Whenever El Osito's men came around, my grandmother always paid her taxes without complaint.

"She was a remarkable woman, my grandmother. She managed to feed and protect five children through the Hard Years, all on her own. Had a knack for squeezing sixteen ounces from a twelve ounce can, as she used to say. Whatever humble little I know about running a proper homestead, I got that from Nana Tucker. Resourceful, that's the word. That's how she kept her family together even after the old ghost cities fell apart.

"Sad to say, out of all her children, my mother was the only one to survive the Second Hyperflu. Must have been quite a blow, having already struggled through so much. She never let misfortune overwhelm her, though. Always pushing forward, with a mind for how to make it through the day and then the next, that was how she lived.

"One evening in early winter, Nana and I were alone in our little brick boarding house. Outside, a thick curtain of snow had begun to billow. The blizzard was unseasonable, for in those days the winters were a good deal warmer. We had a fire crackling in the big common room downstairs, and we sat beside it, her weaving a basket from cedar bark and me helping when I could, though truthfully I did little more than watch. Suddenly, there was a banging on the front door.

"Cut into the door, there was a square peephole with its own hinge. My grandmother swung it aside and lifted her candle up, trying to shed some illumination on whoever was outside. Standing on the porch were three men. They were dressed in furs, but they shivered nonetheless. Snow clung to their beards and dusted their caps. Nana Tucker did not recognize any of them and peppered the men with sharp questions.

"Eventually, one of them held up a pair of silver pieces, pinched between gloved thumb and forefinger, rubbing them in circles around one another with a metallic scrape. My grandmother squinted pointedly at each of the men one last time.

Then she clacked her tongue and unlatched the door, telling the men that they must hang their guns up on the rack beside the door and remove their boots before entering.

"The men thanked her and unshouldered their rifles as they were told. As they squatted awkwardly in the doorway, wrestling with their boots, my grandmother remarked that her two sons were both already asleep upstairs. It was a lie I had heard her tell before. One of the men apologized for the late hour, explaining that the blizzard had caught them unprepared.

"My grandmother waved away his apology and said that she would fix them a warm supper if they were hungry. She took their wet coats and, in a single fluid gesture, directed them towards the fireplace, while driving me off into the kitchen to light the stove.

"I knew well enough that I was to keep my distance from guests, and when she joined me in the kitchen, Nana warned me anew not to talk to or linger near the strangers. I assumed at that point that she would send me upstairs, as she had in the past, perhaps to look after my imaginary uncles. Instead, with Nana Turner's attention consumed by the task of improvising a supper, she sent me back into the common room with a pitcher of warmed cider and three cups.

"The men had shaken off the chill by then and were in good spirits. They greeted the arrival of the cider with delight. All three of them were clustered around one end of the common room's long dining table. I set the pitcher and the cups down between them.

"The cups were antiques. Smooth and glossy and painted in the sorts of vibrant colors you only find in lectricmade porcelain. Unfortunately, they were hopelessly mismatched. One was decorated with a drawing of an orange cat, another with an intricate checkered pattern. The third was bright pink, covered all over in little white hearts, and it had letters across its face that spelled out the word 'princess' or some such if I recall correctly.

"Immediately, two of the men commenced a playful quarrel over who would take which cup. Before I could retreat, one of them turned to me to settle the dispute. Mindful of my Nana's warnings and not knowing how to respond, I said nothing and dashed back to the kitchen, the men's laughter filling the room behind me.

"I found my grandmother peeling carrots. Without looking up, she set me to work stirring a saucepan of gravy that sat simmering on the stove. On the counter nearby, I saw that a bundle of mincemeat had been brought in from the icehouse. Grease had stained the cloth wrapped around it a deep cherry red. Beside it waited a pie tin lined with barley dough. Nana Turner's meat pies were famous, and my mouth watered, though I knew that this pie was not for me.

"After the pie crust was filled and baking inside the oven, my grandmother took the gravy spoon from me and told me to bring a few extra cords of wood inside for the fireplace. I was embarrassed to return to the common room but did as I was told.

"I returned from the woodpile with my boots caked in snow, hugging an assortment of split hardwood logs to my chest. I set down my load long enough to unlace my boots. From down the hall, I could hear the men's boisterous voices. I kept my eyes down as I shuffled past them to the fireplace and stacked my firewood beside the hearth.

"The men seemed to pay me no mind. They were playing cards now. The pitcher of cider was empty, but they had a flask of doju that they passed back forth, splashing the liquor into their porcelain cups.

"The man seated at the head of the table, closest to the fire, was quieter than the other two, I noticed. While his fellows seated on either side of him bantered, he studied his cards and took small, thoughtful sips from his cup, the one with the orange cat. As I passed on my way back to the kitchen, I looked up momentarily and caught his eyes. There was something intense about those eyes. Cold and motionless, even as a flicker of reflected firelight danced within them. They made me feel afraid to look into them and afraid to look away at the same time. I can't quite describe it.

"'Girl,' he said.

"Immediately, the other two stopped talking, as if their comrade were about to make an important speech. Instead, the man just lifted the empty pitcher of cider. I nodded and took the pitcher from him. He rapped a knuckle on the table in thanks. The card game and the men's banter then resumed, and I was invisible once more.

"When I told my grandmother that the men wanted more cider, she grumbled about how the barrel was nearly tapped but had me refill the pitcher right to the brim. Two silver pieces was a lot of money in those days, you understand. I could tell that my grandmother was making a special effort to accommodate the travelers.

"The man at the head of the table again rapped his knuckle on the table when I brought the cider in. The man next to him took the pitcher from me and deferentially filled up his companion's cat cup before refreshing his own checkered cup.

"By then, the smell of Nana's meat pie was wafting into the common room. How much longer would they have to sit there starving, the man at the head of the table demanded of me. His voice was not angry, but it was not amiable either. One of the other men chuckled nervously and began shuffling his cards. Avoiding their eyes, I muttered that supper would be out in a moment, though in truth I knew that it would be some time yet.

"Back in the kitchen, there was little left to do but wait for the pie's crust to crisp and darken. Still, to my surprise, I was not sent upstairs. While my grandmother puttered about, returning occasionally to the stovetop to stir the gravy, I sat on a stool in the corner and returned to my basket weaving.

"Ten or twenty minutes passed. Suddenly, the door of the kitchen swung open, and one of the men burst in. It had been over an hour, he complained. They were hungry. Where was their supper?

"There were some rougher words sprinkled in there as well, I hate to say. The man had his pink princess cup in hand, and, as he spoke, a splash of amber liquid sloshed out onto Nana's clean kitchen floor. Waving her gravy spoon at him in irritation, my grandmother told the man that supper would be ready when it was ready and to wait patiently in the common room.

"Still the man didn't leave. Visibly drunk, he leaned against one of the counters and continued to talk. My grandmother did her best to ignore him and went about her business.

"A moment later, the kitchen door swung open again. It was the man who had been seated at the head of the table, the one towards whom the other two seemed so deferential. Seeing him standing there, I was struck by how much shorter he was than his companions. He was stocky, broad shouldered, with a thick muscular neck beneath his black beard. When he entered, the man with the pink cup straightened up and made an effort to appear more sober.

"The discussion about supper was repeated, to my grandmother's rising irritation. Again, she urged them to return to the common room, but both men lingered. While the man with the pink cup resumed his effort to engage my grandmother in conversation, the shorter man began to wander about the kitchen. Those intense eyes of his inspected everything.

"As my grandmother was checking on the pie, the short man approached the stovetop. He peered with interest down at the simmering pool of gravy. Then he extended a meaty index finger and dipped it into the saucepan. Before he could lift his gravy-coated finger to his mouth, Nana was upon him. She gave the back of his hand such a slap as you've never heard in your life.

"The sound of that slap seem to echo off the walls of the kitchen. You could almost feel the sting in the resounding *pop* it made. The man with the pink cup abruptly stopped talking. His mouth fell open. The short man seemed no less surprised. He stared at the hand my grandmother had slapped, its finger still wet with gravy. His thick black eyebrows were arched in astonishment, but he said nothing. Slowly, he raised his intense gaze towards my grandmother.

"Nana met those piercing eyes without flinching.

"'Listen here, Mister,' she told him. 'This is my house, and there's rules. Now you and your friends can either go back to the

239

fireplace and wait patient like I told you or you can go back out in the snow. It's nothing to me one way or the other.'

"The silence in the kitchen hung heavy. The man with the pink cup seemed to hold his breath as he watched for the short man's reaction, as if the tiniest disturbance in his companion's facial muscles might be the signal to fight or flee.

"The short man opened his mouth to say something, then abruptly thought the better of it. He shrugged, nodded to himself, and left the kitchen without another word. The man with the pink cup watched him go in surprise. Turning back to my grandmother, he gave the gravy one last look of longing.

"'Smells good,' he said, before hurrying out the door in pursuit of his companion.

"Well, I really was sent upstairs after that. The sounds of carousing from the common room continued well into the evening before gradually fading, replaced by the howls of the blizzard outside.

"The next morning, I helped Nana prepare a road breakfast of barley biscuits. She handed each of the men their own knapsack and a jar of pumpkin jam to share between them.

"The men buttoned up their coats and filed out the door to retrieve their weapons from the rack on the porch. As he left, one of the men—it was the one who had ended up with the pink princess cup the night before, I believe—pressed a letter into Nana's hand.

"'Thank you for your hospitality, Ma'am,' he said. 'It was the finest fare we've had in some time. I don't remember when I last saw Osito in such good spirits. If anyone 'round these parts tries to make difficulties for you or your people, you show them this.'

"With that, they were gone. My grandmother gave the letter a cursory glance, grunted dismissively, then tucked it into her apron and went about tidying up the common room as if nothing remarkable had happened. I followed after her, mouth agape. I couldn't believe what I had just heard. Had she known all this time that the gruff little man whose hand she had slapped was the notorious caudillo El Osito himself?

"Nana thrust a broom into my arms before answering.

"'No, I didn't know,' she said. 'And all to the good. If I'd have known, maybe I mightn't have acted as I did. I'd have been afraid. These caudillos, they're used to folks being afraid. When he saw I wasn't, I reckon he was just too surprised to be angry.'

"'Now, I don't suggest you go around slapping warlords willy nilly, Caroline. It's good to be afraid sometimes. Fear helps a body make sensible decisions. But sometimes you have to set aside your fear just so as you can move forward. Fear doesn't change any of the dangers out there, just how you respond to them. When there's a warlord in your kitchen, then there's a warlord in your kitchen. There's nothing that being afraid is going to do about it.'"

TWENTY-THREE: WHEN THE SAP RISES

It was a cold night. The elevation, that was part of it. The Great Eighty Road had sloped upwards all day, gently but steadily, and Laura supposed that they were camped higher up than they had been. Even so, no one seemed prepared for the sudden chill. Ever since the Ghost City of Damoyne, the nights had been unseasonably warm, so warm that Laura had found herself kicking aside the last of her blankets and sleeping uncovered beneath the stars.

That night, even under her blankets, she shivered. In the morning, she could see her breath, and, on the tips of the cedar branches that hung down low beside her bedroll, she saw that a thin dusting of frost had turned their needles pale. In the dawn twilight, as Mr. Chavez prepared a breakfast porridge and everyone readied their cargo for the day's journey, gloves and long-folded coats came back out from wherever they'd been tucked away.

Yet, once the sun was well and up, staring down at the convoy as they resumed their journey westward, the spring warmth returned. Soon, coats were shed once more and stowed again right back where they came from.

"I ain't ever seen weather so fickle," Bill Keo complained, as he stopped by the side of the road to stuff his outer garment into his carrysack. "Reminds me of a girl I knew back in New Hewston. Engaged to be married, we were. Then one day out of the blue she tells me, 'Bill I can't be with you. I aim to take vows and devote my life to Jesus.' Then, not six months later, I find out she and her roommate from sem'nary have run off together. I told you that story yet, Ingalls?"

Pa had stopped nearby to shrug off his own coat. He regarded the cloudless sky thoughtfully.

"'The sap is rising.' That's what my Uncle Freddie used to say when we'd get weather like this up in the Wisconsin. When the days get warm but the nights are still cold. That's the time to tap the sugar maples. Barely have to drive your spile in past the bark on a morning like this, and out she comes like a canoe that's sprung a leak. Golden brown and sweet as any cane sugar."

Pa folded his coat across his arm and walked to the back of the handcar to find a place to tuck it inside the cargo box. Laura watched him and thought of last spring, when she had helped Pa tap the sugar maples that grew in the Big Woods. Suddenly, she was homesick.

Pa had showed her how to hammer the hollow iron tapper into the tree trunk. She remembered sitting and watching the brown sap rise up out of the tree as if by magic. The liquid would gather along the tapper and then come drip-dripping down into their waiting bucket. Pa explained that the maples had been storing their sap down in their roots all winter. Now the tree could feel the seasons changing, and it was pushing the sweet lifeblood upwards, up through its tall trunk, all the way up into its branches to help make new leaves and buds and start a brand new cycle of rebirth and decline.

Ma made syrup from the sap and hard maple candy. Laura scanned the Yowa countryside that rolled along beside the Eighty Road. Looking back in the direction from which they'd come, the hillside was spotted with the prickly shapes of cedars. In the distance ahead, she saw a grove of squat and spindly trees that she did not recognize. The taste of maple candy was on her tongue now, as real and immediate as if she had just popped a piece into her mouth. The flavor was unmistakable, sweet but also burnt and earthy, the flavor of the Big Woods. She wondered if she would ever taste that taste again.

~ ~ ~

The weather grew even warmer as the day wore on and the convoy continued westward.

At one point, Laura heard Devonte quarreling again with his

mother. Laura looked back and saw with surprise that the boy had stripped off his tunic. He stalked down the road bare-chested, the ink cross beneath his collarbone on prominent display. Ms. Aguilar walked beside him, quietly berating him to put his clothes back on, but Devonte exploded at her, yelling that the tunic was too hot and itchy.

Devonte's quarrels with his parents seemed to be growing ever more heated. Everyone's spirits had darkened after the incident beside the flooded village, but the change in Devonte was particularly sudden and striking. Every day of late, he seemed to find something to be angry about. For hours, he would glower sullenly from beneath a wide straw hat he had taken to wearing from sun up to sun down, only to erupt without warning to engage his parents in another argument. Then, at other times, a giddy energy seemed to come over him. In these moments, he would pace the convoy from back to front and back again, as if it were not moving fast enough for his liking. He would leap across gaps in the creetrock road and pull branches off passing vegetation, grinning to himself all the while.

There was much she didn't understand about teenage boys and their moods, Laura supposed. As the angry voices behind her grew louder, she turned back around and tried to pretend not to have noticed the scene.

It was a long, tiring day of travel for everyone. Laura walked the whole while. Ma said that she did not need to go back in the bisox wagon as long as she kept up. Laura did, but by the end of the day her feet were aching and her legs felt like they were made of jelly.

That night, they camped in a clearing up in some wooded bluffs overlooking the Eighty Road. Down in the lowland on the other side of the camp, there was a pond surrounded by a gnarled thicket of swamp oak. There, Pa managed to shoot a duck with a mottled green head, and Caleb and Bill Keo caught a whole sack full of plump frogs.

Mr. Chavez cooked those frogs and Pa's duck together, along with the last of the turnip chips and some soymeal for thickening, in a hot greasy stew. Everyone was glad of the fresh meat. With their destination nearly in reach, the convoy was coming upon the ends of their provisions, and suppers of late had been limited by whatever ingredients happened to lie uneaten at the bottoms of their barrels.

Gratefully, the travelers set down their loads and rested their weary muscles. As the stew bubbled and its rich scent wafted over the camp, Laura heard the sounds of laughter. The atmosphere was not merry exactly, not like it had once been, but a sense of tranquility, perhaps even hopefulness, seemed to be returning to the convoy.

It was not just the smell of meat and the pleasure of a well-earned rest, Laura knew. Their journey was nearly at an end. Another day and then another, according to Captain Syed, and they would be in Lildaka. There, Ma and Pa could trade for fresh provisions and they would begin scouting the Wastes for their homestead.

Everyone seemed to feel the closeness of their destination. The road had been long. They had endured its trials and nearly made it through to the other side. Not unscathed, but they had survived. It was impossible now to look backwards.

Only Devonte seemed to be in a foul mood. He and his mother continued to raise their voices as the convoy made camp. Finally, Devonte stormed off, down towards the frog pond. The others watched him go. Later, Laura saw Captain Syed speaking in private with Mr. Aguilar, a sober expression on her face.

Eventually, Mr. Chavez took a careful slurp from his spoon and gave a nod of approval to the duck-frog stew.

Laura brought a bowl over to Pa. He was helping the Khan cousins repair their handcar, shaping a lumber plank to reinforce the car's undercarriage where it had cracked. He ate his supper standing up, in between swings of his hatchet. Mindful that the last gray traces of daylight were slipping away, he worked quickly. Every now and again, he paused to take a short swig from his stew, then went back to his work, hewing away the rough edges from a log of young swamp oak that he and Bill Keo had felled.

Ma sat beside him on her stool, nursing Baby Grace and handing Pa his bowl whenever he set the hatchet down. That left Mary and Laura, sitting cross-legged across from one another, eating their greasy stew as dusk settled around them.

Laura was scraping her bowl clean when Mary began scanning the camp for Devonte. Apparently, the boy was still off somewhere sulking, and Mary worried that he would miss supper entirely.

"We should bring him a bowl of stew," she told Laura.

Laura said that he could get his own stew if he wanted it, but Mary wouldn't let it go.

"He barely touched his breakfast this morning. I watched him. What if he starves, Laura?"

Laura thought that if Devonte starved, then it was his own fault for being a picky eater and a grouch. But then she saw the concern swimming in Mary's eyes, and Laura felt ashamed. Mary had a kind heart. As she had so many times before, Laura resolved to try and be good and caring like her sister. When they had both emptied their bowls, the girls approached Mr. Chavez together to ask for more stew.

Laura knew Mr. Chavez wouldn't refuse them another helping. The bisox driver was always trying to sneak Mary and Laura extra portions, usually over Ma and Pa's objections. He raised his eyebrows a little in surprise when Mary held up her bowl to him, but then he lifted the lid from his big iron pot to peer inside. He reckoned there was plenty enough to spare for growing girls, he said as steam rose past his face. After checking to see if Ma and Pa were watching, he dipped Mary's bowl back into the pot and brought it out full of hot stew.

With a wink, Mr. Chavez handed them the bowl. Mary and Laura both thanked him. Then they turned and began walking down the hill towards the pond, careful to step over the lines of hemp twine that guarded the camp.

They could still hear the *thwack* of Pa's hatchet. Mary stole a nervous glance backwards. They both knew that Ma and Pa would not like them wandering away from camp, especially when it was growing dark. But Laura wasn't particularly worried about getting in trouble. The pond wasn't far, and they would come right back as soon as they'd given dumb Devonte his dumb stew.

At the edge of camp, they passed Bill Keo, resting flat on his back with his head propped up on his carrysack. Dog lay curled up at his feet. He regarded the girls curiously as they walked by but said nothing.

Soon, they reached the thicket of trees where Devonte had retreated. They stood there for a moment, looking around and listening as a chorus of frogs called out to one another, back and forth, like a creaky car wheel spinning round and round. *Reet reet. Reet reet. Reet reet.*

Finally, they saw him. Devonte was sitting on a tree stump down near the edge of the pond, hunched over and half-hidden in shadow. He was naked from the waist up. Laura imagined she could feel Mary blushing beside her.

As they drew closer, Laura saw that his boots were off too, and he seemed to be scratching beneath his pant legs while he rocked slowly back and forth.

"Devonte?" Mary said as she and Laura approached. "We brought you some supper. Aren't you hungry?"

Devonte's head jerked up suddenly and whipped around towards them. His face was masked in shadow, but something about his posture made Laura stop in her tracks. Mary continued towards him, but her steps slowed to an uncertain crawl.

Devonte seemed to roll off the tree stump, collapsing into a crouch amid the marsh grass.

"Who?... Get out! I ... Let me be!"

His voice was hoarse, his words so guttural and garbled that Laura could barely understand them. He sounded like another person entirely. Mary stared at him mouth agape. Her chin beginning to quiver, she held up her bowl.

"It's ... it's stew?" she said.

Devonte took a step towards them. His movements were stiff, his shoulders hunched. Laura looked down and saw that his hands were balled into tight fists by his sides. They seemed to be

247

shaking in fury.

"Mary," Laura whispered. "Mary, let's go."

But Mary seemed unable to move. She just stood there, still holding up her stew bowl, as Devonte came closer, into the light. He was muttering something to himself.

"...spying on me day and night always spying spying..." Laura heard him hiss under his breath.

Laura could see the ink cross now on his chest, stark against his pale skin, pale skin that seemed to take on a yellower and yellower tinge the longer that Laura stared. It must be a trick of the light, she told herself, the dying sunset reflected off the pond, painting them all in unnatural hues. But then she saw Devonte's face. She saw his eyes. And she knew. With a terrible certainty she knew.

"Mary!" she screamed.

It was too late. Devonte sprang towards Mary. He shoved her to the ground.

Instinctively, Laura ran towards her sister. Immediately, Devonte's flailing elbow caught Laura in the ribs, sending her stumbling. Her foot snagged on a tree root, and she tripped, crashing violently into the pond's muddy shallows.

Sputtering, she sat up and tried to wipe the mud from her eyes. Mary was screaming. Laura blinked and blinked, ignoring the sting, trying desperately to regain her vision. Two blurry shapes wrestled on the ground beside her. As they drifted in and out of focus, Laura saw Devonte looming over Mary as she tried to crawl away. Squinting through her single unobstructed eye, Laura saw him grab her sister by the ankle.

And then, with a horror that would haunt her forever and always, she saw the boy sink his teeth into Mary's leg.

Somehow, a stone had found its way into Laura's hand. Still half-blind, she lurched towards Mary and Devonte. She smashed the stone as hard as she could down on Devonte's back. The boy snarled in pain. Dropping Mary's leg, he turned on Laura. He pushed her. Laura was back on the ground, back in the mud. She curled into a terrified ball, shielding her face with her hands, waiting for the teeth and the fingernails to come.

But they didn't come.

Instead, there was a growl. It did not come from Devonte. This was the sound of an animal, not the sound of a person acting like an animal. Laura lifted her head. A black shape was standing between her and Devonte. Its shaggy hair bristled.

There was a great commotion as Bill Keo burst from the bushes. Devonte screamed something at him, his voice a hoarse wail. Laura saw Bill Keo swing his poleax. It looked as if the flat of the ax caught Devonte in the side. A moment later the boy was writhing on the ground, Bill Keo pinning him down with his boot.

Others arrived. There was shouting all around her. She heard Pa's voice. She tried to look for him, but by then her eyes were clouded with tears.

"Mary," she sobbed. "Oh Mary."

TWENTY-FOUR: THE CITY OF MOUNDS

The door that covered the entrance to the dugout creaked cautiously open. Its misshapen wooden boards scraped the dirt floor as a sneaky shaft of daylight slipped past. From the narrow earthen passageway beyond, the light pushed eagerly through the widening doorway, growing bit by bit.

Instinctively, Laura and Ma both looked to Mary. They studied her face, trying to judge her reaction to the daylight seeping in, creeping its way up the eight walls of log and mud that formed their little house under the ground.

The house belonged to a great uncle of Janice and Oprah Khan. Or perhaps he was a second cousin. No one seemed sure exactly. In any case, the man had recently left on convoy, upriver to Wolf Point in the Northlands. He would be grateful for someone to look after the place while he was away, the Khans had assured Pa.

Like most of the houses in Lildaka, it was hidden beneath the earth, burrowed into the gentle bluffs that rose and fell above the Suri River floodplain. All that dirt hugging tight around its walls and packed atop its roof kept the house warm in winter and cool in summer, Laura knew. And they weren't like to topple over in the harsh winds that were said to sometimes blow in from the Wastes.

The only problem with underground houses was they were so dark, Laura thought. Some of Lildaka's more elaborate structures had a window cut into the mound, sometimes two or three or more. Not Mr. Khan's little dugout.

But, of course, darkness had been just what Mary needed these past months. That morning, when the first sliver of sunlight reached her bedside, Mary winced and rolled her head to the side, but she did not cry out as she once had. Laura sighed in relief.

Mary no longer struggled or thrashed about. She recognized them now and could speak when she wasn't feeling too tired. She had begun to spoon her own porridge, and, yesterday, she had eaten a whole biscuit with apple butter.

Laura hadn't been allowed to see Mary during the worst of it. Those first few days after they had arrived in Lildaka, Laura had been sent to stay with the Khan cousins on their compound on the outskirts of town while Ma and Pa sought a doctor for Mary. But the parts she had seen had been dreadful enough. When Laura was permitted at Mary's bedside at last, the person she'd seen lying there had not been her sister. Gentle Mary, the most mild mannered of little girls, had wailed angrily and bucked against her restraints.

She had been tied down to the bed, her wrists bound together with strips of cloth. It had frightened Laura to her very core. But when Pa asked her if she wanted to stay, she nodded without hesitation.

Mary's arms and legs were free now. To Laura's great relief, the worst of her illness seemed to be well past.

A face peeked around the corner of the dugout door. It was the doctor. Laura was disappointed. When she had heard the footsteps approaching, she had thought it might be Pa.

Pa had been gone for days. Mary's sickness had put pause to their journey to the Wastes. Soon after arriving in Lildaka, Pa had found work in town. He spent his mornings helping the owner of the metalworks, a man named Mr. Hasan, pound out nails and brackets. He took odd jobs mending fences and digging irrigation ditches. And, whenever a river convoy arrived, Pa would join the men down at the docks to haul goods up to the marketplace. In between, he never left Mary's side.

Even so, Pa never stopped thinking about the Wastes and talking about claiming a homestead. As the weeks went by, he grew more restless. It was already late in the planting season. If they didn't get seeds in the ground soon, there was little chance of a harvest that would see them through their first winter.

251

Ma said that perhaps it was for the best, that they could settle there in Lildaka for a time and set out for the Wastes the following spring, but this idea did not seem to suit Pa at all.

"Do you expect to keep on living in this dugout?" he'd said. "You know how uncomfortable this charity makes me, Caroline. For Mary's sake, I accepted, but I don't want to linger under the Khans' roof a day longer than we have to. Besides, we can't count on the work here in town keeping steady. We can't rely on Hasan to feed us. We need something dependable. The only thing a body can depend on is what he can grow and make and scav himself."

Thus, as soon as it became clear that Mary would recover, Pa set out into the Wastes to scout for a suitable plot of land to stake out their claim. He promised he would be gone no more than ten days. Today was the tenth day.

"Good afternoon, Doctor Eagleshadow," said Ma, beckoning the doctor inside. "It's alright. Mary's not as sensitive to the light as she has been."

Doctor Eagleshadow smiled at them and pushed the door open a little wider. He was young for a doctor, bare-faced, with wavy black hair tied up in a neat bun atop his head. He was apprenticed to an older doctor, but Laura had never seen her. It had been Doctor Eagleshadow who had cared for Mary since they had arrived in Lildaka, coming to check on her nearly every day.

"Good afternoon, Ma'am," replied the doctor. "If Mary can tolerate it, I'll leave this open for now. Gradual exposure may do her good."

He sat down beside Mary to examine her energies. Nodding to himself, he pulled a bundle of needles from his bag and began to insert them along the outsides of Mary's ears. The sight of the needles pricking into the skin made Laura flinch, but they seemed to have a calming effect on Mary. Almost immediately, the tension seemed to leave her body, and her breathing became deeper and more regular. After a while, Doctor Eagleshadow began asking her questions in a soothing voice. When he asked her if she felt she could sit up, Mary nodded and said she could.

Mary sat up and scooted around to face the doctor. One leg swung off the bed and dangled above the floor.

"Let's just see how your bandages are holding up," said Doctor Eagleshadow.

Gently, he pushed Mary's blanket aside. There it was. The stump where Mary's other leg should have been. It had been cut off above the knee, above the spot where Devonte had bitten her on that terrible night all those weeks ago.

The memory of it was still raw. That was the night that Pa had set out, carrying Mary in his arms, racing ahead of the convoy, through day and night as fast as he could, to reach town before the infection spread.

Bill Keo had gone with him. Pa and Ma were grateful for that. Later, though, it occurred to Laura that the man might have had his own reasons for departing the company of the convoy. No one knew it at the time, but Devonte Aguilar would not recover from the blow he had taken from Bill Keo's ax. Bill Keo might well have sensed that it would be best if he put some distance between himself and the Aguilars.

Mary scooted further towards the edge of the bed. As much as Ma and Pa had tried to prepare her for it, the sight of Mary's missing leg had still come as a shock the first time Laura laid eyes upon it. The two of them had slept side by side their entire lives, spent nearly every moment of every day together. Laura knew every part of her sister as well as she knew herself. And now one of those parts was missing. It would never be back.

That morning, however, when Doctor Eagleshadow pushed aside Mary's blanket, Laura's sense of loss was tempered by hopefulness. The strips of cloth that wound around the blunt stub of Mary's thigh were dry and clean. When Doctor Eagleshadow looked beneath the bandages, he said the wound was healing nicely. He told Ma to keep using the ointment he had given her and to start leaving the leg uncovered for a few hours in the evening. Finally, he stood and smiled down at Mary.

"I brought something for you," he said. "I wasn't sure how

you'd be feeling, and I didn't want us to get ahead of ourselves. But you're coming along so quickly. I think it's time."

He went to fetch something he'd left outside the entry to the dugout and returned with what looked to be a pair of wooden shafts, joined at the top and middle by short cross-pieces and bound together at the bottom to form a skinny triangle. Doctor Eagleshadow gripped the top cross-piece and tapped soundly against the dugout's dirt floor with the pointy tip. The object seemed sturdy.

"Have you ever seen someone use a crutch?" he asked Mary. "If you're feeling strong enough, I can show you how it works."

With Ma and the doctor's help, Mary rose from the bed. She wobbled there on one leg at first, supported by Ma, but after Doctor Eagleshadow tucked the crutch beneath Mary's arm, Ma was able to let go and step back. To Laura's delight, Mary was standing, all on her own. Her leg continued to shake. She swayed a little, leaning against the crutch. But when Laura looked into her sister's eyes, there was no sign of unsteadiness. What she saw there was determination and resilience.

Without warning, Mary lifted the crutch and took a stumbling step. Ma and Doctor Eagleshadow both lunged forward to catch her, but Mary regained her balance before they reached her. The doctor laughed.

"Whoa now," he told her. "Take it slow. Gothim wasn't built in a day after all."

He told Ma to call on him if Mary's condition worsened but said he reckoned that the Ague was now well and truly beaten back. Now it was up to Mary to get strong again. He handed Ma some powder, folded up in a sheet of hemp paper, and explained how to brew it into a tea that would help rebalance Mary's energies.

Ma thanked him and told Laura to fetch her buckskin purse, the one with the pretty buttons made of vibrant blue-green hardmold. Laura knew right where it was, hidden at the bottom of a clay jar beneath a layer of smooth round soy seeds. Ma dug out a silver piece and handed it to the doctor.

Doctor Eagleshadow bowed and wished them good fortune. Then he left them, leaving the door ajar to welcome in the daylight. Mary lay back on the bed, and Ma resumed her sewing. After a time, though, Mary spoke again.

"May I go outside, Ma? Just for a moment?"

Ma's needle paused.

"Oh, Mary. I don't know. Do you think you can manage?"

"I just want to see."

Ma nodded. Laura felt a little thrill.

They helped Mary pull a loose-fitting tunic over her head and tie a patchwork skirt of lectric fabrics around her waist. Then they helped her up onto her crutch.

With Ma and Laura at her sides to steady her, Mary began to hobble experimentally around the dugout. She visited every one of its eight corners in turn.

Finally, she approached the doorway, planting her crutch into the pool of light that spilled across the dirt floor. Baby Grace chose that moment to awake, sitting up in her basket beside the bed and demanding attention. Ma turned to her, telling Laura and Mary to go ahead.

"Watch her, Laura," she said. "And stay beside the house."

Laura took Mary's arm, sharing some of her sister's weight. Together, they stepped past the wooden door, between the narrow earthen walls that flanked the entrance to the dugout and towards the bright world beyond.

Mary grunted when the sunlight fell upon her, closing her eyes and turning her face towards the entryway's sloping dirt wall. But when Laura asked her if she wanted to go back inside, Mary shook her head.

"I'll be alright, Laura," she said softly. "My eyes just need a moment."

Finally, squinting, she turned back and continued to hobble forward. The dugout walls fell away, and Laura and Mary were enveloped by blue sky and green grass. Mary stopped. She lifted a hand to shade her eyes and looked around. She breathed deep.

Lildaka's smell was not pleasant. There were too many people.

It smelled of drying fish and human waste and who-knew-what burning from a hundred stoves and hearths. But today the wind was blowing in the right direction, and here on the far edge of town the air was crisp and fresh.

Laura felt something nudge against her leg. It was Jack. The brindled pigdog tilted his head back and forth, pointing his one big round eye at Mary then Laura. He looked concerned. But when Mary smiled at him and told him what a good boy he was, Jack's tongue fell happily out of his mouth. He spun in a circle and gave a yip.

Shuffling in place, Mary turned to look back at the dugout.

"Oh my," she said. "Is that what I've been sleeping under this whole time?

Laura smiled. Apart from a slice that had been taken out to make way for its wooden door, the dugout could have been any other little hill. Grass covered its sides, decorated with streaks of red and yellow flowers that had only just blossomed. There was even a small patch of shrubs, sinking their roots right into the dugout's roof.

"Come on," said Laura, taking Mary's arm and leading her up the side of the mound. She watched Mary's expression, remembering how strange it had felt the first time she had walked across the top of the dugout, knowing that Ma and her sisters were down there right beneath her feet.

Mary struggled up the hill. Grunting, she would pivot on her crutch and leap one-legged towards uncharted ground, climbing imperceptibly higher with each effort. Gasping, she would land and fight to win her balance. In between, she would need to stop and catch her breath. Several times, she nearly fell, but Laura was always there to catch her. Together, they made it all the way to the top.

There, Mary turned, looking exhausted but happy. Laura ducked beneath her sister's arm and helped her down to the ground. They sat there in the grass, side by side, on the little hill that was also their little house. Jack lay down beside them.

Mary was squinting less now. Laura could barely contain

herself. It felt so good to have Mary back. There were so many things she had wanted to share with her these last few months.

From their seats atop the dugout, the City of Mounds stretched out before them. There were few trees in Lildaka, apart from the long straight row to the south that the townsfolk called the Windbreak, and so their view was unobstructed. It was an astonishing sight, and Laura felt another tingle of jubilation watching Mary take it in for the first time.

On its own, perhaps their dugout might be mistaken for an ordinary hill. Seeing so many buried houses all together was something different. Pa liked to compare the landscape to a toad's back, green and brown and warty. Yet, that wasn't quite right. The mounds were like nothing natural. Orderly and symmetrical, they bubbled from the earth in purposeful bursts, gathering more densely together as they approached the center of town.

Smoke spires rose from the mounds, escaping from chimneys hidden in their otherwise featureless slopes. A few peaks away, a group of children ran up one hillside and down the other. Further off, other figures could be seen, like ants on their anthills going about their ant business.

Laura pointed out the long mound in the distance where the smoke was thickest. It was a good deal taller than the ones around it. That was where the town's central committee gathered, she told Mary. There lived Marius Ortega, the one they called the Wolfdog, supervisor of the Clan Ortega's westernmost territory.

Laura's finger leapt excitedly onward. She pointed to the swath of white on the far side of the town, out beyond the green and brown ripples of the dugouts. That was the Lildaka Market. It was so much bigger than the Laketown Market, Laura told Mary. There were so many tents you couldn't count them all, with all manner of trade goods and people speaking in all sorts of strange accents.

And somewhere out there, across the Suri River, was the Ghost City of Oma. They couldn't see the ruins from the dugout's roof, Laura explained. Laura had seen them, though, when she visited the market with Pa. On the other side of the river, directly across from the docks where Pa hauled cargo, there was the most splendid dome, rising up through a thicket of trees to loom high above their canopy. It was made of iron bars woven together like lace.

"It all sounds so incredible," said Mary. Her voice sounded tired and distant.

Laura stopped talking. She and Mary sat quietly, looking out upon the wide open outside and breathing it in. After some time, they heard Ma calling to them. Laura called back, and soon Ma was climbing up the side of the dugout with Baby Grace in her arms. They sat beside Laura and Mary and Jack. Laura squeezed Mary's hand with one hand and squeezed Ma's with the other. It felt good to be here, up above the dark, stifling walls of their little underground house. All together. Or almost.

No sooner had she thought this thought, something made Laura turn her head, away from the town and its market and towards the plains to the south where the Windbreak stood. Off in the distance, she saw a lone figure emerge from behind a gap in the long wall of trees and continue up the dirt path towards the town.

Laura leapt to her feet.

It was Pa.

TWENTY-FIVE: BEYOND THE SURI

Laura picked up the jar once more and held it up, letting the sunbeams bend around and through the curved, lectricmade glass, illuminating the layers within.

Pa was very happy with those layers. He had returned from the Wastes exhausted but triumphant.

It was only after telling Pa all about the miraculous improvement in Mary's condition that they had finally asked him about his expedition. In response, Pa had pulled the jar from his satchel without explanation and laid it at their feet like a trophy.

"What is it, Pa?" Laura had asked.

"It's home," he replied.

When Laura lifted the jar towards the sun, the murky water at the top of the jar glowed with a happy chestnut hue. But it wasn't the water but rather what had settled to the bottom of the jar that interested Pa. At first glance, it just looked like plain dirt. Holding the jar up at eye level, though, Laura could see the distinct layers that Pa pointed out.

At the very bottom, the dirt was yellow and gritty. This was sand. A crooked line cut across the top of the sand, separating it from a layer of darker, finer dirt. This layer was called silt. Finally, there was a top layer. It was lighter than the silt and looked almost creamy compared to the coarse sand. That was the clay.

The three layers were nearly equal in size. Pa said that meant good soil.

He had nearly despaired of finding a good piece of land on which to file a claim, Pa told them. By his fifth day out in the Wastes, he'd found a few spots that might support a homestead, but none of them had been quite right. He knew he needed to turn around, but something kept telling him to go just a little further.

"So I tacked east a ways," he told them. "All the while thinking to myself 'Ingalls, you're a blasted fool. If you don't turn around soon, that beautiful wife of yours is going to wring your neck when she sees you again.' But also thinking 'maybe just a little farther. Just another kim or so to see what's over the next horizon.' And then, just when I was about to yield to my more sensible notions, there it was.

"There's a creek nearby. Not big, but big enough for us, at least until I can get a well dug. There's a billabong a ways upstream with a bit of shrubland surrounding. A rare enough sight out on the Wastes I can tell you. 'Wattle' the little trees on the banks are called. Decent wood if you can harvest enough of it I'm told, and the bean pods are edible. There's a few ruins as well scattered about the wattle, half-buried mostly. No one's come within fifty kims of that place since before the Hard Years I'd reckon. Nothing much to look at. But there's materials enough to scav for a simple lean-to I reckon. That'll give us a bit of shelter until I can return to Lildaka for supplies and build you a real house.

"We won't have an easy time of it. Not at first. But just have a look at that soil. Uncle Freddie'd have been pleased to find soil half that rich back in Upstate, and I'd stake it any day against those rocky patches we scrabbled over for so long back in the Wisconsin. Comes of the land sitting untouched so long, that's what I put it down to. Why, even late in the season as we are, if this soil's as fertile as it looks, we may yet manage a harvest this year to see us through the winter."

"It sounds perfect," said Ma. "It must have been the Prezdent Above guiding your footsteps for you to find it as you did."

Pa scratched his beard at that. Ma said these kinds of things more often lately. She had been going to prayer meetings led by Lildaka's conduit, a woman named Mother Imani. It had been at Ms. Aguilar's invitation at first, but Ma continued attending on her own even after Mr. and Ms. Aguilar left for their claim. The meetings had seemed to bring her comfort during Mary's illness, but Pa always seemed unsure how to respond to Ma's newfound piety.

"Well, yes. I suppose that's as may be," he said.

Pa wanted to go straight down to the supervisory the moment he returned, that very afternoon, to file paperwork on their claim. As remote as the homestead was, Pa just couldn't seem to shake the fear that someone might snatch the land out from under him. Finally, though, Ma convinced him it was too late in the day and that, clothes dusty and eyes bleary from travel, he was in no shape to visit Marius Ortega's land clerks. So instead Pa carried Mary back inside the dugout, hung his rifle and satchel beside the hearth, lay down on the bed, and fell immediately fast asleep.

They all slept sound and cozy that night, side by side on that big bed inside their little house beneath the ground. But Pa was up again before first light, fetching a gourd of water from the rain basin outside and trying to comb his hair by candlelight in the black reflection of Mary's handscreen. By the time a pink sunrise began to speckle the City of Mounds in dramatic patterns of light and shadow, Pa was already on the dirt path that led towards the town center.

He was gone all day. They waited for him so long that Ma began to fret that something must have gone amiss at the supervisory. When Pa finally returned, though, he unrolled a sheet of hemp paper. In the corner was the Clan Council's seal. The bisox face was distorted and seemed to grin crookedly from within the ridges of wax. Beside the seal was Supervisor Ortega's signature. Above was a neat block of slanty ink letters made by one of the supervisor's clerks. Pa said those letters described the location and boundaries of their claim.

The paper seemed to have a reassuring effect on Pa. Holding it, he seemed to visibly relax.

"I wasn't the only one there to file a claim, not by a stretch," Pa said. "By late morning, there were half a dozen folks lined up outside the supervisory. When I finally got called inside and saw the stacks of records, my heart sank for a moment. Talk is there's been a deal of speculation, townsfolk and traders who spend one night in twenty out on their claim just to keep it alive, that sort of thing. Not to mention big swathes of land been set aside for the Wolfdog's cronies, to hear some tell it. Well, however it is, I got to worrying about how fast the good land's going.

"We pored over her maps a good while, the clerk and me. Turns out that creek of ours isn't where it ought to be. Whether it's the maps or the creek that's wrong I couldn't say. Lucky for me, I kept careful notes out there, and I'm satisfied we eventually got that parcel pinned down within a stone's throw. Well, you can imagine my relief after the clerk finally finished shuffling through her records and told me no one's filed on it yet."

Pa's relief did not give way to complacency. The race to the claims office might be won, but now came the race against the seasons. The sooner they could get seeds in the ground, the better the chances of a harvest that would see them through the winter. There was no time to lose.

Ma and Pa spoke at first of two trips. Pa would haul a load of supplies out to the homestead alone, he said. He would return later, when Mary was stronger, after the planting was finished perhaps. Laura did not care for this idea, and she could tell that Ma didn't either. But it was Mary's own insistence, soft but certain, that she was well enough to travel that finally won the day. Pa relented. The plan was changed. They would all set out for the Wastes together.

It took another day to get their affairs in order. Pa walked back down to the town center the next morning to see Mr. Hasan about his back wages. Meanwhile, Ma and Laura and Baby Grace made a trip out to the Khans' farm on the outskirts of Lildaka.

The Khan homestead was a bustling place. A dozen or more people lived there, all related to one another in ways that Laura could never seem to quite keep straight. Most of the sleeping quarters were underground in the Lildakan manner, but a number of unburied wooden structures were scattered around the property as well. There was a barn, where an old gray bisox slept, and all over were arched hoop houses, draped in loose hemp netting, sheltering delicate berry vines.

There was even a gazebo for entertaining guests. It had no walls, but its large, square platform was raised above the dirt, and timber posts held up a thatched roof for shade. That was where they met with Janice and Oprah Khan, to thank them for their kindness during those difficult months. The Khan cousins made Ma promise to come back and visit once they were settled in the Wastes.

Laura heard buzzing nearby. A short distance from the gazebo was a row of boxes, circled by dark trails that looked like wisps of smoke. She noticed a lone bee, fat and orange, sitting happily on the bench beside her. The hives had survived their journey west, Laura realized with delight. Here they were, thriving in their new home.

Ma declined an offer to stay for supper. There was still much to do. They returned to their dugout. Pa was back already, packing up the handcar.

Laura ran her hand down the car's stout carrying shafts,

thinking about how Ma had managed to pull it all on her own to Lildaka after Pa had gone on ahead with Mary.

Those final days on the Great Eighty Road had been painful for everyone. Laura remembered the sickening feeling that had sat in the pit of her stomach as she'd held Baby Grace tight in her lap in the back of the bisox wagon, watching Ma strain against the weight of the heavy handcar, falling further and further to the back of the convoy. Later, Ma would say that she was thankful for those physical trials. The exhaustion had distracted her from her anguish over Mary.

Laura sat on the slope of the dugout and watched Pa shove a sack of seed soy into the narrow gap between two barrels, trying to use up every last pocket of empty space. Soon, the handcar was once more piled up with their belongings. Missing were the bundles of furs they'd brought with them from the Big Woods, which Pa had managed to sell at the Lildaka Market. That let them clear a small empty space near the back of the cargo box where Mary would ride.

That evening, they all sat together on top of the dugout and watched the sun set over the Suri River. Then they went below and climbed into bed to spend one last night in their little house beneath the earth.

~~~

It was still dark when they departed Lildaka the next morning. Laura walked beside Ma. Riding in the handcar ahead of them was Mary, with Baby Grace in her arms. They made their way through the predawn stillness, down the rocky path towards the Windbreak.

They reached the line of trees just as the sun was beginning to brighten the eastern faces of Lildaka's dugout houses, leaving their western slopes in shadow. Laura took one last look before following Pa through a gap in the Windbreak. The City of Mounds vanished behind the branches.

They continued south of the Windbreak for some time, tracing the eastern banks of the Suri River. Sometimes, they could see it from the trail. Other times, it curved away and hid over the horizon. Finally, around mid-morning, the path took them all the way down to the river's muddy edge. As the Suri's shoreline appeared ahead of them, Laura spied a ferry dock and, tethered alongside it, the raft that would carry them across.

Upriver from the dock was a small, secluded dugout, almost invisible amongst the tall rivergrass. Pa went up to bang on the door, and a few moments later a woman opened it. As she and Pa spoke, Laura turned towards the marshes beside the river and was startled to see a face staring back at her from among the reeds.

It was a small boy. He was no older than three or four and completely naked. He stood there, knee-deep in the river's shallows, and regarded Laura suspiciously. When Laura waved and smiled, he waved back. Then, with a conspiratorial sparkle in his eye, he raised his other hand to show her what he was holding. It was a skinny black snake with a pink belly. It coiled around his wrist and twisted through his fingers, bobbing its head in tiny circles as if confused how it had found itself dangling so high above its marshy home.

Laura was just about to approach the boy, to take him up on his offer to have a closer look at the snake, when the woman at the dugout door began calling. Apparently hearing his name, the boy untangled the snake from his wrist and flung the poor creature back into the reeds without a second look. Then he splashed through the mud towards the woman's voice.

"Go find your daddy," the woman hollered at him, and the naked boy took off running down the trail.

A few moments later, a man arrived, carrying a fishing pole slung over his shoulders. The little boy skipped along at his heels. The man and the woman helped Pa load the handcar onto the ferry. Then, when they were all aboard, the man joined them and he, Pa, and Ma all took up the rope the ran from the dock to the far side of the river. Hand over hand, they began hauling the raft across.

Laura held tight to Baby Grace. Mary stood beside her, leaning on her crutch, her other arm linked with Laura's. Mary's face was invisible, shrouded by the wings of the bonnet Ma had made to shield her eyes from the harsh daylight, but Laura smiled into the darkness beneath Mary's bonnet and imagined her sister smiling back.

They disembarked on the other side onto a dock much like the one from which they'd left. As Pa paid the ferryman and Ma helped Mary back up into the bed of the handcar, Laura pulled her carrysack higher on her shoulders and looked out over the land that stretched out before them.

It was the Suri River that marked the border of the Great Merican Wastes, Laura knew. They had finally arrived.

~ ~ ~

There were no more old number roads in the days that followed. There was no need for roads on the Wastes. The land west of the Suri was as level as any creetrock road and a good deal less impeded by vegetation.

The earth here yielded up nothing but short grass. It covered everything from horizon to horizon. Laura had never seen such unrelenting sameness. It seemed the only respite came from the subtle changes in color, as the grasses faded from green to brown and back again.

It was one thing to know that the Wastes were flat and empty. To experience that flatness and that emptiness all day, from waking to slumber, that was something else altogether. As they ventured further beyond the Suri, there were no more hills. There were no trees, no streams, no ruins. There was only sky and grass, as far as Laura's eyes could see in any direction. It made her feel small and hopelessly disoriented.

With no number road to follow, Pa had to use his compass and the stars to make sure they weren't going in circles. "We should head further south," he might say or, "We'll be keeping to a more westerly bearing today." But who could tell? Out in the vast grass ocean, all directions blurred together as one.

For a time, even the grass abandoned them. The thin layer of green gradually lost its color and then receded entirely, revealing the naked earth beneath. Dry and hard, the ground was crisscrossed in fissures, forking through the rocky soil like bolts of lightning. The wheels of the handcar kicked up clouds of dust as they crackled over this desolate landscape.

Ma made them all facemasks out of strips of old lectric cloths she'd packed away for just such a purpose. She showed Laura how to fold the cloth just so, first into a square and then a triangle, with two pointy ends to tie around her head and enough loose material hanging down to cover her nose and mouth and tuck into the front of her tunic. They all tied on their masks as they trekked across that dusty country, even Baby Grace, who fussed at having her face covered up like that.

Laura wished that they could make a mask for Jack. His little flat pig nose offered no protection at all from the dust. But there was nothing to be done. The poor little dog lay beside Mary and Grace in the back of the handcar, snuffling piteously.

Pa said not to worry. They were just passing through a small corner of the desert lands that stretched off to the west. Greener pastures lay before them to the south. And, indeed, by the next day, the grass had returned. Laura even began to see the occasional flower. One had a bright yellow center, surrounded by long pink petals, and Pa said that it was called a wasterose.

Late that afternoon, Pa stopped, set down the handcar, and examined the ground. Laura looked where he was looking, and then she saw it too. The grass around them had been trampled down.

Pa suggested that they take a short rest, so Laura helped Mary down from the back of the handcar and Ma sat down with Baby Grace to nurse. All the while, Pa was studying the tracks. Eyes on the ground, he wandered in a slow, deliberate arc, pausing every so often to look up and scan the flat expanse from his feet to the distant horizon.

Jack trotted alongside, face buried in the grass, snuffling with excitement. He had snuffled a good ways out ahead of Pa when the little pigdog began circling one particular area. He yipped. Pa looked over at what Jack had found and then immediately followed.

Laura wanted to run after them right then, but she knew she must wait for Mary. One arm over Laura's shoulder and the other on her crutch, Mary vaulted one-legged across the wastegrass towards the dark patch where Pa crouched beside Jack. As they approached, Pa waved, beckoning them on.

"Come have a look," he called.

Pa seemed to be squatting in the middle of a clearing. It was queer to talk of a clearing in a land so wide and open, but that was how Laura thought of it. The area all around Pa and Jack was discolored. The grass had been stamped down and the soil disturbed.

Laura spied a blackened circle that must have been a firepit. Strewn around it were charred objects, sticking up out of the wastegrass like strange weeds. Mary and Laura nearly tripped over a little pile of them and stopped short. They were bones.

"Nomad camp," said Pa. "Just a few days old by the looks of it. Wasn't here last I passed this way, I'm near certain."

He held up a long, curved rib, twirling it with his wrist like a sword.

"What kind of bones do you suppose these are, girls?" asked Pa.

Laura looked down at the long, thin leg bone at her feet. It had been snapped in two, and its edges were burnt an oily black. A thought had occurred to her about what kind of bones they were, but she did not want to say it.

Pa handed her the slender rib. Laura was surprised by how light it was. Not like deer bones or wolfdog bones or other bones that were best not to think about. Laura reevaluated the blackened piles.

"Wastebird?" guessed Mary.

"That's right," said Pa. "See those feathers there?"

It was true. On the other side of the firepit, Laura saw something bristling in the wind. It was black and bigger than any feather she had ever seen. Nearby, there was another. It was white. The more she looked for them, the more feathers she saw. Some black and some white and some gray. The wind wanted to blow them away, but they had all gotten stuck, half-buried in the dirt. Laura went to pull the white one up. It was as long as her arm.

"That's a fine one," Pa said, admiring Laura's feather. "The nomads make cloaks out of wastebird feathers. I suppose these must not have been up to their standards. Or perhaps they have cloaks enough. All this is just from one bird, I judge. A single kill can feed a whole nomad crew for a week."

Pa knew all about nomads. Back in Lildaka, he had met Yaya traders, come to market to sell their feathers and leatherworks and the scav they had unearthed from forgotten ruins hidden deep in the Wastes. He had told Laura and Mary about the intricate patterns that the Yaya scarred into their skin and about the queer version of the Merican language they spoke, nearly incomprehensible to the other traders.

The Yaya were a strange people, Pa said, but they did not seem as fearsome as the stories. He did not believe that they ate human flesh. Laura hoped that Pa was right, but she thought that if she was a cannibal, she probably wouldn't go around telling everyone about it either.

While Pa studied the Yaya camp, Mary and Laura gathered wastebird feathers. Mary would spot them, and Laura would pick them up. They also found torn scraps of animal hide and a sharpened piece of iron scrap that Pa said was a spearpoint.

Finally, it was time to go. Pa said that Mary and Laura could take their feathers with them. They could be used to make bedding or a broom to keep away the dust. Laura looked at her long, white feather. She ran her fingers through its soft strands. She did not want it for bedding or a broom.

When they returned to the handcar, they showed the wastebird feathers to Ma, who remarked on how pretty and soft they were. The little bundle was tucked into the car, but Laura kept that long white feather separate. She tucked it through the straps of her carrysack. As they continued their journey, she would catch sight of it from time to time out of the corner of her eye, fluttering behind her.

The big sky spread out all around her, but it no longer made her feel so adrift. She marched onwards, chin held high, imagining herself a weathered nomad of the Wastes.

TWENTY-SIX: BY THE SHORES OF CRESCENT POND

The claim was just as Pa had described it. Nearby, a trickle of a creek meandered this way and that across the flat wasteland. Small plants sprouted along the creek's banks. They swelled tumorous above the endless grasses like the ridge of a badly healed scar. Laura thought of it as a distinguished scar, one which lent character to the otherwise featureless expanse.

They built their homestead south of a place where the creek spilled over into a body of still water. The little pond was shaped like a crescent. It curved away from the creek. Then abruptly it stopped, trapped by the unyielding wasteland. Pa said that such ponds were common in the Wastes. They were called billabongs, and they formed whenever the course of a river or stream suddenly changed. The old part of the stream would be cut off, and its water would have nowhere to go. Stranded, that old riverbend would just have to get used to its new life as a pond.

Spindly wattle trees grew around the crescent pond. They leaned out over the billabong from all sides, dipping their roots into its murky water. Their tiny leaves were chained together in long, slender fronds, which hung down from their branches in uneven clumps like a scraggly bisox mane. Bean pods could be found amid the wattle trees' branches. They were longer than soybean pods and turned a dark red if left to ripen. Mary and Laura learned to gather the wattle beans. When they had gathered enough, Ma would grind them into a flour. Laura found that wattle bean flour had a sweeter, nuttier flavor than soymeal.

The sight of the little wattle trees was the first sign that they had reached their new home at last. The trees were nothing but a

271

blurry knot when they first appeared in the distance, but they were the only check upon the horizon's boundless sprawl. Out on the Wastes, trees always meant water, Laura knew. And so, although they could not see the billabong from so far away, they knew it was there.

When they reached their claim, Pa started to work building a shanty. Every day, he took the handcar and his felling ax to the scrubland around the billabong and came back with its cargo box loaded up with wattle logs and branches. He would dump the logs in one pile and the branches in another. Then he would turn right back around with the empty handcar and go chop down more wood for the shanty.

They drove pegs down into the soil where the corners of the shanty would be. The pegs made a rectangle. While Pa chopped and hauled and chopped again, Laura and Ma pulled up all the grass inside the rectangle. Then they packed and smoothed the sod beneath. Soon, there was a bare strip of earth amid the wastegrass. That was the first sign that this place was different from all the other places they had camped along the old number roads and on their journey across the great dry Wastes. This was a place that they would begin to make their own.

Until the shanty could be built, their belongings sat in piles beneath the open sky, and Laura's family slept under the stars. The days on the Wastes were hot, but at nights the winds could blow in a frightful chill that would make Laura pull her blankets tight.

The scrubland gave them fuel in abundance, and every night their campfire burned sweet and fragrant with the crackling wattle branches.

When it was too dark to work anymore, Pa would lie with them beside the fire. Sometimes, he would say, "I feel like some music." Then, Laura or Mary would hand him the two-string, and he would play and sing.

She had rings on her fingers and bells on her shoes
And I knew without asking she was into the blues

She wore scarlet begonias tucked into her curls
I knew right away she was not like other girls

It wasn't only wood that Pa hauled back with him from the billabong. There were old lectric ruins hidden around Crescent Pond, half-buried and nearly invisible amongst the shrubs. Pa would scav up chunks of creetrock and thin strips of hardmold and whatever else he found that might make good building material for the shanty.

One day, he left the handcar behind and set out for the billabong with a length of rope coiled around his shoulder. He returned dragging something behind him. It was a big sheet of iron. It made a raucous scraping sound, plowing up the wastegrass and kicking up clouds of dust as Pa pulled it along.

Pa let it flop down beside the pile of wattle logs. The metal was thin and crinkled and marbled in deep shades of orange. Streaks of black seemed to bubble up from between its ridges, but the big iron square seemed sturdy enough. Laura stomped one of the edges with her boot, and it made a satisfying *clang*. Pa said there was a second one just like it, and between the two they would make the job of roofing the shanty a good deal easier.

When Pa felt he had everything he needed, he set to building. First, he chose the longest logs he had and began to hew them with his broadax. The trunks of the wattle trees were gnarled and crooked, but Pa did his best to hew them into straight, square beams.

The little trees were so short that even the longest beams Pa cut were not long enough for his liking. He did not want to bump his tall head on the shanty's ceiling. So he notched the ends of two logs with his chisel. Then he made matching notches in two other logs. Then he fit one log into another so tight and perfect that they were like one very long log. For good measure, he nailed boards across the joints to keep them together, and those were the posts that would hold up one end of the shanty's roof.

Next, Pa took his spade and sunk it down into one corner of the land that Laura had helped Ma clear and level.

"One thing I don't miss about the wooded country," he said, as he dug into the soil. "Pulling up stumps and roots every time a man wants to build something. The land here yields easy. Why, it will make tilling these fields a lark."

When the hole was nearly a meter deep, Pa went across to the other corner of their flat sod rectangle.

"Mud sills will serve us for now," he told Laura as he started a second hole. "But once the planting's done, I'll make a trip back to town and buy some good stout wood from the Northlands. Then I'll lay a proper foundation. By harvesttime, we'll have us a real house. We'll have wood floors and bottleglass windows. You can help your ma and me make sod bricks for the outer walls. That'll keep us right warm come winter. This old shanty here we'll use as a shed once we move into our real house."

With his pick and hammer, Pa broke up the chunks of creetrock he'd scavved, until he had a pile of gravel. Then, with Ma's help, he dragged over one of the tall wattle posts he'd fitted together and stood it up in the hole. Pa held the post straight while Ma filled in the hole with creetrock gravel and packed it tight with earth.

More holes were dug and more posts set. Then Pa laid beams across the tops of the posts. The beams had teeth notched into their edges that sat snug in the grooves Pa had chiseled into the tops of the posts. Across the beams, Pa nailed rafters, and the shanty began to take shape.

It had only three walls. The whole front of the shanty was left wide open. It faced northeast, away from the winds that whipped across the Wastes at night, snuffing out the cookfire and scouring Laura's cheeks until they were raw and pink.

The roof was made of the crinkled iron sheets that Pa had found. From its peak above the shanty's open face, the roof sloped sharply downward. The ceiling was so low near the back wall of the shanty that even Laura could not stand up straight.

The crooked wattle boards that Pa nailed together for the shanty's walls refused to lie flush together. There were many gaps. In places, the ramshackle boards were filled in with strips of hardmold or smaller iron sheets scavved from the shores of Crescent Pond. Slivers of light penetrated the little patchwork shanty, casting pretty patterns across the dirt floor whenever the sun sank low in the late afternoon sky.

Pa did not rest for moment. As soon as they had moved their belongings beneath the shanty's crinkled iron roof, he began digging a well. The creek was muddy and shallow, and Ma did not trust the deadwater from the billabong. So Pa set to work with his spade. By the end of the first day, the hole was up to his chest. By the end of the second day, he had disappeared entirely within it. From the threshold of the shanty, the only sign of Pa was the dirt, bubbling up from the hole in spurts. Soon, he was climbing down into the hole by rope, and Ma had to pull the loose soil up in buckets.

One day, before climbing back down into the well, Pa called Laura over to show her something. In his hand was his powder flask, but Laura did not see his rifle anywhere. She watched him shake a few pinches of powder into an old scrap of hemp cloth. Then he inserted a wick of waxed string and tied the tiny bundle up tight.

"Bad air likes to settle at the bottom of empty wells," Pa explained. "It can knock a man out if he's not careful. This will clear it out."

Pa then reached into his satchel and pulled out his burning glass. He held the glass above the end of the wick until it began to smolder. Then he carefully held the bundle of powder over the well. When the wick had burned almost the whole way, he let go. A moment later, there was a flash and a marvelous *bang*, and smoke drifted up from the mouth of the well. After the smoke cleared, Pa climbed back down and resumed digging.

A few days later, when Pa decided it was time again to scare the bad air out, he let Laura light the wick herself and drop the exploding bag down into the darkness.

Pa kept digging. The longer the well stayed dry, the graver the look upon Pa's face whenever he climbed back up to the surface, bare-chested and covered in dirt.

"How much deeper do you suppose?" Ma asked one evening, as Pa combed clumps of soil from his beard.

"No telling," Pa replied. "The groundwater's a good deal further down than I'd hoped. We just won't know until we get there."

Then, one day, the earth that Ma hauled up in her bucket was damp to the touch. By that afternoon, Pa was sending up buckets of muddy water. When he climbed up out of the well, his pants were rolled up past his knees and soaked to his thighs. He and Ma took turns then, tossing the bucket back down and inspecting whatever they dredged up. At one point, Pa emptied the bucket over his head, laughing like a child as the water cascaded down his bare torso, cutting trails through the dirt.

Finally, Ma dipped a ladle into the bucket. She sniffed its contents. Then she lifted it to her lips. Beckoning Mary and Laura over, she gave them each a sip from the ladle. The water was cold and pure, and Laura thought that she had never tasted anything so fine.

Next came tilling the fields. Someday, Pa said, they would buy a bisox and plow, and then they would sow their whole claim with crops from one end to the other. For now, he and Ma tilled with spade and rake.

First, they tilled a field for the soy crop. Into the ground went Pa's spade, chopping right through the tangled layer of wastegrass roots and turning the sod over heap by heap. Ma followed behind with the rake. She dragged its three iron prongs through the trench that Pa was digging. She poked and stirred the soil, getting it ready.

When the time came to begin sowing, Pa emerged from the shanty with the sack of seedsoy cradled like a baby in the crook of his arm. He set it down beside the field. In respectful silence, Mary and Laura watched Pa open the sack. That seedsoy had travelled with them all the way from the Big Woods. They had not eaten it, even when they were very hungry. Pa dipped his hand inside and came up with a fistful of the round yellow seeds. He opened his hand and poured them slowly back into the sack.

"Such small things," was all he said.

Ma filled a pouch with seeds and tied it about Laura's neck. She showed Laura how to plant them. Then Ma and Pa each began sowing one of the field's rows. And Laura, all by herself, took the row in between.

Ever so slowly and carefully, Laura moved down the furrow of earth that Ma and Pa had prepared. She knew she must not spill any of the precious seeds. She must not plant them too deep or the soy plant would not be able to wiggle its way to the surface. She must not plant them too shallow or the seeds would dry up in the sun or get washed away by the rain. She must not plant them too close together or the two plants would quarrel over light and water and both would come out the worse for it.

Crops were a bit like people, Pa said. A few hearty ones might survive no matter the hardships. But a healthy field, like mankind itself, required certain conditions to thrive and careful cultivation.

Squeezing all of her fingers together like a bird's beak, Laura pressed a hole into the tilled soil. Then she took one single soy seed from the bag around her neck and placed it inside. She covered the hole with the seed back over with dirt and gave it a *pat pat* for good measure. Then she stood up and took two careful steps forward, placing one foot directly in front of the other. One step then two. Where her toes landed on that second step, that was where she made her next hole.

Laura felt proud to be helping with such an important job. Between seeds, she looked up and saw Mary sitting at the edge of the field. Her crutch lay beside her. Nearby, Baby Grace crawled about in the grass. Mary's face was hidden deep beneath the shadow of her bonnet. The bright sun still caused her discomfort.

For a moment, Laura felt bad that Mary could not take part in sowing the crops. But she supposed that someone needed to look after Baby Grace. Grace's crawling was growing more vigorous and adventurous by the day, and Pa said that he reckoned she would crawl straight across the Wastes all the way to Deseret if they let her. Ma just sighed and shook her head, lamenting that Pa's wanderlust had infected another of her children.

Whenever Grace crawled too far, Mary would scoot after her and guide their baby sister back in the opposite direction. It was a job every bit as important as sowing the fields. Laura hoped that Mary understood that. She tried to wave, but Mary did not see her.

In the end, Laura was so slow and careful sowing her seeds that she was barely halfway down her row by the time Ma and Pa had finished with theirs and moved on to the next. Laura gave a cry of dismay when she saw, embarrassed to have fallen so far behind and feeling rushed and panicky. But Pa came over to reassure her, adjusting the brim of her straw hat and wiping a smudge of dirt from her cheek with his thumb.

"Now don't you go trying to keep up with your mother and me, my little soybean," he told her. "You're a good deal less than half my size, and here you are with more than half a row of soy in the ground before I can start my second. Why, if anything, I'm like to get cross with you for showing me up."

In the days and weeks that followed, more land was tilled. They planted kale and carrots. They planted sugar beets and blue peppers. They planted hemp and squash. By the time the hot winds of summer began blowing across the Wastes, their little shanty, with its three walls and its slanted iron roof, was surrounded all around with rows of furrowed earth and the promise of a harvest that would sustain them in their wild new home.

TWENTY-SEVEN: WASTEBIRD

One morning before sunrise, Pa went out hunting. He was gone the whole day. When he returned at last, he came bearing two rabbits and some astonishing news.

It was Jack who first spotted Pa approaching, a dark speck crossing the empty wastegrass. All day long, Jack had waited there at the edge of the soy field, watching the horizon.

He had been upset to be left behind. Jack had wanted to go hunting with Pa, but Pa told him he must stay and look after the homestead. So Jack waited and watched. He waited and watched until the shadows of the little soy seedlings grew long and the whole field was striped in light and dark just like his brindled coat.

Laura was playing by the creek when she heard Jack bark. There was even less water in the creek now than when they had first arrived on their claim. What remained was a skinny ribbon of mud dribbling down from Crescent Pond, one that Laura could easily step over without getting her boots wet. Still, hidden within its diminished banks, there were things to be seen. That afternoon, Laura had found a fat brown water beetle, and she was watching it intently as it attempted to crawl from her hand only to fall into the palm of her other hand.

Oprah sat on a nearby rock. Lately, Laura had been conscious of outgrowing her ragdoll. She had carried Oprah with her all the way from the Wisconsin, but somewhere on the long journey across the old number roads her attachment to the doll had begun to feel less essential. She did not confide in Oprah as she used to. Some days, she forgot about her companion entirely. It made Laura feel a little sad, and perhaps that was why she had made sure to include the doll in her exploration of the creek that afternoon.

When she heard Jack bark, Laura jumped up, for she knew that meant Pa had returned. She set the beetle gently back down into the mud, grabbed Oprah, and ran towards the shanty.

Ma and Mary stood outside the shanty. Laura ran right by them and out into the soy field. Jack continued to bark. "Come on, Jack," Laura told him as she passed, and together they ran on towards the speck on the horizon that was Pa.

When she reached him, Pa showed Laura the rabbits. They hung from the barrel of his rifle, tied together by their feet. They were long-eared jackrabbits of the type that made their home in the Wastes, smaller than the jackrabbits that lived in the Yowa and the Wisconsin but still much bigger than an average cottontail.

"I'm sorry I've been out so long," Pa told Laura. "But I hope to make it right when you hear all the news I have to tell."

Laura wanted to know the news right then, but Pa would not say another word.

"All in good time, my little soybean," he told her. "If I don't hurry up and get this meat back to your mother, she's as like to skin me as she is these rabbits."

So Pa took her hand, and she walked with him back to the shanty. A cool breeze rolled in from the west, sending ripples across the wastegrass.

"Thank goodness," said Ma when she saw the rabbits. "We'll be needing plenty of game if we're going to make our stores stretch to harvesttime. I baked biscuits today, and we're down to our last sack of soymeal. I ground up some of those beans from the billabong to cut the soymeal. But it's a trick I can only use so many times."

"Pshaw, I'm not worried," said Pa. "We'll find a way if it comes to that. And as for meat, the hunting out there's fair enough when a man has a chance to get to it. If I could just let these fields alone, we'd have fresh meat on the table every night. A bit of rain, that would make all the difference. Ah, but rain or no, I have news that will set your mind at rest. I don't reckon we'll have much trouble filling our bellies once I bring home a wastebird."

Pa looked up from untying the rabbits and raised his eyebrow at them with a sly smile.

"Did you see one, Pa?" Laura asked, in excitement.

"A whole flock of them," said Pa as he reached up and began to hang the rabbits from the eaves of the shanty. "Just over the horizon. A dozen at least."

This was marvelous news indeed. For weeks, Pa had been trying to track the great flightless birds, following their migration trails across the plains, but so far he had not seen so much as a feather.

"They were too far off and it was too late in the day to give chase. I took note of the direction they were heading, though. Reckon I can pick up the trail easy enough once I'm properly provisioned. Anyhow, that wastebird flock's not all the news I have for you. No, it's not the half of it."

Laura and Mary and Ma all looked at Pa, waiting for him to tell them what the second half of the news was. Instead, he calmly finished hanging the rabbits. Then he asked Ma to hand him a knife. Ma groaned in exasperation. She fetched the bone-handled carving knife from where it hung from the rack nailed to the shanty wall and thrust it towards Pa.

"Well?" she said. "Out with it, Charles!"

"We have a neighbor," Pa announced, as he reached back up and began skinning one of the rabbits. "And you'll never guess who it is."

"Who, Pa, who?" Laura and Mary asked in unison.

"Why, it's good old Bill Keo! That dog of his to boot. Both still as mangy as ever. Spotted his footprints first off and knew there was another man tracking that same wastebird flock, but you can imagine my shock when I finally caught up and saw who it was. Turns out Bill's filed on a claim a ways to the southwest, not a half day's walk from us if I understand its whereabouts. Says he found a good patch of scav to build himself a hut. Even has a garden going, though he says he can't recall just exactly what he planted."

Laura and Mary could not believe their ears. Out of all the lands in the great wide Wastes, they had settled right next to the scruffy bachelor that they had met on convoy.

"Oh, Charles, that *is* amazing news!" said Ma. "We owe Mr. Keo so much. Perhaps now we'll have a chance to repay him. What a blessing. It can only be the work of the Prophet, guiding the hand of the Prezdent Above."

"Well, yes, it's quite a stroke of luck, that's certain," Pa allowed. "After all, it may well take two men to bag a wastebird. Yaya crews work in groups of half a dozen or more. This flock's trail cuts across country near about midway between his claim and ours. Bill and I agreed to take the hunt back up first thing in the morning."

The next morning, Pa was gone again before the sun came up. His carrysack was filled with biscuits, and a blanket and bedroll were tucked through the straps. He was determined to bring back a wastebird. That meant he might need to spend several days out on the Wastes.

Ma did not like it, but she knew it must be done. So she wrapped the biscuits in cloth and stuffed them inside Pa's carrysack and made sure that Pa's waterskin was filled. In the pre-dawn darkness, Laura stood at the threshold of the shanty, still in her sleeping tunic. She watched Pa go. Like Jack, she wished she could go with him. Like Ma, she wished he could stay.

From the shadows behind her, Laura heard the creaking of Mary's crutch as she rose and shuffled softly across the dirt floor. Ma sighed. Since they were all up anyway, she said, they might as well begin the day's work. With Pa away, there was much that would need doing.

~~~

Those were hot days on the Wastes. The remorseless sun glared down at their fields and shanty from a cloudless sky. Even the winds seemed hot, rolling in, low and angry, across the dry grasslands.

The young soystalks sagged beneath the heat. By midmorning, their delicate new leaves would crinkle and fold downwards. Pa had been digging irrigation ditches to help water the fields, but even if these channels had been complete, the creek was now running too low for them to do much good. For now, the crops needed to be watered by hand. Every day, Laura helped Ma haul buckets, fill watering cans, and sprinkle moisture across the soil splash by splash.

When they were not at work in the fields, they were gathering wood from the billabong or washing clothes or sweeping out the shanty. They were so busy that the days passed quickly, and it seemed like Pa had hardly left when suddenly, late one morning, there he was, striding triumphantly back across the faded plains.

Laura set down her watering can when she saw him appear in the distance. It took a moment staring at his far-off shape before she realized that someone was walking behind him. It was Bill Keo. They made a strange sight as they approached, so strange that Jack couldn't decide at first whether to bark. He just watched them, his big ears stiff and alert.

They had two long poles hoisted up on their shoulders, like servants transporting a queen. Bill Keo was shorter than Pa, and so the poles slanted downwards towards the rear of the procession. Their load bounced and swayed as the two men trundled it across the wasteland. As they grew closer, Laura could see that something was dangling in between them. It looked like a dead snake, limp and swinging back and forth with every step.

Beside Pa and Bill Keo, there was another shape. It was Dog, trotting apace. When Jack saw that, he could contain himself no longer. With a yip, he raced out to meet the returning hunters.

Ma had set her work down by then, and Mary emerged from the shanty as well. Somehow, she managed to hold Baby Grace against her hip as she worked her crutch with her free arm.

When Pa and Bill Keo reached the shanty, they set down their cargo. Both men were dripping sweat. Bill Keo doffed his hat and bowed low to Ma. Then he made a show of not recognizing Laura and her sisters on account of how much they had all grown. He kept calling Grace "Mary" and Mary and Laura "Ma'am" as if they had never met. Jack sniffed round and round Dog, who simply gazed stoically into the distance. It was as jolly a reunion as ever there was.

All the while, Laura kept looking down at the wastebird lashed between the poles. It was bigger than any bird she had ever seen. Bigger than the turkey Pa had shot in the Yowa hill country. Bigger even than a person, maybe twice as big. Its feathers were brown, not black and white like the feather Laura had found at the nomad camp. Pa said that was because the bird was female.

Its wings were pinned to the sides of its plump round body by the rope that bound it to the carrying poles. Its long legs were folded beneath it. Each leg ended in two fat, scaly claws as big as Laura's head. Those, too, were tied tight to the poles.

The wastebird's head and neck hung free, and these were its most extraordinary features of all. It was that snakey neck that Laura had seen swinging between Pa and Bill Keo as they approached. Now it coiled in on itself, lying halfway across the animal's torso. Beneath patches of downy white feathers, the neck's skin was pink and leathery. The bald head that sat at the end of that long pink neck seemed tiny in proportion. Its beak lay open in a silent squawk. Between heavy, half-closed lids, the wastebird's eyes were deep and black.

It was marvelously ugly. Laura imagined how the bird must have looked in life, striding across the wastegrass on those fearsome claws, that neck held tall. Squatting down beside it, she looked into the blackness of its eyes and felt a sudden pang of sadness.

Bill Keo and Pa sat for a spell in the shade of the shanty, exhausted from hauling the heavy carcass across the Wastes. Ma brought them a pail of cool water from the well, and they ladled it eagerly into their cups. They drank and drank until that whole pail was empty and Laura was sent to fetch another.

As Pa and Bill Keo addressed their thirst, they discussed what to do with the wastebird. There was no salt to preserve the meat. Smoking it was the next best thing, but Pa had not yet begun work on building a smokehouse. Finally, they decided that they would make a pit oven. And so, as soon as they were rested, Bill

Keo and Pa set to digging.

Laura and Mary went off to the billabong to gather up as much wattle wood as they could carry. Mary tied a big hemp sack on her back, and, as they picked their way through the scrubland, Laura helped her stuff sticks into the bag. That way, they both had a load of wood to bring back with them.

When the hole was deep enough, Pa built a fire of wattle logs at the bottom. More and more wood was added, until the flames rose high above the surface. While the fire grew, Mary and Laura went to creek with Ma and Bill Keo to look for stones. They needed to pick the flattest, smoothest stones they could find to make a nice, even surface for cooking the meat. Ma and Laura each picked up a stone, and they put another in Mary's bag. Bill Keo grabbed stone after stone, piling them up in his arms and then lurching back towards the firepit before they could all spill to the ground.

Pa laid the stones one by one on top of the burning logs at the bottom of the pit. The fire shrank back down beneath the ground, tamed by the stones, and the flames were replaced by a thick column of sweet-smelling smoke. While the stones heated up, Pa turned to butchering the wastebird.

First, they plucked the animal clean. The feathers were laid in two careful piles. One pile was for them and one was for Bill Keo, because he and Pa had worked together to kill the wastebird. Ma spoke of making a broom from the feathers or perhaps stuffing for pillows if she could find the cloth. Laura wished that there were enough feathers that she could have a cloak like the Yaya wore.

They cleaned the wastebird of its squishy inside parts. These too were set carefully aside. Everything had a use. Some of those guts they would stuff up with meat and spices to makes sausages. Others they would boil for gravy. Not a bit would be wasted.

As they worked, Bill Keo told them stories about all that he and Dog had done since that night in early spring when he and Pa had walked through the night to hurry Mary to Lildaka.

Towns had always made him feel cooped up, Bill Keo said,

and he had stayed no longer in Lildaka than it took to trade for fresh supplies and get his bearings. By the time the rest of Captain Syed's convoy arrived, he was already preparing to strike out into the Wastes. Carrysack on his shoulders and Dog at his side, he departed the City of Mounds the very next day.

With Bill Keo, it was difficult to know what to believe. He said that he had traveled with a crew of Yaya for a time. They had accepted him as one of their own and treated him with a bewildering respect. Only later did he learn that it was all on account of Dog. Apparently, the nomads had regarded his shaggy black companion as some sort of omen, Bill Keo claimed, the fulfillment of a vision that one of their shamans had seen on a spiritwalk.

All was well until one night when Bill Keo was playing cards with three Yaya men. He had taught them a game called dodeejoo, and they were gambling for wastebird feathers. That night, one of the men accused him of cheating. It was true, but Bill Keo insisted that cheating was an integral part of dodeejoo. In any case, the Yaya tied him up inside one of their tents, and Bill Keo expected them to drag him out at any moment and eat him.

Fortunately, the chief's daughter had fallen in love with him. She untied him and helped him escape, with Dog and carrysack and all. After that, he wandered the Wastes for many weeks. He had just about made peace with a slow death of thirst when he stumbled across a small cluster of ruins near a creek. There he settled.

It was lonesome, living in his little bachelor shack on the edge of nowhere, but Bill Keo reckoned it was a mighty fine piece of land for a homestead and could be worth a good deal if the Wastes did get settled up. As soon as he was able, he meant to make a trip up to Lildaka and file a claim. He promised to bring them back anything they might need from market, and Ma said that she would be grateful and would make a list.

When the stones at the bottom of the pit oven were good and heated, they covered them with a layer of wattle leaves. The wastebird now hung from the eaves of the shanty, just where the rabbits had hung a few days before. Pa carved off thick strips of pink flesh and broke off ribs in big meaty slabs. All of it went right on top of the bed of leaves, as ringlets of smoke continued to wriggle their way up through the stones.

Pa tossed a leg bone to Dog and another to Jack. Dog lay down with his bone between his paws, gnawing thoughtfully, but Jack could not fit his mouth around his bone. He approached it from one side, then the other, but his little jaws just could not open far enough.

While the meat was being carved, Bill Keo asked to borrow Pa's spade, then wandered away, out into the grass beyond the soy field. He returned a short while later carrying a fistful of purple flowers. They were the same purple flowers that blossomed here and there all over the Wastes. He held up the plants in satisfaction. Only then did Laura see that, dangling down at the end of their stalks, each one had a fat dirt-covered root. These roots were called wasteturnips, Bill Keo told them, and you could eat them.

Wasteturnips are hard and flavorless, but when slow-cooked with meat in a pit oven they become soft and delicious. Ma washed and sliced the roots and threw them in on top of the wattle leaves, while Laura and Mary went out to find more.

When all the meat and wasteturnips were in the hole, Ma covered them with another layer of leaves and a damp hemp cloth. Then Pa shoveled dirt on top, and they all sat back to let the food cook beneath the ground. Bill Keo patted his stomach and declared that he was hungrier than a fiend, before glancing at Mary and muttering a sheepish apology.

While they waited, Pa plucked a few buds from a bushy hemp frond that hung drying behind the shanty and packed them into his pipe. The plants that Pa had uprooted from the hemp field and moved off to their own corner of the homestead had only just begun to flower, and so the pipeleaf was fresh and pungent. As Pa and Bill Keo passed the pipe back and forth, the smoke from the newly harvested buds rose strong and sour from the pipe's wooden bowl and Pa began to tell the story of their hunt.

THE STORY OF THE HUNT

"Bill and I met at a spot we'd agreed on about halfway between his claim and ours. That first day, we followed the wastebird flock's tracks until sundown without a sighting, but it wasn't too long into the following morning we finally caught up with the beasts. They were a good ways off, but we counted fourteen adults, plus three chicks.

"Problem was, every time we'd get close to rifle range, the flock would move off. They're smart animals. They keep a watchful eye out for danger. They're far too fast for a man to run down, even the chicks, and there's naught for places to sneak up on them out on the plains.

"I've heard it said the nomads hunt in groups of six or more, and now I understand why. With just Bill and me and the dog, we had to think careful about how to approach the problem. I figured our best chance at it would be our first, for if we went charging in like fools we were like to spook the birds and make things a deal harder on ourselves after that.

"We settled on a plan where I'd make a wide arc and try to get out in front of the flock. Then I'd hunker down in the grass with my rifle while Bill came up on the birds from the other direction. He'd chase them my way, and I'd take my shot.

"Well, Bill played his part just as well as anyone could have. He snuck up on those wastebirds and got just as close as he could before he started barreling in, yelling and waving his hands, Dog running at his heels and barking the while. But a flock of wastebirds is no easy thing to steer, we learned that right away. Bill tried to force them left, but they went right. As I saw them passing wide of my hiding spot, I decided to fire anyway. But I missed of course. They were just too far off and moving too quick in the wrong direction. I felt foolish then, for the crack of my rifle had them dashing off faster than ever. They ran off to where we lost sight of them again, and I feared I'd blown our chance at a kill right there.

"We camped that night by a lone cottonwood. The next morning, I wake up to find Bill whittling away with his knife at a dead limb he's found. A good-sized stick, about the length of my arm, and it's got a thick knot at one end.

"Before I can even rub the sleep out of my eyes and ask just what the blazes he's doing, Bill throws a blanket over his head. Then, he hunches over like this and out pops that stick from underneath the blanket, and Bill starts waving it around above his head. And I thought to myself, the Wastes have gotten to him, the poor man. It's what comes of not staying better hydrated. I was slowly reaching towards my gun when Bill tossed the blanket off and explained his plan.

"At first, I'll admit, your plan didn't go very far to convince me of your sanity, Bill. Dressing ourselves up as wastebirds? I'd never heard of such a hare-brained way to hunt. But Bill insisted it was an old nomad trick, and after the previous day's misadventures, well, I figured anything was worth a try.

"We pulled down another limb from that old cottonwood, making sure to hack off enough trunk to shape into something that might look halfway like a wastebird's head, at least if you were half-blind and came across it in the dark of night after a few cups of doju.

"When we caught up again with the flock, we made our way upwind, and Bill and I both disguised ourselves under our blankets. Hunched over and holding our sticks up in front of us, we crept awkwardly towards where the birds were clustered, rooting around with their beaks in the wastegrass.

"Well, I'll be hanged if the ruse didn't seem to fool them. A short while later, my back was feeling mighty sore from all that bending over, but when I peeked out from under my blanket, I could see the wastebirds' legs up ahead, still just shuffling around.

"I had my rifle tucked under my spare arm. When we'd gotten just about as close as I figured we were likely to get, I dropped to my knees beneath the blanket.

"I was trying my best to get my gun ready without making too much of a stir. I could hear the animals around me, moving about and grunting. Finally, I started easing my way out from under the blanket and prepared to take aim.

"I was expecting the wastebirds to startle and run. What I wasn't expecting was for one of them to charge me. As I doffed my disguise, I had a hen in my sights. But I hadn't yet begun to raise the barrel of my rifle when I heard this terrible hiss from off to the side. I turned my head to find an enormous wastebird rushing towards me at alarming speed. Panicked, I fired at it, but my angle was poor, and the shot went wide. It was all I could do to roll out of the way as its claws came crashing down.

"The beast might well have stomped me dead if Bill hadn't come rushing in. I look up, and there's Bill, shouting to get the wastebird's attention and swinging his stick round and round his head. At that point, it was pure pandemonium. The one that attacked me fell back, hissing all the while. At the same time, all the other wastebirds are racing around in every direction. Dog's gotten himself into the mix too, nipping at their heels.

"I stumble to my feet, trying to reload my gun. By the time I'm ready to fire again, though, it's too late. The birds have all scattered across the Wastes.

"My heart sank, but then I heard Bill calling out to me. He's standing a ways off with Dog, looking down into some sort of ravine. Neither of us had noticed it, but there was a dry riverbed, fairly deep, right there beside where we'd snuck up upon the wastebird flock. It seemed that, in the chaos, Bill or Dog or both had managed to chase one of the hens over the edge of the ravine. We found it with a broken leg, and I put a quick end to the creature's suffering.

"Uncle Freddie used to say a man should always aim to be prepared, but there's no substitute for lucky. I dare say there's a thing or two I'd do different next time around. But meat is meat, and I reckon that'll do for today."

TWENTY-EIGHT: A VISIT FROM THE BLACK SNAKE

Midsummer came and went. Still it did not rain. The creek beside the shanty was now no more than a damp streak darkening the bottom of a dry gully. Crescent Pond was a sliver of its former self. The billabong had retreated from the wattle trees that surrounded it, leaving cracked earth behind.

The wattle leaves were brown. The wastegrass was brown. It seemed to Laura as if the whole world was brown.

The soy field was withering beneath the heat. Already, many of the stalks had shriveled and collapsed, never to rise back up. The other crops were faring hardly better. The carrots they had harvested had come out of the ground short and stubby, and just a single pepper had ripened on the parched little vines that sagged against the wattle stakes Pa had pounded into the soil to prop them up.

Only the hemp field seemed to be flourishing. Back behind the shanty, a grove of plants had sprung up, taller and taller with every week. Laura and Mary could hide and seek among the foliage or pretend that they were back in the Big Woods, hidden beneath its dense canopy.

One day, when the grove had grown nearly as tall as the shanty roof, it came time to harvest the hemp. Pa went through with his sickle and chopped the plants down, stalks and all. When all those tall hemp stalks lay in piles on their sides, Laura helped Ma and Pa hunt through them and pluck out all the seeds. They came away with baskets full of hemp seeds, which Ma would use to make oil and milk and flour.

Only Pa's three pipeleaf plants remained standing where they were. Earlier that summer, Pa had uprooted them and moved them off by themselves. All three were female, Laura knew, for only female hemp flowered and only if the plants were not too close to the male plants.

When all the seeds had been collected, the plants were left in the field to ret. At night, Pa would sprinkle water over the cut stalks to make the retting go more quickly. After a week, all the hemp leaves had decayed, and the bark had turned from green to a dark gray like new-forged iron. Now the fibers would be soft enough to separate from the stalk.

Pa constructed a hemp break, which was a tool made up of several thick wooden boards. One board would swing downward on a hinge, and the hemp stalks would be pounded and crushed between the boards. Another board was lined with iron nails, their sharp ends all sticking up like a row of teeth. This was called a hackle. After the hemp stalks had been crushed, they were run through the hackle, and their silky hairs would begin to unravel.

The previous summer, when Ma and Pa had processed their last hemp harvest in the Big Woods, Laura had only watched. Now, she was old enough to help. She helped beat the stalks over the hackle and helped unwind the strands and peel them away from the woody core. Then, as the hemp fiber began to accumulate in a corner of the shanty in tangled piles, she helped make rope.

Laura liked rope-making the best. She and Mary worked together. First, they drove a stake into the ground. Then Mary looped a bundle of hemp fibers around the stake and stretched them out as far as they would go. She twisted and twisted that hemp until it started to kink and coil. Meanwhile, Laura did the same thing with a second bundle of hemp. When both lengths of hemp were twisted up, they would twist them both together. Then they tied knots on both ends to make the strands stay put, and that was the rope.

They were making rope out in front of the shanty one morning when Laura looked up and saw something that made her drop her half of the rope mid-twist. The coiled hemp fiber sprang away from her hands and burst apart into dozens of individual hairs. Mary turned to her. Beneath the darkness of her bonnet, there was a look of scolding on her face. But then she saw the alarm in Laura's eyes and followed her gaze.

There, out beyond the brown grass, moving across the otherwise empty plains of the Wastes, there were people. Not one or two or even ten people. There were thirty or forty of them or even more. Laura tried to count all the distant figures and gave up. And amongst the procession there were bisox as well. The animals all had large bundles tied across their hairy backs. Sticking out from both ends of these bundles, Laura could make out the shape of long tent poles.

Nomads. Yaya. Laura ran to tell Ma.

Ma followed Laura out to the edge of the retting hemp field. As her boots crunch-crunched over the drying stalks, Ma's gaze stayed latched tightly to the figures in the distance. By then, the nomad procession had stopped. The people and their bisox just stood there on the horizon. A faint breeze whisked a lock of Ma's hair across her face. She made no attempt to push it away. Her eyes only stared. No one moved. It seemed as if the wasteland itself was holding its breath.

Finally, several of the distant figures turned and split away from the group. Their shapes grew and then grew. They were walking straight towards the shanty.

"Laura, go get your father," said Ma. "Hurry."

Laura ran as fast as she had ever run. Pa was harvesting wood by Crescent Pond. When Laura told him about the nomads, he dropped his ax and ran with her back towards the homestead. When Laura's legs could not keep up, he hoisted her up onto his back, and she held tight as Pa bounded across the wastegrass.

When the shanty came into view, Pa stopped short. Laura slid from his back. Standing there beside the shanty were three Yaya men.

Pa wiped the sweat from his forehead with his sleeve. He watched the men. His hands fidgeted open and closed, and Laura knew that he wished he had his rifle with him.

"It's alright," he told Laura, before advancing towards the men, his stride swift but controlled.

Laura knew that Pa probably did not mean for her to follow, but he also hadn't told her to stay where she was. And so she followed close behind him, taking three steps for every one of Pa's. As she hurried to catch up, she struggled and stretched to see past Pa and get a look at the three strange men.

One leaned against a spear, planted tall and straight into the soft soil. At the very top of its shaft perched the spearpoint, which looked to be a made from a sharpened piece of lectric iron. A bundle of feathers was tied just beneath and fluttered in the wind above the man's head.

Two of the men wore feather cloaks. Downy gray feathers fanned outward in stiff tendrils from the men's shoulders like tangles of wild uncombed hair, while a hem of longer wing plumage hung down across their otherwise bare backs.

The three men stood in a circle. They did not speak. The expressions on their faces were unreadable.

At first there was no sign of Ma. Perhaps she had run away with Mary and Grace, Laura thought. Perhaps they were all hiding down by the creek. But then Ma emerged from the shanty. She saw Pa approaching and gave him a nod as if to say that she was okay. When Pa saw that, his pace slowed.

Ma was carrying three cups. She handed one to each of the nomads. By then, Pa was at her side. The nomads looked him up and down but said nothing. One of them eyed the contents of his cup suspiciously before giving it a sniff.

"It's hempseed milk," said Ma. "It's quite refreshing."

The one with the spear brought his cup to his lips and drank the milk down with a single gulp. Then he turned and said something to his companions. Laura listened in amazement. In Lildaka, she had sometimes had difficulty understanding the locals when they would talk quickly in their melodic drawls. But the way the Yaya spoke was something different entirely. Some of the words Laura thought she recognized, but they were so jumbled up and peppered with so many unfamiliar phrases that it hardly sounded like they were speaking Merican at all. She found she couldn't understand a bit of it.

The one with a feather cloak but no spear gave his hempseed milk a delicate sip and smacked his lips. Then he lifted his chin towards Pa in greeting.

"How bodi, bruv?" the man said to Pa.

The man extended a closed fist towards Pa. Pa hesitated awkwardly for a moment, as if unsure how to politely respond. Then he raised his own fist and tapped it lightly against the nomad's.

"I'm Charles Ingalls," said Pa. "You've met my wife Caroline."

Laura peeked out from behind Pa to get another look at the Yaya. Their clothing, such as it was, appeared to be made completely from wastebird leather. Unlike the buckskin hides that Laura was used to, the material had a bumpy texture from where the feathers had been plucked. It was a light brown, almost pink. The nomads' pants were stiff but loose-fitting, and they wore sandals on their feet with straps that wound around their blackened heels and between their toes. Various leather bands were tied around their forearms or biceps. Otherwise, apart from the black-and-gray cloaks that two of them wore, they were naked from the waist up.

"Chief Bobby. Dem me crew," said the man who had touched fists with Pa, nodding towards the remainder of the Yaya tribe, who remained out in the distance just where Laura had left them.

Laura found Chief Bobby's speech easier to follow than his companions'. If she listened closely, she could almost make out his meaning.

"You dey be live here long?" he asked Pa.

"We arrived last spring," Pa answered. "We have a land claim backed by the Lildaka Supervisory on a square kim west of the creek there and running north up to the billabong yonder."

Chief Bobby exchanged a look with one of his fellows, the bare-shouldered nomad with the matching leather armbands around both biceps. The other man said something, but it was incomprehensible to Laura. Chief Bobby shrugged and turned back to Pa.

"Make I tell you Deshi paper no get juice wit we, bruv. Only ting you dey no vex dis crew, we finna go sweet. Sabi?"

Now it was Pa and Ma's turn to exchange a look between them. Laura thought that the Yaya chief was saying that he wouldn't bother Laura's family if they didn't bother his tribe. Pa seemed to sense the same meaning.

"We just mean to raise our crops in peace," Pa told the nomads. "We welcome the Yaya to pass through our land."

To Laura's surprise, the men laughed. Chief Bobby shook his head.

"Yaya? Nah. Das Deshi talk, bruv. Nah no ting Yaya. We Black Snake Crew, sabi?"

At the mention of his tribe's name, Laura noticed for the first time that there was a black snake painted on the leather band around Chief Bobby's forearm. As the nomad chief scanned the homestead, taking in their shanty and their well and their fields, Laura examined him further. His hair hung down in tight braids around a face that was clean-shaven but nearly as leathery as his clothing. Laura had difficulty guessing his age. And there was something else strange about the texture of his skin. When she looked closer, Laura realized that certain patches were covered in decorative scarring. The ridges of Chief Bobby's cheekbones were studded with a trail of dots that coiled back behind his ears, disappearing behind the curtain of his braids. As his head turned, the sun glinted off collection of silver jewelry that studded his ear.

"So you got ting for deal, bruv, or nah? We got dem birdskin threads suit you well well. Or you dey finna want grub grub, make you try Black Snake jerkmeat. Other crew dey no got dem spice same Black Snake. Nah so?"

"Blas'nake jerk well well," the nomad with the spear agreed.

Pa scratched beneath his beard. He suddenly looked disinterested. That surprised Laura, for she knew that her family needed food. They had finished the last of the smoked wastebird meat, and Pa had been too busy trying to salvage their soy crop to go out hunting.

"What do you think, Caroline?" he said to Ma. "I know we have plenty of food, but it never hurts to have a little extra meat around. At the right price, I reckon we might trade for a bit of this spiced nomad jerky."

Ma shrugged.

"We have cloth," he told the men. "And a few lectric artifacts we could part with perhaps. And pipeleaf if your people smoke the stuff."

At the mention of pipeleaf, the nomads perked up. The man with the spear raised an imaginary pipe to his lips to make sure he had understood Pa correctly. Chief Bobby said something to the bare-shouldered man, who nodded and began making his way back towards the Black Snake's main group.

At that moment, Pa seemed to realize for the first time that

Laura was standing behind him.

"You should be inside, Laura," he told her.

Laura nodded and began walking slowly back towards the shanty. She looked one last time over her shoulder at the two remaining nomads. The one with the spear was watching her. When Laura looked at him, he gave her an amused half-smile and tilted his spear slightly in a kind of salute. Chief Bobby and Pa had begun to talk about the weather.

"Dis summer rains dey no come long long," Chief Bobby was saying. "Dem two three years be come plenty rains. Now every ting dey dry same way for when I be young young. I no sabi nah. Only ting world she dis way, now dat way, now dis way. Nah so? Make I tell you, bruv, Mother Sky, she no go sweet quick quick, you dey farmers finna go plenty vex."

When Laura reached the shanty, she found Mary and Grace huddled just inside the threshold. Nearby, Jack had been tied up so that he would not attack or bark at the strangers. Mary's face was pressed flat against the wall, her eye at a chink between the slats from which she could watch Ma and Pa and the nomads out in fields. Hearing Laura approach, she looked up.

"Oh Laura!" she whispered. "What's happening?"

Mary scooted aside so that they could both look through the chink in the wall. Cheek-by-cheek, they pressed their eyes to the narrow gap.

"One of the men went back to the big group," Laura answered. "I think Pa is going to trade with them."

"Will the Yaya try to eat us?" Mary asked breathlessly.

"They don't like being called Yaya," said Laura, relishing the opportunity to correct her sister's ignorance. "They're called the Black Snake. But that's only the name of this tribe I think. Their chief is called Chief Bobby. That's him talking to Pa. He has a leather armband with a snake painted on it and lots of earrings and a line of dots on his face. They speak Merican but different. The one with the spear smiled at me. And their clothes are all made of wastebird skin I think. Their sandals too maybe. They like Ma's hempseed milk. Pa is going to trade them pipeleaf for

298

wastebird jerky I bet."

"Oh," said Mary.

They both continued to watch Ma and Pa and the Black Snake men through the gap in the wall.

"They seem terribly frightful," Mary said eventually. "Weren't you scared, Laura?"

Laura thought about that. She turned her head so that she could look through the gap in the wall with her other eye. Beside her, Grace pulled herself to her feet and babbled as she tugged on Laura's hair.

Laura *had* been frightened by the three strange men. Even now, watching them from the safety of the shanty as they spoke to Ma and Pa, she did not feel completely at ease. The Black Snake seemed so different. It was hard to tell what they were thinking or what they might do next. And there were so many of them. If the nomads did mean them harm, who would stop them?

"A little," Laura finally admitted. "But I don't think they're really so frightful as all that. They're mostly like us I think. They just want to live their lives."

"Oh," said Mary again.

Laura turned away from the wall, blinking and rubbing the side of her face. She leaned back against the shanty's slats and allowed Grace to tumble into her lap.

TWENTY-NINE: DARK CLOUDS

One day, dark clouds appeared on the horizon. At first, Laura felt a thrill. The rains had come at last! Pa would be so pleased.

The soy crop had continued to struggle. They had survived on meat and wasteturnips and a meager harvest of gourds and carrots, but Ma and Pa had begun to fret over what they would do come winter.

With rain, perhaps it was not too late for a bountiful harvest. Laura ran to tell Pa about the clouds. She found him kneeling beside the firepit, melting down spent bullets and molding them into fresh ones. When Laura bounded up to him, full of excitement about the coming rain, he set down his mold. He stood, eyes on the distant horizon where Laura was pointing. He stared off for a long time. Slowly, his brow began to crease. A look came across his face, as dark as the approaching clouds.

Then he said, "Laura, find your mother. And your sisters. Get everyone inside the shanty. Quickly now."

Pa's voice was soft, but there was something frightening about it. Laura hurried to find Ma and Mary and Grace and tell them what Pa had said. As she raced across the fields, she looked back at the clouds. They were closer now. On second look, they were not like any rainclouds she had ever seen. They did not seem to float above the earth as other clouds did. Instead, they seemed to rise up from the very surface of the wasteland itself, towering tall and black into the sky.

"Laura!"

Laura turned. There was Mary. She was heading towards the shanty. Grace toddled beside her, holding Mary's hand, but Mary was having trouble managing both her crutch and her sister at the same time. Laura ran to them. She scooped up Grace, and the three of them hurtled towards the little shanty as fast as they could.

The wind had suddenly picked up. It whipped Laura's tunic this way and that. Mary's bonnet was knocked clean off. It dangled behind her from the strings around her neck as she raced alongside Laura, her one leg hurrying to keep pace with Laura's two.

As they neared the shanty, they saw Ma, ripping drying clothes from the clothesline and piling them in her arms. She shouted to them. Her words were snatched up and carried off by the wind, which roared fiercer and fiercer all around them.

When they reached the shanty, Laura set Grace down. Laura turned, and there was Ma. She thrust her bundle of damp laundry into Laura's arms.

"Stay inside," she told Laura and Mary.

Laura stood there at the threshold. Her breath was caught in her chest. The slats of the shanty were beginning to rattle, and the wind was whistling through the gaps. The noise rose and rose into a horrible shriek. Inside, Grace started to cry.

Looming out beyond the soy field, bigger and bigger, was the cloud. It stretched from north to south, a great towering wall of darkness, brown and gray and ominous. As it billowed towards them, it seemed to writhe and throb like a living thing.

Laura had heard of dust storms on the Wastes, but in her wildest imaginings she had not pictured anything so big and terrible. She retreated into the shanty and set the laundry down in a corner. Then she sat with Mary and Grace beside their bedrolls and watched Ma and Pa run outside and then back in again. Anything fragile or precious, Ma and Pa grabbed it and pulled it back under the protection of the shanty's crinkled iron roof.

At one point, Pa climbed up onto a stool and began nailing their old lectricmade tarp to the eaves of the shanty. It was the same tarp that they had camped beneath so many nights on the long road to the Wastes. Now it hung down over shanty's open front like a curtain. Pa worked quickly. When the tarp was stretched out as far as it could go, he crossed to the other side and began hanging hemp sheets from the opposite corner of the roof. Sheet by sheet, he tried to enclose the shanty as best he could.

Meanwhile, it was growing darker outside. Laura could see trails of dust blowing past Pa's legs as he tried to hammer his mismatched curtains into place. Finally, Ma and Pa both ducked inside.

"Best we can do, I'm afraid," said Pa, as he shook the dust from his hair and beard.

Ma came to sit beside them. Pa inspected the slats on the western-facing wall, trying to plug up the gaps with whatever scrap he could find. Then, he too came to sit with them on the dirt floor. He put his arm around Laura, and together they all held their breaths, listening and watching.

Suddenly, there was a great *whoosh*, and the whole shanty shook. Afterwards, the wind seemed to calm. The slats ceased their rattling and whistling. As these sounds quieted, however, new ones rose to take their place. From all around, there began a soft hiss. It thrummed against the walls and roof of the shanty in a steady patter. It almost sounded like rain.

At the same time, everything grew suddenly darker, nearly as dark as night. Pa's improvised curtains did not quite reach the ground, and there was an open slit between the hemp sheets and the tarp. Through these gaps, Laura saw the darkness crash down around them. One moment, she could see all the way to the pile of firewood and to the heavy lid that covered their well and, beyond, the flat expanse of the Wastes stretching endlessly off into the distance. The next moment, it was all gone. Laura could see nothing outside but dust, as thick as soybean soup.

"Jack!" Mary suddenly exclaimed. "Where's Jack?"

They had forgotten all about Jack! There was nothing to be done, said Pa. Jack was a sensible animal and would surely find shelter.

The curtains flapped and jerked, straining against the nails that Pa had pounded into the eaves and posts. The dust storm was blowing from the other direction, pounding against the shanty's back wall. Even so, clouds of dust began curling around the tarp, invading the shanty and depositing streaks of loose grit across Ma's clean dirt floor.

Dust was also leaking through the gaps in the shanty walls. Mary started coughing. Then Laura started coughing. Ma helped them tie handkerchiefs around their faces, and that helped some.

The hiss of the dust storm grew louder as coarser bits of debris began to strike the walls of the shanty. Then it seemed to soften for a time, only to flare back up, rolling over them in waves.

Finally, just as it began to feel that the outside world had disappeared for good and all, leaving their little house suspended in a fathomless void, the hiss of dust truly subsided. Through the gaps between the curtains, Laura saw fissures of clarity start to breach the murky nothingness. And then, all at once, the dust storm had moved on. The familiar landscape of the homestead reappeared, and all was still and quiet.

They stood. Ma shook her head at the piles of dust that fanned out in a dirty arc across the shanty floor. Pa pulled back the tarp.

Outside, it was as if all the color had been drained from their homestead. The shapes were all there where they should be, but someone seemed to have come through and repainted everything in shades of brown and gray.

A layer of dust coated every surface. In places, it gathered like snowdrifts. The wheels of the handcar were sunk down between hills of dust. They seemed to grip the car from beneath, holding it immobile and lifeless. The craggy peaks and valleys of the woodpile had been smoothed as its crevices filled with dust. A great hill of dust climbed the shanty's western wall.

Pulling his handkerchief tighter around his face, Pa went to inspect the soy field. Laura watched him walk slowly down the rows, threading his way through the soystalks. He looked this way and that as he walked. Every few steps he would stop and just stare, like a man lost. There was a knot in Laura's stomach as she approached.

The damage was unmistakable, even from afar. All those poor fragile soystalks. If only their strength hadn't already been sapped by the long dry summer, Laura thought, perhaps they would have found it in them to stand up to the dust storm. But that was the way of misfortunes. They didn't tear you down all at once. They weakened you, bit by bit.

Dust clung to the leaves and beanpods. The stalks bowed beneath the weight. One plant in three had snapped or uprooted itself completely. Near the center of the field, Pa stopped. He brushed the plant beside him lightly with his hand and rubbed one of its leaves thoughtfully between thumb and forefinger. His handkerchief still masked his nose and mouth. The expression on his face was unknowable.

Just then, a small pile of dust that sat by the edge of the field began to stir. Laura blinked in surprise and took an apprehensive step backwards as the dust pile appeared to rise and come towards her.

As the gray-brown shape drew closer, tiny clouds of dust leaking out behind it, it sprouted ears and legs. Then it sneezed. A great burst of dust erupted from it, and, when it cleared, Laura saw Jack's bulging black eye looking up at her. She let out a joyous yelp.

Jack sneezed again and then again. His handsome brindled coat had turned to dusty drab from snout to tail, but he seemed unhurt. He had just been guarding their crops from the dust storm like the good watchdog he was. Laura knelt beside him and began wiping the dirt from his face with the sleeve of her tunic. In that moment, it seemed to her as if perhaps things weren't so dire after all.

~~~

Pa harvested what he could of the soy. It was too late in the year now to sow another crop. Winter would be upon them before long. Most of the soy, they ground to flour, but Pa set aside a small sack for seed. If they could just make it through the coming winter, they would need that seedsoy to start again.

Weeks passed. Pa went out hunting as often as he could manage. He went alone, for Bill Keo had gone to Lildaka to file his land claim. It didn't matter, in any case. Pa brought back pigeons, grouse, and rabbits and, once, a long-tailed pheasant with a bright red head, but he never saw any sign of wastebird. Chief Bobby had said the flocks were all heading southwest and might not be back until the following spring. Laura supposed the Black Snake would follow. That was the way of nomads.

When they had no fresh game, there was the Yaya jerky they had gotten from Chief Bobby's tribe. The jerky was hard, too hard to bite right into. Mostly, Ma would boil it, but, sometimes, she would carve off thumb-sized strips for Mary and Laura to suck and gnaw on. The Yaya spices, tangy and sweet, were always overpowering at first, dulling slowly as the meat softened in Laura's mouth. It took her a long long time to eat even a small piece of unboiled jerky, and the drawn-out effort helped trick Laura's stomach into thinking she had eaten more than she had.

The soymeal they tried to save for winter. And, of course, there could be no touching the seedsoy. To accompany the jerky and pigeon, there were always wasteturnips. Ma had become an expert in cooking them all manner of different ways. Laura's favorite was thin-sliced wasteturnip chips fried in hemp oil. It was Laura's job to go and dig up the little tubers. There were plenty at first. Soon, though, she found she had to stray farther and farther from the homestead to find the purple flowers that announced the wasteturnips hidden beneath. She began to worry that one day before long she would go out to find the land picked clean.

More and more often now, Laura overhead Ma and Pa quarreling. When it became clear how little flour they would get from their soy crop, Ma had suggested that they go back to Lildaka, at least for the winter. Perhaps Mr. Hasan would give Pa his job back. The Khan cousins might take them in until they could find a place of their own.

Pa did not like that idea, not one bit. If they left the homestead, they would put their claim in jeopardy, he argued.

Even Laura knew that wasn't the whole of it, though. Pa didn't want to work for Mr. Hasan. He didn't like having to pound iron nails all day for the old smith to sell. He wanted to live on his own land, to be free and to enjoy the fruits of his own labor.

One evening, Pa returned empty-handed from hunting. That evening, he and Ma spoke again of what they would do when winter arrived if their stores kept dwindling at the rate they were. Ma insisted there was no way about it but to abandon the homestead.

Neither of them raised their voices, but Laura could see that Pa was frustrated. After cleaning and hanging up his rifle, he went out to split firewood. Ma gave Mary and Laura each a strip of jerky to tide them over and told them to watch after Grace while she went to draw water from the well and soak the handful of wasteturnips Laura had gathered that afternoon.

Mary convinced Grace to stop toddling around the shanty and come sit by her. Together, the two of them paged through *A Children's Illustrated Book of Animals,* marveling at the strange creatures from far away and long ago.

Laura felt restless. She left Mary and Grace and went to eat her jerky outside. She found Jack beneath the handcar and sat down beside him. Nearby, Pa chopped logs with a regular *ka-thunk.* Ma sat next to him, scrubbing the wasteturnips.

"We've always managed," Pa was saying to Ma as he set up another log for his ax. "You know that as well as I do. All on our own. Never asked for help from anyone. A family like ours, with the will and ingenuity to use what nature provides, we don't need anyone to bail us out. We'll find a way."

Pa's ax *ka-thunked* again. Laura rolled her jerky between her teeth. She thought on Pa's words. It was true. They had come so far, survived so long despite such adversity, all without needing to rely on other people.

Yet, the more that Laura chewed and thought, the more that didn't seem quite right. She thought of all the people they had relied upon during their long journey from the Big Woods to the Wastes. People who had traded with them, like the Black Snake

306

tribe or even Marco, the boy soldier from the Illinoy. People who had welcomed them into their homes, like Tobias Goatherd and Mabel the wildgirl back in Happy Valley Orchards or like the Khan family and the little dugout where Mary had recovered her strength. People who had kept them safe, like Bill Keo or Captain Syed or the others they had met on convoy. For all that Laura had grown up far from any society, for all that going west had plunged them yet deeper into a wild and unpeopled country, she and her family had never been truly on their own, not completely.

For a time, neither Ma or Pa spoke. Pa soon ran out of wood to split. Then he sat beside Ma, watching her scrub the wasteturnips. The little round roots were practically bone white, but Ma kept right on scrubbing. Pa twisted the handle of his ax in his fists. The iron head turned haltingly round and round, brushing the ends of Pa's beard as to swept past.

"What about this," Pa said finally. "You and the girls could stay and look after the homestead while I go to town. Just for a month or two. Three at most. I can try and find some temporary work. At the docks or . . . or maybe with Hasan if he'll have me. Then I can buy supplies enough to last us the winter and . . ."

Pa trailed off as Ma let go of the wasteturnip she was scrubbing and let it fall into the water bucket with an angry *plop*. She didn't look at Pa. From her seat beneath the handcar, Laura thought she could see Ma shaking.

"Don't," she said. "Don't you leave us, Charles Ingalls. Don't you do that."

Her voice was soft but it was terrible. Laura had never heard her speak that way before. It seemed to catch Pa by surprise as well. He stared at Ma, his mouth open. His jaw gave a few hesitant, wordless stretches as he chose his response.

"Of course," he said. "You're right as always. It was just a thought. I only meant . . . But no. You're right of course. We'll manage somehow. Like we always do."

A few days later, Bill Keo and Dog paid them a call. He had just returned from town and had brought them the items Ma and Pa had asked him to buy for them at the market. Digging through his carrysack, he first produced an old hardmold jar with a wooden stopper, full of powder for Pa's gun, and then a new iron spade head to replace the one that Pa had warped trying to break up a particularly rocky patch of sod. From his vest pocket he fished out a new iron sewing needle and handed it to Ma.

He'd not been able to find any salt, not at a reasonable price, he said as he handed them back the rest of the copper pieces they'd given him. Ma and Pa said that was quite alright and that he'd done more than enough.

Dog made a noise then that might have been a woof or maybe just a sneeze. Bill Keo looked to him and snapped his fingers.

"Good lookout, pal," he told the animal. "I nearly forgot."

He unbuttoned a side pocket of his carrysack and pulled out a small bundle wrapped in a handkerchief. Inside were three bright orange rings glistening with sugar. It was a type of sweet Laura had seen people cooking in Lildaka, but she had never tried one. They were made from lentil paste, squeezed into a pan of frying oil in a delicate ribbon that weaved and looped in and out until it formed the shape of a flower. Then they were dipped into sugar syrup. There was one each for Laura, Mary, and Grace.

Laura cradled hers in her hands. She sat with Mary, just looking at the little orange flower cakes. They were almost too pretty to eat, Mary whispered. Laura wasn't so sure. She felt her mouth water as she turned the treat over, watching the way its sugary glaze caught the light.

While Laura and Mary admired the sweets he had brought them, Bill Keo turned back to Ma and Pa, and his manner grew serious. He had quite a bit of news to share from town, he said, and little of it good.

Lucius Ortega was dead.

"Passed away some time late last spring, folks reckon," he told them, "but word only reached Lildaka a month or two back. Well, it looks to be a full-blown succession crisis, just as everyone was afeared. The sister's seized control in Davenport, but old Wolfdog Ortega, he's thrown his lot in with the nephew. Rumor is, there's an army, two or three hundred strong. Maybe five hundred, some say. Marching down the Great Eighty Road towards Lildaka.

"Make matters worse, the Merchants Guild's been disbanded. Those Deshi traders don't want no part of Marius Ortega's war but some of them, they think they smell a chance to buck the Clan for good. Seems they tried to stage some sort of power grab, only the Wolfdog, he got wind of it. Now you've got some of town's most prominent citizens locked up and the supervisory taken over direct control of the market. I tell you the tension there's so thick you could butter your toast with it.

"I did my tradin' and got myself out of town quick as I could. Didn't even bother to try and file on my claim. Figured they'd be a sight too preoccupied to find time for the likes of me. Anyways, stock in them Ortega land claims is falling fast. Settling the Wastes, that was Marius Ortega's scheme. Davenport backed him, sure, but with the Old Man dead and Lildaka in revolt, what's the chances the Clan Council is like to honor a bunch of papers with the Wolfdog's signature? Assuming they win, that is, and I wouldn't lay no bet against it."

Laura watched Pa's face as Bill Keo spoke. He didn't react to the news, but the look in his eyes seemed to grow darker and darker.

If their claim wasn't any good, did that mean that people could come and drive them from their land after all? And if an army was marching towards Lildaka, was it safe for them to go back there? If not, where would they go? Laura had many questions that she knew she was not supposed to ask.

Her fingers had grown sticky where they clutched her flower cake. It was still pretty, but it no longer seemed so tantalizing. She followed Mary's lead and wrapped it up to save for later.

Bill Keo said he had better be on his way if he wanted to make it back to his little bachelor shack before dark. As he shouldered up his carrysack, he told Ma and Pa that he'd had just about his fill of the Wastes. If he could find a convoy heading west for Deseret, he reckoned he'd join them, try to find some town in the foothills where he could hole up for the winter. Ma and Pa thanked him again and said they hoped that if he did decide to leave, he would stop by first to say goodbye.

They all gathered outside the shanty and watched him walk off across the plains, Dog trotting behind him. As he walked, he sang an old tune to the wastegrass.

By the rivers of Babylon, where we sat down
Yeah, we wept, when we remembered Zion

For they that carried us away in captivity
Demanded from us a song
But how shall we sing the Lord's song in a strange land?

He grew smaller and smaller and his singing fainter and fainter until at last he disappeared.

~~~

It was the day after Bill Keo's visit, early in the afternoon, that the second dust storm arrived.

Laura was playing a game of chase and fall with Grace out in the brown grass by what remained of their soy field. Grace would lift herself to her feet and begin to toddle away from Laura, arms outstretched as one unsteady foot after the other sent her careening forward with a momentum barely under her control. Without looking back, she would call to Laura.

"Rolo! Rolo!" she cried breathlessly, her gaze fixed on the horizon.

Laura would hop up then and stumble in a silly zig-zag after her sister. When she saw that Laura had caught up, Grace would fall down into the grass, and Laura would flop down beside her. Grace would laugh and laugh at that, before lifting herself up and starting the game again.

The sky had been a cheerful blue that morning. Warm sun and cool breeze had come together in pleasant union, almost enough to dissipate the cloud of apprehension that had hung over the homestead since Bill Keo had brought news of the unrest in Ortega country.

Laura tumbled once more onto the grass, laughing right along with Grace at the fun of rising and falling and rising again, when she looked up and saw the darkness gathering in the distance. Immediately, she picked her sister up and raced her back to the shanty. There, she found Ma already unfurling the tarp. Pa arrived soon after.

Laura set Grace down inside, next to Mary. She tied her handkerchief around her mouth and nose. Then she helped tie on Grace's handkerchief. Grace fussed, but Mary and Laura soothed and cajoled until their little sister finally accepted the mask wrapped around her face.

When Grace was settled, Laura dashed back outside to see if she could help with covering up the front of the shanty or bringing their belongings inside. To her surprise, Ma and Pa were not running around frantically as they had during the previous dust storm. Instead, Laura found them just standing there, with their backs to the shanty, as still as creetrock monuments. Pa's hammer was in his hand, ready to nail up the tarp, but it hung limply at his side like a crippled limb. He and Ma watched the coming storm, motionless but for their hair whipping about in the wind.

Laura walked up beside them, so soft and cautious that Ma and Pa did not seem to notice her approach. They did not turn their heads to her, nor did they look at one another as they spoke.

"Well, it's not as if there's crops it's like to ruin," Ma was saying. "There's that."

Her voice was not bitter. It was simply weary.

"What's a little dust? What more can it do to us?"

Pa didn't answer. His eyes just watched the horizon. Not a muscle on his face moved, even as his whiskers leapt wildly about his cheeks and chin like the surface of a tempestuous sea. Laura followed his gaze towards the gray-brown clouds growing and churning in the distance.

The dust storm was still far off, but already this one seemed bigger than the last. It yawned, deep and dark and indifferent, consuming both earth and sky. Great plumes of dust erupted here and there from its body like a faceless beast flexing its claws.

They had weathered the last dust storm and trials much worse than dust storms, and Laura knew deep down that this one too would pass. But staring into the coming darkness as it loomed, closer and larger every moment, it was hard not to imagine this as the end of all things.

Together, they watched the dust storm approach, Ma and Pa and Laura too. For a moment that seemed to stretch into forever, there was no sound but the whistling of the wasteland, the dull hiss of a billion little blades of grass all shaking in their shallow roots. Then, without taking his eyes from the horizon, Pa spoke. His voice was soft, his words not intended for Laura's ears. Many years later, when sitting down to record her memories of that time, Laura would wonder if truly she had heard him right.

"Caroline, I've made a terrible mistake. I'm so sorry."

EPILOGUE

Cold swept across the wasteland as the convoy stopped for the night. The cold lingered, settling over the semi-circle of wagons and handcars that ringed the camp. Earlier, flurries of snow had followed them westward across the flat expanse, but now it seemed as if it was too cold even for that. The evening sky was clear, and, as it darkened, it filled with stars.

The mountains of Deseret rose in the distance. The convoy's destination was in sight at long last. Their journey across the unforgiving Wastes was nearly at an end. And so, despite the cold, the mood around the fire that night was quietly hopeful. Someone called for music.

Laura nudged closer to the fire. Beside her, Pa removed his hands from the pockets of his coat. Folded inside one of those pockets, Laura knew, there was a letter from Oprah Khan. One of her cousins owned a general store in a mining town in the Deseret foothills, and he needed someone to look after the storefront over the winter.

Pa flexed his fingers and rubbed his hands together to warm them. Then he picked up his two-string and set its barrel on his knee. Several of the faces huddled around the fire smiled at him. He tuned. Then his bow began to slide up and down the instrument's neck. Softly at first, Pa began to sing.

The others seemed to know the song, for more voices soon joined with Pa's. From that tiny flicker of firelight on the wide empty wasteland, their music swelled, keeping the darkness at bay.

Laura listened. She looked westward, and her eyes were drawn to that place where the great canopy of stars above them disappeared behind the black silhouette of the mountain range ahead.

Somewhere beyond the far side of those mountains, though Laura had no way to know it then, there was a boy who lived with his family in a little house by the seashore. The name on the identification papers issued to him by the Tang occupational authority was Wei Manli, though his mother always called him Almanzo.

Laura stared into the shadow of the peaks ahead. She knew that the future was uncertain, that more trials awaited them. But Ma and Pa and Mary and Baby Grace were all beside her, and that was what mattered.

ABOUT THE AUTHOR

 Laura Ingalls-Wei currently lives with her husband and daughter in the Free and Independent Republic of Merica, in a little house in the countryside southeast of Jiujinshan. *Little House on the Wasteland* is her first attempt to preserve and share her memories of a childhood spent on the margins of civilization, travelling far and wide with her family across the wild and lawless country left behind by the collapse of the Old Merican Empire.

Made in United States
Troutdale, OR
03/04/2024

18193574R00195